Sunder had once been a magical melting pot where
the creatures of the world would fill its streets
with their ideas, powers, cultures and cuisines,
firing off each other like a box full of fireworks
and mousetraps.

Now it was falling under the command of a company who
couldn't be trusted. We'd handed over our future to a rich
man with no morals, and people were too content and
comfortable to see the cost.

I didn't know what Niles was up to. It was a question
too big to crack on my own, and every person in this city
was too concerned with punching their timecards and
begging for promotions to help me out.

I needed some way to snap them out of it. I needed to
prove that there was still a way to change things back.

Praise for
Luke Arnold

"Arnold's universe has everything, including the angst of being human. The perfect story for adult fantasy fans—a tough PI and a murder mystery wrapped around the mysticism of Hogwarts, sprinkled with faerie dust."

—*Library Journal* (starred review) on *Dead Man in a Ditch*

"Superb. . . . With a lead who would be at home in the pages of a Raymond Chandler or James Ellory novel and a nicely twisty plot, this installment makes a strong case for Arnold's series to enjoy a long run." —*Publishers Weekly* on *Dead Man in a Ditch*

"A marvelous noir voice; Arnold has captured the spirit of the genre perfectly and wrapped it around a fantasy setting with consummate skill."

—Peter McLean, author of *Priest of Bones*, on
The Last Smile in Sunder City

"A richly imagined world. . . . Winningly combining the grit of *Chinatown* with the quirky charm of Harry Potter, this series opener is sure to have readers coming back for more."

—*Publishers Weekly* (starred review) on
The Last Smile in Sunder City

"This off-piste detective story set in a magical world, now in meltdown, has verve and charm in abundance and a rough-diamond hero with quite a story to tell."

—Andrew Caldecott, author of *Rotherweird*, on
The Last Smile in Sunder City

By Luke Arnold

The Last Smile in Sunder City
Dead Man in a Ditch
One Foot in the Fade

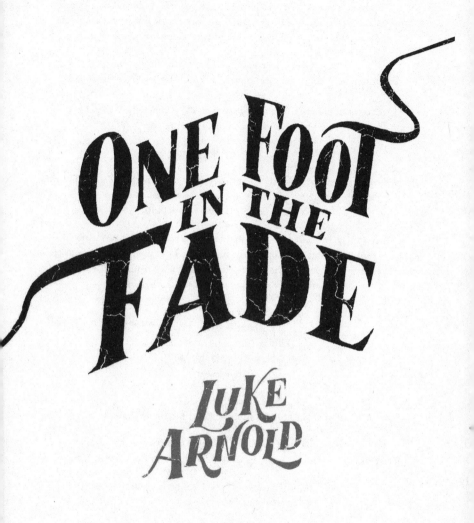

ONE FOOT IN THE FADE

LUKE ARNOLD

orbit

orbitbooks.net

Copyright © 2022 by Luke Arnold
Excerpt from *The Mask of Mirrors* copyright © 2021 by Bryn Neuenschwander
and Alyc Helms
Excerpt from *Sixteen Ways to Defend a Walled City* copyright © 2019 by
One Reluctant Lemming Company Ltd.

Cover design and illustration by Emily Courdelle

Orbit
Hachette Book Group
1290 Avenue of the Americas
New York, NY 10104
orbitbooks.net

First Edition: April 2022
Simultaneously published in Great Britain by Orbit

Orbit is an imprint of Hachette Book Group.
The Orbit name and logo are trademarks of Little, Brown Book Group Limited.

The Hachette Speakers Bureau provides a wide range of authors for speaking events. To
find out more, go to www.hachettespeakersbureau.com or call (866) 376-6591.

Library of Congress Control Number: 2021948634

ISBNs: 9780316668774 (trade paperback), 9780316668743 (ebook)

Printed in the United States of America

LSC-C

Printing 1, 2022

To
Mum
Ashley
Granny
Nanna
x

Get up.

Get the fuck up, Fetch.

Get your ass out of bed and go fix the fucking world.

That's what you said you were going to do, right? Isn't that why you killed him?

So, get to work. Bring the magic back, you stupid bastard. Do some good like you said you would and get your ass out of the goddamn bed!

Clang!

Down on ground level, metal rapped against metal, and the sound resounded all the way up to the fifth floor. It was a pewter mug striking the outside stairs: Georgio's way of getting my attention without paying the price of a phone call.

Clang!

Wiping the residual nightmares from my eyes, I dragged myself out of the sheets and over to the Angel door. The key was in the lock. I turned it and stepped out onto the fire escape; these metal monstrosities had been bolted to the front of every building on Main Street courtesy of the Niles Company and their city-wide redesign of Sunder City.

Every day she looked a little different. It wasn't just the new paint or the neon signs. Not only the asphalt roads made to accommodate the multiplying automobiles, or the identical uniforms that strangled every filthy factory worker, blending them all together in an amorphous mix of grease, beer and obedience. It was more than the assembly-line firearms that dangled from the hips of cops, criminals and anyone who could afford them.

Her soul had shifted. Her smells and sounds. The way she moved. With every bite the Niles Company took from Sunder, the memory of her magic-filled glory days became harder to hold onto.

I stomped down every step, waiting for the day when I'd finally break through.

"Fetch, look!"

The silver-haired café owner waited on the street with his ever-present smile, crooked back, and a shiny brass plaque in his ancient hands.

"What is it, Georgio?"

He handed me the slab of brass. Etched into the front were the words:

> Fetch Phillips: Man for Hire
> Bringing the magic back!
> Enquire at Georgio's café

I held back the flood of sighs and eye rolls that attempted to pour down my face.

"What is this?"

"It's a sign! If people come around and they need your help but you're already off doing your investigations and your adventures and looking for clues, then they will come to me! I will take their information and you can call them when you get back!"

Georgio wielded his smile like a lance, sharp enough to pierce even my prickly disposition. His glory days as Gorgoramus Ottallus, pacifist adviser to wayward adventurers, were technically behind him, but he still managed to dispense his fair share of ancient wisdom over plates of greasy bacon and increasingly edible eggs. I'd humored him at first, then I'd learned to appreciate his insight, and I was getting dangerously close to relying on him as a friend.

Georgio's nephew, Gerome, came out of the café and handed me a cup of coffee. A couple of sips brought some life back into my eyes and a more tolerant tone to my voice.

"Thanks for the sign, Georgio. I appreciate the thought. Though I could have done without the exclamation mark."

"No! That's the point! It must be done with gusto! No more talk, talk, talk."

He laughed, and I had to laugh too. Georgio had spent many a generous hour listening to me yammer about all that needed to be done and how hard I was going to work to do it. He'd also watched me drink too much, sleep too late, and scrape my shoes along the sidewalk when I should have been running into action. He was right. There was no time for excuses. Not anymore. No more wasted days or half-cocked attempts at turning things around. If Hendricks had died so that this city, our magicless world and my dumb ass would have a chance at becoming something better, then I needed to spend every waking moment making it happen.

"Get a drill," I said, "and let's put her up."

We screwed the plaque into the stone wall halfway between the revolving door of my building and the entrance to the café. It looked good, even with the overexcited punctuation mark.

Georgio, Gerome and I stood back to admire the sign, drinking more coffee and trying our best to believe that a few words etched into a slab of brass might make a lick of difference.

But they did.

It took a while, of course. Change doesn't happen in a straight line; it's a series of loops. Most of the time, you think you're moving forward, but you end up right back where you began. Unless you work really hard. Then, when you loop around, you come back to a place that's a few inches ahead of where you started. Then you do another loop and, if you keep working hard, that loop finishes farther ahead again.

That's the most you can hope for, as ambitious as you need to be. If each time you come around, you've learned a little something, then you might wake up one day and find yourself doing the thing that you always said you were going to do.

And that's when you're really in trouble.

1

"C'mon, pal. Be a hero."

The panhandling Ogre was a foot taller than me and twice as wide. His jaw was strong, but his left eye was cloudy, and he probably couldn't see out of it too well. If I had to hit him, I'd hit him right around there.

"No," I said, but he'd been told that word too many times and had become inoculated to its effect. He shook his tin can in my face and I fought the urge to slap it from his fingers.

"Just a couple of bits, mate. For the parade. Year of the Phoenix!"

He proclaimed it loudly, as if I hadn't heard him give the same pitch to every other table at the Beggar's Bread, Sunder's complimentary kitchen for those of us who weren't making bank in the city's recent boom. The Ogre had moved from bench to bench around the Sunder streetcar, saving me till last. Maybe he'd seen me sneer every time *Year of the Phoenix* passed his lips: a stupid, flamboyant title to celebrate the anniversary of the Niles Company bringing the fires back to Sunder City.

"I don't have any money," I told him.

He scoffed, and all the pretend-friendly tone fell from his voice.

"You're eating here for free, mate. The least you can do is cough up some change."

"Ask me again and I'll have you coughing up all kinds of things."

The Ogre flared his nostrils, and his head was just as empty as I'd expected. Inside my pocket, I slipped my fingers inside my brass knuckles.

"You want a hero?" I asked him, putting my weight on the balls of my feet. "I'll give you a fucking hero."

"Brothers!" A soothing voice interrupted us. "Both of you know that there are no conditions put upon a meal at the Beggar's Bread." The Ogre and I turned to find Brother Benjamin, one of the winged monks who cooked and served food from the old streetcar, waiting with a paper plate in each hand. Like the rest of the Brothers Hum, he had an unflattering bowl-cut hairstyle and wore a hooded red robe with holes cut into the back to expose his featherless wings. "Here you are. I've added some extra sausage because the stars have been kind to us today."

The Ogre looked from my face to his free meal, and his stomach finally won out. He took his serving of bread over to a table where another grubby panhandler, a Gnome, sat staring at me with an ugly smirk across his face. I was about to ask him what his problem was, but Benjamin sat down opposite and slid the second plate under my nose.

"Eat, Brother Phillips. I feel it may be the first time today."

He wasn't wrong. It had been seven years since the Coda. When the magic first left the world, I'd found plenty of work helping creatures who were struggling to adjust to the change. It rarely made much of a difference but it paid me enough to get by. In the last few months, as more Sunderites surrendered themselves to a magicless existence, fewer clients were interested in enlisting my services. I wasn't bothered. I'd collected enough loose ends and tantalizing rumors to keep the investigations ticking over on my own time, but it was easier when someone else was supplying the funds.

Luckily for me, the Brothers Hum hadn't changed with the times. Every night, without fail, they served free food to anybody who turned up to claim it, and I'd become their most loyal customer.

I took a mouthful of the fried bread – made from restaurant scraps and grass flour – and thanked Brother Benjamin for his charity. As always, he waved away my words.

"I tell you every night that your thanks aren't mine to receive."

"And every night I tell you that I'll give them anyway. But can you spare your thoughts on something?" The monk nodded sagely, and I opened up the little leather-bound notepad I'd made a habit of carrying around. "Things are going missing around town: artefacts, once magic, that we all assumed had lost their spark." I flipped through the pages, showing off my amateur illustrations of ancient wands, jewel-encrusted ornaments, and other rare trinkets. "If someone's gathering these things up, perhaps they know something we don't. Dozens of items have gone missing in the last few weeks. Some have even been stolen from displays at the museum. The thieves are rarely seen, but there have been three reports: a red-scaled Reptilian teenager, an elderly Werecat gentleman and a Wizard with mutton chops. I think they must be some kind of collective: a gang of thieves, working together to steal ex-magical treasures." I opened up the page where I'd drawn my impressions of the criminals, taken from the witness accounts. "Have you seen anyone like this around here recently?"

Benjamin's smile pulled tight, and his eyes were patronizingly apologetic.

"Look around you, Brother. The Beggar's Bread collects Sunder City's most needy and its most misunderstood; those in the process of regaining their footing, as well as those who may never find their feet. There are no judgments here. No questions. The police know to leave this place alone so that anybody, no matter their situation, can receive our offerings without fear."

"Yeah, but I'm not a cop." Benjamin raised a questioning eyebrow. "I'm *not*."

"You are known to work alongside them, though. You share information. But it matters not. Police officer, debt collector, estranged family member or overenthusiastic investigator, it is not my place to share the information of any of our guests. The bread must come with no conditions, lest our operation be compromised."

"Benjamin, this is important. I'm not trying to arrest anyone or get them into trouble, I just want to know what they know. If these things are magic, they could be the key to fixing everything!"

Benjamin stood up.

"Then I hope you find them, Brother Phillips. Until then, enjoy your meal, but please respect the privacy of your fellow guests as I have always respected yours."

I was about to enquire as to who might have bothered asking about me, but my eye was drawn to the table where the two panhandlers were waiting. Watching. The Gnome was talking at the Ogre, who was looking at me with his one good eye. I had a strange feeling that they were discussing some part of my history and wondered which chapter it might be. Was it the one where I defected from the magical alliance known as the Opus to join the Human Army? Or how that betrayal led to the invasion that turned the sacred magical river to crystal and killed all the magic in the world? Maybe they were talking about the time I found a mutated Vampire in a library basement, or perhaps the Gnome was telling the tale of the time I teamed up with the cops to squash a violent revolution, allowing Niles Company goons to take the city unopposed.

Whatever story it was, the Ogre didn't like the sound of it. He was getting ready for a confrontation and it wasn't a good idea to let him make the first move. I pushed back my seat and got ready to jump over the table.

"There you are."

The glare from my gossiping neighbors was interrupted by the far more pleasant face of Eileen Tide: librarian, bartender, one-time Witch, and occasional accomplice in my quest to bring the magic back. It had taken her a while to forgive me for the part I played in burning down her old library, but we'd managed to patch things up over the previous few months; more because of her love of a good mystery than any of my pathetic attempts to apologize.

She sat down, pulled her long braid into her lap to keep it off the filthy cobbles, and leaned over the table with a conspiratorial smile.

"I've got something for you," she whispered.

"I hope it's not another two-hundred-page tome of Dwarven history. Can't you just give me a summary this time?"

"Don't worry, this is something tangible. Maybe. I overheard a couple of customers at the bar talking about buying a rock of Hyluna."

"And you believe them?"

"I don't know, yet, but they gave me the number of the guy who sold it. I was thinking we could invite him down here and find out for ourselves."

I agreed, and Eileen went over to the pay phone to put in a call. A rock of Hyluna was on my list of stolen artefacts. Only last week, I'd been at the apartment of an old Elven lady who'd had one pilfered from her mantelpiece.

I was distracted by the eyes of the panhandlers: twin death stares over gritted teeth as they did the math on how much trouble I'd give them if they decided to follow me home. They might be respectful enough not to start anything here, but once I'd left the relative safety of the streetcar, I was fair game.

I stared back, unblinking, and made a few calculations myself. They were too cheap to buy pistols, but they could have acquired them through less lawful means. Despite the early spring weather, they both wore bulky jackets capable of hiding an untold variety of weapons. If I waited for them to make their move, I'd be toast before the fight even started.

"Brother Phillips?" Benjamin was standing beside me with a jug of milky tea and a stack of cups. "I need to quench the thirst of our guests. Could you work the fryer in the meantime?"

Begrudgingly, I left my table and the gaze of my enemies and stepped up to the giant fryer that was fixed to the back of the streetcar. A nickel pipe ran from the mechanism beneath the pan to the nearest streetlight, stealing some energy from the lamps that lit up the night sky. I dipped a ladle into the bucket, spooned some mixture onto the sizzling surface, and watched it turn from slurry to a crispy, brown sheet of flatbread.

It didn't take long for me to get agitated. I was wasting my time cooking kitchen scraps instead of focusing on the job that I was supposed to be doing. When Eileen returned from the phone, I tried to get her attention, but she went straight to sipping tea with a mangy Werewolf and didn't even look over. I wanted to ask her if the seller was coming down here and who he thought he was meeting, but she was lost in some frivolous conversation and didn't bother to fill me in.

There was no doubt that Eileen was helpful and that she'd saved my neck a number of times, but she didn't understand the stakes. She liked playing the game, though I was pretty sure that she didn't believe we could actually win. It was just something to pass the time. A way to keep her spirits up until something better came along. It wasn't life and death. Not to her, and not to anyone else. There was only me, the last real soldier tasked with turning back the hands of time.

"You're running hot, Brother Phillips," said Benjamin, picking up a sizable spatula and sliding it beneath the bread. "Better flip it."

He turned the portion over to reveal a blackened underside.

"Sorry."

"No bother. The Gnomes like it like this. I'll put this piece away for them."

Embarrassed at failing such a simple task, I let Benjamin take over. He gave the frying pan every bit of his attention, rotating pieces, pushing them down, and then piling them onto the plate with the focus of a rogue disarming a bear trap.

As he moved around the pan, his wings dangled lifelessly from his shoulder blades. They looked heavy: thick spikes of cartilage webbed with featherless, pockmarked sheets of dry skin that flapped against each other in pathetic applause. In recent years, most flying creatures chose to have their wings amputated. Without magic, the appendages were nothing but a burden. The Brothers Hum ignored such customs and continued to wear their featherless wings as if nothing had changed.

Good, I thought. At least a few of these creatures haven't given up completely. They might not be working to fix things like I am, but when I get the job done, at least these Brothers will be able to appreciate it.

"Fetch, he's here."

Eileen grabbed my arm and turned me toward a mustachioed Cyclops. He had the look of a sailor about him, someone who once made a living on the seas and still hadn't adjusted to life on land. He wore big brown boots, a dozen leather pouches dangling from his belt, and a black jacket that had been waterproofed with beeswax, giving him the slick, wet shine of a walrus.

"You're looking for a rock?"

We both nodded. Eileen clearly enjoyed playing the part of a dangerous, underground artefact merchant.

"Shall we go somewhere private?" she asked.

The Cyclops shrugged. "I'm fine here. Nobody's gonna mess with us at the Beggar's Bread."

We sat down at one of the tables, Eileen and me on one side with the Cyclops sitting opposite. I waited for him to reveal his merchandise, but he just said, "Five silver leaf." If I'd been drinking, I would have spat it all over him. "That's a hundred bronze bills if you don't have the big boys."

"I can do the math," I said, though I'd never had occasion to count that much cash before, "but it seems a little steep for a useless stone."

The Cyclops groaned.

"If you want to see it in action, you only need to ask. But you're not just here for a show, are you? You got the dosh?"

Eileen pulled a leather-wrapped bundle out of her jacket. She let the Cyclops admire the size of it before she tucked it away again. She was perfectly careful with her actions, as if it really was a fortune in bronze and not just a couple of small books wrapped in canvas.

"All right," said the sailor, pulling a towel from his sleeve, "you better finish that drink. Wouldn't want it spilling on the merchandise."

Eileen slammed back her tea and placed the cup on a neighboring table. The Cyclops wiped down the surface, untied one of the leather pouches from his belt, and pulled out a bundle of waxed material. When he unfolded it, there was a little, brown, utterly unremarkable rock inside.

I resisted the urge to make some kind of slight, knowing that it would further reveal my ignorance. Eileen took the lead.

"Can I touch it?"

"Wipe your hands first," said the merchant, handing her the towel. "Make sure they're completely dry."

Eileen did as she was instructed and then picked up the stone.

"I thought it would be lighter," she remarked. The Cyclops shook his head; this was a conversation he'd had a hundred times over.

"They used to be. Ancient Dwarves enchanted these rocks to hold up the lake-top city of Hyluna: a platform that was as tough as granite but utterly unsinkable."

"Then why can't we get it wet?" I asked.

"Because the Coda screwed all that up. When the magic left the rocks, they stopped floating, and Hyluna sank to the bottom."

"You wanna hold it?" Eileen asked me.

I wiped my hands on the towel and she dropped the rock into my palm. It was uneven, rough and . . . well, it was a rock. The rockiest rock I'd ever seen. I put it down on the table.

"So, it's a stone that doesn't float," I said. "Should we call the papers?"

The Cyclops's single eye squinted at me.

"You're the one who wants to buy it, right?"

"I'm sorry," interrupted Eileen. "This is my bodyguard. I don't bother filling him in on all the details. He's a simple fellow and too many facts will overwhelm his little head. Please, continue."

The Cyclops returned his attention to the stone and Eileen gave me a twinkling smile. If I'd had this meeting on my own, I likely would have blown it to pieces several times already, so I was lucky to have someone more amicable at my side.

The Cyclops flattened out the material beneath the stone, licked his finger, wiped away some excess spit onto his sleeve, and pressed his fingertip against the little rock. Then he sat back and said, "Go on."

Eileen grabbed the rock again.

"Shit." She wrapped her fingers around the stone and pulled, but the rock of Hyluna remained right where it was. "It's heavy."

She laughed and removed her hand so that I could have a try.

I anticipated some kind of joke, like this whole meeting was an elaborate schoolyard prank and when I hoisted the thing up, expecting it to be heavy, I'd fall backwards with nothing but a pebble in my hands, giving everyone a good laugh. So, I was careful at first. I slid my fingers around the edge and tried to pry it off the table. It wouldn't budge. I clenched it tight between my fingers and pulled harder and harder until I was leaning right back on my stool, but it stayed stuck on the table as if someone had nailed it down.

"Is this a trick?" I asked, panting.

The Cyclops chuckled, enjoying my confusion.

"No trick, just a twist of the old magicless magic."

I stood up and really put my back into it. The rock slid to the side, and I could tilt it a little, but I couldn't get the whole thing off the table at once.

"That's incredible," I said. "How does it work?"

"How should I know? Five silver leaf, take it or leave it." He took a lighter from his pocket and waved the flame over the stone for a few seconds to evaporate the moisture, then wrapped it up in the waxy cloth again. He left the bundle on the table to tempt us.

Eileen wrinkled up her face, pretending to think it over. We didn't have the money to buy it, of course, we were just gathering information. When the sailor saw that she was stalling, he shrugged and picked up the bundle.

I grabbed his wrist.

"Tell me where you got this," I demanded, keeping my voice low.

"What are you doing?" He was more offended than afraid. "You think I came here alone? Take this any further and I signal my friends."

"Do it. I've got questions for them too."

Eileen's hand gripped my leg under the table. This was not the plan.

"Fetch," she warned.

"Tell me where you got it, or I take it from you."

Our guest tried to pull his hand back.

"Let go," he warned.

I pulled harder.

Maybe the rock wasn't anything truly special – just the shadow of a miracle that used to mean something – but then I could follow this stepping-stone to someplace that mattered.

"This is something that I haven't seen before," I told him, "and I've been looking harder than most. Maybe the guy who gave it to you has something more interesting for me to look at. If a straight answer from you could bring me closer to what I want, then I'm not letting go of your arm until you give it to me."

There was real fear in his eyes now. He was no longer trying to bluff a potential buyer; he was hoping to survive an encounter with a madman.

"This is the Beggar's Bread," he stammered. "You wouldn't dare."

A smile climbed my unshaven cheek.

"You're holding magic, my friend. You think I'll let that go rather than disturb somebody's dinner? You think I care about being polite? After what I've done? No. I dare do more than you can imagine."

Eileen released her grip on my leg and leaned back. Either she'd sensed that I'd gotten through to him or she was just too afraid to touch me. Likely, it was both.

The Cyclops nodded.

"I have a cousin who travels the trade roads," he said. "Brought them back from Hyluna himself. The whole thing dried up and you can just pick them out of the lakebed. He brings a sack-full every time he visits."

I leaned in.

"Bullshit. This is stolen. Taken from the mantelpiece of a little old lady on Lark Street by the same gang of thieves who've been lifting similar pieces all over the city. Who gave it to you?"

He looked to Eileen, hoping to find a friendlier ear.

"Please. I'm telling the truth."

He kept his voice down; less afraid of my fists than the fact that I was willing to create a scene. This man's business required a level of secrecy, and I was holding his reputation over the fire.

"I told you," he said. "I got it from my cousin, but . . ."

He looked over both his shoulders. I jolted his arm to regain his attention.

"But what?"

"But . . . but I know what you're talking about. The thieves." He leaned right in and made his voice as quiet as possible. "Go to the Mess."

Eileen and I looked at each other, and the sailor used the moment to yank back his arm and get to his feet.

"Next time you want a show-and-tell, you go to the museum," he growled, loud enough for those around us to hear. "Don't call a meeting if you don't have the cash."

He stuffed the bundle back into the pouch and moved off,

playing the part of a busy trader who was frustrated with us for wasting his time. Even though he'd offered up some sort of clue, I hated the thought of him taking that miraculous little rock away from us.

I turned to Eileen.

"Do you believe him?"

"I don't know. I guess we go look."

The Mess. A whole block of market stalls and carts stacked with imported produce. Just the place to send some inquisitive pests if you wanted them out of your way.

"I'm going after him."

"Fetch, wait!"

But I was already off, squeezing through the crowded tables. The Cyclops's bald head bobbed its way up Main Street and he looked like he was about to turn east. I pushed past a group of Dwarves – and then my feet came off the floor.

The panhandling Ogre spun me around. He had both my lapels gripped in his thick fingers and his face pressed right up to mine.

"My friend told me something about you," he snarled, sprinkling my face with beer-flavored spit. "He told me you worked for the Army. That you were there when the Coda happened. That it's your fault."

"If he was a really good friend, he would've have told you about that bit of spinach in your teeth. Let me get it out for you."

I had my brass ready to go and his blind spot all figured out. My fist hit his temple before he felt me move. He growled in pain and dropped me. I landed, crouched, and came up under his chin with another metal-wrapped attack. Hitting Ogres with your bare hands will break your fingers, but brass knuckles do a good job of evening the odds. The panhandler grabbed the table for support and tried to shake the stars from his eyes.

The gossipy Gnome reached into his jacket for something. I didn't wait to see what it was, I just kicked him in the chest so that he rolled off his chair onto the floor.

Then the Ogre's arms were around my waist. He squeezed like he was trying to break my back, but he wasn't as strong as he would have been in the old days and he hadn't managed to pin my arms or legs.

I couldn't land a good punch – he was tucked in too close – but my elbows were happy to take over. I'd marked his temple with a bloody cut, so I made it my target and struck him over and over. He dropped his head, so I introduced my knee to his chin, then used a perfectly aimed haymaker to turn out his lights.

He fell back, and the eyes of Benjamin, Eileen, and a few dozen other disapproving patrons tried to make me feel remorse. It wouldn't work. I had a half-decent lead on my team of thieves and my heart was hot and beating.

"Let's go," I said to Eileen, and marched off towards the Mess.

2

The sign said "Primrose Markets" but it had been called the Mess for as long as anyone could remember, and it only became messier with time.

The semi-permanent stalls on the outside of the square sold everything from clothing and paintings to herbal tea and indoor toilets. The center of the square was stocked by different sellers every day of the week. Some days it was fish, others it was fruit or spices or salted meat. They took turns, day after day, leaving behind the residual scraps that gave the Mess its name along with its unique aroma of rotten cabbage, shellfish, cinnamon and blood.

Eileen and I arrived to see the farmers loading up their remaining fruits and vegetables onto carts and harnessing them to donkeys and oxen.

"He screwed us," I said.

"Not necessarily."

"Or we heard him wrong."

"We both heard him say the Mess."

There was nothing useful here. In half an hour, it would be empty of everything but corn husks and horse shit.

"You go clockwise," said Eileen, "I'll meet you at the other end."

She took off without giving me a chance to argue, moving swiftly around the outside of the vegetable stalls with her long braid of brown hair trailing behind her.

I grabbed the closest fruit-seller – a heavyset farmer with the facial tattoos of a retired warrior – and asked him if he knew anything about a hideout. He wrinkled up his face.

"Buddy, I'm just selling lemons. Three for a bit or two bits a bag."

I ignored his offer and moved through the other stallholders, who all answered in much the same manner, then turned my attention to the more permanent stores on the outside of the square.

The first store was a cartographer. The door was locked and everything in the window was dark and dusty. The next store was a watchmaker and then a massage parlor; both lacked any signs of life. Two doors down, there was a little hut with wooden masks in the window: all kinds of different creatures, including costumed characters, a smiling Unicorn, and a cat burglar. I pushed open the door and was met with the hollow eyes of a hundred wooden faces balanced on pegs around the room. Behind the counter, a prune-faced Elf on a stepladder reached for a box on the top shelf.

"Excuse me," I blurted. The Elf startled, lost his footing, and grabbed the cupboard for support. The store was just a rackety old shack, so the whole place wobbled, causing a couple of the façades to fall to the floor.

"Blast you," shouted the mask-maker, still gripping the cupboard. "Don't startle an old man like that."

"Sorry. I'm looking for a thief. A gang of them, actually. Apparently, they're hiding out in the Mess."

The Elf came down from the stepladder, muttering expletives to himself.

"The only thieves around here are the landlords who just upped the rent for this termite-ridden wreck. I don't know anything about any gang."

He hunched over to pick up one of the masks and examine it for cracks, groaning and swearing under his breath.

"Sorry," I said. "Didn't mean to intrude."

I went next door and knocked on the entrance to a shop that made oil lamps. The door swung open, but the place was abandoned. I didn't spot any obvious entrances to sewers or basements, and there were no signs proudly announcing "Secret Thieves Club", so I moved on. Everything else was closed. It was too late in the day. The Mess opened at sunrise and did its best business before noon. We were wasting our time.

I met Eileen at the opposite entrance and she hadn't found anything more interesting than I had.

"What were you expecting?" she asked.

"I don't know. Maybe we get a higher vantage point. Stake it out and wait."

"For what?"

"One of the culprits: a crimson Reptile, an old Cat or a Wizard with sideburns. Then we just—"

I stopped. While I'd been rattling off the descriptions, I'd seen the images of the thieves in my mind clearer than ever before. I could picture them perfectly: the lizard, Sorcerer and feline. *The cat burglar.*

"Come on."

We stood outside the mask-maker's workshop and Eileen, for a change, was impressed.

"There isn't any gang of criminals," she said. "It's just one."

There they were: all our thieves, waiting quietly in the window with their faces balanced on wooden pegs. There was no organized team of burglars, just the old Elf that I'd met inside a few minutes earlier, when I'd stupidly revealed that I was looking for him.

The door was closed. I tried the handle.

"He's locked it."

"We should call the police," Eileen suggested, but I shook my head and took two steps back.

"He already knows we're after him."

"Fetch, think before you—"

Eileen jumped back as I ran my shoulder into the mask-maker's door. The wood around the latch splintered and split. I shouldered it again and the door swung open. I stumbled inside.

I expected the mask-maker to be running. Trying to escape. No.

He was waiting for me.

When I'd come around asking stupid questions, the thief had been careful not to show me his whole face. He'd kept his head turned away and his body hunched over in the shadows. If he hadn't, I might have noticed that his lips didn't move when he talked.

The mask was finely carved and expertly painted. It covered his whole face and wrapped around the sides of his head to adorn him with tall, pointed ears. When I'd found him on the ladder, he'd been wearing a wig. That was gone, and the top of the wooden mask now cut across his forehead, revealing pale skin behind it. The face was sculpted into an expression of despair but the eyes peering out from the sockets were full of fury.

"You're nothing," said the voice behind the mask, far deeper than the croaky one he'd affected when playing the elderly Elf. The thief stood up straight – his hunch forgotten – and drew a pistol from his belt.

I jumped back and pushed Eileen out into the square, dragging the door closed just in time to feel the shudder of two bullets embed themselves in the wood.

"Round the back," I told her. "But be careful."

I waited for her to move. She didn't. She had her back against the wall and her eyes were glazed over.

"Eileen, you okay?" Her eyes found mine. She nodded.

"Yeah."

"The back door. Quickly."

Eileen took off, searching for a gap between the shacks. I drew my own pistol – the prototype machine that every other gun in the city was modelled on – kicked open the door and stepped to the side.

As anticipated, the thief's third and final shot went through the open door and executed an innocent watermelon in the stall behind me. The owner of the melon screamed, and her startled horse kicked out the supporting beam of her neighbor's berry stand. The commotion escalated as I ran inside, ready to tackle the mask-maker before he had a chance to reload.

A crowd was waiting for me: a wooden ensemble of strange faces staring with empty eyes, the unstable walls and floorboards made them shake like they were all cracking up at some great joke.

At the back of the room, there was a hallway with two doors off to the left and one that went straight out into the alley. That door was wide open. He must have just ducked out. I ran towards the hall, hoping that the thief hadn't gone too far, when someone moved behind the counter.

Shit.

The thief hadn't tried to escape; he'd been ducking down, waiting for me to do the exact dumb thing I'd just done.

That's the problem, isn't it? I can work harder, sleep longer and take better care of myself, but I still don't know how to be any smarter today than I was yesterday.

I expected to see the pistol in his hands. Instead, he held two golden rods shaped like small rolling pins. They were engraved with swirling turquoise patterns and were blunt enough to appear quite harmless. They didn't look like weapons. Certainly not weapons to be worried about. Then, the mask-maker clanged the rods together and the room turned upside-down.

I landed on the splintered floorboards, but I felt like I was dangling from the roof, then the wall. Someone had stuck the store in a giant tumble-dryer, but the thief didn't seem to notice. He came around the counter – unaffected by the somersaulting room – then reached behind his mask and plucked the stuffing from his ears.

He said something that I couldn't hear over the reverberation in my brain, and slammed the door shut. He thought I'd come alone. That I was trapped. If Eileen didn't find the back entrance, he was right.

"I see you're quite taken with the golden rods of Rakanesh," he said, as the ringing started to abate. "They really take your inner ears for a spin, don't they?"

The sound was dying out, but the unbalancing effect remained, making the world do another loop-the-loop. Stomach acid rose into my throat.

"Maybe I can interest you in a rock of Hyluna?" He leaned down close, looked me over with his hate-filled eyes, and dropped a pebble onto my chest. When I reached for it, he swatted my hand away. Nausea had turned my muscles to mealworms. "Doesn't feel like much, does it?" He brought a finger up to the lips of his wrinkled mask and the tip of a pink tongue pushed through a slit. "But the smallest bit of liquid and . . ."

He prodded the stone with his wet finger, and it was like he'd put his knee on my chest. Not even *his* knee: more like the knee of a Giant. My breath rushed from my body and the floorboards creaked and bent beneath my back.

"Not all magic needs magic," said the thief, his voice muffled by the mask. "To forge these artefacts, the creators used the talents of their time. The Coda may have killed the artists but the art itself is far more resilient."

I tried reaching for the stone, or kicking him off me, but the thief grabbed my wrists, stood on my knees, and held me to the floor.

"If only *we* were so lucky, us creatures of the old time. All our powers, drained away. You've been lucky, though, haven't you? Before the Coda, you were nobody. But me? I was *everyone*."

A shapeshifter. I'd only heard about them in stories: cautionary tales of travelers who were led from their path by villains in disguise, or conspiracy theories about important men and women being replaced by doppelgängers.

"I lost a million lives when your kind took the magic. Now, I claim only what I am owed. You dare to try to stop me, Human? No. Despite your efforts, I will be whole again."

My vision sparkled and blurred from lack of oxygen. I couldn't make out much of the mask-maker's true face, just the wrinkles around his bloodshot eyes, but it was enough to see that he was smiling.

"Maybe I'll make a mask of you," he said. "It can be useful, sometimes, to go out into the world as a nobody."

I spat. Not at him – I'd been called far worse things than *nobody* – I spat at the little gray rock that was sitting on my chest.

The weight was unbelievable. If I had any breath left, I would have screamed, but my lungs were all wrung out. I heard something crack, prayed that it wasn't my ribs, then summoned all the strength I could to lift up my elbows and slam them back against the floor.

The eyes inside the mask went wide as the floorboards caved in.

"No!"

The fall didn't last long. I had just enough time to twist to the side. That way, when the rock of Hyluna hit the basement floor, my body was no longer beneath it. It was a small mercy in an otherwise unforgiving outcome. I collided with the sharp corner of a tall wooden box, scraped the edge of another box that was shorter than the first one but just as sharp, and landed upside down behind a heavy chest. The mask-maker was somewhere nearby, and both of us were groaning.

"Please, don't get up," I grumbled. "Let's just stay here for a second and nurse our wounds before you make me chase you aga—"

The chest shifted as he got to his feet. The candle up on the ground floor gave me just enough light to see the shadow of the thief as he stumbled through toppled crates towards the staircase. I coughed out a lungful of dust and scrambled after him, shins and elbows finding every available corner. I tripped over some unknown piece of junk and grabbed the mask-maker on my way down, gripping him by the ankle. He came down hard and his bones rapped against the stairs like the world's worst drum roll.

He kicked me right in the face. The thief might be light on his feet, but his legs were damn strong. I caught his foot on the second kick and pulled him towards me.

He stopped struggling. Never a good sign.

I looked up to see what he was doing, which, once again, played right into the mask-maker's hands. He tore open a tiny parcel and pure white light flashed out of it, adding blindness to my growing list of artefact-induced ailments.

He kicked my forearms against the stairs, knocking both funny bones, and my fingers lost their grip. I reached out to grab him, and left myself open to another crack across the face.

My balance was all wobbly and I couldn't see a thing, but I could hear his footsteps, so I felt my way upwards: sloppy and scrappy but managing not to fall on my face. Something must have slowed him down because when I got near the top of the stairs, I reached out and found a handful of cloth.

I pulled him into me; one hand around his throat, the other around his waist. He tried to pull away, so I brought us both down onto the floor – half on the stairs, half on ground level – and wrapped my legs around him. I had no idea how long it would take for the blinding effect to wear off, but all I had to do was hold on until Eileen arrived.

"Fetch . . ." said her voice from between my arms. "What are you doing?"

Shit.

I released my grip.

"Where is he?" I asked. "The mask-maker?"

"I don't know," said Eileen, obviously annoyed. "I ran in and you grabbed me."

"Well, go look. I can't see a thing."

"Oh, right. I thought you'd just wanted a cuddle."

She went off and I collapsed on my back, letting all the little aches turn into proper pains. When Eileen returned and told me he was gone, I was honestly thankful. She pulled my eyelids open, and I could just make out her bleached silhouette.

"What did he hit you with?"

"Some silver paper . . . thing. That was after the heavy wet rock and the golden sticks of . . . whatever."

"The golden rods of Rakanesh? They were stolen from the museum. Did they work?"

"If by work, you mean did they make my stomach think the roof is the floor, then yeah, they work."

"Oh. They used to control flying machines by creating points of temporary gravity. I wonder what else he— Holy shit!"

Her footsteps rattled down the stairs.

"Eileen, did you just step over me?" She was giggling. "What is it?"

Her giggle turned into full-on laughter.

"Treasure!"

3

Eileen found more candles and placed them around the mask-maker's basement. While the sparkles faded from my eyes, she opened up the crates, squealing with delight every time she spied some new piece of stolen loot.

"There's more than we knew about," she said. "A lot more."

When the light had left my eyes, and I could finally see what she was talking about, I almost squealed myself.

Treasure. There was no other way to describe it: chests full of old coins and crates full of gemstones, jewelry, goblets and gold. There were jade figurines that glowed of their own accord, rings of polished stone, and a bracelet woven from the skins of tiny snakes. It wasn't all pleasant to look at. One box was full of shrunken heads and jars of pickled fingers. Eileen opened a little red pouch, gasped, and dropped it on the floor.

"Teeth," she explained, scrunching up her face.

Some of the pieces were familiar to me. I'd seen them at the museum during my regular visits to prod Baxter Thatch for information and advice, but they seemed different down here. When they'd been tucked away behind glass or pinned onto walls, it had looked like they'd always been there, just facsimiles of the real thing or props from made-up stories. Seeing them all bunched together in a candlelit basement made it feel like we'd discovered these wonders for ourselves.

It was an embarrassment of riches. Of course, plenty of them belonged to the city, and it wasn't my style to steal things from Baxter's museum. Other items had been stolen from individuals, but maybe not everything. There was a real possibility that some key item was sitting here amongst the ill-gotten gains.

"I suppose we should call the cops," said Eileen.

She saw my reluctance. Detective Simms and I had been working on this case together, in the "off the books" manner we'd become accustomed to. Even so, I knew that our motives weren't as perfectly aligned as we pretended they were. Simms wanted to keep Sunder safe and stable while I wanted to turn the world on its head.

"It's the right thing to do, Fetch. Besides, we just ran around the Mess shouting our intentions and getting into a shootout. We couldn't keep this under wraps even if we wanted to."

She was right. I was tempted to tuck every piece away so we could investigate their powers on our own, but this case was too high profile and I'd carelessly given the game away. If I pushed back against Simms, I'd be putting us both on the wrong side of the law, and Eileen didn't deserve that.

And yet . . .

"What if we go through the boxes first? Quickly?"

"And then what? Smuggle the best stuff out of here? I thought you trusted Simms."

"I don't trust anyone to go all the way. Especially not the police."

"What do you mean, go all the way?"

I didn't have the words to explain myself, and the look on Eileen's face made me question whether it was worth finding them. If I wanted to keep myself involved in the case after the cops got here, my best option was to stay on their good side. I swallowed my desire to risk it all for the sake of some unknown stolen trinkets, and stepped back from the crates.

"I think there's a phone upstairs," I said.

The floor beneath the telephone had caved in. To use it, I had to straddle the gap with one boot on a shelf and the other on the edge of a broken floorboard.

It rang twice before a high-pitched voice answered. It was Sunder City's most sickeningly polite police officer, Corporal Bath.

"Is Simms there?" I asked.

"Can I ask who's speaking?"

"You can give it a try."

There was a pause. I would have let it go on longer if my foot wasn't cramping.

"Bath, it's Fetch. Just let me talk to her."

Eileen shouted from below.

"Fetch, look!"

She'd unwrapped something from inside a large piece of canvas.

"Just tell Simms to come down to the Mess."

"The Mess? We had a report of somebody firing a pistol down there. Was that you?"

Of course. Even in a city as wild as Sunder, bullets fired into a fruit stall are bound to be noticed.

"I didn't do the firing but I know who did. I'm in the basement of the mask-maker's store with something Simms will want to see. Don't tell anyone else, okay? This is for her ears only."

"Sure. But—"

I hung up and rushed back downstairs to make the most of our last few minutes alone. Eileen and I were two kids unwrapping our birthday presents and we didn't want to put down our toys for a moment.

Eileen was holding a wooden sword over her head like a character on the cover of a children's story, with the tip pointing up through the hole in the floorboards into the room above. It was three feet long, made from dense, dark, knotted timber.

"It's a Fae sword," she said. "I've read about them in stories but never seen one for real."

I ran my finger along the edge. It was kind of sharp, but not enough to cut my skin. I brought it near one of the candles to get a better look at the grain and saw that there were no joins or separations; the pommel, handle, crossbar and blade were all constructed from a single piece of wood. This sword hadn't been carved, it had been shaped by a talented Wood Sprite; grown from a living organism by a creature who could sculpt with nature itself.

"I thought the Fae favored magic over wielding weapons by hand. Or—"

As I tilted the sword to examine the hilt, the blade tapped against the leg of a metal table. As soon as it made contact, the leg bent, then snapped. The table collapsed and the candle hit the floor, splashing hot wax all over us.

I was left stunned and confused, staring at the pieces of shrapnel lying beneath the broken table and wondering what had happened.

Eileen picked up the candle and lit it again.

"During the Third War, after Humans forged the first iron weapons, the Fae crafted these swords in response. You can't kill anyone with them, but . . ."

The broken table was sideways on the floor. Eileen put the tip of the sword on another one of the legs and pushed down. The thick metal bent easily, like it had been heated up to an incredible temperature, then snapped in two. We both giggled in amazement.

"It works like it used to!" I said.

Eileen shrugged. "Not quite. In the stories, it shattered armor with the slightest tap and broke swords into millions of pieces. This seems to have diminished somewhat, but it might be handy around a construction site."

She laid the sword down on the canvas and we kept searching the crates, hoping to find another rare treasure ripped from one of her stories. Gold and silver shimmered in the darkness. Some items smelled like distant oceans, others like old smoke or musty caves. We left Sunder City behind, adventuring out across Archetellos as it used to be: a world that was barely big enough for its own amazing creations, full of magic and danger, with unpredictable wonders tucked into every square foot.

We were so wrapped up in our discoveries that we didn't notice the footsteps above.

"Hello? Mr Phillips?"

It was the courteous Corporal Bath. His pale face peered down from the hole over our heads.

"Hey, Bath. Is Simms up there?"

Another, deeper voice responded.

"She'll be along shortly, Mr Phillips, but we can handle things for the time being."

Goddamnit.

The sound of leather-soled shoes brought Thurston Niles down the stairs. His suit was tan, his shoes were spotless, and his eyes were as warm and welcoming as a shallow swamp.

"Well done, Fetch. Baxter will be pleased."

When he looked to Eileen, she tensed, as if preparing to defend herself. I grumbled out introductions.

"Eileen Tide, this is Thurston Niles of the Niles Company. From his shit-eating grin, it looks like he's here to try and take the recovered artefacts for himself."

"I don't *try* to do anything, Fetch. Just leave everything where it is and we'll take care of it."

"Some of these pieces belong to my clients."

"Then they can file a claim with the House of Ministers and apply to get them back, but they'll have to prove that they won't be used for nefarious means." He walked up to the closest box and examined a stone figurine of an archer. "We can't just let things like these loose on the streets, can we?"

Eileen snorted.

"You're the one who put killing machines in everyone's hands."

"Yes, but that's *fair*. The pistols create an even playing field for all of us. It works the same, no matter who wields it. Something like this," he picked up a golden bracelet and twirled it in the candlelight, "well, who knows what kind of trouble it might cause?"

He stood there, saying nothing, waiting for one of us to officially cross the line. I wanted to slap the treasure from his hands, chop off his fingers and crush them under my boot. Each item in the room had the potential to bring the world we lost out of the darkness, and Thurston Niles was determined to stop that from happening.

A year ago, I saved this city. It cost the life of my best friend to do it. Hendricks believed that if Niles could control this city, he'd use that power to take over all Archetellos, but I believed that the people of Sunder wouldn't give him their souls so easily. I had faith that they could resist the easy comfort that Niles offered them, and find a way back to the world we all wanted.

I was wrong.

Every day that goes by, Niles digs his claws deeper into this city. Every day, fewer folks dream about ever going back.

Niles and I were in a race – I needed to prove to everyone that the magic wasn't gone for good before Niles created a world where even a miracle wouldn't matter – and Niles was way out ahead.

"Drop it," I said.

Niles grinned, his mouth full of artificially whitened teeth.

"No," he replied. No explanation. No defense. He didn't need one. Thurston Niles owned Sunder City. He'd purchased it a year ago by bringing the fires up to the surface, heating homes, and filling factories with well-paid workers. He built houses on the outskirts to get people out of the slums, and mansions on the hill so they had something to aspire to. You couldn't fight him. You might as well try to fight the sidewalk or the smog or the lantern-light.

But that didn't stop me from trying.

"I said, drop it."

One of Thurston's lackeys came down the stairs in his charcoal suit. He stood behind his boss and tried an unconvincing scowl. I couldn't tell any of those fuckers apart. They all had the same haircut, same charcoal suit, same black tie, and same slap-attracting face.

"Settle down, Mr Man for Hire," said Niles, spinning the

bracelet on his finger and adopting the patronizingly rational tone that all powerful men use when they want their opinions to come across as fact. "The police are upstairs, and this is all above board. We just want to make sure these valuables find their rightful home."

He was goading me, and I was more than happy to take the bait.

I grabbed the Fae sword and brought the tip up to Niles's throat. The point wavered under his dimpled chin, tilting his head upwards. The charcoal suit froze, his hand not yet on his weapon. Everyone in the room held their breath, for just a moment, before it all came out as laughter.

Niles first, then his lackey, then another charcoal suit on the stairs. Even Bath up in the bleachers had a chuckle.

"Whatever people say about you, Fetch, you certainly know how to paint a heroic picture." Niles dropped his chin against the harmless tip of my weapon. "A lone man going up against the fully-armed might of a more powerful enemy with nothing but a child's wooden sword. Your efforts are as ineffective as always, but I appreciate the symbolism."

Fuck him. I pulled back my shoulder and bent my arm. The sword might not be sharp, but the wood was hard enough to hurt if it came down on his head. There was a hint of surprise in Niles's eyes that pleased me, but the jackets of the charcoal suits slipped open, and three pistols were pointed in my direction.

"Stop!" screamed Eileen.

Shit. I'd almost forgotten she was there. I relaxed my arm.

"Now *you* drop it," said Niles, who was no longer smiling. He was used to being ten steps ahead and resented anything unpredictable.

"Fetch, do as he says."

The unmistakable lisp of Detective Simms dropped down from above, the words landing on my head like unhappy little raindrops.

Fuck this. Fuck her and fuck them all.

I dropped the sword. Niles found his shiny grin again.

"There's a good boy."

Between my feet, the rock of Hyluna sat in the divot it had made when it hit the floor.

"Fine, but I'm taking thi—" I tried to pick it up but the rock hadn't dried all the way. "I'm taking this. For my – hnghh – for my . . ." It took all my effort to get it up to the height of my outer jacket pocket. "For my client."

Niles was about to protest, but a ripping sound stopped him. The rock tore its way out of my coat and smashed back onto the floor, making another dent.

As they laughed, I wiped it with my sleeve – which made it slightly lighter – and kept it in my fist as I marched up the stairs. Eileen huffed for a few moments before following me.

"Lovely to finally meet you, Miss Tide." Thurston's smile didn't make it past his top lip, let alone his eyes. "I hope you're enjoying the new library we built for you. Education is so very important in a flourishing civilization."

We left him with his room of precious treasures, and I wondered if there was anything in the world that had the power to change things now. Could any of those trinkets truly make a difference in a city where Thurston had brought his brand of prosperity to the streets? Even if they could, would anyone want to hear about it?

Simms was waiting at the top of the stairs: a thin figure in a black coat, hat and scarf, absently rubbing a loose scale on the side of her hand.

"What the hell, Simms? I called you, not Niles."

The detective didn't have a habit of apologizing, but her eyes were something close to sorry. She leaned in close and said, "Let's take this outside."

4

"Eileen Tide, meet Detective Lena Simms."

They shook hands. Eileen's long fingers wrapped around Simms's reptilian scales.

"Nice to meet you, Ms Tide. I'm sorry to be rude, but would you mind if I spoke to Fetch alone?"

Eileen nodded.

"As long as you're gonna kick his ass for almost getting me killed down there. Next time you want to start a scrap with your boyfriend, Fetch, wait until I've left the room."

Simms raised an amused eyebrow.

"Actually, this one can stay."

"You're kidding!" I looked between them, mouth hanging open. "Why the hell wouldn't you back me up?"

"We can't," said Eileen. "The new library is funded by the Niles Company, and we all know the influence Thurston has with the mayor. Simms can't be seen arguing with him in public."

"So, I'm the only one who's willing to put myself on the line?"

"Yes," hissed Simms. "That's the point of your whole Man for Hire act, right? Not having to answer to anybody?"

"No. The *point* is to find the magic again. Magic that could be down in that basement right now, but we'll never know because neither of you has the guts to stick your neck out."

"Fetch, you know I can't . . ." Simms trailed off, with a side-eye to Eileen that sent a message.

"I should get back," said Eileen, on cue. "Gotta be up early to open the library for the school kids."

She swanned off down the street. Simms watched her go for a few beats longer than was polite.

"Damn Witches," she said finally, and pulled the scarf away from her mouth. Her serpentine face was cracked, and her lips were dry and bloody. A year ago, she'd only ever uncovered herself around me as an intimidation tactic when she'd take me downtown to threaten me with things that never worked. Now she exposed her pockmarked checks and missing scales when she wanted me to feel like there wasn't any barrier between us. It was a gesture of friendship, but I still didn't know whether to believe it. "What happened in there?"

"You screwed me. That's what happened." I took out my pack of Clayfield Heavies, and Simms held out her hand. I passed her a twig and put another between my lips. "I called your office but Niles and his goons showed up instead."

"He's got security suits at the station now. Officially, they're supposed to be representatives for the mayor, but since the mayor answers to Niles it's all the same thing. From now on, you call me at home or get me to meet you at another location if there's anything important you want to tell me."

A couple of the charcoal suits came out of the mask-maker's store and headed uptown. I sneered at their backs, liked the feel of it, then turned to sneer at Simms a little more.

"Thurston is walking off with a fortune in magical artefacts and nobody in this city gives a damn. Hendricks was right. The world would have a better chance if this whole stinking city got buried."

Simms chewed her twig, not liking the fact that I was voicing regret for the case that had seemingly put us on the same side.

"Fetch, there are ways we have to do things. This isn't the old world where you solve problems by picking up a sword and charging into battle. We've got laws and policies to consider. People need this city functioning if they're going to survive."

"Screw your politics, Simms, and screw you too."

I spat my Clayfield at her feet and marched out of there. Did I mean what I'd said? I don't know. What Hendricks had wanted was horrible, but teaming up with the police to crush the last gasp of Sunder's true believers was its own kind of crime.

Sunder had once been a magical melting pot where the creatures of the world would fill its streets with their ideas, powers, cultures and cuisines, firing off each other like a box full of fireworks and mousetraps. Now it was falling under the command of a company who couldn't be trusted. We'd handed over our future to a rich man with no morals, and people were too content and comfortable to see the cost.

I didn't know what Niles was up to. It was a question too big to crack on my own, and every person in this city was too concerned with punching their timecards and begging for promotions to help me out.

I needed some way to snap them out of it. I needed to prove that there was still a way to change things back.

I walked the long way home, imagining Wizards tearing down the powerlines with tidal waves and lightning. I pictured great beasts charging up Main Street, shattering the asphalt. Giants rocking the foundations till the factories fell apart. Dragons and Wyverns breathing fire into the banks, and bursting pipes with talons and tails.

An impossible idea, of course. It was all over, and I was wishing for a future that would never come.

Then, I turned the corner from Twelfth Street onto Main, and found a miracle splattered on the sidewalk.

5

There was a halo around the Angel's head. The force of the impact had cracked his skull, spraying blood and brain matter in a near-perfect circle on the freshly set concrete. His jaw was twisted to the side and his teeth had broken through the skin of his lips. His arms were spread wide with one elbow bent the wrong way, and the other snapped open, exposing the bone. His abdomen had ruptured, freeing his organs and deflating his belly like a badly stuffed scarecrow.

He'd fallen at an angle that put one leg in the gutter and the other out on the street, both bare beneath his heavy brown robes.

All the Brothers Hum wore the same robes. All of them had the same haircut. There was no way to know that it was Benjamin.

Except I knew that it was.

I knew it even though he was facedown without a face. Even though his eternally patient voice would never say another word. Even though I couldn't feel his comforting hands on my shoulders. I knew it was him, even though the wings that protruded from his back looked nothing like they had a few hours earlier.

They poked through the holes in his robe, same as always, but different in every other way. Where they'd once been limp and twisted, they were now stretched out, reaching for the end of the world. The skin that covered them, which at dinner had seemed bald, pale and sickly, now sprouted tiny white feathers. The cartilage that came out of the bone was long and straight and the webbing was as taught as a well-made sail, barely seen beneath a glorious plume. Benjamin's wingspan was three times his height, spread out on either side of him.

He was illuminated by the headlights of a taxi. The driver had stepped out of the automobile but hadn't gotten any further. He just stood there with his mouth open, shaking.

"What happened?" I asked.

The driver looked towards the sky.

"He fell."

I looked up into the empty, endless night. I looked back down. The breeze blew across Benjamin's fallen body, causing his feathers to flutter as if the poor fellow was trying to take flight.

I wish I could tell you that the tears were for my friend. That I was heartbroken by the knowledge that we would never again sit down to dinner. That his selfless heart would be forever closed to the most vulnerable members of the city; the ones most of us ignored because our attention was focused on finite and fleeting things.

I felt all of that, but I wasn't crying for my friend. I was crying for the miracle that had sprouted from his back and the first evidence I'd seen since the Coda that the world could become whole once again.

An Angel had fallen in Sunder City: bloody, broken, and the best thing to happen in seven long years.

6

Within minutes, Brother Benjamin's body was surrounded by cops, charcoal suits and excited onlookers from all around town. As word spread from one ear to the next, I was pushed back from the scene until there was no point being there unless I was interested in examining the back of someone's head.

The longer I lingered, the more frustrated I became at the way Niles Company suits commanded the cops, and the way most of the cops listened. There were no witnesses with anything useful to say, just the taxi driver who was stuck in a loop.

"He fell."

I left them to their questions, confident that I could take a shortcut to the answers the very next day.

"What do you mean he's not here?"

Portemus stood at the morgue entrance, behind the bars of a recently installed security gate.

"Like I said, he never arrived."

I slammed my fist against the bars, and Portemus stepped back. I'd startled him. Considering he was a Necromancer used to dancing with the undead, that was some task.

"Sorry. It's Niles, right? He has the body?"

"They haven't told me anything. I want to see the specimen as much as you do, but this is out of my hands. I—"

Somebody coughed down the hall, deeper into the underground mortuary. It was a harsh and repetitive sound, like they were trying to dislodge a fishhook from their throat. Portemus looked over his shoulder, then back at me with an uncharacteristically somber expression. In my frustration, I took it as guilt.

"Portemus, are you screwing with me? Who's in there?"

His dark look only got darker as he unlocked the gate.

"Come in. I was going to call you anyway."

Portemus had a habit of making people uncomfortable. He was a sharply dressed Necromancer mortician with a too-sweet smile and unblemished skin. I enjoyed the fact that I was one of the few locals who wasn't unnerved by a trip into his lair. This was different. He was pensive. Troubled. His brow was furrowed like a freshly plowed field, and his jet-black hair was firing off in all directions. The clearest indication that all was not well was the state of his suit: no tie, no pocket square and his shirt as creased as a used napkin. There was even a crusted stain on the lapel of his jacket, the source of which was not wise to think about. This city had been to hell and back since the Coda, but Portemus had always stayed immaculately styled through it all.

Something was terribly, terribly wrong, and it wasn't any of the things that might *seem* wrong to someone who hadn't been inside the morgue before. I expected the endless rows of cadavers, uncovered and cooling on the sheeted slabs in all their post-Coda glory: the ancient Elves whose once-youthful forms had collapsed into reams of wrinkles, Reptilia reduced to half their scales, and Gnomes whose brittle bones fell in on themselves once the magic drained away.

One wall was lined with Lycum: creatures who were half animal, half Human. Pre-Coda, both elements worked together to make these beings stronger and smarter than their non-magical counterparts. Now, for the unlucky ones, the two sides were coming apart like a badly sewed suit.

I used to avert my eyes when I went down there. Now, I force myself to take them in; this is the cost of leaving our world the way it is. This is what gets forgotten when we measure our success by new roads and job numbers but ignore the fact that in a world without magic, a lot of good people won't ever see the shining future we're supposed to be working for. I see their pain and their suffering and their early demise and I drink it all up.

I looked over every cold body, flat on their beds, until my eyes fell on the final figure at the back of the room: a corpse, propped up on a wooden chair, with straight dark hair hiding her face. Her shoulders were slouched, and her head was tilted to one side as if she'd died while sitting in a doctor's waiting room and the rigor mortis had set in before anyone noticed.

She was a tiny little thing in a black skirt and sleeveless top, with tattoos all over her mottled flesh. Her skin was an uneven pattern of pink, brown and green; decaying in some places and rotted away in others. Surprisingly, there were some parts that were perfectly smooth, as if blood still coursed through arteries beneath the surface.

I wondered what could cause such a horrific death. Some cruel disease, perhaps? Maybe one of those little infections that was trivial in the old days but spread uncontrollably in a magicless body if no new medicine was found for it. Maybe she'd been blessed by a spell when she was young; something to protect her from the elements or strengthen her skin, but it had been corrupted by the Coda and turned against the person it was supposed to protect. In this twisted, limping world, untold miseries could have been visited upon the poor girl. To my mind, not enough people were trying to stop it from happening again.

"What happened to her?" I asked.

Portemus stepped forward and placed a gentle hand on her shoulder.

"Mora, I'd like you to meet my friend."

The corpse raised a skeletal arm and pushed the fringe from her face, revealing one empty eye socket and a single baby blue.

In Sunder City, you get plenty of opportunities to practice your poker face. I liked to think that mine was better than most, but, in this instance, I was startled enough to jump back in shock.

"Sorry, Mister. Didn't mean to freak you out."

"No, uh . . . I'm sorry," I stammered, unsuccessfully trying to cover up my surprise. "I'm Fetch Phillips. Pleased to meet you, Mora."

She snorted, wobbling a piece of cartilage behind her bare nostrils.

"Yeah, you sure look pleased."

"Mora is undead," explained Portemus. "Half-undead to be precise. I met her a decade ago, when I was passing through a mountain village plagued by creatures of the night. Mora had been bitten by a Yakanese scorpion, the venom of which, if untreated, will eat through flesh in a matter of hours. By the time they gave her medicine, much of the damage was already done. I could not save the parts of her body that had been affected by the poison, but I thought that maybe I could revive it. I had never used my powers this way before, but as I had brought whole creatures back from the dead, a few recently deceased bits of meat on a still living body was no problem at all. Until the Coda, of course."

Of course. Aren't we all a little sick of every story ending the same way?

"Does it hurt?" I asked.

Mora shrugged – granting me a biology lesson through the hole in her shoulder.

"You learn to live with it."

She smirked to show that she was being ironic, but I was still too shocked to share in the joke.

"So," said Portemus, "you think you can help?"

Oh shit.

I'd struggled to even retrieve a stolen rock. How was I supposed to solve something that stumped the town's resident Necromancer?

"I'll try," I said. "If we set things right with the world, the spell should come back into effect, right? You just need magic again, and that's what I'm trying to do."

"Oh, of course," said Mora. "Why didn't we think of that?"
Portemus nodded unconvincingly.

"Yes. If you do that, then all will be well – and I hope you do – but in the meantime, we need something else; some way of keeping her body alive without magic. At least, not the magic we once knew. Can you think of anything?"

I ground my teeth against each other so I wouldn't speak too soon. Over the last year, all kinds of creatures had come to my door asking similar things and I'd done my best to help them. But, after coming back empty-handed time and time again, I'd settled on the frustrating truth that the little fixes weren't worth my time.

The world was full of species that were right on the brink. Whole sections of Archetellos were apparently uninhabitable. In Sunder, the Niles Company had covered up this reality with appliances and advertising, making it look like we were all moving forward again. But the foundations were rotten. I could spend weeks looking for ways to patch up Mora – at best, I'd find a way for her to stumble on for a few more years – but what would be the point if the world was dying anyway? The only way to truly help her would be to get the magic moving again, but even Portemus didn't believe that was possible.

I let those thoughts pass through my head before I dared to open my mouth.

"I know some surgeons," I said. "They might have a solution. Something to buy us some time. I'll talk to them for you."

"Thank you, Fetch," said Portemus.

"Yeah, thanks, fella. Let me walk you out."

When Mora stood up, her joints creaked like she was unfolding a rusty ironing board.

"You sure?" Porty and I asked at the same time.

"Yeah, if I don't stretch my few good muscles, they'll soon be just as useless as the others. As long as you don't mind a saunter?"

"No, you set the pace. Good to see you, Portemus. Call me if you find out where they took the Angel. I'm sure we'd both like a better look."

"I'll ask around. Let me know when you've spoken to your surgeon friends."

Mora led me out, wheezing through a hole in her neck.

"Thanks for humoring him," she said. "He's getting sentimental in his old age."

"I'm not humoring him. I really will do my best to help you."

"And how is your best working out so far?"

The scars on Mora's face gave her a perpetual smirk. Even without them, I had a feeling her expression would be much the same.

"Mixed results, if I'm honest. But there's a chance this Angel could change everything. If Portemus finds out where the body is, I'll make sure we get a look at it."

I tried to say it with certainty and hope, but she rolled her eye and closed the gate.

"Good luck with that," she said, and limped away.

Fine. She didn't need to believe me. I was used to that. Not long ago, I was moving just as slow as she was, with just as much hope in my heart.

I'd seen a few wonders since then. Most of them more monstrous than magical, but enough to jumpstart my faith that the world wasn't quite as solemn as it seemed. Like a marrow-sucking Vamp, a rabid Unicorn, or two Succubae lovers who knew how to get under your skin.

It was time I paid that pair a visit.

7

Even though I was Sunder City's one and only Man for Hire, I'd been neglecting my duties over the last few months. The insignificant ventures frustrated me if I couldn't see how they'd lead to more substantial steps towards real redemption. Helping out an unfortunate Half-Zombie wasn't the clearest path to bringing the magic back, but since I could investigate it alongside Benjamin's transformation, I wasn't too worried about expending the extra effort.

I went all the way to the wrong side of town before I remembered that the Succubae surgeons had relocated their business yet again. A year ago, as their unique brand of body modification became more acceptable, they moved from their underground lair into the building above. This prompted the papers to start running stories about how garish it was to get your features artificially adjusted to look the way they did before the Coda. Rather than deter customers, the stories mostly served as free advertising. Not every creature is comfortable with the idea of a full-body reconstruction, but these days, plenty of ex-magical creatures are open to the idea of a little touch-up to make the mirror easier to look into. Thanks to Thurston's fire-filled factories, employment is at an all-time high, and Sunderites are more accepting of the idea of putting some of their savings towards a new piece of their old selves.

The new surgery was a red-brick cottage with a freshly painted fence, centered on a plot of land that was decorated with imported shrubs (another business that had boomed in the last year). The fixtures of the building were painted white, and the plants had all been trimmed into neat geometric shapes, giving the surgery an air of pristine cleanliness.

I went up the steps through the front door into a waiting room that was bigger than my office. Half a dozen patients sat on expensive cushioned chairs and, when she saw me, the girl behind the counter stretched her smile extra tight in anticipation of trouble.

"Hello, sir. Do you have an appointment?"

"No, I just want to talk to the surgeons for a moment."

"Of course. We have several doctors who specialize in a variety of areas. Please fill out this form and we can match you with the practitioner who can best accommodate your needs."

She held out the form. I ignored it and took a free mint.

"Exina and Loq. They here?"

"Dr Exina's next free appointment is in . . ." She flipped through a thick book. "Three weeks. Dr Loq is available a week after that. Do you have a preference?"

Her smile was so tight I could have plucked her lip like a banjo cord.

"Look, sister, a friend of mine just fell to his death sporting a brand-new set of feathers that didn't do much to soften his impact with the sidewalk. So, before word gets out that this surgery gave my friend a set of fake wings and told him to try them out, I thought your bosses might want a chance to defend themselves."

"Sir, if you're a reporter, you can leave your card with me, and the surgeons will get back to you when they have the time."

"Forget it."

There was only one hallway out of the waiting room, so I went down it.

"Sir!"

I pushed open the first door on the left to find a Werecat woman reclining in a chair with her head tilted back, and an Elf in scrubs scraping something against her teeth.

"Sorry, wrong room."

"Sir!"

The next room was empty. "SIR!" The one after that was filled with intense yellow light that almost blinded me. I wish it had. I might have been spared the sight of the naked Ogre asleep in a strange apparatus that spread his legs wide, allowing Loq to sit on a stool between them, stitching up his nether regions.

"Oh, hey, Loq. I . . . I need to talk to you . . . when you've got a minute."

Loq nodded, unfazed by the interruption. When your job involves flaying an Ogre's junk first thing in the morning, it takes more than an impolite intrusion to get you rattled.

"Perhaps we should give Mr Jenkins some privacy," said a seductive voice behind me that was an octave deeper than the shrill cry of the receptionist.

"Hello, Doctor. Aren't you looking sharp?"

Exina's crisp black suit concealed the more distinct parts of her Succubae body, projecting pure professionalism that was accented by tiny square reading glasses and a black bun.

"This is a respectable business, Fetch, with appointments and a discerning customer base. Why don't you come back after hours?"

"You read the papers?"

"Rarely. They're not fond of our operation and the feeling's mutual."

"You might want to check today's edition. A monk jumped to his death with a brand-new set of freshly feathered wings. Surely you didn't tell one of your clients to take their ornaments for a test drive."

"What makes you think he was our client? Plenty of new surgeries are cropping up around town, now that we've made it fashionable."

"Because the work was good. The Brother's body was a mess, but the wings were a thing of beauty."

Here's a top tip for any future Man for Hire: flattery works wonders on a Succubus.

"It wasn't us. Nobody asks for wings. They're impractical."

"When did that ever worry you? I thought you were all about

helping people express their true selves. Making the 'outer you' look like the 'inner you'. No Angels ever ask you to dress their wings up to look like the old days?"

She shook her head.

"If someone comes in with wings, they're here to have them removed."

"And you do that?"

"Of course."

I sensed a sore spot, and I couldn't help putting my finger on it.

"That's a little conservative for you, isn't it? Hacking off their proudest features just so they can fit in with modern society?"

She rubbed two of her fingernails against each other. It sounded like a knife being sharpened.

"We do what is asked of us, Fetch. That's all."

I looked over her shoulder. Posters lined the hallway walls advertising the various surgeries on offer: horn reduction, prosthetic scale replacement, fang filing and fur removal. They were undressing the inhabitants of Sunder City, stripping them of the elements that once made them magic. It pissed me off because they were removing the parts of their bodies that they'd most miss if I ever found a way to fix things. Not because those parts were painful or dangerous, but just so they'd better suit Thurston Niles's new world.

"Dr Exina," called the receptionist, her eyes locked on me, "your nine o'clock is here."

"Thank you, Sandra. Fetch, I have to go."

"What's the job? Sawing off the back half off a Centaur so he can fit inside a phone booth?" I was enjoying being a brat, but I'd almost forgotten my side mission. "One last thing. I know a Zombie who needs some help. You dealt with their kind before?"

She would have waved me away if I hadn't piqued her interest.

"Not since the Coda. The undead didn't make it."

"This one did. She's a Half-Zombie. A mortal woman patched up with reanimated pieces."

"Send her in and I'll take a look. No charge for the first consultation but tell her to make an *appointment*."

We went out into the waiting room where Exina greeted a Gnome lady with a limp. I left the surgery and stepped back out into the spring morning where sunlight bounced off the windshields of the passing cars: washed, waxed and purring their way to somewhere important. Hordes of uniformed workers weaved past each other, checking watches and straightening ties with the self-satisfied expressions of people who'd been promised a paycheck. A vendor in a stall swapped sandwiches for copper coins, and a cop stood on the street corner serving smiles and the illusion of safety. The sky was clear, and the sun was out, and the city skipped along like it was all set to music.

You could almost forget we were living through the apocalypse.

8

I fought the crowds back east and every pedestrian seemed determined to get in my way. They were all too slow, too distracted, or wandering along the wrong side of the path, messing up the flow of foot traffic. As I cut through Five Shadows Square, weaving between lines of meandering tourists, I tripped over a bald man who sat cross-legged on the ground.

"What the hell are you doing?" I growled.

The collision brought his distant eyes down from the sky and he took me in. There wasn't a hair on his head or face, just wrinkles, dust, and five red scabs: four across his brow and one on his right temple.

He stared at me for a while, like he was struggling to bring me into focus. When he did, his laugh lines and crow's feet deepened before he cackled at the top of his lungs. He stared right at me, howling in joy. I backed away, watching his spit catch the morning sun. Just another of Sunder's looser units waiting to be left behind by our increasingly complicated world.

I turned towards Main Street and his laughter eventually merged with all the other madness of modern life.

The wings of the chalk outline touched the brickwork of the corner store and stretched all the way out to the middle of the road, passing through the gutter where water from an uptown carwash had already swept some of it away. Footprints had smeared the hard lines, creating short, white streaks, as if the cop who'd drawn it had been overcome by artistic inspiration and attempted to capture the feathers in more realistic detail.

I looked towards the sky.

Until recently, Sunder City had spread itself out more than it had ever built up. Over the last year, Niles Company construction had been laying the foundations for apartment blocks and offices that would, apparently, be taller than even the Elven spires in Gaila. On the corner where Benjamin had met his fate, the buildings on either side of this road were only two stories high.

I'd spent more hours than most doing the math on how high you'd have to fall to make sure the landing was fatal. Two floors weren't enough; he'd barely break a bone, let alone spread his insides across Main Street with the explosive exuberance I'd seen the night before.

The cab driver had told me he'd fallen, but Benjamin couldn't have come from any of these nearby buildings and done that kind of damage. Perhaps the wings were strong enough to glide on and they'd carried him across the city from a nearby perch before giving out.

I used the fire escape to get up on the roof and take in a view that was unobstructed on all sides. The closest platform that was more than three stories high was my own building, old 108, three blocks south. Benjamin would have had to jump out the Angel door and glide at an even height, then drop like a stone once he'd reached this spot. A stunt like that already pushed the boundaries of what I believed was possible. If you can accept that as an option, then Benjamin flapping his wings isn't much more of a feat.

I needed to see his new appendages up close. If Niles, Simms or the city were hiding Benjamin's body, they knew that they had something to suppress, which only increased my curiosity.

Down below, more footprints kicked through the outline, wearing it thin without even glancing down. Not a thought spared for the potential miracle; all too busy rushing off to punch their cards and kiss their boss's ass before the lunch bell.

It was busy, but not like it used to be. It used to be kinetic. Dangerous. Loud like good music, not loud like the relentless drone of those new engines. We'd bounced off each other and, when we did, we made sparks. We made memories. Even in the dark days, when the streetlights were empty, I could see the light that emanated out of every brick of this damn city. When I couldn't see the light in myself, I felt it all around me. Now the lanterns were on, and the factories were full, but somehow it managed to feel emptier every day.

It looked wrong. It felt wrong. *I* felt wrong. I was out of step and in the wrong damn shoes.

I spat over the edge. It missed the pedestrians and cracked against the pavement.

Only two stories high. Not enough. Not by a long shot.

9

"I'm here to see Simms."

"Do you have an appointment?"

"What is it with everyone and appointments all of a sudden? When did this city start running by the second hand?"

"She's busy, sir."

"Don't give me that 'sir' shit. You know who I am. If Simms is busy, I'll see Richie instead."

"Who?"

"Fuck off. Sergeant Richie Kites."

"He no longer works here, sir."

"Call me *sir* again and I'll crack you."

"Then we'd have to arrest you . . . sir."

It took everything I had to swallow my anger and keep my fists at my sides. Fine. I'd wait for Simms. I'd ask her about the body and find out what happened to Richie.

How could he not work here anymore?

I took a seat in the waiting area, picked up the newspaper, and swore some more. A picture of Benjamin filled one corner of the front page. Beside it, as a smaller insert, there was a photograph of the plaque outside my front door.

At sundown last night, Owen Benjamin, a follower of the Brothers Hum and long-time attendant at the Beggar's Bread, fell to his death on the corner of Main Street and Twelfth. The events that led to his demise are still under investigation, but authorities have suggested that Mr Benjamin may have been attempting to glide on a set of surgically attached wings that failed to support his weight.

If so, this would make Mr Benjamin another statistic in a string of misadventures that have taken the lives of once-magical creatures attempting to recapture their pre-Coda powers. Some will likely see this as more evidence to support, or even strengthen, Mayor Piston's city-wide ban on unregulated magical practices.

Even with the new laws in place, there are many businesses operating in Sunder City that prey on desperate citizens by promising a return to the old days. We have reported at length on the Succubae surgeons who will indulge any paying customer's desire to appear how they did in the past (with varying results), and the self-professed "Man for Hire" Fetch Phillips, whose advertisement boasts his ability to "Bring the Magic Back". Perhaps these kinds of statements are precisely the encouragement Mr Benjamin and the like needed to take absurd risks in the hope of rediscovering the life we all know is lost.

Mayor Piston has not yet commented on this latest tragedy, but after two Werewolves poisoned themselves with underground potions last month, he put out a statement saying:

"We are at a crucial turning point for Sunder City, and indeed the world. If we can accept the reality that we are in, instead of clinging to lost glories, we have a chance to build a future that is brighter than the one we lost. I understand that the temptations offered by these charlatans, who are willing to capitalize on their community's pain, can be too great for some to resist; which is why it is our job to snuff out these exploitative practices and protect our citizens, so we can all work for a better tomorrow, together."

Perhaps this latest death will encourage the mayor to finally live up to his promise and shut these dangerous businesses down for good.

"Oh, fuck off!" I screamed. The smarmy cop went to chastise me, saw my face, and thought better of it. Even that couldn't lighten my mood.

"She here?" I barked.

They shook their stupid head.

"She's out on business, sir. Can I take a message?"

I marched out, taking the paper with me.

"Have you seen this?"

I threw the *Sunder Star* onto the counter, covering a customer's change.

"Sorry, sir," said Georgio, as the guest retreated with his take-away sandwich. "This oaf works above my building and he somehow believes that the whole place belongs to him." Georgio collected the coins, handed them to the patron, and reluctantly read the article. "Amazing. Free advertising. You're a better businessman than I thought."

"They're blaming me for Benjamin's death. Using it as a reason to bring in more ridiculous laws."

"It must mean you're doing a good job. If your adversaries are trying to slow you down, then they must be afraid of what you're trying to do."

Georgio never stopped moving while we talked. He wiped down tables and picked up dirty plates as I followed him around, brandishing the offending paper.

"It's a whole organized operation," I insisted. "They *know* that there's no explanation for what happened to Benjamin, but they want to make sure that nobody asks any questions."

"Very peculiar," he muttered.

"I know!"

"No, I mean *you* are peculiar. He was your friend, wasn't he?"

"Yes."

"Aren't you sad? You keep talking about what happened to him, but you haven't said how it makes you feel."

He stared into me with those all-seeing blue eyes.

"It doesn't matter how I feel. It matters what I do about it. If he found a way to fly again, imagine what that would mean for this place. For everyone here!"

Georgio gave me a pitying smile.

"You know what you are?" When I didn't respond, he poked a long, bent finger in my chest and said, "You're a Ponoto."

"What did you call me?"

He chuckled.

"A Ponoto! When I was the leader of Shay-men, in the old days, in my birthplace up north, warriors would come to us when they learned that a life of fighting would get them nowhere. As I helped them to put down their weapons, I would hear of their customs and their codes. A common tradition with warrior tribes was that if you were snatched from the jaws of death, you owed your life to your rescuer and must serve them for ever more. Not the Ponoto. If a Ponoto saved somebody's life, it was the Ponoto who did the serving: dedicating their life to the one who was saved." He pointed his craggy finger in my face. "YOU are a PONOTO!"

He cackled. I looked at him like he was mad, and he only cackled more.

"I'm going to talk to Niles," I said.

"If you're heading uptown, take the scraps for the streetcar on the way."

"Georgio, I need to see Thurston and—"

"People need food!" He shoved a canvas bag of scraps into my chest. "People need to eat and have a place to sleep and to feel safe. After that, you can worry about the rest of it. Go on, you old Ponoto."

I left him cackling and took the canvas bag outside. Every pub and bar spilled onto Main Street as workers did the sums of how drunk they could get and how late they could be without starting a fight with whoever was waiting at home. The answer was usually three drinks and one hour less than what they ended up indulging in.

That was the way our minds always worked, wasn't it? Knowing the right thing to do but always unable to convince ourselves to do it. Surely we couldn't have started civilization like this. We never would have managed to climb out of the mud. It must be a side effect of industry. We know that the machine will move forward, with or without us, down a path that won't change in the slightest whether we help it along or not. For most of us, if we get up earlier and push ourselves a bit harder, our own little lives might change, but the world on the whole won't care in the slightest, so why bother?

At least I knew that my ridiculous occupation wouldn't exist without me. I made a difference, for better or worse, and that somehow made it easier to get out of bed in the morning.

I saw the streetcar the same way. If the Brothers Hum stopped serving, it would leave a vacant space on Main Street and in the stomachs of all its customers. It *mattered*. Maybe that's why I liked going there.

"Hello, Brother Ryan."

The Beggar's Bread wasn't as busy as the bars, but the usual modest crowd had taken their seats. I approached the window and looked in at another monk with the same bowl cut and brown robes as the others, and held up the canvas bag.

"Got a delivery. I'm so sorry about Benjamin. How are you all holding up?"

It was strange not to see a smile on the monk's face. I'd expected grief, of course. But this wasn't just sadness, it was anger. Brother Ryan didn't say anything. He didn't even move to take the bag. He just stared at me silently, biting his tongue.

"Do any of you know what happened?" I asked.

Brother Ryan shook his head and went back to chopping tomatoes, so I approached Brother Kim who was working the fryer.

"Kim, I'm so sorry. I've got some scraps from the café. Do you need any help tonight?"

Brother Kim wore the same expression as Brother Ryan.

"Not from you," he said.

It was so out of character that my first instinct was to laugh. Brother Kim, like all the winged monks, was generous and cheerful to a fault. They'd been a constant light in Sunder since before the Coda. Nobody had ever been turned away from the Beggar's Bread, no matter what they'd done, where they were from, or how bad they smelled.

It seemed that I, once again, was the first.

I turned around to see the eyes of all the customers on me; copies of the *Sunder Star* in some of their hands. Well, there you go. All it took was a suggestion stamped in ink to make somebody's idea an undeniable truth.

Screw 'em.

I dropped the canvas bag and headed north to talk to the man that I knew was responsible. I went all the way uptown till the cobbles turned into smooth asphalt streets, and approached Thurston Niles's front gate.

"Evening, Mr Phillips," said the guard. "Go right in."

10

Thurston Niles filled the first glass, then held the bottle of whiskey over the second, testing my resolve.

"Still off the sauce?"

It had been nine months, not that I was counting. I doubt that it had made me any more productive, and I'd doubled my Clayfield intake to make up for it, but it gave me back my mornings and allowed me to enter the parts of Sunder that tended to turn away a drunk.

"Yeah."

"How about a cigar?"

"Sure."

He pulled two cigars out of the box beside his armchair, cut off the tips with a bejeweled guillotine, stuffed one between his lips and handed the other to me.

"Are they expensive?"

"Obscenely."

I threw the whole thing in the fire.

Thurston rolled his eyes.

"You really are a child."

On the table beside him, there was a bottle of water that he used for mixing with whiskey. I snatched it up and sat down opposite. There was a copy of the *Sunder Star* on the table beside me, clearly intended to rile me up, and doing so rather successfully.

"Is there a point to this whole thing?" I asked. "Or are you just screwing with me for the fun of it?"

He lit his cigar and puffed away thoughtfully, perfuming the room with bonfires, brandy and power. I almost regretted throwing mine away.

"A little bit of both, actually." He licked his lips. "What we're creating here is a system that sustains itself. The more it grows, the more it needs to be fed. We can't power this week's growth with last week's work. If it pauses or, God forbid, goes backwards, it begins to crack. We can handle a few kinks in the machine – parts that don't quite fit the whole, like you, because you sometimes serve a purpose – but if too many parts start moving in the wrong direction or perform functions that don't align with the rest of us, then the machine becomes unstable and collapses back into a million separate pieces."

I tried not to stare at the whiskey as he rolled it around in the glass.

"That's why you're trying to stop me?" I asked.

"Don't flatter yourself. You're not a threat on your own. I'm just making sure your ideas don't spread. The people of Sunder have recognized their potential and are looking toward the future. I need to ensure that the future they are looking toward is mine, not yours."

The race. Niles was way out ahead, but it was encouraging to know he was still looking over his shoulder.

"So, you believe that my future is possible?"

"I believe you are the least useful person in this entire city and, while I find it entertaining, I can only handle one of you. We need a workforce, not a city of dreamers."

I took a swig of the water. It was crisp and clean, unlike the copper-tainted stuff that came out of the taps in town. Goddamnit. This prick could even ruin water for me.

"I don't believe you."

"With the things you do believe, I'll take that as a compliment."

"You wouldn't risk all this just to sway the story: commandeering artefacts, locking up local mages, and ghost-writing articles for the *Sunder Star*. You could just let me embarrass myself until the whole idea of reviving the magic fades away. You're scared. You know that there's a chance I might stumble onto something real, and when that happens, this tin city you've built will come crashing down around you."

He blew a smoke ring over my head.

"Why do you come here?" he asked.

"Because I hate you."

"Now you're just being mean."

"I can't be mean to you. Nobody can, because you're not a real person. Every other soul out there makes me feel guilty, or embarrassed. Even after everything I've done, I'm always worried that I might say the wrong thing or make a fool of myself. Not with you. The only thing I worry about here is whether anyone else will see me coming and going. Other than that, I couldn't be more comfortable."

He lowered his cigar onto a crystal ashtray.

"You don't need to like me, Fetch, but you'll soon realize that I'm the best thing to ever happen to the people of this city."

"You're a life raft, I'll give you that. You got our heads above water long enough to get some air, but it won't last. Once everyone's bellies have been full for long enough, they'll realize that the future you're offering isn't any kind of future at all."

"Forget the future, Fetch. You can't even remember the past. Not like the rest of them. They don't pine for the days of Dragons and Fae, they fear the hunger and the cold that came afterwards; the dark times when they never thought they'd be useful again. You never lost what they lost. From the old world, through the Coda, to now, you've been exactly the same. You could have hung up your hat and your jacket and done a hard day's work any time you wanted. To those out there who believed they might never work again, I'm the hero, and your actions become more dangerous to them every day."

A satisfied smirk had moved onto his face and made itself at home. I decided to try and kick it out.

"You talk about Sunder as if it's the whole world," I said. "It's a nice distraction, and it gives us something to trade jabs over, but it's not really the point, is it? Not to you. There are too many trucks full of metal coming in. Too many trucks full of ammo going out. You like to talk, Niles, but don't pretend like any of this is about the welfare of Sunder's citizens."

The smirk didn't leave, but it looked less comfortable. Hendricks had been investigating the shipments going between Sunder and the other Human cities. We'd broken into Niles Company warehouses together and found their first pistols. Those factories had only expanded in the previous year, but I hadn't been able to learn any more on my own. There were more weapons being made than what I saw on the streets, so I was pretty sure they were being sent off to some dangerous land, in preparation for something terrible.

I needed to bring back the magic before we found out what it was.

The race.

Niles shook his head.

"You want to see what we're making?"

He reached down beside the chair, picked up a foot-long cardboard box and threw it over to me.

"What's this? The new improved killing machine? Takes out your entire extended family with the press of a button?"

"Just open it." I cracked the box to find a long strip of metal with rounded edges, folded up a dozen times. "It's a clothesline," said Thurston proudly. "Incredibly sturdy but extremely flexible. You can fit it anywhere; in your bathroom, on a windowsill, or out on the fire escape, then fold it up and stick it in a drawer when you're done. This is only one of the inventions that our factories are making. The more of them we make, the cheaper they are to sell, which is better for everyone, don't you think?"

I had no interest in newfangled clotheslines or the benefits of overproduction.

"I want to see the body," I said.

Thurston relit his cigar.

"The Brothers Hum have decided that they don't want the body on show, in case it inspires more vulnerable souls to follow in Benjamin's footsteps. The police are holding onto it until the funeral, where it will be cremated. Even if I wanted to help you, Fetch, it wouldn't be my place to go against the wishes of a sacred brotherhood, especially in their time of grief."

Arrogance dripped from every word that passed his tobacco-stained lips.

"Thanks for the smoke, Niles. I'll see myself out."

I got up but, as always, Thurston wanted the last word.

"Are you ready to work for me yet? It wouldn't take much. I'll give you a new suit and one of our signature charcoal ties. You'll keep doing what you're doing, except you bring the information you find back to me. Say yes, and I'll take you to see your friend right now."

And he wondered why I hated him.

"How about I shoot the both of us instead? Then the city can find its future without the two of us interfering."

He stubbed out the cigar.

"You were a lot more fun when you'd drink with me."

"Sorry, but I'm working now. See you later, Niles."

"Take the side exit. Less light. Wouldn't want anybody to spot you and ruin both of our reputations. And give the clothesline a try."

Though I hated doing a single thing that Thurston asked of me, I took the clothesline and the side exit out into the darkness.

Did he actually think I'd ever work for him? Impossible. I'd given up too much to hand over this city now.

Eliah Hendricks had seen Sunder as a poison; a toxic, fire-fueled monstrosity that would suck the life from Archetellos until nothing was left. In our world without magic, he believed that the temptations of this place would stop us from fighting for a better tomorrow. He bet the lives of everyone here on his hunch.

But I'd bet against him. I'd saved this city, so now it was mine to protect.

I guess I am a fucking Ponoto.

Fine.

Let's go take a look at this body.

11

"Yes! Of course! Let's go!"

Portemus stepped away from the splayed Dwarf he'd been working on, grabbed a black cloak from the wall, and made for the exit.

"Portemus, wait! We need a plan!"

He turned, and his shiny shoes squeaked on the tiles.

"A plan?"

"So we don't get caught. The body is somewhere inside the police station. The Brothers can't know we've been in there, and if the city or the cops find out then they might stop sending you bodies altogether."

His expression was shocked, then hurt. Nobody had adjusted to life after the Coda as enthusiastically as Portemus. Before the factories were full or the carts were loaded, our local Necromancer was caring for our recently deceased. If Portemus couldn't do his work, I wasn't sure what would happen to him, but it probably wouldn't be pretty.

"Yes," he said solemnly, "we must be clandestine."

"Do you know anything about the room they're keeping him in?"

"I have been there before, to pick up specimens sometimes, when the police are too busy to deliver them. It is a room beneath the station. Not as nice as mine, not as chilled, not as kind to the bodies, but it is fine for a night or two."

"How do you get in?"

"There is a stairwell inside the station, on the left. Down two levels."

"Damn." I was familiar with some areas of the station but nothing below ground level.

"It is not very busy, this room, and it is kept locked when it is not being used."

"So, we need to get the keys."

"Or," said a voice from the shadows, "you need someone inside."

Mora used a slab to pull herself up to standing. The flesh of one of her legs was all the way gone, and her femur was visible beneath the hem of her skirt.

"Eyes up here, Mr Phillips. It ain't nice to stare at a girl's skeleton."

She winked, but since she only had one eyelid, it was a common occurrence.

"Sorry, Mora. Those Succubae are happy to meet you, by the way. If you can get down to the surgery."

"Let's worry about your little infiltration adventure first." She turned to Portemus. "That room can probably be unlocked from the inside, right?"

Portemus made a face as he tried to remember.

"I'm not sure."

"What about you, Phillips? You're friends with the cops, ain't you?"

It sounded like an accusation, though I don't think she meant it that way.

"Occasional reluctant collaborator. I've never been down to the morgue, though."

"If I'm going to go in there, I want to know that I can get out. Any cops you trust that can give us the lowdown?"

I shook my head. Even though I'd fought alongside them against the uprising a year ago, the cops tolerated me at best. Simms couldn't be counted on, she'd made that clear, and Richie . . . Well, apparently Richie was no longer a cop. If that was true, he might be the one person with inside knowledge of the police department who wouldn't be worried about losing his job.

"I might have someone who can help."

The phone rang and rang, and I wondered whether Richie might have left town. I was just about to hang up when he finally answered.

"Hello?"

"Richie, it's Fetch. What happened?"

"What do you mean?"

"You're not a cop anymore."

"It's been over a month."

"Well, I don't keep tabs on the hiring and firing process of the Sunder PD. You retire or what?"

He grumbled into the receiver for a bit, then said, "Meet me at the Ditch and I'll tell you all about it." He waited for me to agree to the plan. When I didn't, he offered up another idea. "Or maybe come over here. That place is too crowded these days."

"Works for me."

He gave me his home address and I stopped by the corner store to pick up some of his favorite Orcish cider. When I came out, there was a man standing in the middle of the road.

It was the guy I'd tripped over in Five Shadows Square. He was wearing nothing but a filthy pair of trousers, his five red scabs, and a wondrous expression, as if he'd just witnessed something incredible. There was nothing incredible anywhere around us, just the usual pedestrians and an old, refurbished automobile that was driving up on the curb to avoid the smiling wanderer, the driver yelling obscenities from the window.

I watched him as he watched the world go by, waiting for him to do something. Anything. But he just stared at the people as they passed like they were part of a parade put on in his honor. Eventually, his eyes fell on me and his smile widened.

It made me uncomfortable and then it made me angry, so I stepped out into the road to confront him.

"Do I know you?" I asked.

The question only increased his amusement. I thought for a moment that he didn't understand the language, and might just be reacting to the strangeness of sounds, but eventually he shrugged and said, "Why ask a question that only you know the answer to?"

Oh shit. A two-bit street-corner soothsayer.

"What's your problem?" I asked him. "Is that some kind of injury?" I pointed to the red spots on his forehead and temple.

"Quite the opposite," he said, and looked at me like that meant something.

"Get off the road," I snarled.

"All right."

He walked past me, still grinning maniacally, and weaved through the river of pedestrians like a fish through water, not letting any of them get in his way. He was light on his feet, but something had come loose in his head.

I kept going west, struggling against a city that was focused on going north and south, bouncing off pedestrians or waiting impatiently for gaps between the cars.

Why did it feel like everybody else was going the wrong way?

The house was small for such a big fellow; one of those places that used to be bigger until they ran a wall through the middle of it and split it in two to double the rent. When Richie opened the door, he filled the frame and then some.

I held out the paper bag of booze. He peered in, saw that it was the kind that I couldn't stomach, gave an understanding nod and said, "Come on in."

I'd never been to Richie's home before. He'd only been to mine because it was also my place of business. It was a long half-house with a living room at the front, a kitchen visible through the door behind it, and presumably a bedroom at the back. Whenever Richie stopped moving, and the floorboards stopped creaking beneath his weight, you could hear the neighbor's radio through the wall.

He sat on the couch, I sat on an armchair, and he opened one of the bottles.

"You want a glass?" he asked.

"No. That's all for you."

He sat back and took a satisfied slurp.

The couch was too small for him. The house was too small for him. Seeing him out of his police uniform, wearing worn woolen pants and a loose threadbare sweater, the whole city seemed too small for him. The table was covered with open tin cans, the dregs of ready-made meals stuck to the bottom. I was thankful that having Georgio beneath my building meant that it had been over a year since I'd been reduced to eating tinned dinners.

Richie took another healthy sip, and I felt a sliver of judgment slink into my head. What a joke; I was the last person who should be allowed to judge someone for drinking too much during the day. Besides, he was a Half-Ogre whose constitution could handle a lot more than mine, even with all my practice.

My eye was drawn to a coat rack in the corner that held his police-issue trench and a couple of winter coats beside a familiar blue jacket. It matched the one I was wearing, except it was twice the size and without the fur lining. It was the Shepherd's uniform he'd been wearing when we'd first met: two optimistic boys tasked with protecting the magical creatures of our world. Now we were two tired men with gray in their whiskers who still didn't know how to talk to each other.

"Nice place," I said, to fill the silence. Richie looked around as if he was also on his first visit.

"No it's not. A nice place has warmth and a view and someone else to share it with. This is the place you end up in when you spend your life chasing things that can't be caught."

I would have argued with him if he wasn't so right. It wasn't the kind of place you plan for, it was the kind of place you find yourself in when you don't make plans, or the plans you make go south and you never get around to making new ones. It was where most of us would end up. Men especially, but by no means exclusively. These musty little pockets are tucked into every corner of the world: flats, townhouses and trailers where nobody ever goes except for the quiet, solitary souls who call them home. Uncles, widows and widowers, and the single parents who got the short end of the stick. The ones who never found themselves after school, and the romantics who risked it all on that first great love and never mustered up the energy to try again.

Richie attempted to resurrect the stub of a cigar and I sat back, soaking up an overwhelming feeling of inadequacy. Richie had pulled me back from the brink countless times. The first conversation we ever had happened because he chose to reach out to me, a near stranger, and offer some guidance when he saw that I was struggling. Now, he was the one who was struggling, and I felt pathetically inept in my ability to lend a hand. Who was I to offer advice? Why would compliments or words of kindness mean anything from a screw-up like me? Anything I said to make him feel better would likely make things worse, if history was anything to go by, so I just asked, "What's with the retirement? Was pushing papers too much exercise for you?"

It was one of my usual jabs and it fell limp and awkward out of my mouth. Richie gave up on the crumbling cigar and went back to the cider.

"I couldn't do it anymore, Fetch. It's gone rotten. Maybe it always was."

"The police force? You know I'm not the biggest fan of the pig pen, but you're a good cop."

"I'm not sure there's any such thing. There are good people, but once you put on the uniform, it does all kinds of crazy things to you. Any kind of uniform, really. I've worn enough to know. So have you. All these patches, jackets and tattoos, they're just excuses. Ways to blame the things we've done on someone else."

He was talking the way I used to, a year or so ago, before I forced myself to fight for the future that I wanted. I should have had something to say that would help lift him up, but instead, I could feel him dragging me down towards a familiar place; a comfortable, lazy darkness that was waiting with open arms.

The bottle looked more appealing by the minute.

"Richie, this isn't like you." My words sounded unconvincing, even to me. Had I ever spent time trying to find out who Richie really was? "What changed?"

He dropped the first empty bottle on the coffee table.

"We shouldn't have done it, Fetch."

"Done what?"

"Stopped him. Hendricks."

"He was going to destroy the city."

"I know, but . . . there must have been another way. We could have put an end to his stupid plan without having to go to war with our own people. We were so full of adrenaline and the excitement of some big bad guy to fight that we didn't see what was happening."

I didn't need him to tell me that. I was well aware that I'd led the police into a battle to put down the last great fight for old-world creatures that this city might ever see.

"That was Niles's first move on this city," Richie continued, "and we helped him make it. Since then, half the job of the police has been enforcing his new rules about banned magical practices. All this talk about keeping people safe and bringing order to the city: it's a pile of bullshit, but it's too late to go back."

"Maybe it's not." I leaned forward and tried to sound convincing. "Everyone's going along with it because they think there's no other way. As long as they believe that the magic is gone for good, they'll accept that Thurston's future is the only option. But I'm not giving up. If you want to keep fighting, I could use your help."

He shook his two-ton head.

"That's not what I mean, Fetch. Whatever pipedream crusade you're on, you keep at it, but I can't muster up that kind of optimism anymore. There's no big secret waiting to be unlocked. No relic we can find that will solve our problems. That's not how life operates. It takes work. Constant work from a community of people who care about doing the right thing. We lost that. Now we just have a city full of people who want to get paid, and are willing to do whatever it takes to make that happen. It's over."

"Oh, fuck off, Richie." He raised his eyebrows in surprise. It was the liveliest he'd looked since I'd walked in the door. "Last night, an Angel landed on Main Street, splattered on the sidewalk from a greater height than could be reached by climbing any of the buildings nearby. That doesn't fit into Thurston's story. That's our story, if we can put all the pieces together."

"Yeah, I read the paper."

"Screw the paper. You know the *Star* has become another Niles bullshit machine. Benjamin's body is some kind of secret, and they don't want it getting out. Right now, it's inside the police station. Tomorrow, it'll be taken out and cremated. That's why I need to get to it tonight."

Richie stared me down.

"Why are you like this?"

"Like what?"

"So worked up. So angry."

"I'm not angry. I'm just trying to do the right thing."

"For who?"

"What?"

"For who, Fetch? Who are you doing it for?"

"Everyone!"

"Bullshit!" He slammed his hand down on the table, rattling the beer bottles and empty bean tins. "You're doing this for you, just like you always have been! You killed Hendricks, and because you can't handle the fact that you might have made another big mistake, you're going to run around town kicking everyone in the teeth until the world lines up the way you want it to. It's not for Sunder or for the world or whoever you say it's for, it's for *you*."

The neighbor's radio began an upbeat number that did nothing to lighten the mood.

"Richie," I began carefully, "you know that Niles is up to something big, something that spreads out across the whole continent. We have to do something."

"You're not Niles."

"I know that."

"No, you don't!" He took a big gulp of cider to drown his frustration. "You can't fight the fight like he does. He's a faceless fucker in a house on a hill, moving a million little pieces all around us. Of course he can make this city dance to his beat. Of course he has people thinking and talking the way he wants them to, when he's the one putting pay in their pockets. You can't do things the same way, so stop trying to."

"I'm not."

"You bloody are! You want everyone to think the way you think and want what you want, but how can that happen when you don't actually talk to anyone? When you don't listen? How can you change this city if you won't be part of it?"

"I am this city!" I shouted, finally snapping. "I spend every waking second working to protect the people who won't protect themselves. I'm the only one who gives a shit."

"Then why didn't you call?"

His question caught me off guard.

"What?"

"It's been a month since I left the force, Fetch. A month."

"I only just found out."

"And whose fault is that? I left a message with Georgio the day I quit, and I only hear from you now you want something."

Fuck.

There was a note, on a page torn out from Georgio's notepad, still sitting on the top of my desk. I was supposed to get around to it.

"Richie, I'm sorry. I thought you were just going to bust my balls about some cop bullshit."

He bit his lip to hold back his frown.

"You're my friend, Fetch. Doesn't that count for something?"

I couldn't look at him. Not with those big, watery eyes staring back. I grew up in Weatherly, of all places. We didn't talk about friendship or feelings – not even with my adopted father, who went out on every limb he could for me. I didn't know what to say in response, except for the truth.

"I don't know, Rich. Would a call from me really matter? I'm not really one for a pep talk."

Richie rubbed his stubbled chin.

"Fetch, I've known you longer than anyone else in this city. I've known you since we was kids."

"I know."

"So think!"

"I do! I just . . . I'm sorry. I don't think I matter, in that way. I'm working hard, and that seems valuable to me. But I'm not good at that stuff, you know?"

"No," he said flatly, still holding his gaze at my darting eyes. "Because this is how you find your value. Not by forcing some new future down our throats, but by being a part of our lives. All right?"

It was my turn to bite my lip. To keep my mouth shut. I felt bad for not calling him back. Of course. I felt terrible. But Richie didn't believe that I could fix anything. Of course he thought I should spend my time getting to know my neighbors and investing in their lives. But those lives wouldn't last very long if I didn't find a way to fill them with magic again.

I kept that in, nodded slowly, and said, "All right."

He leaned over, put a heavy hand on my shoulder, and we shared a smile.

"See, now *that's* hard work," he said. I laughed, and he thankfully released me. "After eight o'clock, the bottom and top floors of the station are shut down. That leaves just the reception, the waiting area and the on-site jail cells open."

Finally.

"Who has the keys?"

"Whoever's assigned to night watch. Two special officers stay on duty at the station in case anything wild springs up. You won't be taking the keys from them without bringing the whole force down on your head."

"Can the morgue be unlocked from the inside?"

"What do you mean?"

"If I was inside the morgue when they locked it up, would I be able to let myself out?"

"No, because if you were inside the morgue when it was locked up, you'd be dead."

"If I wasn't."

He closed his eyes and glanced around at his memories.

"Yeah, I reckon you could. Too many morons in the force not to have handles on the inside, or someone would have locked themselves in by now."

It wasn't an airtight endorsement of the plan, but it was something.

"How many cops in the station at night?" I asked.

"No way of knowing. Depends on what the day's been like because that determines how much paperwork needs to be filed. If it's rowdy, they'll all be on the street, but then they'll have to come back to report each incident. Could be anywhere from a few to a few dozen."

"If an incident calls them away, it'll empty the place out, right? Other than the receptionist and the night watch?"

"Maybe. Most likely, they'll put a call out to cops on standby. Then the other officers on hold will come on down, and you'll have more trouble than you did before you blew up the water tower, or whatever juvenile plan you're concocting."

I might not know Richie as well as I should, but he certainly knew me.

"I thought I'd run one of Niles's trucks into that building site on James Street."

Richie shook his head.

"Cops are exhausted. Always. If they think it's just a usual night, you might find a way to slip past them. But if you give them a reason to think that trouble's afoot – whether it's in the station or on the other side of town – they'll be all full of adrenaline and searching for someone to shoot. Keep them sleepy, keep them bored, and you might get down there without getting yourself arrested for the millionth time."

He started on the second bottle.

"Thanks, Rich. That helps. If you want to help some more, I could really use you. This case feels like the big one."

He sighed, the way an adult does when they're sick of answering the questions of a child.

"You're never fighting alone, Fetch. Even when you think you are. But I have no interest in working for a world that doesn't exist anymore. Let me know when you want to work for the world that's here."

Richie sat back in a way that made it clear he had no intention of moving anytime soon. He'd given up, just like the rest of them. They'd all accepted that Niles could steer our city wherever he wanted. Either they were going along with it or they were checking out, but I was the only one left who was willing to fight.

I left him to his cider and his early retirement and went off to recruit another player, hoping this one would be more helpful.

Eileen quit working at the Roost after her librarian job became fully financed, but I could still find her there most nights, helping herself to some shots from behind the bar.

"I don't know, Cowboy. This one feels wrong."

"Why? Because it's going against the cops?"

"Because it's messing with the dead."

I got her meaning. Breaking into a police facility to look at a recently deceased friend wasn't the kind of caper that made you excited to turn up the music and start drawing maps.

"Maybe wait a couple of days," she said. "I know the Brotherhood are angry at you now, but give them time to grieve and I'm sure they'll soften up."

"The body will be gone by then. If we want a good look at those wings, we have to get in there tonight. Nobody else cares. Nobody else is looking for what we're looking for. It's just us."

Eileen bit her lip.

"And what would my role be?"

"Well, do you know the term *honeypot*?" Eileen cracked a wide grin: shocked, and perhaps a little flattered. "Meet me outside the station in two hours. I have one more person to invite." I stood up, then realized there was a problem with the last part of my plan. "And would you mind if I borrowed some cash?"

She scoffed at the audacity.

"What'll it go on this time? Drugs, booze or tobacco?"

"Oh, nothing like that," I assured her. "I just need to hire a sex worker."

12

The Kirra Canal had never been clean, but an oily film now lived on the surface, mixing pink and green swirls in with the brown. I crossed the bridge into the Rose Quarter, noting that the crowds were quieter than they used to be. That would all change at sundown. In the early post-Coda, it was much the same all day: folks would come down to the Rose, looking for company at any hour. Now, it had found a new rhythm that was a counterweight to the routine of the factory and office workers. It simmered through the daytime and reserved its energy for the night, when more money would cross the canal than ever before.

"Hey, Fetch," came a sweet voice from above. "You coming to pay me a visit?"

On the balcony of The Baroness, a slender Wood Elf was balancing her book on the railing, reading and soaking up the sun.

"Not today, Delilah. Work to do."

"When you get paid, make sure you come down here and tell me all about it."

I nodded and tried not to contemplate the idea of stopping at The Baroness instead of continuing on to The Heroine. It would be a more pleasant visit, no doubt, but it wouldn't help me get into the police station morgue that night.

At the front door of The Heroine, the lady Dwarf who owned the place looked me over.

"How can we help you?"

"I'd like to see Gabrielle."

She checked her watch.

"She hasn't started yet."

"But is she here?" She didn't answer, which I took as a reluctant "yes". "Would you mind asking her if she has time for an early appointment?" I brought one of Eileen's bronze leaf bills out of my pocket. "I can pay."

"Of course you can pay. Wait here."

She went inside and a suited-up Ogre stepped out to take her place. He looked me over with a quizzical expression.

"You been here before?"

"Once or twice."

His expression remained suspicious as he tried to remember what our last meeting was like. I was hoping he wouldn't remember, because my last trip to The Heroine ended with me being drugged, beaten up, and throw out on my ass. They wouldn't have expected me to ever come back. I never expected I would either, but I hoped that a more sober and focused Man for Hire might make a better impression than I had the last time.

The Dwarf came back out and held the door open.

"Last door on the left. She's waiting."

"Well, this is unexpected," said Gabrielle, reclining on a chaise longue, wearing unglamorous comfort wear and no make-up. "But you never know how some people get their kicks. What part did it for you, champ? The insults, the hooch or the pain?"

"I'd like to forgo those elements this time, if it's all right with you. I have a proposition."

Gabrielle sighed and leaned back, arching in a way that was either intentionally provocative or just a force of habit.

"Did the goons knock the memory out of your head last time you were here? That's exactly the kind of carry-on that got you kicked out. I gotta get ready for the real work and I don't have time to play your little games. Drop the money and drop your pants or leave so I can get my face on."

I took a seat.

"You're a singer, right?"

"So, it *was* the pain you were after."

She reached out towards a little bell on her dresser. Ringing it would call the Ogre, and then I'd be in all kinds of trouble. I had to talk fast.

"My name is Fetch Phillips and I spend my time searching for ways to help ex-magical creatures find a way back to their old selves. Last night, an Angel flew over Sunder City on a brand-spanking-new set of feathered wings. Impossible, I know. So, to find out what really happened, I need to get into a locked room at the police station and take a gander at the body. That means I need somebody to distract the cops long enough for me to get downstairs."

"And what? You want me to flash my tits while you sneak behind their backs?"

"No. I want you to sing them a song."

She looked skeptical but at least she wasn't ringing that bell. Yet.

"I'm a Siren."

"I know."

"Folks don't like it when Sirens sing these days."

"Especially with the mayor's new laws. Everyone's getting all uppity when ex-magical creatures don't fall into line. I think a singing Siren on the street, right outside the station, would be a nice way to remind the cops what they're stomping on."

Her hand came away from the bell and went back into her lap.

"You want them to arrest me, then?"

"For what? A singing Siren is a social taboo, but there's no law against it."

She licked her lips.

"Not yet. What do you think they'll do?"

"I have no idea. I just want to see what happens when a Siren sings on their doorstep. They can't legally do a thing to you.

They'll feel like they *should* do something, to please their leaders in the shadows, but they won't know what. Doesn't that sound like fun?"

From the look on her face, she did indeed think it sounded like fun. Sirens had been given a rough ride since the Coda. Not only had their powers been taken away, but society had come to see the Siren song as a questionable practice of the past. Gabrielle had attempted to use her voice after the Coda, but the world wasn't ready for that, and so she'd ended up here. It wasn't exactly an invitation to a concert hall, but I would have been the first person in years who'd asked her to use her talents.

She got up from the chaise longue and took a seat at the vanity, examining herself in the mirror.

"Things have gotten busy down here. I'll lose a lot of work if I step away."

"No doubt. What's it worth to you?"

She gave me a price that wasn't wholly unreasonable, but was more than I had on hand, so I used her phone to call Portemus who agreed to float the rest. She'd get a third of it now, a third outside the station at the agreed-upon time, and a third when it was done. I shook her hand, gave her the first payment, and was about to leave when she asked, "Why me?"

It was a fair question. In our only other interaction, she'd beaten me with her words then called her guards to follow it up with their fists.

"Because I see what this new Sunder is selling, and I'm not satisfied. Too many people are. To fight back, I need allies who are just as dissatisfied as I am. Folks who can't help themselves when they see something that doesn't sit right. I remembered the way you saw through me the last time I was here – how you couldn't humor a self-pitying ex-soldier trying to play hero – and I thought you might be seeing things the way I see them now. If you did, maybe you wouldn't mind kicking up a stink to help me out. I'm glad I was right."

She gave a little shrug.

"Maybe you were. Or maybe you just knew the right price." She took off her sweater – there was nothing underneath it – and opened a drawer full of perfumes and powder. "You want to hang out while I get ready? We could have a drink. A real one, this time."

"I wish I could, but you're not the only performance I've got lined up for this evening, and it's almost time for the opening act."

13

Eileen and I waited across the road from the police station, in the shadows of the alley between Eleventh and Twelfth. We both checked our watches, as we'd been doing compulsively every few moments for the last fifteen minutes.

"Go in at five to eight at the latest," I said. "It might take a while for you to get Simms out of there."

"Then I'll go now."

"But if she comes immediately, you'll have to keep her entertained for at least fifteen minutes. Maybe more."

Eileen looked up at the sandstone building and chewed her lip.

"What else do you know about her?" she asked.

I shrugged.

"She's a dedicated cop but she's willing to buck the system when she thinks it's right, in both good ways and bad. Some days that means illegal beatings, other days it means helping out citizens against her orders from above."

"Is she a believer?"

"In magic, you mean?"

"Yeah. Does she still think we can fix things?"

Last year, it was Simms who hired me, unofficially, to look into a murder that couldn't be explained. She sensed that the police wouldn't be able to do their job properly, so she put me on the case.

"Yeah, she's still looking for a way back."

"Then I can keep her talking."

Eileen marched across the road, up the steps, and into the station. She was back out in under a minute with Simms at her side. I couldn't hear what they were saying but I enjoyed watching Eileen buy time by pretending that she was afraid of prying eyes and ears. She'd start talking, look around nervously, lead Simms a bit farther down the steps, then up the street, and start her story all over again.

Simms was well and truly on the hook. Whether it was the believability of Eileen's performance or just her natural charm, Simms obediently followed her every move, leaning in close to absorb Eileen's secrets.

I checked my watch: seven fifty-eight.

Simms asked questions then furrowed her brow and nodded. She looked around too, having absorbed Eileen's paranoia about people listening in. Simms even got her little pad out and made some notes. She was still writing things down when the doors of the station burst open and a young Human cop came out. He bounced down the stairs and stood at the curb, anticipating the arrival of the Niles Company automobile that came screeching from the north.

The car hit the brakes in front of the waiting officer, lowered its windows, and the driver and the cop exchanged a few words. I couldn't hear them, but I was pretty sure I knew what the police officer was saying. He'd be passing on the information that he'd just received from Portemus: a story about a body that I'd delivered to the Necromancer's door. Portemus would have told the police that the corpse was marked with signs of magic, and that the impulsive Man for Hire had mentioned something about bringing reporters down to take a look.

Eileen was here because I didn't want Simms inside when the call came through. She might have tried to do the right thing and keep it under wraps until she could investigate it herself. Without her around to remind the cops that they worked for the citizens – not for the man in the mansion uptown – Niles's little lackeys had sprung into action.

The car screeched away before Simms could reach it, so she ran after the tattletale officer to ask him what was going on. She got some version of the story, berated him a little, apologized to Eileen, shook her hand (for a longer time than was necessary) and marched back inside.

Eileen returned to the alley.

"Good job," I said. "What story did you tell her?"

"A true one. Seemed to be safest. I've been doing some research on those artefacts we found in the mask-maker's basement. The ones I remember, anyway. A lot of knick-knacks but, if I've done my research correctly, there are some truly precious pieces there too. Simms tells me they've mostly been handed over to Baxter at the museum, but I wouldn't be surprised if a few went missing along the way. She's open to the idea of helping me catalog the pieces, as long as I keep her informed about what I find."

I liked what I was hearing for a few reasons: one, it showed that I was right to use Eileen to open up Simms's softer side (and it was always nice to be right about something); two, I realized that the case of the missing artefacts might not be over; and three, it appeared that Simms was still open to bending the rule of law in search of a better Sunder. She might be reluctant to do it for me, but who knows what she and Eileen could uncover if they started working as a team.

It didn't take long for a police wagon to arrive, followed by the same silver automobile full of charcoal suits. Simms came back out to watch with dubious interest as the cops unloaded the covered body from the back of the wagon and carried it on a stretcher up the steps. The suits got out the car to smoke cigarettes and watch them take the "corpse" away.

"You think she'll be all right?" asked Eileen.

"It's almost knock-off time. She might get a couple of uncomfortable pokes and prods, but she's in the hands of public servants now; they won't bother doing a real investigation until morning."

Just in case Simms, a curious cop, or any of the suits decided that they felt like putting in the overtime, it was time for me to offer up a distraction. I gripped the empty bottle in my hand, slouched my shoulders, let my eyelids go lazy, and stumbled across the street.

"Where is she?" I yelled, when I was a few steps away from the trio of charcoal suits. "Where's the girl?"

Their hands instinctively reached inside their jackets, but I was close enough to have the upper hand.

I swung my bottle at the head of a goon that I recognized from the mask-maker's shop. He still had the same cocky smirk, and I enjoyed wiping it from his face.

They were more concerned with getting out their guns than defending themselves, which made my job easy. I dropped the bottle, gave one a crack in the ribs and the other a sock across the jaw. I ducked a right hook and punched the wind out of the guy who threw it, knocking him to the ground. I felt a lazy punch hit my side and responded by breaking his nose with my elbow. The other one kicked out, but I grabbed his foot and kicked his other knee. He screamed as it bent the wrong way and fell on top of his friend. The one I'd winded was trying to get up and I readied my boot to stomp down on him.

"FETCH!"

Simms was at the top of the stairs with her pistol out, flanked by two more officers mirroring her pose.

I put both feet on the ground and swayed a little, affecting the drunken characteristics that, not long ago, had been a regular part of my repertoire.

"You fucked me again, Simms! Where is she?"

I expected to see fury and frustration in her face: the exhaustion of having to deal with my chaotic aggression once again. Instead, she looked from the dropped bottle to my sweaty face, and her expression was mostly of disappointment. I was touched. Rather than being angry, she was sad that I'd stumbled back into the old habits that she'd thought I'd put to the side. It almost made me feel guilty that we were screwing with her, but we had no choice. She might not be all bad, but we still couldn't trust her not to toe the line.

"Fetch, what are you doing?" she asked, pity dripping from her forked tongue.

"I'm investigating a case! At least I would be if you hadn't sent your goons to steal my evidence!"

Two senior officers came out to see what the commotion was. They must be the night watch that Richie had mentioned, charged with keeping the place under control till it returned to full duties in the morning.

"Throw him in the cage till he sobers up," Simms told them.

"You can't do that!" I shouted.

"I just watched you assault three men!"

I threw up my hands in protest, stumbled back over one of the fallen suits, and landed on his moaning body.

"Get their statements," Simms instructed her officers, "and charge Mr Phillips when he's sober enough to remember it."

I let them take me in, keeping my eyes on the pistols as if they were the only reason that I wasn't making a break for it.

The night watchmen held my arms as they pushed me up the stairs. They led me past reception and opened the door of an empty iron cage that I was already quite familiar with. I stumbled in and grabbed the bars for support. The other cops moved away, leaving Simms to look down on me with pity.

I stared at her, eyes in soft focus, and head lolling from side to side.

"Can I get a drink?" I asked.

"Sure."

"Thanks. Whiskey, neat."

She wasn't amused.

"How about water?"

I pretended to think about it, nodded sheepishly, and she fetched me a paper cup. I took a little sip.

"When did you start dodging punches?" she asked.

"When did you start sucking Niles's dick? I never thought I'd see you on your knees for anyone."

It was just the kind of dumb, crude comment to get her to leave me alone. I didn't need her feeling sorry for me tonight. I didn't want her looking for ways to help me or wondering whether my cause was the right one. All I needed was for her to walk away.

"Leave him till morning, we'll process him then," she said to the night watchmen. "Ice up the morgue and lock the doors. We're going to have guests here first thing."

She left, and I leaned back against the wall to wait for things to die down. The suits spoke to the cops but didn't press charges. I knew they wouldn't. They'd want to sort me out on their own terms, some other time, when the law wasn't looking over their shoulders. Without their statements, I'd be able to walk out of the station first thing in the morning with nothing but a fake hangover to act my way through. I curled up in the corner of the cell and pulled my hat down over my face like I was going to sleep, leaving a thin gap for me to peek out of. I was just another sleepy drunk to be ignored till morning. The receptionist got comfortable behind his desk, and the night watch went out the back to do as much of nothing as possible, only throwing a cursory look in my direction before they left.

Before we'd settled on asking Gabrielle to help us, we'd thrown around a lot of fun ideas about how to distract the officers. We wanted something that would last long enough for me to get down to the morgue and back without being noticed. Drugging their coffee seemed a fun one, or creating some kind of crazy disturbance, but I'd already have enough hard questions coming in the morning and if it was anything too conspicuous, Simms would see right through me. Anything violent would put them on edge, so it needed to be something more subtle. Something that they wouldn't go blabbing about as soon as Simms reappeared.

After half an hour of sitting in my cell, Gabrielle started singing.

There was no mistaking it. She'd been bolder than I'd imagined. I thought she'd go with some kind of modern standard: the sort of song you hear on street corners, sung by blind crooners and kids too young to use tools. Maybe something jazzy, like the songs she would have been trying out in her post-Coda career as a nightclub act. If she'd done that, the realization of what kind of creature she was would have taken some time to register.

But this wasn't any feel-good radio number written to blow away the blues. It was undeniably ancient. I couldn't interpret the words, but I could understand the meaning because the emotion spoke clearer than language alone ever could. It was a Siren song, in its purest form. A beckoning, pining chant that seemed to skip your ears and go straight to your heart, forcing tears down your cheeks and shortness of breath, carried by a voice that had been told the world no longer wanted it.

I kept my head down as my plan played itself out perfectly. The cops exchanged glances with each other and, one by one, made their way towards the door. I lifted my head and saw them standing, transfixed, staring out at the street. A younger officer asked a question of his senior – perhaps enquiring whether they should do something to stop this not-quite-illegal transgression – but he was shushed by a hand on his shoulder and, absolved of responsibility, joined the others in silent appreciation. As the sound continued, growing in dynamism and heart-wrenching beauty, they stepped outside to watch the performance, bathed in the golden light of a setting sun.

With the coast clear, I stepped up to the cage door. Most of the station had been renovated during recent years, but the cage hadn't been touched in decades. It was nothing but rusty iron bars bolted into the ground, and an uneven gate fixed with a heavy lock. It was thick enough to hold an Ogre for a night but far from state-of-the-art.

I plucked some sandy pebbles out of my trouser pocket. They were pieces that I'd chipped off from that Rock of Hyluna I hadn't got around to returning yet. I shoved them into the keyhole, added a second and third pinch, then followed it up with some water from the paper cup.

As the small pebbles increased in weight, I heard them press against the mechanisms inside the lock: scraping, twanging and eventually snapping the tumblers. A ping of broken metal echoed out from the keyhole and a stream of water leaked down the bars. When I gave the door a shove, it slid open, and I was free.

Before leaving the cage, I removed the wire clothesline from my trousers. Thurston's high praise for the gizmo was deserved, as it had been pressed against the outside of my thighs for the last hour and had only caused minimal discomfort. I twisted it into a triangle that supported my coat and hat when it was leaned against the wall. When I stepped back, it looked similar to the way I imagined I had when I was all curled up. Not if you inspected it for more than a few seconds, but if you walked past and gave it a cursory glance, the general shape wouldn't draw any attention.

I scurried past the unmanned reception. Outside, I could see the back of the cops' heads as they watched the show out on the street. I bounced down the stairs and rapped against the heavy metal door, a new addition with a Niles Company lock that would have taken more than wet crumbs to crack.

There was a screeching sound, then the handle turned, and Mora peered out of a gap, her breath visible in the chilled air.

"Are you okay?" I asked. "They didn't hurt you?"

"They were perfect gentlemen. Seems that if I want a fella to treat me nice, I'll just have to wait till I'm dead."

I pulled the door closed behind us.

"Any chance you've found Benjamin?" I asked.

"Well, he's kind of hard to miss."

He was the only other body in the room; facedown on a gurney with a trolley on either side to support his wings. He was naked except for the full set of feathers that covered his wings. A collection of cords hung down from the roof and were attached to different parts of his body.

"What are they for?" I muttered, not expecting an answer. Mora went over to the wall and grabbed the end of a thick rope that dangled from above.

"It's actually pretty cool," she said. "Stand back."

She pulled the rope, slowly, and it moved through a series of pulleys strung along the ceiling. The cords pulled tight and lifted the wings from Benjamin's back until they filled the whole room. The tips touched the corners of the roof in an unbelievable show of old-world beauty.

I stood beneath his wings and examined the perfect curve that went from his shoulder blades to the final feathers. It was a work of art. There was no mark or scar where they attached to his back, and I was sure that no surgeon or twisted engineer would have been able to sculpt these from scratch. As far as I could tell, it was the closest thing to real magic that I'd seen since the Coda.

The rest of him was far from a thing of beauty. He was marked with bruises, after lying there for a day with his internal organs leaking inside his skin. Other areas had emptied. There was blood on the gurney, in his bowl-cut hair, and smeared across his perfect feathers. He smelled like death and he was cold to the touch.

"What are we supposed to learn from this?" asked Mora.

I shrugged. "I don't know."

What was I hoping for? If this was a regular old murder, I'd know the kind of clues to look for. But how do you check the details of a bona fide miracle?

Benjamin's face was flat to the ground, just like it had been when he'd landed. There was no doubt that his underside was going to be something horrible, but since we'd come all this way, the least we could do was look.

I plucked one of the cords.

"You think this will hold him?"

Mora looked worried.

"What are you going to do?"

I found the lever on the side of the gurney, put my foot on it, and stepped down.

The gurney dropped an inch. I took my foot off the lever, and everything seemed to hold. He was being raised up by his shoulder blades, with his head and legs still resting on the bed. Nothing had broken, yet, which was all the assurance I needed to keep going.

I pressed down on the lever again and, little by little, it dropped away. As the ropes and wings bent to support him, it looked less like the gurney was being lowered, and more like Benjamin was taking flight.

Richie's words came to mind, when he tried to tell me that the best way to make a difference is by listening to those around you and meeting them on their level. That was Brother Benjamin's whole life. He was dedicated to the simple act of serving food and smiles to those who came to him for help. He'd listened to me, tried to talk some sense into me more than once, and never met me with impatience or judgment. The city was a darker place without him, and one of the few reliable lights in my life had gone out.

When the bed reached its lowest point, he was left dangling from the roof by his incredible wings. With his head slumped over, and some weight still on his knees, he looked like he was kneeling in prayer.

There was nothing but misery beneath him: open wounds and stained skin. Crusted blood. Glimpses of bone and intestine.

Mora looked away. I almost made a crack about her being the last person I'd expect to be squeamish, but she'd risked a lot that night, so drawing similarities between her and an actual cadaver would have been a terrible way to show my thanks.

"Anything useful?" she asked.

What are you doing, Fetch? Why do you always search for answers by looking death in the eye?

"No," I said. "I don't think so." I put a hand under Benjamin's broken chin and lifted his face up towards mine. "I'm sorry, friend. I'll let you sleep now."

"Wait." Her surprise made my skin crawl. Had she just seen him move? Or breathe? Being in a morgue with one Zombie was bad enough. "What's that?"

She directed my gaze to Benjamin's neck. It was red, but not like the rest of him. His body and face were an abstract painting of gore, but there was a shape around his throat that was unmistakable once she'd pointed it out: a handprint, wrapped around his jugular, made of bright red blisters.

Mora looked up at me from under her fringe, excitement in her eye.

"What's tha—" she started, before we both turned our heads. The door had been left ajar, and somebody outside was shouting.

"You better get back," said Mora, so we raised the gurney, lowered the wings, and let Benjamin rest. I peered out. The shouting was clearer now. It was a male voice that I didn't recognize. Not one of the cops. The singing had stopped, and that worried me. I crept up the stairs, hunched over, until I could see the ground floor. It was still empty, but the crowd of cops had thinned out, likely involved in whatever commotion had stopped Gabrielle's performance. There was nobody else inside, so I came up into the room and went towards my cell.

"She's not supposed to do that!" shouted the voice, coming up the outside steps towards the entrance. There was no time to get myself back to where I was supposed to be, so I jumped behind a vending machine as the ranting man entered the station.

"They're not supposed to sing. It's not right."

His voice echoed off the sandstone walls, whiny and entitled. I peeked out to see the one who was doing the ranting: a middle-aged Human wearing some kind of sports jacket branded with the Niles Company insignia. It didn't look like a uniform – at least, not any I recognized – so it was likely one of the fashion items that the company had started pumping out. I was baffled as to why anyone would go around with corporate marketing on their clothes without any financial incentive, but apparently it was all the rage.

"It's against the law!" he continued, becoming even more agitated. "You have to do something!"

"It's not exactly against the law," said the cop, who clearly wished that it was. "There's no real magic in it. But don't you worry, she's stopped now."

"Only because I stopped her. You weren't going to do anything."

"Sir, she's gone, and it's time for you to go too. We appreciate your concern."

"But you need to charge her! You know what she was trying to do, don't you? Control your minds!" He launched into a tumbling, nonsensical ramble that I feared would never end. Worse, I was worried that the cops, bored with his monologue, would let their eyes drift over to my cell and notice that the body in the corner was more of a crumpled coat rack than a Human prisoner.

The officers were standing on all sides of the man, eyes in every direction, making it impossible for me to step out from behind the vending machine without getting caught. Then one of the cops, a Werewolf, finally snapped.

"That's enough, sir. The Siren's gone and it's time to leave. If you don't, we'll be forced to charge you."

"For what?" he yelled. "For demanding that you do your job? The job our taxes pay you to do?"

"For disobeying police orders. Everyone agree?"

Oh shit. If the entitled anti-Magum asshole pushed his luck, and they threw him in the cage, the clothesline would be spotted for sure. I had no suitable excuse for why I was out of my cell, hunkered down near the snack machine. I looked around the corner to see the other cops nodding in support of the Werewolf, got ready to run out of the station in panic, when—

"Excuse me." It was Mora, standing at the top of the stairs, performing the role of a disoriented and frightened girl more believably than I'd played my relapsed drunk. "Where am I?"

All eyes turned to look at the talking corpse that they'd dragged into the morgue only an hour earlier. I seized my moment and sprinted silently across the room, behind their heads, and slipped into the cell, closing the door behind me. I put on my hat and coat and slid the clothesline back in my trousers while the police officers stuttered through their confusion.

Mora explained her condition – no need to stretch the truth – and the cops called Simms, who rushed in to investigate and apologize. The angry bystander was harshly dismissed when he tried to comment on the proceedings, vowing to report his treatment to the mayor.

Eventually, Simms asked for Mora's address so they could return her home.

"Don't tell them," I finally piped in.

Mora looked at me, and her face broke out in relief.

"Oh, Mr Phillips!"

She delivered her lines perfectly. All eyes turned to me, then back to her.

"You know him?" asked Simms.

"Of course!"

"I told you, Simms. She's my case! I've been trying to find a way to help her. That's what I do." I lost the slurred speech but stayed wobbly on my feet so as not to give the game away. "Mora, don't tell them anything. You hadn't been here two minutes before someone called up Niles's guys to come take a look at you. You're a special case, and they might not be done with you yet. Just get out of here."

Mora looked from me to Simms to the exit.

"What if they're out there?"

Simms looked hard at the girl. Was she starting to doubt her? Was she onto us?

"Would you feel better if Mr Phillips took you home?" asked Simms.

Mora almost cried with relief.

"Oh yes, please. Since I arrived here, people have hassled me constantly. Mr Phillips is the only one who's tried to help."

Simms glared at me, her suspicion not fully quashed.

"You knew she was alive? Why didn't you say anything?"

"I thought she was dead because that's what you idiots were saying! How was I supposed to know you just hadn't checked properly?"

"I'm sorry," said Mora sweetly. "When I sleep, I kind of shut down. Not all of my body has a pulse, you know. If you checked the wrong place, you wouldn't have felt anything. It's an easy mistake."

One of the officers, seeing that Simms might be willing to set me free, chimed in.

"You can't just let him out, Detective, he assaulted people outside!"

"Not according to them, I didn't." I tried really hard not to sound smug. "Nobody filed charges, right? How about you book me for drunken disturbance and let me take this girl home before the goons come back."

I did my best to sound earnest and direct, as if getting this girl home, safe and sound, was my only priority.

Mora looks up at the cops with her one good eye, her face a painting of vulnerability, and you'd have to be a real asshole not to break at that.

"Let him out," said Simms to the night watch. "And I don't want anyone here making any calls to any connections outside this police station, understand? I'm sick of Niles men showing up at our door every time someone takes a piss."

The sheepish officers nodded, and one of them came over and put the key in the lock. As soon as it made a sound – just the grinding of metal and stone, rather than anything actually unlocking – I kicked it open with my toe and stepped out.

"Come on, Mora, let's get you home to bed. Somewhere where these amateurs won't drag you out from under your blanket and put you on a slab." I turned to Simms. "Was Portemus part of this?"

"Yes, and I'm sure he's very sorry."

"He will be. Night, night, Simms. Make sure none of these guys follow me. I don't want them telling Niles where they can find her. He has a problem with anyone too special walking the streets of his city."

Mora and I went out the doors, down the stairs, and around the corner.

"Are you smiling?" I asked.

"Yeah. That was fun."

"It was, wasn't it?"

"You're a terrible actor."

"We fooled them, didn't we?"

"Only because I squeezed out some tears. You know how hard that is with only one eye?"

"All right, don't go picturing your name in lights just yet. We should go tell Portemus what we found."

14

Portemus almost flung the gate off its hinges when he welcomed us back.

"You're okay! You did it? You got in and got out?"

We took him through our adventure, and he gasped and applauded at every turn. Then, when we came to describing the handprint, he actually jumped into the air.

"What is it?" I asked. "Do you know what it means?"

"No! But look at this."

He led us down the aisle, between slabs, until we came to the corpse of an elderly man whose body was scarred with burns and black patches of soot. Blood vessels had burst in his cheeks and eyes, but the damage on his hands was the most severe.

"Did he lose his thumbs in the fire?" I asked.

"No, that happened before the Coda. He was a Lumrama: a very powerful Wizard. He removed his thumbs by choice decades ago."

"So, what happened to him?" Mora asked.

Portemus cracked his knuckles and launched into his explanation, looking more like his old self every minute.

"This is an electrical burn. Our first hypothesis was that it was caused by some kind of malfunction with the Niles Company power supply: a surge, perhaps, or faulty wiring. With so many new inventions, and the speed with which the energy is being implemented, these kinds of accidents are to be expected. That seemed to make the most sense. Now, I am not so sure."

"What changed your mind?" I asked.

"Come look." Portemus pointed to the man's naked shoulders where two red handprints had blistered the skin.

"It's like some kind of brand," said Mora. "But it couldn't be metal. Look at the way the fingers curl around."

She was right. The handprints wrapped around his skin, as if they'd been burned onto him while someone was giving him a shoulder rub.

"What kind of creatures can burn someone with the palms of their hands?" I asked.

"Fire Sprites," said Portemus. "But there are none of them left. Some Sorcerers, Wizards and Mages could have done this, but only using Ditarum, which died with the Coda. At least, that's what we thought."

Portemus moved his attention back to the Wizard's hands.

"You think the handprints were made by a spellcaster?" I asked.

"I have no idea how those burns on his shoulders were made, but I have some ideas about his hands. This Wizard, once upon a time, would have been able to conjure all kinds of magic from his fingertips: fire, frost and *lightning*. Many an amateur Sorcerer, attempting to perform a spell beyond their training, has wounded themselves in a manner such as this, leaving their fingers scolded, frozen or electrified." We all looked at the streaks of black and red that ran up the dead Wizard's arms. It was easy to imagine a ball of blue light in his hands, surging out of control, and flaring out. "I would never have considered that this could happen today. It is a thing of the past, as you are well aware. But if an Angel has met their demise after the apparent return of their powers – and they bear the same markings as this man – well, perhaps it is not so impossible after all."

We all looked down at the Wizard; his missing thumbs, his burns, and the handprints on his shoulders.

"What does it mean?" I asked.

Portemus shrugged. "I have no answers that will not sound insane."

"Let's hear them anyway," I said.

"Well, perhaps somebody knows how to give people their

powers back. When they do this, they also brand them for . . . some reason."

"Like a gang?" Mora suggested. "Maybe these prints are the new version of the tattoos."

"But whoever is giving them their powers, it isn't working properly," Portemus added excitedly. "It's overloading their systems, surging through their non-magic bodies and destroying them."

"It destroyed this fellow," I added. "And it destroyed Benjamin, but how do we know they're the only ones?" I got up close to the blisters. Despite the painful appearance of the burn, the handprints seemed delicate in nature: slender fingers wrapped around his shoulders, the way you would touch someone if you were trying to comfort them. The same couldn't be said for Benjamin, who had been gripped around his throat, but they certainly weren't the meaty hands of an Ogre. Perhaps Mora was right. Maybe the marks weren't wounds as much as they were symbols. But of what?

I'd never seen marks like that before. But then again, I hadn't been looking.

"Ask around," I said. "But only people you trust. We don't want Niles or the cops knowing anything about this. If they saw the mark on Benjamin's body, then they'll want it destroyed before anyone else knows about it. Portemus, check the other corpses in case you missed anything and call the café if you need to leave a message. I'm going to hit the streets and see if I can find anyone else who bears the same brand."

15

I went to the café to let Georgio know to expect a potential call from Portemus, as well as to ask him if he knew anything about the magical history of red handprints. When I entered the café, he turned to me, held out his hand and said, "Here he is!"

The person he was addressing was the kind of young man who would spend most of his life being called a "young man": round, boyish features on a gangly body that looked, and always would look, like he'd experienced a growth spurt the previous week. He was wearing a clean shirt, pressed trousers and new shoes. His collar was too tight, so there was a red ring around his neck that blended nicely with his shaving rash.

He stood up from his chair, dusted crumbs from his lap, and dangled his hand out between us.

"Mr Phillips. My name is Lazarus Quintin Symes. A pleasure to meet you."

I ignored his hand and turned to Georgio.

"I need to run a few things by you."

"Master Symes has been waiting. He has been most patient."

Lazarus Q. Symes nodded politely.

"Fine. Come upstairs. Georgio, I'll be back in a few minutes to brief you on new developments, and . . . I'd love a coffee."

I sat down at my desk. Lazarus sat opposite. I was impatient and irritable. He acted as if the meeting had been planned weeks ago and things were all happening right on schedule.

"So, what can I help you with?"

Lazarus smiled.

"Everything." He pulled a velvet-covered jewelry box out of his trouser pocket and placed it on the desk.

"Is this a proposal?" I asked.

"In a manner of speaking." Inside the box there was a circular silver badge etched with an intricate design.

"What's that supposed to be? Some sort of circle?"

The kid was disappointed that I wasn't immediately impressed.

"It's a stone bridge over a river, reflected in the water. You see? And the Dwarvish writing around the outside says, 'Connecting one world to the other' on the top, and, 'Returning to the original' on the bottom. You know, like a bridge in music."

He was obviously proud of the whole thing.

"And why are you showing this to me?"

"It's a proposal, as you said. I represent an organization – known as The Bridge, you see – who have charged ourselves with guiding the world back to the magical existence we've left behind. I've been authorized to offer you membership."

His opening pitch had a rehearsed, made-by-committee sound to it. I wanted to throw things at him until he started talking straight, but I started by saying, "No."

There was nowhere on his fresh, pale face for him to hide his disappointment. He gave himself a silent pep talk and continued.

"We heard about you some time ago and have thought long and hard about our decision. We, like you, are dedicated to restoring the world to its former glory. The Bridge is a union of all species, but I believe that humankind – who caused the Coda and yet are unaffected by the consequences – are in the greatest position to put things back. Of course, you know this more than anyone."

I'd heard that last line before. Usually, it was delivered with snide accusation, but this kid was being frustratingly sincere.

"What do you mean by that?" I asked, expecting an insult that would put me back on familiar ground.

"I mean, you know what we lost and how we lost it. More importantly, you know that many of our kind are capitalizing on this broken world for their own profit rather than trying to make amends. You, Mr Phillips, *are* trying to make amends. So are we. Which is why I believe that we should be working together."

He spoke too loud for my liking. He was overexcited and it made the whole idea seem rushed and ill-advised; less like a well-thought-out plan and more like a scheme he'd put together with friends after too many drinks.

"So, what do you do? You and this *Bridge*?"

"It's a two-pronged attack. First of all, we find ways to help ex-magical creatures continue on. This involves researching and sharing new technology as well as appropriating old-world principles for modern use. The kind of things that you get hired for, sometimes: patching up the needy using modern versions of potions and spells. But that's just to buy us time. Ultimately, we want to turn things all the way back to the way they were. We want the magical river to flow again. We want Dragons in the air, immortal Elves, and for all Magum to live the life they deserve." He was sitting forward in his seat, damn near shouting. He must have seen me wince, because he caught himself, gave an embarrassed cough, and sat back. "I know it sounds grand. I try to temper my speech in front of most people but, with you, I feel like I can risk speaking my truth."

He was flushed. Nervous, even. It made me uncomfortable.

"So, what would this entail? Us working together?"

"Well." He opened up his folder, took out a stack of papers, and passed them over my desk. "This contract contains all the details but, in short, we share information, plan missions, and designate assignments, all with the intention of finding a way to revive the old world as efficiently as possible."

"You want to give me orders?"

"No. Not exactly. We encourage an open dialogue between all

members of The Bridge, no matter their position, and foster an egalitarian culture with minimal hierarchy."

"Does everybody in The Bridge talk like you?"

"What do you mean?"

"Like you want to sound smart without saying anything at all." I pushed the papers back over to him. "You might think you know about the Coda, but you were still in school when it happened. I was there, as you seem to know, and the worst mistake I made was handing over my choices to somebody else. I'm done with orders and tattoos, badges and groups, Master Symes, but thanks for the offer."

I closed the jewelry box and it snapped shut with a satisfying clap. Lazarus, once again, wore his disappointment like a feather bonnet.

"Mr Phillips, think of what we can do if we work together. This is bigger than any one of us."

"If you've got some information that you want to share with me, I'm happy to hear it."

An expected look of uncertainty crept across his face.

"We have a policy of only sharing sensitive information with members. We don't want—"

"You don't want other people getting all the credit and leaving you out in the cold? Or you want to control me because you don't like the way I'm doing things? Or you've gone so far up your own ass you think you're the only ones who can put things right? Well, I don't want any part of it. But you and your friends go forth with my blessing. The way I see it, the more idiots we have searching for magic, the more chances we have of stumbling over something important. You play your game. I'll play mine. If we're really lucky, one of us might actually win."

The young man nodded and went to get up, then stopped himself. He sat back down, leaned forward, brought his hands together, and rested two fingers on his lips. If it still wasn't clear that he was supposed to look deep in thought, he squinted up his face and made a frustrated "Hmmm" sound.

"Careful, kid. You're gonna sprain something."

"I wasn't meant to tell you this, but I think it's only fair. I was the only member of The Bridge who wanted to offer you membership. The others don't think it's a good idea. They think you're not really on our side. That you just exploit people like the papers say. Others think you work for Niles and the whole magic thing is just for show."

"So why did you come to me?"

"To give you a chance to prove them wrong. If you sign up with us, and share your information, they'll know that you really want what we want, but—"

"I've got better things to do than convince a bunch of kids that I'm trying to do something most people think is impossible. If The Bridge don't like me, fine. I'd never even heard of you until today. Thanks for the invite but I need to get back to work."

"But—"

"Larry Dicky Remington the Third – or whatever your name is – we're done. Take your silly names and your expensive badge and get out of my office."

He finally did as he was told and took the fire escape down to the ground floor. I gave him a few minutes to clear off before I went down to the café, which had closed up for the night.

"Georgio, you in here?"

"Yes," echoed his voice from the kitchen. "Back here!"

I went around the register into the kitchen, crammed full of fridges and fryers. Georgio was hunched over the sink, scraping leftovers off plates and dunking them into soapy water.

"We found a link between Benjamin's body and another corpse in the morgue."

"Mm-hmm," he replied, hinting that it was too late in the evening to engage in crackpot magical theories, but I continued on. I told him about the handprints and the feathered wings and the Wizard's charred fingers, but he didn't do much more than nod and mumble. "Georgio, have you seen anything like that before? Someone who can burn people with only their hands?"

"Wizards, yes. Could be."

"But it looks like the victims are regaining their powers, just for a moment. The magic was forced back into them, somehow. Wizards can't do that, can they?"

"I don't know."

"Well, of course they can't. Not anymore. But maybe something got twisted. Was there ever some kind of spell that could boost the magical properties of a creature?"

He sighed and hung up his dishcloth.

"Let me sleep on it. Maybe something will come to mind."

"Thanks, Georgio. I'm going out to see what else I can dig up. I've told Portemus to call here if he finds anything, so I'll check in with you first thing in the morning."

"Of course."

Georgio sat down on a stool, exhausted, and caught his breath.

"Are you all right?"

"Just tired. Big days."

"Maybe you need a break."

"Maybe. Too busy."

"Take a day off. People can eat elsewhere, can't they?"

He looked up at me, and his kind blue eyes were ringed with disappointment. I could feel them trying to release the steam from my engines and ask me to slow down. I resisted them. Too much to do. Too few people to do it.

"You okay, Georgio? Can I get you anything?"

"Do you remember the story I told you about the Ponoto?"

I did my best to squash my impatience.

"The guys who, when they save someone's life, dedicate themselves to serving that person?"

"Yes. What do you think happens when a Ponoto's life is saved by another warrior? Someone with the opposite belief system?"

Frustration rose up in me. More time wasted.

"You mean when the other warrior thinks the Ponoto owes him his life, and the Ponoto thinks the opposite? I have no idea. They fight it out?"

He shook his head.

"Nothing. They part on peaceful terms. No problem."

"Oh, right. Interesting. Well, good night."

"It is the *other* situation that causes problems."

"What? The Ponoto saves someone's life, so now they both want to serve each other?"

"Exactly!" He had a tired chuckle to himself. "The Ponoto wants to dedicate his life to the one he saved. The warrior wants to dedicate his life to the Ponoto. Neither will relinquish and neither can walk away. It is a catastrophe!"

"I don't get it."

"Because you haven't thought about it. What would you like more, Mr Fetch Phillips, Man for Hire? Some stranger following you around all the time, never leaving your side, or to know that you've dedicated your life to something noble and true?" Georgio didn't wait for an answer; he just smiled like he knew what it would be, and wiggled his long finger in my face. "Go on, you Ponoto. Be safe out there."

"Sure. Thanks, Georgio."

I'd had enough of his nonsense advice. It was time to get back into action.

So, I walked out onto Main Street and got hit by a car.

16

I heard the car coming from the south. Expecting it to pass by, I reached into my pocket for the pack of Clayfields. But it didn't pass. It ran right up onto the curb and hit me before I had any idea what was happening.

Luckily, it wasn't going that fast. It must have been waiting on the corner and had only accelerated when I'd stepped out of the café. The gutter would have taken the edge off the impact too. Even so, it made a right mess of me in a myriad of ways.

The car hit my left side, launching me off my feet. My head hit the front of the vehicle, somewhere near the windshield, and my body got all bent back like a slingshot ready to snap. Then they hit the brakes and I went skidding off the side, onto the ground, and landed on my hip, shoulder and the side of my head.

Before the pain could set in, I heard footsteps. I reached for my pistol, but I was seeing stars, and my fingers were slick with blood. Two sets of hands dragged me inside the very same car that had just made friends with my internal organs.

My assailants were a couple of the goons from outside the police station. I recognized them by the black eyes and bruises I'd left them with, more than any defining features of their own. They shoved me into the center seat and held my arms, though I had no intention of fighting until I worked out just how badly I'd been injured.

"You're not hurt too bad, are you?"

Yale, one of Niles's top henchpeople, was sitting in the driver's seat, her head twisted just enough for me to see the side of her face.

"Only my feelings, pride, reputation, skin and bones."

"Good. The boss wants to have a little talk."

The guard at the gates pushed them open with perfect timing, allowing the car to glide through. Rather than stop at the front door, we went around the house to the expansive backyard, lit up by torches as impressive as the ones that lined Main Street.

Between the immaculately mowed lawns and the carefully pruned hedges, there was a circular platform. It was only a foot high, built from wood, and covered with soft matting. It was a stage, of sorts, currently hosting a single performer: Thurston Niles, wearing peculiar armor, and swinging a shining rapier.

One of the suits opened my door and I stepped out, still nursing a sprained left wrist and a headache.

"Fetch! What do you think?" He spun on the spot, showing off the strange attire. "We're bringing plate mail into the modern world. No need for the gambeson because it has its own lining, and it doesn't require three men to get you into it. It's lightweight, flexible and just as tough as the old stuff. Here!"

He threw me a sword. I stepped away and let it hit the car, scratching the paintwork. Yale swore and the suit grabbed my lapels.

"Drop him," ordered Niles, picking up a second sword. "That was my fault. But Fetch, if you don't play along from here on out, and give it your all, that will be the last time I hold the boys back."

This wasn't my first invitation into Thurston's backyard to engage in a bit of sport, but every other time, I'd been handed a pair of boxing gloves.

"What are we doing?" I asked.

"Dueling. Like men. I want to test the armor – and myself – against your skills."

"Is that why you had Yale hit me with your jalopy before she brought me here? You wanted to soften me up so you won't lose as badly as last time?"

"She did?" He feigned surprise. "That must be related to your exhibition match outside the police station. Nothing to do with me. Now, get up here."

The other times we'd duked it out, I'd had more of a say in the matter. We'd knock back a few drinks and, when the war of words became too heated, we'd come out here to put our grievances into our fists. Despite myself, I'd kind of enjoyed those matches. This had a different energy to it – and it was the last thing I felt like doing when I had a real case to get back to – but as far as I could see it, there were two options: a real fight with the goons or a play fight with their boss.

I picked up the sword and climbed onto the platform.

"There's a good boy."

"Where's my armor?"

"Oh, come now. You're a soldier. I'm nothing but a puffed-up businessman who sits on his ass all day. We must keep this sporting."

I didn't like getting hit anymore. It used to be bad enough, back when the pain was all I had to worry about. Now, it meant recovery time. It meant moving slower, sleeping more, and standing out in a crowd. I needed people's trust, and a black eye or bloody nose could be the difference between someone confiding in me and not.

I did not want to play this game. I didn't want to be here. But if I *had* to play, I'd be playing to win.

"All right, Niles. What are the rules? What do I gotta do to you before you'll let me go home?"

"First to draw blood?" he suggested, putting his helmet on.

"Well, you've got the advantage there, in your fancy metal suit. How about we go until someone calls Uncle?"

"Sounds fair. Sword contact only, though. No closing the distance and kicking me. Wouldn't be fair."

"And you do love being fair."

"Deal?"

"Deal."

We moved at the same time, both trying to get that first cheap shot, same as the start of every one of our boxing matches. Unfortunately, his suit gave him the advantage in a game of chicken. My sword clanged off his helmet, while his hit my left shoulder and sliced through my jacket and my skin.

"Shit!" I jumped back and created some distance. "You keep your practice swords sharp."

"Who said they were practice swords?"

Emboldened by his successful hit, he attacked again, but I was ready for him now, and aware of how I had to play the game. He didn't need to block me, so I could only attack when I had him disarmed, caught off balance, or if his sword had been batted away. Till then, I had to bide my time.

He attacked in a rehearsed, triple-move flurry, and I parried them all at the last moment.

"When I was last here," I said between dodges and deflections, "you asked me why I visited."

"Yes. And you told me it was because you hated me."

"I respect you too much to lie to you."

He feinted an overhead cut. When I went to block it, he twirled his sword around and switched to a stab that just touched my side as I jumped back.

"What about you?" I asked. "Why do you keep inviting me?"

He had me backed into the corner.

"Well—" He went for a clean belly slash that I couldn't move out of the way of. I had to block it and push past him. Having the upper hand, and not being worried about a counterattack, he kept the pressure on, and as I moved away from the edge, back towards the center of the circle, he ran the edge of the blade along my right upper arm. Not deep, but damn painful. I had some room to move now, but I couldn't let myself get cornered again.

"Well," he repeated, breathing hard already, "I find you amusing."
Slash. Back away.

"Why's that?"

"Because you think you're something better than the rest of them."

Another rehearsed routine. Musical, almost. I parried the first two, pushed the third strike aside and gave him a jab under the ribs. Can't let him get too comfortable.

"Rest of who?"

"The Humans. You believe that you'll actually make the sacrifice. That you'll put everyone else's happiness above your own. Their lives above yours." Slash, dodge. Stab, parry. "But it's all a game. A way to let yourself sleep at night, after what you've done." Feint, lunge, riposte, parry. "When it comes down to it, if you ever have to make that call and give your life for their cause, you, like all of us, will ensure your own survival first." Slice, lean. Slice, block. "I invite you over because I know that one day, whether you deign to wear a uniform or not, you're going to realize that you and I are on the same side." Stab, parry. "And lucky for you, because of me, our side is going to win."

He did another one of those rehearsed routines. They were the sort of things we'd do as drills at the Opus, but not the kind of moves that would serve you in a real battle. We'd practice them for months before facing each other in the dueling circle. Then we'd go a whole year before finally being bestowed with our real swords and sent out into the field.

I was surprised at how quickly the skills came back. Of course, any real swordsman would have me in ribbons, but Niles was a long way from being a real swordsman. I had a feeling that whoever he'd hired to train him had been overly complimentary, which gave him an inflated sense of his talents. I played along – not blocking too soon or hitting his sword away too hard – until I'd finally had enough.

I was close to the edge again. It made him cocky. He lunged.

I deflected it and brought my sword up under his armpit. He yelped.

"I think I see some weak spots in your armor."

I whacked the back of his knee. The mesh stopped it from cutting through, but the impact buckled his leg. He stumbled, almost off the edge, then spun around, uneven in his footing.

He slashed, desperate to make room. I hopped back to let the blade pass, then stepped in and punched him in the face with the hilt of my sword.

Shouts erupted from the goons as Thurston tumbled off the platform and fell onto his back, the weight of the armor dropping him hard and fast.

I looked down at him.

"Ring out don't count, right? You gotta say Uncle." He struggled to roll over.

"No punches, remember?" He rolled onto all fours and struggled to get onto two.

"You said sword contact only. The hilt is still the sword."

I jumped down and socked him in the back of his head, knocking the front of his helmet into the dirt.

Pistols appeared from out of the charcoal jackets.

"Woah, lads. This wasn't my idea." I stepped back. I was technically correct, but nobody would care if they shot me dead, buried me beneath the platform, and pretended they'd never seen me. "How about we reset? Unless you want to call Uncle."

Thurston got to his feet. There was dirt in his visor. His gauntlets were too thick to wipe it out, so he resorted to hitting himself in the back of the head.

"Reset," he coughed, like he was tough.

I got back on the platform and offered Thurston my hand.

"Wanna lift?"

He swatted it away, then made a right ass of himself as he climbed clumsily up on his own.

"Before we get going," I said, "can you order these guys not to shoot me if I win? Fight goes till one of us says Uncle, right?"

"Right." He turned to his men. "Nobody interrupt the fight until it's done."

"Thanks. We good?"

He got into a stupid-looking en-garde position.

"Good."

He attacked as he said it. I blocked, trapped his sword, slid in, and gave him an uppercut with my hilt. Twice. He fell back, too heavy, and when he landed, I punched him in the guts (with the handle of the sword, of course).

"Anything to say?" I asked. I waited for a breath, then hit him again. "Anything?" I hit his helmet again, and again, and again. It dented nicely; the metal was made for blade hits but nothing like this. "ANYTHING?!"

"UNCLE!" he screamed. It sounded sloppy, like his mouth was full of water. I stepped back.

All those guns were pointed on me again. They wanted to use them. Any longer, and they would have. Then Niles would have got his answer about what I was willing to die for: a lot less than most.

I dropped the sword. There was blood on my left hand, dripping down from that cut he'd given my shoulder at the start.

"We done here?" I asked. Nobody said anything. I jumped off the platform and headed for the side exit. "Thanks for the fun, Niles. Next time, I'll drive myself."

17

I'd hurt my wrist and my arm was bleeding, so I didn't much feel like wandering the streets, searching for more handprints. Instead, I went north until I got to the shell of a prison once known as the Gullet. A tree had burst from its walls about a year ago. The plant had once been a Sprite, then a statue, and was now a towering landmark looking over all of Sunder. She'd gone bare during the winter, but now her branches were budding, and her trunk was shedding bark to reveal fresh, pale layers underneath. She was huge, and she was still growing, her limbs reaching out towards the lights of the city. Insects buzzed between her branches. Her first new leaves opened like beckoning hands that unfurled from each other, ready to return her to her fullest glory over the coming weeks.

Often, I would climb into her arms. Not tonight. I needed to get to bed. I needed to see a doctor. But no medicine could make me feel better than being beside her. Even in silence. Even like this.

I'd hated Hendricks for what he'd done to her: stolen her soul from her frozen body and delivered it here. Now, I thanked him every day. She could breathe. She could feel the sun and drink the rain; watch the days rise and fall and the city turn, and her old idiotic friend run around in circles waiting to figure things out.

I put my hand against her. Her trunk was thick, and her roots were deep. She was strong. Yale could run a car right into her and it would barely leave a mark. Whether I won or lost, it wouldn't matter to her at all. I couldn't convince myself that I was doing it in her name or for her sake or anything like that. She was finally free from the burden of having me try to make her happy.

I brought my hand back from the bark and, lit by the residual glow of the fire-filled lanterns, a bloody print remained. Unlike the burns that had been left on Benjamin and the Wizard, it was an uneven image, with more blood on my fingers than on my palm.

I took out my lighter to get a better look. My fingerprints glistened: five red spots, similar to the ones that I'd seen on that strange man's face. That smiling guy who spoke nonsense and kept wandering the streets aimlessly, always getting in everyone's way.

He'd been marked like Benjamin.

Well, he had the spots, but not the rest of it. Why would that happen? If somebody had gripped his head from the front, the mark would have covered his entire face, leaving a print that would be clearly noticeable to anyone.

Unless, of course, he'd been wearing a mask.

18

The next morning, I went to the medical center and got my arm sewed up and my wrist strapped, then I restocked my Clayfields and spent the day searching for the strange little man. He wasn't outside the corner store this time, and he wasn't back in Five Shadows Square. Around sunset, I finally found him down by the Southern-most lamp.

He was on a bench, finishing off a serving of beggar's bread. Oil dripped from his fingers, and he wore ragged clothes and those five red spots around his face. He didn't seem to care when I sat down beside him. He just kept munching on his dinner, allowing me to get a good look at the red mark on his temple, which, now that I could see it up close, was undeniably a thumb print.

"You seem happy," I said.

The pleasant pauper looked at me and laughed.

"And you most certainly do not."

With his face turned toward me, all sparkling eyes and laugh-lines, I had my first proper chance to weigh it up against my hypothesis . . . and it seemed impossible. When I'd fought the mask-maker down at the Mess, I'd never seen his whole face. I'd heard his voice, and though it wasn't dissimilar, I couldn't imagine the entitled, conceited speeches of the artefact thief coming out of the affable, half-asleep hobo.

"What changed?" I asked him, and he did a strange little nod, as if commending me for finally recognizing him. Was that why he'd been laughing all the time? Because he knew something I didn't?

"I was given an opportunity," he replied. "A chance to regain what I'd lost. What I yearned for."

"Somebody told you they could give you your powers again?"

"Yes." He placed his hand over his face and matched up his fingers with the crimson prints. "But she warned me that the gift was uncertain. Many do not survive the attempt. She told me that I should only take her offering if I believed that a magicless life was not worth living. So, I refused."

WHOOSH!

Flames filled the lamp over our heads, coughing a cloud of black smoke into the air. The mask-maker watched it, and grinned, as the light reflected in his watery eyes.

"But you were so angry," I said, "so eager to get your powers back. Why did you say no?"

He laughed. "I was scared, I suppose. I was frustrated that my new life wasn't my old one but, when it came down to it, I didn't want to give it up. Imagine if I had. I'd be missing out on all of this."

He closed his eyes and took a breath of the sulfur-filled air. He licked the oil from his lips and grinned like he was a ruler sitting safe on his throne, instead of a wanted burglar perched on a filthy street-side bench.

"Who is she?" I asked.

The mask-maker opened his eyes and put one hand on my leg.

"You're a soldier, aren't you?"

"I was."

"But now?"

"Now, I help people."

"So say your bruises and bloody knuckles. And how about our first meeting, when you came charging through my door?"

"You fired first."

He chuckled. "I suppose that's true."

Without warning, or any apparent reason, he slid off the bench and started walking. I went after him, weaving through the Main Street crowds. He smiled at every person we passed like he'd never seen another living being before.

"What were you after," he asked, "when you came to my store?"

"The artefacts you stole."

"Why?"

"Because I believed they could help people."

"How?"

"I thought they might be able to fix things."

"Fix what things?"

"Creatures. Magic. The world."

"The world?" He tittered condescendingly. "You do think highly of yourself."

He turned into an abandoned alley. I followed close behind him, watching the shadows for any signs of an ambush.

"Why did you want the artefacts?" I asked.

"I wanted them for power. I was clinging on to a version of myself that no longer existed. It was nonsensical. Like someone who wastes their waking hours being angry about something that happened in a dream." He jumped up on a dumpster to peer over a brick wall, then beckoned me to join him. "Look!"

Whatever this was about, I sensed that it had nothing to do with the case. Some pointless exercise had bubbled out of the brain of this lunatic, solely to test my patience. But I had to humor him if I wanted answers, so I hopped up on the dumpster and looked over the wall.

It was a concrete square behind an apartment block, dust-covered and dirty, with broken furniture and rusty bikes leaning against the walls. Two stray dogs dozed in the center of the square, and one Werewolf kid stood at a doorway, looking inside the building, eagerly bobbing up and down.

"What is this?" I asked.

The mask-maker held up a finger, directing me to wait, but I knew when I was getting dicked around.

"This woman who made you the offer said she could restore your powers. Why did you believe her?"

"Maybe I didn't, not really." He spoke fast; dismissing me, as if this conversation was trivial compared to whatever was about to happen over the wall. "But I thought I should at least try. So, I stole the bracelet for her, and then—"

Ding! Ding! Ding!

A dinner bell clanged inside the building; a heavy, slow chime that was immediately trampled by thundering footsteps, shouts of excitement, and the barking of the two dogs who started running in furious circles. The kid in the doorway followed them – his little legs fruitlessly trying to match their speed – before more children, of all species and ages, tumbled out of the building and joined in, forming a tornado of tiny feet, flailing arms and laughter. A young Elf in a wheelchair shot out of the door at breakneck speed, pushed by a grinning Half-Ogre teenager, arms spread wide, and wheels narrowly missing the ankles of the others.

"What are they doing?" I asked.

The mask-maker's face was a perfect match of the grinning children.

"Making the most of the day before it disappears."

The spinning circle existed for only a minute before the bell rang again. Just as quickly, the torrent of adolescent creatures funneled back inside, leaving the two dogs to jump and bark on their own, stirred up by the sudden rush of excitement.

"Every night they do this," said the mask-maker. "Some kind of last hurrah, before—"

I grabbed his collar in one hand and yanked his face forward.

"I don't care about your half-assed lessons from the street or your newfound take on the world. Tell me where I can find this woman."

He didn't resist. Just kept snickering.

"And why do you want the woman? You want to stop her?"

"Perhaps."

"Oh . . . you want to help her? See if she can help you?"

That idea seemed to interest him, so I went along with it.

"Maybe. If it's real. If she can do it properly. Permanently."

"Do what?"

"Make things good again."

He raised his arms, gesturing to the lot with the two riled-up canines.

"Things *are* good!"

"Not for everyone."

"Maybe not. But you really think that you're the one to make things better?"

I jumped down from the dumpster, dragging him with me, and threw him up against the opposite wall.

"I get it. I beat you, so you've had to come to terms with the fact that you lost. Well, I haven't lost yet, and I'm not giving up. People are dying without magic, and more firearms and factories won't give them back what they lost. We need to fix everything. For everyone. Forever. *That's* what I want."

He didn't look so happy anymore. Just a little disappointed.

"She worked out what I was doing before you did," he said. "I'd only stolen a few harmless pieces at that point, and she asked me if I could acquire a particular artefact on display at the museum. I did as she asked, but before I could hand it over, you arrived, and the treasure was lost."

"Which treasure was it?" I asked, remembering the rods that threw my inner ears for a loop, or the wooden sword that shattered metal at the slightest touch.

"A golden bracelet. No rare markings or power of its own, but precious to her and her kind. After fleeing my workshop, she cornered me, asked me what happened, and I told her."

"And she punished you?"

"No. Not at all. Even though I'd lost the piece, she offered me my prize nonetheless."

"And what prize was that?"

His silly grin returned. He grabbed my hand and maneuvered it up to his face, so that my fingertips rested on the five red spots.

"One single wish from a Genie."

19

After the mask-maker filled me in on the rest of his story, my head hurt from the implications. I needed someone to sort through the story with me, but I'd never been good at asking for help. My associates were all too smart, and their intelligence had an annoying habit of highlighting my ignorance. I never felt more stupid than when I was discussing one of my cases with a clever colleague.

I hadn't been a smart kid, not that it mattered. Kids are allowed to be stupid. You get the benefit of the doubt that you'll improve with time. When I first came to Sunder, fresh out of Weatherly, my naivety was to be expected. Back then, I was fine with being on the back foot. What could I expect after being fed a diet of lies all my life? Now, it was different. Once I'd started going around town telling people that I was planning to save the world, I tended to get self-conscious when someone made me look like a fool.

The solution, I'd discovered, was to get two smart friends in the same place. That way, they could bounce their minds off each other like flint and steel, and I could stand among the sparks, even if I didn't say anything.

As soon as I said goodbye to the mask-maker, I called Eileen and asked her to meet me at the café. After it closed, the three of us sat at the back table: Georgio and Eileen with a glass of wine, and me with a fresh cup of coffee. They made encouraging comments about the way I'd tracked down the mask-maker, and listened intently as I recounted the story.

"A Genie?" repeated Eileen with excitement. "Are you sure?"

"That's what he said, though he likes to speak in riddles. Do you think it's possible?"

Eileen went first.

"I don't know. I've read a little about the Genie. Never met one. I thought they all faded away after the Coda. Georgio?"

Gorgoramus Ottallus – once a spiritual leader, now a humble café owner – looked into his glass of wine, then back up with a coy smile.

"You want to know the story?" he asked.

"Yes, please," said Eileen and I together.

Georgio cleared his throat.

"This legend begins between the Second and Third Wars; a time when Archetellos was bursting with magic, and wondrous new beasts were brought into existence. The Wizard Queen, Riverna, was being hunted by her own kind, so decided to build a fortress in the desert sands of the far north. Her followers would venture out into the world, collect whatever treasures they could find, and bring the riches back for her. In return, she gave them powers, purpose and a home. But it wasn't enough. Her followers, believing that they were owed more from their leader, killed her in her sleep and took the treasures for themselves."

Eileen and I sat perfectly still and silent, knowing what an honor it was to hear a living legend deliver one of the great tales.

"The curse was visible the very next morning. When the followers woke, they could see through their own skin, then their own flesh, until they became translucent ghosts. Panicked, they ventured out across the land, searching for someone to undo the curse before they were gone for good.

"Most did not make it. When their bodies dissolved into nothing, the cursed jewelry landed in the dirt, waiting for the next poor soul to stumble upon them. Until, eventually, one of the followers found a way to resist the effects of the curse."

"Good deeds," interrupted Eileen, impulsively. "Sorry."

"No, you are correct! He discovered that serving others would bring his body back to its old form. For a while. If he wanted to remain in this world, he was forced to spend the rest of his existence performing helpful tasks for those around him. Do you know what else he did?"

Georgio asked the question of us both, though Eileen was the only one with the answer.

"Retrieved the other treasures."

"Yes! He made it his mission to find the other pieces of jewelry, lest they fall into innocent hands. Because the curse granted him eternal life, as long as he continued to serve others, he had plenty of time to do this. Once all the pieces were retrieved, he hid them away so that nobody would be burdened by the same affliction that he was."

"But one of those pieces was in the museum," I said. "So, someone must have found out where they were hidden."

"Not quite," said Georgio, kind and patient. "After decades of wandering between cities and towns, helping whoever he could, this man realized that there was more potential than danger in this curse, as long as it was bestowed on the right person. With this knowledge, he formed the Genie: a group of eternal servants who are untethered from mortality and bound to help those less fortunate. They have a strict selection process and an unbreakable code. For centuries, they have wandered Archetellos bringing countless good deeds into our world."

Georgio let the old-world story sit for a while before dropping the inevitable new-world twist.

"The Coda stopped all that, as far as I know. Good deeds no longer power the treasure, so, without any way to feed the curse, the bodies of the Genie have disappeared, leaving the useless jewelry behind."

I chewed on a Clayfield and shared the rest of the mask-maker's tale: how a woman had tracked him down and asked him to steal the piece of Genie jewelry from the museum.

"Why would she want the Genie jewelry if it doesn't do anything?" asked Eileen.

"He didn't know, or he wouldn't tell me."

"And what did she offer in return?" asked Georgio.

"If he wished, she would attempt to restore his old powers."

They were dubious, of course, but I went over everything I knew: the handprints, the wings, and the mask-maker's experience with the mysterious woman.

"Is it some kind of scam?" asked Eileen. "Or does she really think she can do it?"

I shrugged. "Either way, we should talk to her. Unfortunately, the mask-maker hasn't seen her since that night and he has no idea how to contact her."

Georgio cleared away our glasses. I was disappointed that he didn't seem as excited by the case, but luckily Eileen made up for it.

"So, what do we do next?" she asked, and I was glad that I had an idea ready to offer.

"We build her a trap," I said. "But for this to work, we're going to need Baxter Thatch on our side."

20

Baxter had ratted me out a year earlier, and I'd barely spoken to them since. They'd made lame justifications about how they had to prioritize their plans for the city, and keep a delicate balance of bureaucracy and passion, but I didn't want to hear a word of it. If Baxter had given up on magic ever coming back, then we had nothing to say to each other.

Until now, that is, because nobody else could get me what I needed. Niles, maybe, but I'd be damned if I was going to ask him for a favor.

Baxter performed many roles for the city, one of them being curator of the museum. Thurston might have retained possession of the other artefacts, but it was likely that the pieces stolen from the museum would be returned to their home. All I needed was a little bending of the rules, so I could use the bracelet as bait.

I approached the museum feeling optimistic. Baxter was a pragmatist and always willing to see reason. I'd been a right ass throughout our friendship but, if I approached them honestly and made a clear and sensible proposal, I was sure that they'd hear me out. I'd become a more reasonable man over the last year and had learned to keep my personal feelings out of my business, so, if I remained humble and calm, I was sure we'd find a way to work together.

As soon as I stepped into the museum, I started swearing.

It was empty. Almost. No Wyvern skeleton hanging from the ceiling. No suits of armor. No paintings of great leaders. No murals depicting the sacred river and all the creatures that it gave birth to.

The walls were bare, and the hall was full of open crates containing the precious pieces that had once been on display. There could be a reasonable explanation, of course: cleaning, renovations, or perhaps the whole thing was moving to a new building. I would have considered the possibility of those ideas if there wasn't a squad of pricks in charcoal suits doing all the packing.

At the other end of the room, the bespoke-suited Demon, Baxter Thatch, looked up from their clipboard to see my irate face staring back. They sighed like the bellows of a blacksmith's forge and beckoned me into their office. I managed not to break anything and went in after them.

Baxter had numerous offices around the city to accommodate their plethora of titles in both government and business. This room, to me, was the one that most suited Baxter's nature.

It was a miniature version of the museum itself: a mess of scale models, ships in glass bottles, cheaply made snow globes and irreplaceable, one-of-a-kind, hand-crafted sculptures. It was a neat kind of mess where nothing matched but everything had a place, and though I couldn't determine any kind of order, there was clearly a pattern to the chaos.

Every inch of the wall was covered in art: priceless gifts from long-dead friends alongside the scribbles of grateful students drawn beneath this very roof. The fact that the masterpiece and the doodle shared equal place of pride on the wall reminded me why I'd always been fond of Baxter, even when we were working against each other.

"Are you going to be civil," they asked, "or shall I pack away the more fragile items?"

Baxter's horns had been recently polished, and their eyes were, as always, full of fire.

"Where's it all going," I asked, trying to keep my voice even.

"Away. For now."

"Because of Thurston?"

"Because the city decided it was smart."

"You're half this city, Baxter."

"Not quite. Not anymore."

"You put up a fight?"

Baxter shook their obsidian head.

"I worked with the prominent ministers, the mayor, and other interested parties to design policies that would be most beneficial to its citizens. We need everyone working together."

"You've been spending too much time with Niles."

"I spent years molding Sunder before Thurston Niles set foot here. He has brought prosperity and increased its potential, but he is only one part of what I'm working towards. Unlike you, I learned a long time ago that nothing worth doing can be done on your own."

"Is that why you're letting him take the magic away?"

Baxter threw up their hands. It was always nice to get them animated.

"*You* took the magic away, Fetch, or don't you remember? All we're doing is shifting the city's focus. These pieces from the past will find another home, soon, I assure you, but they don't need to be taking up prime real estate in the center of the city. Their time is done."

It was rare to hear Baxter speak without complete conviction; they didn't fully believe what they were saying, though they were hoping I wouldn't notice.

"What the hell is wrong with you?" I asked, trying to goad some revelation out of them. "You've survived for centuries. Longer, apparently. You lived through more of the magical age than anyone, yet you're willing to let it go?"

"Exactly." Baxter's glasses had fogged up, so they wiped them on their tie. "I've seen ages come and go. Empires rise. Cities fall. I've lived through years of peace and decades of strife, so I've learned what's worth fighting for."

"And what's that?"

"Nothing. Because you cannot fight for peace. You must give in to it. You must let go. Of course I wish that the magic had never left us, but it has. You cannot force something into a world that no longer wants it. You saw what happened to Rye. To Brother Benjamin. You're not helping people, Fetch, you're just telling them that they should feel unsatisfied."

This wasn't going well. Baxter was more deeply entrenched in the Niles camp than I thought, and I was becoming less inclined to play nice. Once one of us started yelling, any chance of bringing Baxter into our plan was hung, drawn and quartered.

I had to try my darnedest to keep my tone conversational.

"So, you're set on helping Niles turn Sunder into his magic-denying, industrial utopia?"

"I wouldn't put it that way, but yes, I am."

"Then you sure as shit need me."

Baxter looked bemused.

"How do you mean?"

"Look at all this." I gestured to the collection of rare treasures they'd surrounded themself with. "You've crunched the numbers, considered the philosophical angles, and come to the conclusion that this is the right way to do things, but you're still a dreamer, Baxter. Just because you're building the safest world you know, it doesn't mean you don't hope for a better one."

"I know when it's time to put my dreams aside."

"Right. You're a realist too." I leaned forward. "You know that your love of peace isn't equaled by the men you do deals with. You know that there will come a day when they decide that a peaceful city full of industry isn't enough for them, and they'll want to cross lines that will no longer line up with your principles. When that happens, you're gonna wish you had somebody out there still looking for a way to fight back."

They took that in. Not enough to convince them, not yet, but enough to get them thinking.

"I deal with today, Fetch, not an imagined future."

"Fine. Then deal with *me* today. Drag my name through the mud. Make me a joke. Make me too dangerous to do business with. Make me the face of failure so nobody else will be tempted to go against the grain. Secure a safe, conformist mindset for all your citizens, but, at the same time, stick an ace up your sleeve for when Niles decides to go all in."

The temptation I saw in Baxter's flaming eyes warmed my blood. I had them on a hook, but I couldn't be careless.

"What would that entail?"

Careful, Fetch.

"A few artefacts, taken out of storage and put on display."

Baxter snorted.

"Oh, so exactly the thing that the city doesn't want to do."

"Not here. A museum is for history. For truth. You can't have that. But history doesn't get forgotten, Baxter, you should know that more than anyone. It becomes a story. How about we turn all these dangerous truths into harmless little children's tales, so they won't cause any trouble."

Even Baxter's granite cheeks couldn't push down their smile.

"And what story, in particular, are you thinking of telling?"

Hook. Line. Sinker.

"Have you ever met a Genie?"

21

Eileen, in her wisdom, surmised that a Genie-focused exhibition would be a bit obvious. Instead, she brought all her librarian skills to bear and curated an exhibition of famous stories, featuring the real-life objects that influenced them.

Baxter willfully forgot to ask about my ultimate goal and focused on the misinformation campaign that I'd pitched them: real stories from history presented alongside known fictions to blur the lines for Sunder's most influential generation.

"Are you sure it's worth it?" Eileen asked, when I told her the details of the plan. "Isn't this exactly what you were fighting against?"

"I don't love it, but it won't last. When kids see magical creatures again – hell, when they feel magic for the first time – all this will fall right out of their heads."

When a reporter and photographer from the *Sunder Star* came up to the library, I made sure to keep well away in case my notorious reputation sullied Eileen's good name. I had to wait until the next morning to see the results.

The new, Niles-built library didn't compare to the old, wooden building that had burned down, but it wasn't without its charms. The outside was made from the same concrete bricks as the other hastily made buildings constructed during the recent boom, but the interior spoke of Eileen's passion and dedication.

It was bigger than the old one and far better organized. The walls were decorated with patterned wallpaper, and the rows of shelves were painted different colors – bright enough to appeal to children but not so wild as to turn off the adults.

The exhibition had been set up at the back of the room, using display cabinets borrowed from the museum. Inside each glass case, an artefact sat on a purple plinth with a segment of a story written beside it. I walked along the line of treasures, reading the tales that Eileen and Baxter had chosen.

First, there was a warped bottle of green liquid beside a story that described how a group of Gnomes used medicine to permanently protect their bodies against the sun, becoming the first family of Goblins. Next, there was the head of a Gargoyle that would have been grotesque if it wasn't so obviously made from paper and glue. The Gryphon feather, which could have been real, sat beside a "dinosaur" egg that, to the best of my knowledge, was invented by a children's author only a few years earlier. Next, there was the Fae sword that we'd discovered in the mask-maker's basement, and, right at the end, the dull golden bracelet that was the true star of the exhibition.

Looking at the display, I was impressed and disgusted with the effectiveness of my idea. Kids would get all these stories jumbled up in their minds before they knew which ones were real and which were make-believe. To adults, it framed the desire to hold onto the glory of older days as a childish thing to be cast aside like soft toys and training wheels.

There was no need to dwell on it. Compromises must be made, and if I do my job right, this would all be undone when the magic came rushing back.

"Here's the article," said Eileen, approaching me with the morning's edition of the *Sunder Star*. "I think you'll like the photo."

The inside cover showed Eileen standing in front of the display, taken from an angle that put the bracelet closest to the camera. There was no mention of it in the article, but anyone who was looking for a piece of Genie jewelry wouldn't miss it.

"You look good," I said, handing it back.

"That's not the point, but thanks. You think it'll work?"

"We'll find out tonight. Whose idea was it to use the Fae sword?"

"Mine, of course." She looked into the tall case and admired the weapon. "I just love it. I gave Baxter some long excuse about why the Fae needed to be part of the exhibition for bla, bla, bla, but I just wanted to make sure Niles wasn't going to bury it somewhere. Isn't it gorgeous?"

It was. Mostly useless, but gorgeous all the same.

"Sure. It's the bracelet that matters, though. Let's hope she takes the bait."

I hid myself away early. If anybody suspected a set-up, they'd be smart to monitor the library for as long as possible, taking note of everyone who went in and making sure they all came out. To play it safe, I climbed into the ceiling around lunchtime with a couple of snacks, some water and an empty bucket, and got comfortable.

On Eileen's recommendation, I borrowed a book full of philosophical meditations. It was written by a warrior who wanted to help people adjust to a more industrial world, but I didn't make it past the first few pages. I found the scene below too interesting. Though some would argue that it wasn't ethical to peep on folks who had no idea that I was there, I couldn't resist peering out through the cracks to watch people wander the aisles, thinking they were alone.

A young woman could barely meet Eileen's eyes when she entered. Practically shaking with anxiety, she sat at the back of the building, as far away from everyone else as possible, and gasped and muttered to herself as she plowed through the pages of a new-release paperback.

Two kids in school uniform were delivered into the building as if it was childcare. The mother told Eileen that she'd return after running a few errands, and didn't wait for a response. Though visibly frustrated with the parent, Eileen didn't pass any of that attitude on to the kids, who she warmly directed to the picture-book aisle. As soon as Eileen was back behind her desk, and busy with paperwork, the sister beckoned her younger brother to follow her. Hunched over like pantomime villains, they crept into the science section where, without hesitation, the girl plucked a large biology textbook from the bottom shelf and opened it up to a page she was obviously familiar with. I couldn't see the details from my position in the ceiling, but whatever they were looking at, it put them in fits of uncontrollable laughter that they had to smother with their hands.

Readers came and went, the sun set, and when Eileen shut up shop, she didn't acknowledge me at all, just in case anyone happened to be watching. She put away her papers, grabbed her coat, went outside, and locked the door behind her.

The library seemed louder without anyone else in it. The shelves and floorboards creaked like the books were stretching out their pages after a long day's work. Once the sun had gone, the room was pitch black with just the dull outline of the shelves, counter and the glass of the display cases. I stared into the lightless room, seeing things that weren't there, wondering whether movement was real or just the swirling of my old eyes and overactive imagination.

The more tired I became, the more the nothingness below danced with waking dreams. Real dreams invaded the space as I crossed the line from awake to asleep and back again, unsure if I'd closed my eyes for a split second or an hour, hoping that I hadn't dozed off long enough for the thief to have already crept in and pilfered the artefact.

That fear was lifted when I heard the sound of something metal landing by the entrance. A hole had appeared in the door, letting through a circle of dim lamplight from the street outside. There was a scraping sound as a slender arm reached through the gap. I held my breath. The hand found the deadbolt, and its owner gave an uncomfortable grunt as the door unlocked and swung open.

The shadowy figure stepped inside, closed the door behind them, and was lost in the darkness. Footsteps, barely audible, came closer, and then they struck a match. Light flared below me as they lit a small lantern. I could only see the top of their head, but it appeared to be a woman: small and dressed all in black. Careful not to make any noise, I flicked the electric light switch that we'd pulled from the wall earlier that day.

The wires were connected to the outside light. Yesterday, before the journalists had been told about the story, I'd got up on a ladder and wrapped a tin cone around the globe to stop the light spilling down on to the street. Of course, if you happened to be sitting, say, at a bar a few blocks away, keeping a keen eye on the front of the library, the light would be perfectly clear. I just hoped that Eileen hadn't become too tipsy or tired to notice.

The thief held the lantern out in front of her and moved from one display to the next, pausing at each one as if to read the stories. That seemed a little strange, because there was only one real item of value in the cabinets, and I was pretty sure that the thief knew which one it was. She eventually found the final cabinet and put down the lantern so that she could take off the covering.

I couldn't hear any footsteps. There was nobody else at the door. Maybe Eileen had nodded off.

The thief didn't move fast. In fact, they seemed quite clumsy. It took longer than it should have for them to remove the glass covering, grab the bracelet, and tuck it away.

I was out of time. I pulled back the panel of the ceiling, leaned over the gap and moved my weight onto my hands. The thief turned. Moved back towards the door. She was walking fast. No sign of Eileen. I had to act.

I dropped through the gap and tumbled as I hit the ground.

She ran. I scampered to my feet and ran after her, but my hip found the corner of a table and I bounced painfully off course. She found the door, grabbed the hole with her hand and pulled it open – but the door pulled back, slamming shut. She yanked at the door, but someone was yanking it from the other side, and the other side was winning. I pulled out my pistol.

"We've got you. Don't make me shoot." The thief stopped struggling and slowly turned in the darkness. "Step this way." The thief obliged. "Eileen, you can come in."

She opened the door, backlighting the thief, whose face was still hidden.

"You don't have to be afraid," said Eileen. "We just want to talk."

The thief brought the lantern up to her face, illuminating one blue eye and an empty socket.

Mora.

"Well, shucks. You only needed to ask."

22

Even if Mora had wanted to run away from us, her failing body wouldn't have allowed it. After some introductions, I suggested that we all head back to the bar where Eileen had been waiting, to continue the interrogation.

"You might want to fix your door first," said Mora. "Sorry about that."

"At least it wasn't a window," Eileen replied in her usual good-natured way. "Give me a few minutes."

It was normal for Mora to be hunched over, head down, with her fringe covering up her missing eye, but it wasn't just her usual cool nonchalance that kept her face hidden. She seemed embarrassed, and maybe a little sad. Her healthy arm was holding her undead one, and it looked like it was causing her pain. It had likely been a more active evening than she was used to.

"If we leave here," I said, "will anyone else come to finish what you started?"

She shrugged. "Don't think so, but I don't know."

I held out a hand.

"May I?"

Mora handed over the bracelet, though I sensed her reluctance. It didn't seem any more special than the other objects on display: just a thin, gold-plated band with no jewels or discernible markings. I put it in my inside pocket. If another jewelry thief did come by while we were gone, they'd have to make do with the paper Gargoyle or lizard egg.

We walked the two blocks to The Roost, Mora and I both sluggish, and Eileen still full of adrenaline.

"You weren't waiting long, were you?" Eileen asked me, as if Mora wasn't there. "I was saying goodbye to Sam – he runs the place now – and when I looked back, the light was already on. I came as fast as I could, and when I looked through the hole in the door, she was running right at me."

"Perfect timing as always," I assured her, noticing the way Mora's shoulders slunk even further forward. "You handled the door pretty well, Mora. I'm guessing you've done this before?"

Mora sighed. "I traveled a lot before the Coda, mostly playing music. Some cities found me too freaky, which made it hard to get paid, so I occasionally encouraged their generosity. Only when I didn't have a choice. I'm not a career cat burglar or anything."

Eileen took us behind the bar but kept the shutter down so that we were hidden from the street. Although she no longer worked here, Sam clearly didn't mind leaving her a set of keys. She poured herself a whiskey and offered one to Mora and me, but we both just asked for water.

"How do you wanna do this?" I asked Mora. "We can hit you with the hardball questions or you can just go ahead and spill."

Mora took a sip of water and shrugged.

"I went to those surgeons, like you suggested, but they were all bullshit: cover-ups and concealments. Nothing real. I'd still be coming to pieces, you just wouldn't be able to see it. When I left, I . . . I got emotional. I was standing on the sidewalk, trying to get myself together, and I saw this woman across the street. She was all wrapped up in some flowing, black material. Only her face was showing, and she looked right at me. I don't like anybody looking at me, especially a stranger, and especially if I'm crying, so I flipped her off and left, but she followed me. When I stopped and confronted her, she asked me what I was hoping for when I'd gone into the surgery. I was honest, for some reason, and told her that I wanted them to save my life. When I told her that they couldn't, she offered to take a shot instead."

It was the same way the Genie met the mask-maker.

"How was she going to do that?" asked Eileen. "Save your life?"

Mora scrunched up her face, stretching the dead and living flesh, and pointed to the whiskey.

"I might take one of those, actually," she said.

"Sure."

Eileen poured her a slug, and she took a tiny sip. Alcohol probably didn't mix well with her delicate anatomy, but it wasn't my place to question her choices.

"She said she was a Genie," Mora continued, "but that her powers had diminished. To get them back, she needed pieces of cursed jewelry. She told me one was here and if I brought it to her, she'd try to use her power to heal me."

Everything Mora said was tinged with embarrassment, as if she wanted us to be sure, every step of the way, that she knew how silly it all sounded.

"And you believed her? When she said that she could heal you?"

"No, but I thought, screw it, why not? I didn't expect anyone to be chilling in the roof like a fucking assassin. What's this all about, anyway?"

"I don't think we should be sharing anything with you yet," said Eileen. "Not until we know you're telling the truth."

"Fine, I don't care. You gonna call the cops?"

"No," I said flatly. "Nobody wants to bring them in if we can help it. We think this woman you talked to is tied to those cases at the morgue: Benjamin and the Wizard. If you'd brought her this bracelet, there's a good chance you'd have become her next victim."

Mora nodded. I wasn't telling her anything that she hadn't put together herself. She'd seen what had happened to those bodies. If she hadn't, she might not have risked breaking into the library. The other two had died, but the chance to be the exception would have been a hard temptation to resist, especially as her time was already running out.

"Where is she?" asked Eileen, taking a harsher tone in response to my kinder one. "When were you going to give her the artefact?"

"She said that she'd come to me. That's all."

Eileen and I looked at each other. Could be a lie or could be the truth, and neither option gave us a clear next move.

"She was just going to find you when it was done?" I asked. Mora nodded. "That means she likely planned to watch you from the moment you left the library."

As I said this, the sense of it dawned on all of us. If she was watching the library, she would have seen us leave together. She'd know that Mora was caught and that there was no reason to find her again. We weren't any closer to catching her than we'd been before this whole escapade.

Mora looked tired, or perhaps just weighed down by disappointment.

"Come on," I said. "Let's get you home."

Just in case the "Genie" had discovered where Mora worked and had planned to meet her there afterwards, we let the Half-Zombie leave first. We followed her from a distance, staying to the shadows. Mora got back to the morgue without encountering anyone, and Eileen and I watched her enter from the alley opposite.

"Well, that's that," she said.

"The Genie could still be watching. We should wait."

"Come on, this is ridiculous."

"Fine, go. I'll wait on my own."

It came out harsher than I'd meant it to. I was tired and disappointed and didn't want anyone reminding me that the whole plan had been for nothing.

"Fetch, I was happy to help. I'm sorry it didn't work out, but I'm going home now."

I forced a smile.

"Thanks anyway," I said. "You really did arrive right on time. Sorry it didn't add up to much."

"Early days, cowboy," she said as she walked away. "This story isn't over yet."

I waited all night with nothing to look at but darkness, and nothing to listen to but the warm wind blowing through the streets, jangling the wind chimes on somebody's porch. When the sun rose, bringing street sweepers, bakers and fry cooks, I finally admitted defeat.

That old kind of tired was creeping back in. The one that wanted me to lie down, not for a night, but for a lifetime or two. To stop trying so hard to convince myself that there was some sense to what I was doing. That it really was for everyone else, the way I said it was, and not just a way to make myself feel important. When those thoughts came in, they grew barbs, and couldn't be washed away. I needed to pull them out by force before they dug themselves all the way in and became a part of me, but that sounded like work, and I was all done with work for the day. Maybe I was done for the week. Maybe forever.

That might have been the end of it, if I'd gone back to my office and found the place empty.

Instead, a Genie was waiting.

23

Only three kinds of people come through my door.

Those wanting help.

Those wanting a fight.

And sometimes, when I'm lucky, those who want to dance.

The Genie was wrapped in lightweight, black cloth that covered every part of her body, all tied together in an intricate series of attractive knots and folds. Just like Mora had described, only her face was visible. Her hands were hidden in wide-mouth sleeves that reached past her fingertips and must have made tying her shoelaces a nightmare.

She was leaning back in my chair with the kind of relaxed energy I always hoped to exude but never pulled off. Her eyes were hazel, her cheeks were full of cheek, and one eyebrow was raised in skeptical amusement.

"You don't keep a lot of notes, do you?"

Her question drew my eye to the piles of papers spread out across the floor and on the desk. The drawers were pulled out and overturned, my cupboards open, and my meager belongings in even more disarray than usual.

I tried my own look of skeptical amusement, but, feeling that it wasn't nearly as effective as hers, I took the bracelet out of my pocket instead.

"Looking for this?"

"No," she replied. "I saw you put it in your pocket outside the library. I was trying to find out who hired you."

"What do you mean?"

Her second eyebrow leapt up to meet the first.

"What do you mean, what do I mean? You're a 'Man for Hire',

right? That's what you've got painted on the door, and etched onto the plaque, and printed in the paper?"

"I never asked to put it in the paper."

"But that's what you do, right? Odd jobs for handfuls of cash? I just want to know who paid you to lure me into a library and throw a net around me, or whatever you had planned. I hope it wasn't too costly, considering the results."

"Well, you're here, aren't you?"

"Oh, please. Don't pretend that this was some part of your scheme. No librarian waiting in the alley this time, is there?"

"No. And nobody hired me either."

She crossed her arms and looked me up and down.

"So, what is it? Revenge?"

I saw, for the first time, a crack in her demeanor. She was tough, no doubt, but a moment of pain had broken through when she asked if I was out for revenge. I've spent plenty of time looking into the eyes of men and women who have done terrible things. I've heard them justify their actions with all kinds of causes, plans, paranoia and pain. They dared me to tell them that they'd done wrong. Not her. She knew, or at least feared, that she'd made a mistake.

"Revenge for Benjamin?" I asked. She didn't confirm or deny it. "So, that was you?"

"In a way."

"In what way?"

Her hazel eyes took me all in at once, and she sucked the insides of her cheeks as she contemplated her response.

"In the way that I gave him what he asked for. I explained the risks and he accepted them. At that point, what happened to him was his doing, as much as mine."

There was a challenge in every sentence. She was ready for me to start screaming. Prepared for an attack, perhaps. I had the feeling that she'd already played out this conversation in her head – prescribing my lines, working on her responses – and was waiting for me to play my part.

She'd seen me around town with the trench coat, hat, suit and pistol, and it had given her the wrong idea about me. I saw her surprise when, instead of shouting, I sat myself down on the clients' chair and asked her, "How did you do it?"

My question, and the sincerity of it, had the desired effect. Her demeanor became less defensive and more curious.

"I granted his wish. It's what I do."

"Could you grant my wish?"

"No. Since the Coda, there's only one wish to grant, and it doesn't work on Humans."

"It doesn't work at all, by the sound of it."

A little jab. She didn't flinch.

"That's why I have to regain my power."

"And how do you plan to do that?"

The Genie weighed me up and decided that I was fun enough to play with. She lifted her hands from her lap, and the wide sleeves rolled back to reveal slender hands with rings on each finger: some plain gold or silver, others with jewels embedded into them. Both her wrists were wrapped in metal: one was a warrior's cuff, the other entangled in delicate, dangling chains. She pulled back her hood to reveal even more accessories. Countless piercings studded her face, lips and ears. The material around her neck had been bound like a scarf. She unwrapped it, and more rare jewels glimmered around her collar. One could only imagine what each of them was worth.

The top of her head was the only part of her body clear of jewels. In fact, it was clear of everything. It took grace to sport a bald head with confidence, but the Genie turned it into an art. Her scalp was as smooth as fine whiskey, and about the same color.

She sat back, rested her arms on the sides of the chair, and let me imagine how many other treasures were hidden behind her robes.

I twirled the bracelet in my fingers, and took a shot at putting it all together.

"You think if you get enough of these artefacts, you become a Genie?"

"I *am* a Genie."

I'd offended her a little, but she didn't take it to heart.

"The Genie are gone."

"So's the magic, but you've still got an optimistic little sign screwed onto your front wall, don't you?"

"Good point."

"Thank you."

She scratched her eyebrow, and the bracelets tinkled against each other.

"I thought you'd be more argumentative," she said.

"Yeah, well, I'm pretty darn tired. So, you might as well explain it all to me because I'm too pooped to come up with the right questions."

"I *could* explain, but then I wouldn't have a chance to work out how smart or stupid you really are. Pressure's on, Mr Man for Hire."

I didn't know what I had to gain by impressing her, though impressing her felt like a worthy enough goal in itself.

"When did you become a Genie?" I asked.

"Ten years ago. To the best of my knowledge, I was the last person to be accepted into the clan."

"Is that why you're still around?"

"It's a theory. I wasn't always, though."

"Always what?"

"Around. The Genie make a deal: we gain immortality if we spend our lives doing good deeds for others. If we break that code, we fade away. Or, if some idiot Humans freeze the magic river, we also fade away, no matter how many kind acts we dish out. They never explained that part to me during initiation. Must have slipped their minds."

She knew that her comment might stab me, so she didn't put her weight down on it.

"How did you get back?" I asked.

"Don't you want to take a guess?"

She twiddled her fingers playfully.

"Can we swap seats?" I asked. "You're in my chair. I feel weird on this side."

"No. What's your guess?"

"My guess is that you found another piece of Genie jewelry. Another member of your clan faded away completely, you found their artefact, and it brought you back."

She applauded me.

"Well done, Mr Phillips. You might not be as stupid as your reputation suggested. I was fading from the world, though not as quickly as my comrades. Perhaps, like you said, it was due to the fact that I was only recently initiated. With no way to stop the process, I returned to the Genie temple. The others were all gone by the time I got back."

"But their jewelry remained."

She held up the stone on one of her necklaces.

"My master's piece was lying on the ground. I put it on, just to take it with me, really. To keep it safe. When I went outside, an Elven woman was waiting. Her back was all twisted up and she could barely move. She pleaded for my help."

"What did you do?"

"I tried." She closed her eyes. "I put my hands on her, and I could feel the magic running between us. Her skin went smooth. Her eyes cleared. She *smiled*."

"For a moment, right?"

Her eyes opened, accusingly.

"You get a point for following the thread, Fetch, but you lose a few for delicacy. She had a heart attack. I was still holding her when it happened. One moment she was dying from the Coda, then she was back to her old self, then she was gone."

I let that story sit out in the open for a moment, mentally holding it against the one featuring Benjamin, the few ideas I had about the electrified Wizard, and the one with Mora that I'd interrupted.

"If it didn't work," I said, "why try again?"

"You can guess, can't you?"

"I don't want to this time. I like the way you tell it."

She nodded. "Because afterwards, the ground was a little more real beneath my feet. My mind, which had been drifting out of this world and into . . . some other place, snapped back. It fixed me. Stopped me fading. For a while."

The post-Coda, magicless magic. It weakened some creatures, corrupted others, and occasionally twisted things up like a carnival mirror.

"Was it the extra jewelry or what you did to the Elf, do you think?"

"Both. The curse has been weakened, but it works the same way, only more unforgiving than it used to be. More treasures increase my power, and using that power keeps me in this world."

"I thought you were supposed to grant wishes. Do good deeds."

"That *is* what I'm doing."

"Is it? You think that the curse saw your act as a wish granted, not a woman murdered?"

"Careful. If we're going to be friends, you can't go hurting my feelings every five seconds."

"But that's what happened, right?"

"Yes. Which is why I went searching. The temple kept records of all its members: where they were living or where they planned to travel. I've been hoping to find another of my comrades, but I only ever find more of this." She spread her arms to reveal more cursed artefacts covering every part of her body.

"And each piece you find stops you from fading away?"

I twirled the bracelet in my fingers and watched her eyes. I expected her to focus on the treasure, like a hungry animal tempted by food, but she kept her eyes on me: clear and compassionate.

"Each piece contains some part of the power that kept Genies alive for millennia. With these treasures, we saved whole species from extinction, stopped cities from crumbling, and brought countless civilizations back from the brink. I feel the power in them still. There have been failures, I know that, but if I can bring enough of them together, and I work my fucking ass off, then I'll be able to grant real wishes and make them stick. You want to bring the magic back, Fetch Phillips: Man for Hire? Then help me regain my power I'll show you how it's done."

I closed my eyes for a second. I was getting too excited. She was telling me everything I wanted to hear, and I'd had that happen too many times to trust it.

"Benjamin was my friend," I said. "He did a lot of good in this city, for me and many others. You think your little experiment was worth it?"

She couldn't have looked any more hurt if I'd reached across and slapped her.

"Fuck, man. I don't know!" She lifted her knees up to her chest and curled up in the creaky old chair. "I hate it! I don't want to hurt anyone. I did this whole Genie thing because I wanted to help. The other option is to just fade away. It would be a hell of a lot easier, that's for sure. But what then? I'm the last of my kind, as far as I know. If there's a way to make this magic work again, and I don't even try to help people with it, then what's the cost of that, huh? I'm sorry about your friend. Truly. You have no idea. But if you saw him up there, when it worked . . ." There were tears in her eyes; for the tragedy or the miracle, I couldn't say. "Brother, it was the most beautiful thing I've ever seen."

She covered her eyes with her sleeve, all the bracelets bouncing off each other.

"There's a handkerchief in the top drawer."

"Oh, thanks." She took it out and wiped her cheeks. "I know it didn't last, with your friend, and I don't want to keep doing this if it doesn't. But if we can make it stick, then the sky will be full of Angels again, and isn't that worth a little risk?"

I rolled the golden bracelet along the desk. It clanged against her rings as she clasped it.

"Maybe. But if you're some immortal Genie, what do you need a lug like me for?"

She put her hand through the golden loop, and it fell among its brothers, clinking happily at the reunion.

"Nothing much," she replied. "Just to travel to a distant land, slay a monster and steal a priceless treasure. Sound like something you could handle, Mr Phillips? Or are you too tired?"

Her eyebrow did its little dance, and I wondered if I'd ever be tired again.

24

Her name was Khay. She was a thirty-one-year-old Half-Elf when she joined the Genie, and hadn't aged a day in the ten years since; though time had found other ways to get its hands on her.

I followed her out of the building and, as she stepped into the light, I tripped over my feet.

"Oh, crap," I stammered. "I can . . . I can see right through you."

I looked into her eyes and saw straight through them to the street beyond, where pedestrians passed between her ears. She pulled her hood back over her head. With her face wrapped up tight, the effect was barely noticeable.

"Yes, that happens sometimes."

"Because of the curse?"

"Either that or I have an allergic reaction to stupid questions." She marched ahead, north up Main Street.

"Shouldn't the bracelet help?"

"It will once I do a good deed to power it."

"You want to pick up some litter or give a tourist directions?"

"That might have helped in the old days, but it doesn't cut the mustard anymore. Got to break out the big guns if I want to keep my feet on the ground." Her voice was light and carefree with just a hint of doom.

"That's why we're going to the morgue?"

"Exactly. No good deed left undone. I would have already done it if you hadn't gotten in my way."

Nothing she said was completely serious, nor was it ever flippant. It was the kind of honesty I liked: wry without being cruel, and sincere without being absolute.

"Why didn't you just steal the bracelet yourself?" I asked. "Why get Mora involved at all?"

"I had a sneaking suspicion that there might be a trap waiting for me. The photo in the newspaper seemed a little obvious. Was that your idea?"

"It was my idea, but I wouldn't have been so heavy-handed in the execution."

"Oh, yes. You're an obvious master of subtlety. I'm sure your brass knuckles barely leave a bruise."

I buzzed the door of the morgue and, when Mora opened it, she was embarrassed, then confused, then fearful.

"What . . . what's happening?"

"It's all right," I said. "We've called a truce."

"For now," added Khay.

"Mind if we come in?"

Mora opened the door and we entered to find Portemus wrist deep in a Dwarf.

"This is the red-handed woman, is it?" he said. "Let me get myself cleaned up."

Portemus had woken during the night to find Mora missing, so had stayed up in a panic waiting for her to return. Guilty that she'd made him worry, Mora felt obliged to fill Portemus in on her expedition. His fear had turned to frustration and anger over the last hour, and Khay, who he saw as the instigator of it all, was catching most of the flack.

"Why didn't you get the bracelet yourself," he asked her, "instead of recruiting somebody so vulnerable?"

Behind his back, Mora rolled her eye. This might have been the first time that Portemus had ever flexed his paternal muscles, and he was clearly straining them too hard.

"I expected a trap," she said honestly, "and I couldn't risk getting caught. Being locked up for even a few days could be the end of me."

"But Mora's limited time was no concern to you?"

"Porty, please," said Mora, putting a hand on his shoulder, but Portemus's emotions were getting the better of him. It was a strange phenomenon; for the longest time, I wasn't even sure he had emotions.

Khay kept her voice level, doing her best not to get too defensive.

"Her *limited time* is exactly why I approached her."

"Ah, yes," said Portemus with sardonic flair, "your corrupted wishes. I've seen what happens to people who let you get your hands on them."

"They knew the risks."

"Did they?" Portemus scoffed. "They knew that they would die?"

"They knew they *might*, but they knew there was a chance that they might receive their old powers again. *Which they did*. It was their own magic that killed them, not me. I don't know why their bodies couldn't control it – I'm still working all this out – but I believe there is a way to put magic back into people's bodies and make it stick."

Portemus was unconvinced.

"And you think people will risk this? Risk their lives for a chance to have their powers again?"

"I don't know," said Khay. She turned to look at Mora. "Will they?"

Mora shrank under our collective gaze. To fill the silence, Portemus spoke on her behalf.

"Mora might have considered helping you, but she has come to her senses. It's too risky."

Mora pulled her hair to the side, revealing the hollow where her right eye had once been.

"If I hadn't let somebody else risk unknown magic on me years ago, I wouldn't be alive today," she said to Portemus. "You'd never tried this on anyone else before me, had you?"

Porty's confidence wavered.

"No, but this is different. You were about to die."

"I'm still about to die. That's why you brought this bozo in, right?" She pointed a withered thumb in my direction. "To find a way to keep me alive? Well, he did. He found her. The longer we leave my body the way it is, the less chance we have of it working."

Portemus turned back to Khay.

"What makes you think that it will work this time, when it didn't work with the others?"

"Because I have one more artefact. Each piece I reclaim makes my powers more stable. Also, I think this is different. With the others, I was pushing lost power back into bodies that had grown too weak. Mora's body is already split in two: some of it alive and healthy, other parts dead. Maybe there's a way to revive the decomposing parts without affecting the rest of her."

Portemus threw up his hands.

"See! That's why this is too dangerous. You cannot just revive half of her without touching the rest. It is all connected. You must bring her body together or you could tear her in two. Did you think of that?"

"I guess not."

"Exactly! Mora, when I revived you, I knew what I was doing at a surgical level. I knew the ligaments and tendons. The way the bones connected. The tension of the skin. Even then it was risky. This one," he pointed at Khay like she was a broken piece of machinery, "has been going around forcing energy into bodies without understanding any of the science!"

"Then show her!" said Mora, louder than I'd ever heard her before. "If you know what she needs to do, then show her, because I'm asking her to try." Portemus went to argue, but she drove over him. "I was fine with the pain. With the limping and the loss of movement. But it's gone too deep. I feel death coming closer every moment, and I'll do anything to push it back."

To his credit, Portemus didn't argue with her. He didn't like the idea and he didn't trust Khay, but he wasn't going to take Mora's life out of her own hands.

"Fine," he said, "but you better watch closely. If you don't pay attention, I'm out."

A long day and longer night followed, as Khay, Portemus and Mora made their preparations. I was able to catch up on some sleep in the back room while the three of them went to work. Mora lay down on one slab, and Portemus placed an unidentified corpse on the slab beside her. Piece by piece, he brought Khay's attention to the parts of the body where Mora's undead flesh joined the living, described the way it was connected, then used the adjacent corpse to demonstrate in greater detail. He flayed and sliced the cadaver in ways that matched Mora's two halves, explaining what he would do if it was him that was bringing both sides together. He went through every layer of skin, muscle, bones, nerves and joints. On my third coffee run, I dared to ask a question that had been kicking the inside of my skull.

"So, do you need to actually understand anatomy to make this work? Because that seems . . . ambitious."

Khay explained that it was less about practical information and more about clarity of intent. She didn't need a surgeon's skill, but greater specificity would help things to play out the way she intended. It was hard for me to wrap my head around it, but Portemus and Mora, being magic users in the pre-Coda, thought it made sense. They appreciated the lugubrious, speculative nature of magic; the way it did things that could be understood but never explained, how it responded to suggestion more than force, and that it should be treated as an ally rather than a tool. If Khay had truly tapped into the magic of old, then she wasn't going to wield an imaginary needle and thread, but she needed to tell the energies at her disposal exactly what she hoped to accomplish. That was how they described it, anyway. Controlling magic was an impossible-to-explain sensation, and I had a feeling that they were dumbing it down to its dumbest level to fit it into my head.

After I'd returned with the fourth delivery of caffeine, the team told me that they were ready to give it a try. Then it was my turn to be overprotective.

"Are you sure you don't want to sleep on it?" I asked. "We're not in a rush, are we?"

In response, Khay put her hand between me and one of the lamps on the wall: the flame shone bright through her body.

"This city has been tough on me," she said. "The more I fade, the riskier this becomes. Same with Mora. It would be best to act fast."

It was a fair reason for me to shut my mouth. I sat down silently in the corner of the morgue and watched them work.

Portemus had written a list of every connection point inside Mora's body. Khay looked it over, asking questions and making clarifications.

"Is that a ball-and-socket joint?"

"The liver is in front of that, right?"

"Are there nerves in there?"

The list was pinned to the wall above Mora's head. She had been lying naked on the slab for several hours. It seemed that her self-consciousness had less to do with her body's unique make-up and, like many of us, more to do with the personality inside of it.

Portemus turned down all remaining oil lamps but one, sat on the seat beside mine, and we both fell into respectful silence.

Khay removed her robes. First, from around her head and neck, exposing the earrings and artefacts I'd already seen. She unwrapped herself further, revealing necklace after necklace, from tight collars to loose chains holding precious charms. One extravagant silver necklace had been threaded through a series of rings that mustn't have fit on her already crowded fingers. Her collarbones were studded with jewels. They'd been punched right into the skin, charting lines from her sternum to her shoulders.

A web of golden lattice ran down her sides, around her back, and joined a tight silver belt. She wore thick golden cuffs, matching anklets, and as many rings as could fit on her toes. With the robes gone, the pieces chimed louder, tinkling happily as she climbed on to the slab, straddled Mora, and took a deep breath.

With only the one light burning, Khay should have been just a silhouette, but in her half-formed, translucent state, the light danced through her body; refracting as she adjusted her position, arched back and forth, and put her hands on Mora's shoulders.

"Ah!" Mora gasped.

"I'm sorry," said Khay, "but it won't be long. Can I keep going?"

Mora nodded and closed her eyes, then Khay began talking to herself.

At first, I recognized the words from the list that Portemus had written up. She was going over his instructions, remembering everything she'd been taught. Soon, the language changed into something I'd never heard before: a mixture of singing, keening and animal sounds interrupted by glottal stops and screams. Then some tumbling rush that seemed driven more by emotion than meaning, like an ancient entity was using Khay's vocal cords to travel through time.

Suddenly, she made sense again.

"What do you wish for?" she whispered. "What do you want?"

Mora whispered back.

"I want to be whole," she said. "I want my body again. All of it. I want to live."

Khay returned to her indecipherable song. Her hands never left Mora's shoulders, even when Mora started moaning.

She was trying not to. She was biting down on her lips, struggling to keep the complaints in, but she was hurting. Portemus was about to stand up, but I put a hand on his shoulder. Mora could ask for it to stop if she wanted to. But she hadn't. If she could handle it, so could we.

Khay screamed first. Hers was high pitched and wild, as if in shock or ecstasy. Mora followed: deeper, guttural and hoarse. I could smell something burning, so I looked to the lamplight.

That's when I noticed that the room was getting darker.

The light coming from the lantern hadn't changed, but Khay was in front of it. As she recomposed herself, the flame that had been visible through her body was gradually blocked out.

Mora kept moaning. Khay went quiet. She sat atop Mora's body, fully opaque, breathing heavy, and then toppled to one side.

"Careful!" I said, and jumped up to catch her.

She spun on me, suddenly lucid.

"Don't touch me!"

That stopped me in my tracks. Even Mora went silent.

"I'm sorry," I stammered.

"No, I'm sorry," said Khay, quietly now. "Please, hand me my robes."

I did, and she wrapped them loosely around herself.

"I'm going to lie down," she said. "I'll be fine soon. Just tired."

She moved into the back room. As she passed Portemus, he jumped up and went to Mora's side. The source of the burning smell was clear: two handprints made of red blisters, marked on Mora's shoulders.

"Did it work?" asked Portemus, pulling a blanket over her body.

I looked down at Mora's face, her eyes closed, seemingly unconscious, but still grimacing from the ordeal.

"We'll see."

25

We sat back and waited. I had no idea what time it was, how long we'd been there, or what we were even waiting for. We didn't say anything to each other. I closed my eyes but couldn't sleep.

Portemus raised his head and looked intently at the slab where Mora was lying.

"What?" I asked him.

"Her breathing. It changed."

He got up and went to one side of the slab. I went to the other.

"Changed, how?"

He crouched down and looked across her body.

"Only one of her lungs was working yesterday, but now . . ."

I leaned over as well. Together, we watched her chest rise and fall. Portemus put a hand on her sternum and, after another breath, gave a triumphant squeal.

"It worked," he said, tears in his eyes.

"It did?" Khay was standing in the doorway, her robes wrapped tight around her body and her head uncovered. "She's awake?"

"Not yet, but she's breathing and . . ." Portemus rolled back the sheet to examine the arm that had been giving Mora the most trouble. He tapped it, and her fingers twitched in her sleep. "Yes, I think it worked."

"Yeah, it fucking worked," said Mora, making us all jump. "Quit touching me. Everything still hurts." She kept her eyes closed, but there was a smile on her face.

Portemus burst into tears.

"I'll get something for the pain," he said. "Then, we should let her rest." He looked at Khay with an emotional mixture of gratitude and regret and said, "Thank you."

"No, thank you. I underestimated what it would take to do this right. Thanks for teaching me."

We said our goodbyes and Portemus promised to meet again when Mora was up to it.

"Take this," he said, and handed Khay a thick tome. "Basic anatomy of most creatures. Might come in handy."

Khay and I stepped out into the morning sun, neither of us able to find words that wouldn't diminish what had just happened.

"You want to get a drink?" I asked.

"Not really my thing. Swore off it when I joined the Genie. You can, though."

"I don't really drink either."

"Well, so much for that idea. What else you got?"

"Coffee?"

"I'm all coffeed out, but my taste buds are kicking in hard. They don't work so well when I'm half in the fade. You know a good place for breakfast?"

"You want something fresh, like fruits and things? Or something greasy?"

She bit her bottom lip.

"Greasy sounds good."

"I know just the place."

We weren't the first customers, but we were the first ones who wanted to take a seat. Everyone else was taking coffee and sandwiches to go. Since nobody was at the counter, I went into the kitchen to find Georgio.

"Hey, George, where's Jerome? You've got a line forming out there."

Georgio was standing over the fryer, cooking up a storm, with sweat beading on his face and arms.

"He's gone," he said. "Went back to stay with his parents. Too much work."

"Shit. You'll need to hire someone new."

"I will. When I get the time."

"Are these ready to go out?"

He had a few breakfast rolls open on a tray beside him: fried eggs, bacon and brown sauce.

"Almost." He tonged a lump of onions onto each of them. "Good to go."

I wrapped each of them up in paper and took them out to the waiting customers.

"I thought we were here to eat," said Khay as I collected and tilled the cash.

"We will. Just clearing out the queue ahead of us."

I went into the kitchen again.

"Add two breakfast specials, please, Chef."

"Coming right up."

"And one coffee."

"Can't you make it yourself?"

"I like the way you do it."

I grabbed the extra ingredients out of the fridge and placed them beside the fryer.

"You know, you should really put a window in here," said Khay, as she invited herself backstage. "Open the place up a bit."

Georgio made an exaggerated gesture of exhaustion.

"Oh, you must be with this one. He's also fond of offering unsolicited advice."

I made introductions, and Khay and I helped get Georgio up to speed. By the time our meals were ready, the breakfast rush was over so we could go back to the seating area and enjoy them. When Khay took her first bite of the bacon, she squealed.

"Oh, brother, that's horrendously good. Screw granting wishes, this could thicken me up on its own."

Her hood was still down, and there were no signs of her fading yet.

"How long will it last?" I asked, my mouth full of sausage. She shrugged.

"There's no handbook for it, but it depends on the size of the piece and the success of the wish and what I do in the meantime. Since Mora seems happy with the results, I could get a few weeks out of this one."

"And then you need to try it on someone else?"

"I wish it was that easy. Good deeds will prolong the effects, but they won't save me completely. My abilities fade as I do, so, at a certain point, I won't be able to grant wishes until I find more cursed items."

"What happens when you run out of artefacts to find?"

She lowered her fork and glared at me.

"You don't have much of a bedside manner, do you?"

"Sorry."

"It's all right. I kind of like it. We don't have time for beating around the bush these days." She shoveled some more eggs into her mouth and chewed thoughtfully. "I don't know what happens after I find them all. Maybe there's no way to keep me here for good. But, with each piece I find, the ground feels sturdier beneath my feet and my sense of taste and smell gets stronger. I'm thinking that eventually, if I wear enough of these things, they'll be strong enough to hold me here and they might even let me keep my powers. If that happens, that's when then the real fun starts."

I made sure I'd understood her before I spoke, in case I was jumping too far ahead.

"You think that if we get enough of these things, then you can keep doing what you did to Mora, but to everybody?"

"Shit, maybe not everybody. But I'd like to try."

God damn.

I'd heard all kinds of insane plans since the Coda happened, but they were usually screamed by insane Wizards or scrawled in blood on prison-cell walls. Everyone wanted their powers back – of course they did – but Khay was the first person who wanted them so she could do the same for others. The biggest difference of all was that she had a solid plan for how to make it happen.

"Where do we get more pieces?" I asked.

"Well, it's become a bit of a crapshoot. I exhausted the leads from the assignment book I took from the temple. It wasn't like they had members calling home every week to update their locations. That's why I came here. A few pieces were sitting in pawn shops and jewelry stores, and then there was the one in museum. There might be some more here, if we keep looking, or . . ." Her eyebrows did a dance I hadn't seen yet, and her bright, bejeweled face turned cheekier than ever. "Or, we go straight for the big boy."

"What's the big boy?"

She pushed her plate away and took a sip of water.

"Shit, even water tastes good today. The big boy is the crown of Riverna the Wizard Queen."

"She's the one who made the curse, right?"

"That's right. The Genie believed that the crown might actually be the source of the whole thing. Which makes sense. She kept it close to her at all times, and if she really wanted to curse her potential murderers, the one who dared to wear her crown should surely receive the harshest punishment."

"You think that the crown could be like putting on a whole outfit of artefacts?"

"Perhaps. There's no way to know, because it was the one item that the Genie never recovered. Before it could be brought back to the temple, it was recovered by—"

Khay looked around her, afraid that somebody would overhear.

"It's okay," I said. "There's only Georgio."

"And you trust him?"

"If you're dumb enough to trust me, then Georgio's the least of your worries."

She laughed, throwing her head back and making her earrings jangle.

"I'll tell you the rest while we walk. I want to stretch my legs while I can feel them properly."

We paid for our grub, helped with the washing-up, and headed out onto Main Street.

"Careful!"

I pulled Khay out of the way of a speeding car that had gone onto the wrong side of the road to avoid a fight between two street-food vendors battling over a valued spot.

"Brother, this place is crazy."

"I thought you'd be used to it by now, after sneaking around the place, following the mask-maker, Mora and me."

"I had one foot in the fade most of that time. I move differently then. I lose some senses and gain others. It's not a fun way to get around, but it makes it easy not to be noticed. Also, I tended to stick to the high ground."

She jumped the barrier of a fire escape and climbed the stairs. I followed, nowhere near as nimble, and puffed my way up the side of the apartment block, stealing glances in at the messy or abandoned rooms along the way.

Khay beat me to the top and perched herself on the edge. The building was as high as mine, but it still chilled my blood when I looked straight down.

"This is more like it," she said. "I prefer this city when I can see it from a distance."

I sat beside her, and we watched the little people rush around like someone was shouting orders in all their ears. Once we'd soaked up enough silence, Khay continued her story.

"Riverna was born a Sorceress at a time when only men were allowed to train as Wizards. She traveled to Keats University but was refused admittance. Rather than leave, she moved into the surrounding town and made a habit of luring students, then teachers, into her confidence and stealing their secrets. As soon as one acquaintance had nothing left to teach her, she'd leave them in search of someone more talented.

"Soon, her skills were beyond anything they were teaching at the University, and she formed an institution of her own: a castle in the desert where she would pass on her skills to any Sorcerer who wished to learn.

"The treasures began as unsolicited gifts: presents from new students who wanted to gain her favor. Soon, they became a required entry fee. Longtime pupils would even leave at regular intervals to find greater symbols of their devotion.

"It was one particularly ambitious follower who went too far. He traveled to Incava, the Wizard city, and used the powers that Riverna had taught him to assassinate the king and steal his crown: a triumphant 'fuck you' to the organization that had denied her entry. Riverna accepted the gift but her follower demanded more than her thanks. For delivering such a prize, he demanded a night in her bed.

"The Queen refused, and the follower, having been scorned, built the revolution that would eventually lead to her death and unleash a curse on the traitor and all who aided him."

"So, the horny follower took the crown back?"

"That seems to be the story, but if the power in the crown is as strong as they say it is, he wouldn't have lasted long; he likely wasn't the kind of man to immediately do a multitude of good deeds of his own accord."

"So, he faded away, dropped the crown, and then what?"

"There's centuries' worth of stories that I won't bore you with, but the Wizards made it a priority to get their crown back. Sometime later, they succeeded, and it has been kept in the halls of Incava ever since."

"Great. So we just go there and get it?"

She watched a butterfly float past, then turned to face me.

"Look, fella, I can shine the story up for you but I think it's best I just tell it to you straight. There are Wizards back in Incava and they haven't taken to the Coda too kindly. Not good dudes. At all. As far as I know, they still have the crown, along with all kinds of things that, to be perfectly honest, you shouldn't go anywhere near. If I could, I'd do it alone, but I don't know how to get in and out without bringing anyone else on board. That said, you don't need to do this. I can't pay you, and I don't want you to think you're already roped in, because you're not. I understand if you want to walk away."

"I'm not walking away."

"But you can. You should! You don't have anything to gain, do you? Let some ex-magic creature take the risk. Because then I *can* help them in return. What am I supposed to do with you?"

I started laughing.

"What?" she asked. "I'm not joking."

"I think you've missed a memo somewhere. I'm not the guy you worry about thanking. I'm the guy you kick to the curb when I stop being useful."

"Now you're just being mopey. I mean what I said. How about you find me an ex-magical creature to take the risk?"

"We might need one of them anyway. More than one. If we're going to travel for days to an enemy city and steal their greatest treasure, then I'm not enough to even the odds. But let's get one thing straight: whether you want my help or not, I'm not doing anything else until we get that goddamn crown, stick it on your head, and see if we can't unfuck the world for once."

26

One time, back before I became a Shepherd, I asked Eliah Hendricks whether he believed in fate.

"Time is a painting," he replied.

"What are we, then? The artists? The brush?"

"No. We are merely the warm air that dries the paint."

Some days, I think I almost understand what he meant.

The journey to Incava was the kind of mission I'd spent every day since the Coda preparing for, but it would still be a disaster if we didn't plan for it properly. Khay gave me further details on what she expected to find at the other end, and the clearer the obstacles became, the more she agreed with me: the two of us wouldn't be able to do this on our own.

We needed allies. My ideal first choice was the adventurous Werecat Linda Rosemary, but she hadn't been in Sunder for over a year. She'd posted the occasional letter, so I sent a telegram to her last known address – Keats University on Mizunrum – and told her about our plans. It was unlikely that she'd make it back before we left, but it was worth a shot; she was smarter and tougher than I was, and just as fixated on rumors of returning magic.

After that, I was kind of lost. I knew plenty of people in Sunder City, but most of them only became begrudging accomplices when I offered them some direct benefit, certainly not the kind of people I could ask to go on a weeks-long journey out of town to retrieve a magical artefact that they wouldn't be able to keep.

Though I'd been demanding too much of her time recently, the most obvious person to ask was my faithful librarian, Eileen Tide. We met her at the library as she was closing up.

"So, what's next?" she asked as she opened the door, doorknob properly secured again. "Have you come up with another plan to find your Genie?"

"Yeah. Here she is."

"Oh, shit." Eileen extended a hand.

"Best not," said Khay. "I have this whole burning-hands thing that doesn't make for great first impressions."

Eileen, ever the researcher, jumped on the admission.

"So, you can't control it?"

"Not yet, unfortunately. When I put my hands on a magical creature, my power starts firing off of its own accord. That's why we need your help."

We made ourselves comfortable in the reading corner, and Khay and I explained what we needed: a skilled team of travelers to join us on an expedition to Incava to retrieve an ancient crown from a group of vengeful Wizards.

"Any information you have on the city would be helpful, and we need to chart the safest route there and back."

Eileen brought out the most recent map she could find, and we hunched over it together. Roads shot out of Sunder like the petals of a flower. The Light Road went directly west, in a straight line to the Opus Headquarters. The north roads were rocky, tangled tracks that cut through jungles and carried on to the great plains. Farmland filled the east, until you hit the Vampire city of Norgari, or hopped the ferry to Mizunrum.

When Main Street left the city on the south, it became the Maple Highway, and traveled past Fintack Forest and Sheertop Prison, all the way down to Weatherly. A south-eastern turn-off took you in the direction of another Human City, Mira, and just below that, the secluded Wizard city.

"How are you traveling? Horses?"

Khay and I looked at each other and shrugged. We hadn't got that far.

"Yeah, I guess."

Eileen sighed at our lack of foresight and fetched an atlas, opening it up to the page that featured Incava: a craggy land surrounded by dense forest near the south-eastern coast.

"Even with horses, you won't be able to go the whole way. The Wizards made a point of not building roads in or out to deter others, especially Humans, from getting too close. Horses will have a problem with it, and if one slips and breaks a leg, then it's a long way home on foot."

"What's the alternative?" asked Khay.

Eileen went back to the map.

"Here's our destination," she said, pointing, "and here's the Human city of Mira. This is still well populated, and I hear that they import a lot of Niles Company products, which means they'll need new roads running all the way there. The quickest and safest option is to drive to Mira, hide the car, and go the rest of the way on foot. It won't be quicker than horses in the long run, but it will make the journey home a lot easier."

"Cars don't come cheap."

"This trip won't be cheap. Not if you want to come back alive. Have you thought about food?"

"Not yet. I'm sure Georgio can help us out."

"You're bringing Georgio? He's ancient!"

"Of course not. But he can pack some stuff for us."

"You can't pack lunch for a month-long journey. You can't go hungry either. Not if you're expecting a fight at the other end." She turned to Khay. "Are you much of a hunter?"

"Never had much need for it. Before the Coda, folks were happy to offer me food and lodging wherever I went."

"So, you'll want a tracker. A good one. Your best bet is Hunter's Hall."

"Oh, of course. We'll hire them with all the change left over after buying the automobile."

"I'm certainly not going if you can't guarantee two good meals a day."

"How am I going to afford a hunter and a car?"

Eileen gestured to Khay's bejeweled face.

"If we hit a couple of pawn shops we can be bankrolled in an hour."

Khay was clearly horrified at the idea.

"That's not going to happen," I said. "Unless we want Khay to disappear before we get anywhere near the crown. We need to find a cheaper way to do this."

Eileen sat back and crossed her arms.

"Impossible. Well, it's possible but we won't make it back."

"Then I'll do it on my own."

"No!" said both the women, together.

"It'll be cheaper, won't it? Just me and a donkey. I'll sneak in, get the crown, ride back. If I don't make it, then you can come find me."

Eileen and Khay shared a look, bonding over a mutual belief that I'd be dead if it wasn't for both of them.

"You know Sunder City," said Eileen, "but it's different out there. If you want to succeed, you need to prepare and fund this expedition properly and—"

"What the hell is that?" I pointed to a silver circle pinned to her shirt, half visible beneath her blazer. The broach depicted a bridge over a river, its reflection mirrored in the water.

"Oh," she said, "some kid gave it to me."

"Lazarus, right? An over-articulate beanpole? You actually joined them?"

"The Bridge? Yeah, they seemed harmless."

"They seemed ridiculous. A bunch of kids making badges and writing speeches without actually doing anything."

"How do you know?"

"It was obvious. You don't improve things by spending all your time designing logos."

Eileen unpinned the badge and put in on the desk.

"It is a nice logo," she said, "and well made."

"Exactly. I know that kind of kid. He probably spent a bunch of his dad's money on market research and merchandise and none of it will actually go towards anything important."

The two ladies looked at me, already a step ahead.

"Well," said Khay, "perhaps we should show him a better way to spend it."

Eileen rang the number that Lazarus had given her, and I leaned close to listen in.

"Hello?"

It was a woman's voice.

"Hi, yes, this is Eileen Tide. I'm looking for Lazarus."

"One moment . . . LARRY! SOMEBODY'S ON THE PHONE FOR YOU! . . . He's coming."

There were hurried footsteps and whispers.

"Hello?" said the young man.

"Hi, Lazarus. This is Eileen Tide from the library."

"Oh, hello, Eileen. Sorry, my office is waiting to have a new phone line installed so I'm sharing the utilities for the moment. How can I help you?"

"I'm here with Mr Fetch Phillips; I believe you know him. He's working on a case that has him positively flummoxed, and I thought that you might be able to help. Could we meet you sometime tomorrow?"

"Oh, sure. At Mr Phillips's place of business or the library?"

"Actually, Larry," I cut in, "this is a sensitive subject and I'm not sure either of our locations are secure. How about we do this at your place? You just said you had an office, right?"

"Oh, yes, bu—"

"Does nine o'clock work for you?"

". . . Sure."

"Fantastic. What's the address?"

Lazarus reluctantly gave us the details and we bade him goodnight.

"What was that about?" asked Khay.

I looked at the address and smiled.

"If we're going to approach Mr Symes for some funding, I'd like to check out the depth of his pockets."

27

I knew it.

You would have thought it was five houses if there wasn't only one letterbox. Lazarus Q. Symes lived in an extravagant stone manor house that must have been built in the first years of the city. One of the founding engineers would have lived here, back when space was the least of their worries, and it had been extended and improved by rich asshole after rich asshole until it could only be inhabited by families who could afford an extensive team of gardeners, cleaners and builders to keep it in shape.

The gates were closed and there was nobody manning them.

"Hit the buzzer," said Eileen.

Khay had decided not to come. She was technically connected to a couple of open homicides, and you never know what someone will do when they come upon a creature they'd believed to be extinct.

As soon as I pressed the button, a voice erupted from a metal box embedded in the wall.

"Hello. This is uh . . . this is The Bridge."

"Hey, Lazarus. It's Fetch and Eileen."

"Oh, hello. I'll let you in."

There was an electric honking sound, then a click, before the gate began to open on its own.

"That's new," I said. "Some Niles Company contraption?"

Eileen inspected the metal box.

"It says Mortales."

Shit. Same, same but different. I hadn't seen many new products from them since Niles came to town. Mortales were essentially the Human Army with a new coat of paint and a less offensive mission statement, trying to take over the world with appliances instead of soldiers. I thought the Niles Company was another coat of paint on top of that, but seeing a new contraption with their stamp on it made me wonder if there weren't two Human-controlled mechanical companies at play. It might not mean anything significant, though, just more proof that whoever lived here had the cash to order expensive new products that weren't made in this city.

When the gates were open, we stepped inside, and another buzz closed us in.

The stone walls of the main building were the only parts that appeared to be original. Turrets and towers had been built on each corner, above newly renovated rooms with rows of narrow windows. A wooden balcony covered in climbing vines and garish sculptures wrapped around the second floor and extended out over the driveway above an idling automobile painted bright gold. I was ready to laugh, until I saw that somebody was sitting in the driver's seat: a suited man with a flat black cap over his bald head. He was so busy glaring at us that he missed his cue, as a rotund fellow in a tweed suit came out of the house and opened the rear door.

The driver jumped up in a panic.

"Sorry, sir."

"Not at all, Radcliffe. I can manage it myself. Hello!" he said, when he noticed Eileen and me watching from the middle of the drive. "You must be Larry's friends. He's waiting inside. Make yourself at home."

The driver closed him in, got back in the front, and revved the engine of the monstrosity. The gates opened once more, and Eileen and I stepped aside to let them pass.

"Is this our future?" she asked. "Golden cars and folks too lazy to open their own doors?"

"All the more reason to bring the old world back."

Before we got to the front door, Lazarus Q. Symes opened it enthusiastically.

"Hello! Hello! Please, come in."

The inside of the house was just like the outside of the car: gaudy, glittering and hideous. I couldn't believe the extravagance. Only a year ago, the city was dealing with a firewood shortage. This place was stuffed full of furniture that had never been sat on in its life. It was like a museum of tack, and I felt a strong desire to kick things. I'm glad I didn't, because we were met in the corridor by a waifish woman holding a glass of green juice.

"Oh, hello! Welcome. I'm Tiara. Would any of you like refreshments? I can make you a juice. Some herbal tea? Something heavier?"

Eileen threw me a look to make sure I wasn't going to make any cracks.

"No, thank you," I said. "I'm fine."

"Me too," said Eileen politely.

"Well, just holler if you need anything. Have fun."

"Thanks, Mom." Lazarus swallowed his embarrassment and continued on. "This way."

He took us into an office that clearly hadn't been an office twenty-four hours ago. I got a surge of satisfaction imagining Lazarus throwing it together in expectation of our arrival. The walls were bare except for metal hooks that were likely waiting for paintings to be returned to them once we left.

"Please, have a seat," he said, directing us to two chairs on one side of a large mahogany desk that must have been his father's back-up. We took our seats, and he sat opposite, projecting awkward anticipation. "So, how can we help you?"

Before Eileen could talk, I cut her off.

"We?"

"Yes. The Bridge."

"How many of you are there, exactly?"

"Oh, our numbers are multiplying every day."

"Well, it's easy to multiply by one, isn't it? One by one is one, by one is—"

There was no tactic in the way I was talking; the kid just rubbed me the wrong way and it was messing with my pride that we had to ask him for money. Luckily, Eileen was there to steer things back in the right direction.

"Don't mind him, Lazarus. Yes, we need your help. We need to go on a journey that could take up to a month. If it works, we'll have the best chance I've ever heard of to heal the ex-magical creatures that are suffering the most."

Larry's eyes lit up.

"You want me to go with you?"

I snorted.

"No. We want *The Bridge* to help us. We need a safe way to travel there and back and we need to hire protection, so we need money. What are the coffers of your organization looking like these days?"

He couldn't hide his disappointment.

"Oh. That's not really what we do. We share information and assist in research. We don't have any money."

I threw out my arms.

"I don't know about that, Mr Lazarus Quintin Symes. There's gotta be some stashed away somewhere. Maybe check the glove box in your solid gold sedan."

"It's just paint," he replied churlishly.

I cackled.

"Those are some hairs you don't wanna start splitting, kid."

Eileen put her hands on the desk and tried to make up for my behavior.

"We do want your help. Really. There are things we don't know about the place we're going, or what we're going to encounter there. Your research could prove invaluable. But aside from that, yes, there is the problem of funds."

Larry looked between us, a petulant expression on his pubescent face.

"Where are you going?" he asked.

Eileen glanced over to get my approval. I shrugged.

"Incava," she responded. "We need to retrieve something from the castle."

"And you really think it could help people?"

"We don't know for sure, but we have strong evidence that it could do some good. Maybe a lot of good. Maybe fix everything, we don't know."

He sat back, trying to reclaim some power.

"As I said, The Bridge don't normally do this kind of thing. Even if they did, the back and forth it would take to acquire funding from our headquarters could take weeks. I could, perhaps, unlock some emergency savings of my own." Eileen reached over and gripped my leg, warning me not to make any comments that would change his mind. "Once you share the particulars and we match it up against our own research, of course."

"Of course," said Eileen, ever so politely.

"As far as transport goes, I should be able to borrow something from a colleague." I was pretty sure that this colleague was his mother or father, but I kept that presumption to myself. "But I would have to go along with you. To keep an eye on it, of course."

I opened my mouth. Eileen gripped me even tighter, till she was scraping bone.

"Of course," she said.

"Of course," I echoed.

"Good," said Lazarus, turning to focus on me. "Now, I suppose you'll be wanting a badge."

28

"Has this always been here?" I asked.

"In some form."

"Well, I've never been here before."

Eileen looked me up and down, a sarcastic smile on her full lips.

"Yeah, no surprise there."

"What does that mean?"

She marched up to the entrance of a two-story, red-brick building with a sign shaped like an archer swinging over the doorway.

"Hunter's Hall caters to a different class of adventurer."

The exterior of the building was brick – like most Sunder City buildings that didn't want to turn to ash the next time there was a fire – but the inside walls were lined with thick planks of dark wood that made the place feel like it was out in the forest somewhere, not crammed between a brewery and a recycling plant on the wrong side of Sickle Street. There were long communal tables up front and discreet booths suitable for secret meetings at the back. Apart from the bar – which seemed to sell nothing but mugs of frothy pale beer and red wine – there was another counter, connected to the kitchen, manned by a heavyset Ogre with a mustache like two fox tails glued to his face. He had a huge set of scales beside him, and was wiping a bloody cleaver on an equally bloody apron.

I was just about to ask what that was all about, when the door was shoved into my back by a party of Satyrs dragging a dead Elk.

"Clear off!" said one of them, shouldering me to the side so that the others could follow, each holding a leg of the animal, its antlers dragging along the ground. They stopped in front of the scales and the Ogre gave an impressed whistle.

"This looks like an Apland buck."

"It sure is," said the fellow who'd shouldered me.

"You wanna sell it like it is or carve it up?"

"Carve it up. Keep the pelt in one piece and leave us with the rump and the loin; everything else is for sale."

The Ogre negotiated a price for the meat per pound, with an added fee for his butchering service.

"Come around back and let's string him up."

The leader sent his comrades to the bar while he assisted the Ogre in his work. Eileen and I found a couple of seats at the end of one of the communal tables, and she grabbed herself a wine.

"Told you," said Eileen.

There was a wet slop in the kitchen as the Elk's organs tumbled out of its belly onto the floor.

"What do we do here?"

She pointed to a noticeboard by the bar that had bits of paper pinned all over it.

"That's where we can leave our wanted notice: a short description of the job, what it entails, and how much we're paying. Though our best bet is to approach somebody directly."

The crowd was made up of sweaty, hairy, fur-covered warriors that were needlessly loud and overly vulgar. They had a collective stink that overshadowed the aroma of blood and offal coming from the kitchen and, to be honest, it warmed my heart. I thought places like this had been forgotten. Sunder was all shiny suits and hidden pistols these days. Not here. Here, clubs rested against the backs of chairs and dead rabbits dangled from belt loops. Beer and blood covered the floor, ensuring pencil-pushers with shiny shoes wouldn't risk a visit.

Most importantly, I seemed to be the only Human. The ceilings were high and the tables were spread wide so that Ogres wouldn't have any problem navigating around the room. There were low

benches for the big guys, and stools for the shorter ones. Every
kind of Lycum was accounted for, all with sharpened nails and
wild fur – none of the over-groomed style that had started to
become fashionable. It was loud. Loud like the old world. A
constant cacophony of fists on tables and sword tips scraping
against the stone floor.

"Where do we start?" I asked.

Eileen explained that there was a visual language at play that
I never would have noticed if she hadn't pointed it out. Most
patrons were drinking from wooden mugs. A bunch, like Eileen,
had tin cups, and a rare few sipped from fine copper tankards
instead.

"It's to help with introductions, but also allows the hall to take
their finder's fee. You have to register your interest with the
bartender, pay five bronze to get your tin cup and see the list of
adventurers available, then sit down with whoever seems interesting. Any deal done outside this system will bring management
down on your head."

"Gormon Kinseeker!" shouted a Dwarf at the bar. He had a
tin cup in one hand, and the Hunter's Hall adventurer listing in
the other.

A heavily armored Ogre raised his copper tankard.

"Here! And bring some beer with you!" he shouted in good
humor, and it made many of the patrons laugh and cheer. Eileen
joined in and finished her drink.

"Shall we see what's on offer?"

There were ten adventurers on the books that night, and four of
them specifically listed hunting and tracking as a skill.

"So, we just call out their name?"

"If you're feeling ostentatious, but mostly you can pick them
out from their description. Like this one: Rhiannon Vine. No

other Goblins on this list so she must be the one in the corner drinking from the copper cup. Let's go say hello."

Eileen purchased a flagon of wine and filled both her and Rhiannon's cups. Before we'd even told her what we were planning, she launched into a list of demands and conditions about what jobs she would and wouldn't do. Eileen gave me a look that suggested having her along on an already exhausting trip would only make things worse, no matter her qualifications, and I gave her a look that told her I agreed. We couldn't even get a word in to tell her we weren't interested, but, as she sang the praises of some particular brand of tent that must be supplied if we wanted her assistance, my attention drifted to the table beside us, where another buyer was struggling to fit in.

"The payment really is overly generous," said the Half-Elf on our side of the table, "but that's because we need to get moving as soon as possible."

The gray Werewolf on the receiving end of the pitch nodded, then leaned over to let his companion, a black-furred member of his species, whisper something in his ear. After listening for a few moments, the gray wolf turned back to the Elf.

"What provisions have you made for crossing the marshes?"

The Elf looked between the two wolves, and stammered, "We . . . we plan to cross the bridge through Juda."

There was a knowing look between the Lycum.

"Juda has been occupied by a band of ruthless Half-Ogres for over three months. Have you put aside some *overly generous* payments to deal with them?"

The Half-Elf was clearly caught out.

"I'm sure there's something we can do. We still have some planning ahead of us."

"I thought you needed to get moving as soon as possible."

"We . . . we do."

The gray wolf looked to his black brother, who shook his head.

"Thanks for your time," said the gray.

"You can't—" started the Half-Elf, but a cold look from the silent one stopped him from going any further. "Of course. Have a fine night, gentlemen."

The Elf went about his business and, as soon as the Goblin gave us a moment to cut in, so did we. We had a long conversation with an amiable Gnome who pressed us for details that we were reticent to give. Eileen, Khay and I had all agreed that speaking about our mission in such a crowded place, to a stranger, was unwise. There were Wizards waiting at the end of our quest and if they got word that we were coming, our task could go from difficult to impossible.

While we were dancing around his questions, I saw the gray wolf shake hands with a red-bearded Dwarf who bounded up to the bar to order a celebratory flagon.

Eventually, the Gnome we were talking to decided that a month was too long if we couldn't guarantee a return date, and we filled his tankard to thank him for his time.

Eileen and I sat in an unoccupied booth, considering our options. I had a perfect view into the kitchen, where the skinned Elk was being portioned out into pieces that were small enough to fit on the scales.

"Who's left?" I asked.

"That's it. All the suitable candidates, anyway. We can draw up a note for the board and see if anybody calls. It's only another two bronze bits. I'll get some paper."

While she grabbed pen, paper and another cup of wine, I watched the black wolf. He was sitting silently, one ear cocked to his partner's conversation with the Dwarf, but otherwise he was perfectly still. He wasn't drinking or fidgeting, just waiting, it seemed, for this all to be over so he could get back to something more important.

His gray brother was bigger, with his appearance leaning on the Human side of his heritage more than the animal. Werewolves' powers would fluctuate with the moon, becoming more Human when the moon was new, and more animal when it was full. The Coda scrambled the whole mixture, leaving each of them a mish-mash of their separate forms.

The black one had more fur on him, except for one of his arms that was fully Human and sat in a leather sling (that looked to be a permanent part of his wardrobe rather than a recent injury). Even so, he still seemed the most promising ally in the whole place.

He wasn't like the rest of them. There were plenty of hardy fighters here, but he looked like someone with knowledge, skills, and the temperament to wield them efficiently.

I'd listened in on other conversations and read some of the notes on the board. Other folks just wanted help escorting goods or shaking down people late on payments. I was saving the world, and I deserved the best warrior that this place could offer.

I left the booth, crossed the room, dragged a seat beside the Dwarf, and sat down.

"You much of a hunter?"

The black wolf made eye contact but didn't speak. The gray one looked between us, but knew it wasn't his place to step in. The Dwarf coughed up his beer.

"Hey, now," he spluttered, "there are rules here."

"I can pay you what you need," I continued, "but this isn't some bodyguard mission to move a few toasters out to the prov-inces. This is old school; a small team sneaking into a heavily guarded city to retrieve an artefact that could change the world. If this works, we're going to save a lot of lives, and I need the best people by my side if I'm going to see it through."

I was worried that my speech wasn't that special. Perhaps there were overexcited adventurers with magic-fever in here all the time.

The black wolf's long pink tongue licked his fangs.

"What's the artefact?" he said finally, his voice as clean and direct as a well-fired arrow.

The Dwarf, affronted by the fact that the black wolf had never deigned to speak to him, started stammering. "Now . . . now, look. If Theodor was an option, we'd all be making offers, but he's not, so we let him drink in peace. That's the rules, and the rules—"

"The crown of the Wizard King, imbued with the Genie curse, guarded by—"

"Fetch—" Eileen's hand gripped my shoulder.

"Guarded by Wizards who, we're guessing, will defend it with their lives."

The smallest, smoothest of nods from the wolf.

"That's not all that's waiting for you," he said. "Is it?"

I looked up at Eileen, who furrowed her brow in return. There was one part of our mission that Khay had mentioned to me that I hadn't passed on to Eileen yet, because I feared it might make her reconsider the whole thing. Apparently Theodor was already informed.

"No," I told him. "That's why I want you."

The Dwarf kicked back his stool and moved off.

"Fetch . . ." warned Eileen.

"Who's your team?" asked Theodor, not rushed in the slightest.

"Me, our money guy and my partner Eileen Tide."

Eileen smiled, but her attention was mostly absorbed by the conversation between the Dwarf and the Ogre with the meat cleaver.

"And what are Ms Tide's skills?"

"She's a librarian," I responded, "and she makes a killer martini."

He cracked a smile. While that felt like an accomplishment in itself, it wasn't going to get him across the line.

"Sounds like I'll be doing the heavy lifting," he said.

"There's one more."

"Fetch!"

The Dwarf and the Ogre were approaching, axe and cleaver in hand.

"The last of the Genies is coming with us. With the crown, there's a chance she can use her powers to send magic back into the bodies of creatures who would die without it. My name is Fetch Phillips. Come find me if you—"

"FETCH!"

The Ogre grabbed the back of my jacket and dragged me off my feet.

"My office is at 108 Main Street!" I shouted to Theodor as my ass hit the first step, then every other, until I was flung out onto the street.

"Come back, and I'll gut you, skin you, and sell you by the pound," said the Ogre, then turned around and bumped into Eileen. "That counts for you too, Missy. You're done."

He went inside and Eileen kicked me in the ribs.

"Fuck you, Fetch. I liked that place."

"Yeah," I agreed. "The whole window into the kitchen thing was very cool. Georgio really should do that at the café."

She kicked me in the ribs again.

"Ouch!"

"You shouted our whole plan to every person in there. That means we need to get moving now, before anyone can send word. And that," she went for another kick, but I blocked it with my hands, "is for keeping shit from me."

I stood up before she could have another go.

"What do you mean?"

She locked eyes with me. Properly pissed.

"What's waiting for us in Incava? Other than the Wizards?"

Damn. I really had said too much.

"I know I should have told you earlier, but I wanted to get things moving and keep everyone positive. I was going to fill you in before we set off anyway, so—"

"Fetch. Tell me."

Shit.

"Apparently they have a Minotaur."

29

Khay and Lazarus listened with frustration as Eileen filled them in on our failed recruitment mission. Georgio refilled our coffees and was the only person who seemed slightly amused by the tale.

"It's fine," I said. "They were all useless anyway. The only real warrior there was the guy I was trying to talk to, so it was worth the risk."

"We don't need a warrior," said Lazarus. "We just need someone who can hunt, right? Catch food and scout ahead."

"Oh, that's the best part." Eileen sipped her coffee with attitude. "You want to tell our investor what's waiting at the end of our journey?"

Rather than let me catch all the heat, Khay did me the favor of chiming in.

"They have a Minotaur. The last remaining Minotaur, if the rumors are true. Captain Longhorn himself."

Lazarus nodded, seriously, as if he'd suspected this all along.

"You know much about the Minotaur, Larry?" I asked.

With all eyes on him, he cracked.

"Uh . . . no. Not really."

"They're the evilest creatures ever to set foot on the great mountain."

We all turned to see Theodor, standing at the edge of the café, his black fur blowing in the breeze. Other than the pink and emaciated arm, he was more *wolf* than *were*: practically a canine on his hind legs. He wore dark green leather armor and boots that came up to his knees. There were knifes in his belt, another in his boot, and a crossbow strapped to his back.

"Everyone, this is Theodor," I said proudly.

"You're all going to die," he said in response.

Not the valiant message of support I was hoping for.

"You know about the Minotaur?" asked Larry.

Theodor pulled up a chair.

"Hey, Georgio!" I called, and immediately registered our guest's disapproval at my ill manners. Georgio came out from the kitchen and approached Theodor with his pad and pencil ready.

"Hello, sir! Can I get you something to eat or drink? The special today is lamb pie with fried potatoes."

"Just a tea, please. Mint, perhaps?"

"One fresh mint tea, of course."

Recognizing something of the old world in each other, they exchanged short, respectful bows. It was a glimpse into a time where this warrior and sage might have met under more dignified circumstances.

Theodor put his good hand in his lap and looked each of us in the eye, perhaps to make sure that we were paying attention.

"The Minotaur were a group of Barbarians that attacked the Lycum home of Perimoor thirty years before the Coda. They avoided the city itself and went straight for the sacred peak of Mount Kar, where the first Were creatures were created some millennia ago. It was peacetime, so the city was undefended, and they murdered the guards and any civilians who didn't flee. They knew of the power of the mountain and they thought that they could steal that magic and use it on themselves. Once they had the mountain secure, Captain Longhorn sent his soldiers to find the strongest beasts imaginable, so he could fuse his body with them, just as the Werewolves and Werecats had done before. We are not the only Lycum. Our younger cousins, the Coyala and Ursaro, are rarer creatures, but it had been centuries since Perimoor had permitted any new species to be born from Kar's power.

"Unfortunately for the Barbarians, and the world at large, they had a poor sense of timing. While the soldiers were away, Longhorn waited on the mountain with a band of his closest followers. That night, the moon rose over the water and a transformation took place."

Complementing his silence in Hunter's Hall, Theodor spoke as if every word was important. He chose them carefully and delivered them with considered articulation.

"Unlike Perimoor's true inhabitants, the Barbarians had no animal companions at their side. What they did have were the pelts of many beasts: skins and furs that had been turned into cloaks, coats, or blankets, wrapped around their bodies."

Listening to this story, I was struck, not for the first time, by the river's tendency towards poetic justice. What often felt like a dark sense of humor. As if magic had a mind of its own and decided how to turn its hand depending on the heart of the creature who had dared to dance with it.

"The merging of man and animal is a traumatic process, even when it is performed as part of a ceremony and both participants already share a companionship. I can only imagine the psychological terror of having your soul fused with the spirit of undead animals that you yourself had slain. A war must exist in Longhorn's very self; a beast forever battling his own internal enemy."

Georgio delivered the tea. Theodor gave his thanks, took a sip, and complimented its flavor.

"The Minotaur became monsters after that. All but unstoppable. Ravenous, evil creatures to be avoided at all costs."

Larry spoke up first, and I was surprised to hear him ask the question I was already pondering.

"But what about the Coda? Hasn't that made them more . . . manageable?"

Theodor took a long sip, in no hurry to respond.

"In truth, I have not seen them since. From what I hear, they are just as fearsome, and there is still both a barbarian and an animal battling inside their brain. I have not studied the effects of the Coda extensively, but it is clear that not all creatures were affected in equal measure. Those whose powers were born in darkness seem more able to maintain their strength in this new age. The Human at the center of the Minotaur may be harder to recognize, but the horrific beast he gave birth to could be more dangerous than ever."

There was a short break of silence as we let Theodor's story sink in.

"Fetch?" said Eileen. "Why are you smiling?"

"What? I'm not."

"We really have to fight this thing?" asked Larry.

"No," Theodor said gravely. "It is suicide."

"We have to sneak in and out," said Eileen. "Avoid the Minotaur."

"*We?*" I asked. "Does that mean you're coming?"

She gave a frustrated sigh, as if she knew it was a terrible idea but couldn't help being swept up in the excitement.

"If you promise we're going to be careful, and you're not going to go looking for a fight. We should avoid being spotted at all, if we can help it."

"Which would have been easier before you made your intentions so public," added Theodor. "You really should have kept your mission more secret. Many who frequent Hunter's Hall make their business selling information for money."

"If only we'd thought of that," said Eileen, strangling me with a look. I didn't bother arguing that it had been worth it, since Theodor had decided to turn up, but turned my attention to galvanizing the group.

"Then we should get moving right away. I doubt Incava has phone lines, but someone could be sending a letter as we speak. Larry, you negotiate Theodor's fee, and we leave . . . tomorrow?"

"Day after," said the Werewolf. "I'll need to prepare supplies and tie up some loose ends. You have enough horses for the five of us?"

We all turned to Larry.

"We're looking into an alternative mode of transportation."

30

"This is yours?" asked Theodor with disgust.

"My father's," replied Larry.

"I thought your father's car was that golden monstrosity," I said.

Larry looked even more embarrassed.

"He has a few."

"Why?" Khay sounded genuinely curious.

"Because he can, I think."

It was a large, black luxury vehicle without a scratch on the outside or a scuff mark on the leather interior. Theodor peered in the window, then back at the group, then at our hulking pile of supplies, and then back at the car. He didn't need to put his doubts into words, but Larry turned on the sales pitch.

"There's plenty of space in the trunk, and we can fit some things under the seats too."

Theodor was only half listening. He pushed down on the roof of the car, testing its weight with his fingers, then his fist. The metal bowed a little, but seemed strong enough, so he picked up one of his packs.

"Careful," said Larry. Theodor looked at him, then up at the gargantuan house shadowing us.

"Who does your father work for?" he asked.

Lazarus swallowed.

"Mortales."

Theo threw the pack onto the top of the car. It bulged the roof inward as it landed, but didn't break. Theo nodded to himself, satisfied that he'd solved our problems.

"Please bring me some rope," he said.

Larry gritted his teeth as Theodor and I pulled either end of the cord. It went over a cloth that we'd wrapped our supplies in, then through the windows on either side of the vehicle. We scraped off paint and scratched the metal of the window frame, but I had the same attitude as Theodor: if Mortales had paid for this car, and would pay for any repairs, then any damage done to it was morally acceptable. Perhaps even righteous. At the very least, it gave me a sick kind of satisfaction that was only heightened by Larry's dismay.

The roof was piled high with camping gear and weapons, and the trunk was stuffed full of food and fuel. Despite Larry's promise of more space inside the car, there was barely room for the five of us. Eileen sat in the back seat with Khay and me either side. Theodor rode shotgun and Larry insisted on driving.

When Khay had first pitched this expedition, I had grand visions of leading a team of warriors out of the city on mighty steeds, with bows on our backs and canteens bouncing on our hips, thundering off towards the sunset. Instead, when Eileen lifted up her knees to try to find a more comfortable position, her hand brushed against my ass.

"Sorry," she said.

"No problem. I can't really squeeze over any more."

"It's fine."

She shoved the other way and accidently nudged Khay, making her jewelry jangle.

"Sorry."

"No problem."

Khay was all wrapped up in her robes and even had her sleeves tucked into a pair of gloves.

"Are you cold?" Eileen asked.

"Oh, no. It's just that . . . we really shouldn't touch."

There was a silent pause while Eileen thought things through.

"Do you mean that if you touch any part of your skin, with any part of my skin, it might . . . burn me? And try to shove magic back into my body?"

"No!" Khay reassured her. "I mean, not immediately. The burning, yes, probably, but the whole wish-granting thing takes a while."

Eileen looked at me without blinking.

"Hey, Theodor," I said, "any chance you want to ride in the back?"

We swapped positions and Larry finally put the car into gear and puttered out of the gate. The roof creaked and strained with every bump, and Eileen bounced back and forth between me and Theo. After the first few corners, we forgot the apologies and accepted that the contact was beyond our control.

"I have snacks," said Larry, leaning over Khay and opening a compartment in the dash. Khay opened a bag of jerky, took some for herself, and offered it to the back. Eileen and I each took some, but Theodor politely declined.

While I chewed, I noticed that Khay seemed confused by the taste. She smelled the jerky, then licked it, furrowed her brow, and looked seriously concerned as she took a bite. Larry clocked it too.

"Is it not good?" he asked.

"It's fine. I've just lost my edge, that's all. It starts with my senses. But it's delicious. Thanks."

There were no easy roads through the city. Half of them were being dug up, widened or resurfaced. The other half were so narrow that when you encountered a car coming the other way, one of you would have to pull over to let them pass. It was a jolting, swerving journey, made worse by Larry's touchy right foot and tendency to over-steer when he panicked.

"You done much of this before?" I asked.

"Yeah, but—" *screech* "—but my car is only a two-seater. Easier to maneuver. This one's just a—" *screech* "—a lot to handle on the side roads. I'll be fine when we leave the city."

It took us half an hour to get onto Maple Highway, and we all unclenched our jaws when we saw the wide, straight road ahead of us. All except Theodor, who had his head resting against the back of Larry's seat, and his eyes closed.

"Hey, Theo, you all right, man?" I asked. He opened his mouth, thought better of it, and gave me an unconvincing thumbs-up instead. "Larry, you might want to pull over."

"Oh. Was it all the corners? We should be straight for a while now."

Theo made a gurgling sound and then a beckoning motion with his hand. I asked Khay for the jerky packet, and got it to Theo just in time for him to unload his breakfast into the paper bag.

Larry agreed to pull over.

We stood by the car as Theodor fed the flowers.

"Maybe he should go back up front," said Khay. "I think it's better."

"What about the whole burning skin thing?" asked Eileen.

"It only affects magical creatures, I think. If Fetch goes in the middle, we should be okay."

I looked at the tiny middle seat and tried to look cheerful.

"Of course."

Theodor washed his mouth out with water and apologized profusely for having slowed us down. We all did our best to make him feel like the mighty warrior we'd thought he was before the incident, and squeezed back into the car. I felt bad about pushing my legs into the women on either side of me, so I bent my knees and brought my feet up onto the console between the two front seats. Eileen and Khay both gave me questioning looks.

"It's all right," said Khay, "I'm not going to hurt you."

"I know."

"Put both legs this side if you need to," offered Eileen, shifting over. "You look ridiculous."

"No, this is comfortable. Really."

Their questioning looks intensified until they gave in and decided to enjoy the extra space.

After a while, Eileen fell asleep. Her head dropped onto my shoulder, so I did my best not to move or talk too much in case it woke her up. Khay ungloved her left hand and had it pressed against the window. She was likely trying to see if it was as corporeal as it had been the previous day, or the day before that. To my relief, she seemed satisfied, and put her glove back on.

"What's this *Bridge* thing?" she asked Larry, who straightened himself up with pride at the question.

"Well, The Bridge is a group of community-minded individuals who have charged ourselves with guiding the world back to the magical existence we've left behind."

"Careful, Khay," I warned. "He's got a whole speech memorized."

"But how did you get recruited?" she asked him. "Was it like a form in the mail or something?"

I thoroughly enjoyed her light teasing of Larry.

"I accompanied my father on one of his business trips to Lopari and fell into conversation with a Half-Elf named Dalia who happened to be one of the founding Bridge members. We got talking – about all kinds of things, really – and she invited me to a meeting the following night. As soon as I heard what they were about and got a measure of their character, I decided to join their ranks."

Khay knocked my feet down to the floor and put her legs over mine to stretch out.

"Right. So, why you two?" she asked, pointing at Larry and me.

"I didn't join them," I protested. "You should ask Eileen."

"Yeah, but she's a Witch. I get why this would be her bag. Why are you two Humans so set on finding magic when it won't do you any good?"

I went very quiet, knowing it was the kind of conversation littered with traps. Larry wasn't so reserved.

"Because I can," he said.

It was a line I'd used before, and judging from Khay's face, I was glad I wasn't the one to use it now.

"And you think ex-magical creatures can't?" she asked.

"Of course not. I just . . . It's so much easier for me to put time into this. I didn't lose anything when the Coda happened. In fact, it turned my life upside down in the opposite way. Look at this thing." He tapped the steering wheel with the palm of his hand. "This wasn't my life before the Coda. My dad made electronic gadgets that were only sold in Human towns, to customers who resented using the superior Magum products. When that stuff stopped working, Mortales bought the patents for all my dad's inventions, gave him some crazy job, and sent us here to work with Niles. So, what am I supposed to do? Feel good about that? No. I have to try to give something back. Dad won't. Niles won't. But *I* will."

I watched Khay take that in.

"Honest," she said. "I like it."

Theodor looked between all of us. He'd barely said a word since his bout of travel sickness, but the front seat seemed to be helping.

"Do you truly believe it's possible?" he asked, without making his opinion on the subject clear. "Is your goal actually to see the sacred river flow once more?"

"If we can," said Larry, shy again after his outburst.

"That may be beyond my abilities," said Khay, "but we do what we can, and trust that fate will carry us the rest of the way."

"It has to be possible," I said, "or we're all screwed. We can keep patching things up, but eventually the cracks that we put in the world will be too wide to ignore. Plenty of people just want to build a new world on top of the broken one and move on, but it won't last."

"Some people like this new world," said Theodor.

"Because it makes them money. For now. Let Niles and his allies distract themselves with new weapons and expanding suburbs; when we find a way to bring the magic back, it'll break their experiment right down the middle and none of it will matter."

Eileen slid a hand up my chest and put a long finger across my lips.

"Shhh," she said. "My pillow is talking too much."

I was glad for the interruption; I could tell that I was losing my audience. I didn't know why, but I sensed that they weren't convinced. It didn't matter, though. They were here. If we were successful, I'd never have to try to talk someone around again. They'd all be able to see it for themselves.

We traveled in silence for a while. The world outside was overgrown and colorful: a springtime explosion of wildflowers and fruit that ended in a straight line a few feet from the road, having been trimmed back recently by some kind of machine. There wasn't much else to see from the middle seat, so I rested my head on top of Eileen's and closed my eyes.

Our adventure had begun.

31

The First Fire

When Khay and Larry first learned about my attempt to recruit Theodor, they'd been skeptical. That was somewhat rectified by witnessing his wise and measured energy, and seeing him strapped up with leather and knives, but we were yet to see any real evidence of his expertise.

Out of the car windows, we spotted four seemingly suitable places to camp, but Theodor vetoed all of them, detailing problems that the rest of us never would have noticed: too exposed, in a flood plain, beneath a tree infested with buzzing mites, or without enough nearby scrub to attract animals for hunting. We all stopped offering suggestions after that. For half an hour, we kept our mouths shut as Theo watched the wilderness and eventually said, "Stop here."

Theodor got out, looked around, checked the soil, pulled out his binoculars and examined the horizon. He followed some tracks, sniffed some footprints, then said, "This is good."

We brought the camping gear down from the roof, further scratching the paint job, and set up the tents. Theodor and I were going to share the larger one, Eileen and Khay would have one each, and Larry would sleep in the car. I set them up while Eileen and Khay prepared a fire, and Larry checked the car to make sure we hadn't completely destroyed his father's ridiculous automobile on the first day.

The fire came alive just as the last of the light fled from the sky.

"You think Theodor is all right?" asked Larry.

"I think he'll always be all right," said Eileen, "as long as he's not in the back seat." When Theodor did return, he was holding the hind legs of three dead rabbits, each of them with a bloody hole in their heads.

"That was fast," said Eileen. "You want me to skin them for you?"

"Thanks. Still haven't mastered that side of things." I was wondering how he was such a sharpshooter without his left hand, but knew that it would be insulting to ask.

"How do you shoot then?" asked Larry.

Theodor took it in his stride and pointed the end of the crossbow at his feet. There was a hook on the end of the weapon and a metal loop fitted to the boot of his right toe. He kicked his foot up on a tree stump, used his heel to balance, leaned back, took aim, and fired.

The bolt struck the piece of firewood that Larry was holding. He dropped it and yelped.

"I'll get you some tools," said Theodor, and dropped the rabbits on the stump.

From out of his pack, he pulled a large cleaver and a sharp, slightly curved knife, and gave them to Eileen.

"You done this before?" she asked me. I told Eileen that I'd seen somebody skin a rabbit plenty of times but never done it myself. "Well, it's time you learned, then."

Eileen demonstrated on one rabbit and I mirrored her process on another, chopping off the head and paws, slicing the knees, pulling the legs through the holes, ripping the fur from the meat and emptying the guts.

Theodor had also collected a whole bunch of wild fruits and vegetables that Khay chopped up and seasoned with spices we'd brought from Sunder (another of Theodor's recommendations).

"It makes all the difference," he said. "Never leave home without some salt."

We roasted the rabbits and fried the vegetables, and when the rabbit was being portioned out, Theodor revealed that he wouldn't be having any.

"You don't eat meat?" asked Larry.

"Not when I'm working."

"But you're the one who caught them," said Eileen, as if she was personally offended by his choice. Larry and I had already taken our first bites and shared a look of bliss that threatened to tip us into friendship.

"Exactly," said Theodor. "When you eat meat, it changes your scent. The prey can smell it. Food may be bountiful here but, if hunting becomes harder, I'll be most effective on a flesh-free diet."

I picked a crispy piece of meat out of my teeth.

"Larry, I don't think you're paying this guy enough."

The vegetables were good, but nowhere near as delicious as the rabbit. Theodor made no complaints or showed any sign of temptation. He finished his plate and wiped it clean with some dry leaves.

"It's going to be warm tomorrow," he said, with no mention of how he'd come by that information. "We should start traveling early before it gets too hot. It will be uncomfortable in that thing if there's no cloud cover."

Following his advice, we cleaned everything up and got into our tents. There was just enough room for Theodor and me to keep our canteens and lanterns between us. After he rolled over, he barely shifted his weight all night while I continued to roll around, as quietly as possible, trying to find some position that didn't put pressure on my injuries. I eventually drifted off into a half-decent slumber, and dreamed I was a rabbit on the run.

32

Cannonballs

The next day, the landscape and seating arrangements were much the same, though some of us were stiff and sore after our troubled night's sleep on thin bedrolls. Theodor was unaffected, staring ahead at the oncoming road without any signs of fatigue.

Every now and again, trucks came from the other direction dragging heavy trailers behind them. Occasionally, we'd overtake trucks going the way that we were and I'd have time to look in at the heavyset drivers, all with charcoal suits beside them in the passenger seats. They stared back, perhaps thinking that we were highway bandits looking to steal their cargo.

"Shit, it's muggy," said Eileen, leaning her head out the window.

"No kidding." I fanned myself with my hat.

"Then why are you wearing that shirt?" asked Khay, and I pointed out that she was the one wearing black robes. "This is finely spun Farra Glade fabric, not whatever cheap crap you're wearing. And if I don't keep covered, I could sizzle someone's skin. What's your excuse?"

"I'm comfortable."

"Bullshit. At least roll your sleeves up."

I undid a few buttons and, as she suggested, rolled my cuffs up to my elbows.

"Oh," she said, "that's why you keep them down."

She was referring, of course, to the four ringed tattoos that wrapped around my wrist like black bracelets. The first one labeled me as a guard in the Weatherly watch – the walled city where I grew up – then there was my identification as an Opus

Shepherd, my brand from the Human Army, and my prisoner ID from Sheertop.

Khay was right that I liked to keep them hidden. The first mark made people ask questions and the others delivered some answers. I'd felt proud when I'd got them – all except the prison one, of course – but now they were only reminders of my shame.

"Brother, you've got some ink."

None of my usual witty deflections felt suitable.

"Yeah. I've done some things."

Theodor turned around in his seat to admire the marks.

"You have stories," he said. "Can we hear them?"

We had the time, sure, but I really didn't feel like unloading my complicated past on my fellow travelers. Some of them might know some of it, but giving them the full rundown of my failings felt like a surefire way for them to lose their faith in me, right before a mission where I'd need it most.

"Maybe on the way back," I said.

We made a short detour down a dirt track because Theodor was familiar with the area and knew that there was fresh water nearby. We drove to the edge of a gulley where we could see a creek below, fed by a natural spring that tumbled over rocks into a wide pond.

"Probably a good idea to bathe while the sun's out," said Eileen. "Unless Theo's going to tell us there's some secret swamp creature or parasite in there that will kill us when we dip our toes in."

He shrugged. "If there is, we'll just have to find out."

"Then grab your towels." Eileen led the way down the embankment to the water's edge. We filled our canteens and took a moment to relax, listening to the bubbling water and birdsong, perhaps wondering which one of us would be the first to jump in.

Khay unwrapped the cloth from her body and let it coil around her feet. Eileen pulled her shirt over her head, and Theo began the lengthy process of unclasping his many pieces of armor, untying his bracers and greaves and belts, until there was a pile of leather sitting on the rocks.

I stripped off, awkwardly turning to the side and hunching over as I removed my trousers and underwear, then briskly walked into the water. The pond was damn cold, but I wasted no time getting waist deep.

There was a patter of bare feet against the wet rocks as Larry sprinted, still in his underwear, and stumbled in.

"Oh, shit," he spluttered. "It's freezing."

"Don't worry, kid," said Khay. "Nobody's looking."

"Much," added Eileen, smiling as she ducked her head underwater.

We floated around the watering hole for a while, letting the cool temperature sink into our skin, flesh and bones. We didn't say much or get too close to each other, but there was a relaxed comradery that boded well for our expedition.

Theo was the first one back on the rocks.

"Already?" asked Khay, disappointed that he might want us all to dry off and get moving again.

"I need time to dry myself properly," he replied. "Or the whole car is going to smell like wet dog."

"Avert your eyes," said Eileen. We did, staring into the trees on the other side as she crawled out and got her towel. Larry went next, huffing and puffing, and I followed shortly after, facing the waterfall as I dried myself off, then wrapped my towel around me and found a spot in the sun. There was a little splash as Khay kicked her feet and dove underwater, before reappearing on the other side of the pond.

"It's pretty deep." She looked at the ridge above, which was about ten feet high, and grinned. When she came out of the water, Larry and I turned our heads away. "Oh, don't be such prudes. I barely have a body half the time. Might as well see it while it's here."

Sunlight danced off her jewels and the beads of water that ran over her bald head and down her skin, sparkling as if a hundred flash photographers were capturing her climb. Through her faded body, you could just make out the landscape beyond her; water ran down her spine, a skink scurried between her shoulders, and the clouds passed behind her eyes.

She looked down from the edge. Theodor warned her of a snag near the bank, but she was confident that she would hit her mark. After rocking on her heels a few times, she launched forward, arms outstretched, and plunged into the water, spraying the rest of us.

Ripples spread out and lapped against the sides while we waited for her to reemerge.

"Oh great," said Eileen. "We go off on a mission to save a Genie, but she drowns herself halfway there."

Khay's face broke the surface: smiling wide and spitting water into the air.

"That feels so good!"

She came out panting, stretched her towel out on the hot stones, and lay on her belly, uncovered and smiling.

Theodor might have been worried about his fur taking too long to dry, but Eileen's waist-length hair had absorbed just as much water. She wrung it out like a dishcloth, creating a huge puddle beside her, then splayed it out like a fan as she laid back.

Without a word, Theo shook himself off and went walking, naked, through the forest, with just his pack thrown over one shoulder. The rest of us lay there, rolling over occasionally to cook ourselves evenly under the midday sun. At least, I thought it was midday. Time had become elastic, and I wasn't sure if we'd been out there for twenty minutes or several hours.

"Larry," said Eileen, her voice deep and relaxed, "do you know how to braid hair?"

He looked nervous, like she'd asked him to hold her rope while she abseiled over a cliff.

"Uh . . . no."

"Come on. I'll show you." Eileen tore a leaf into three strips and demonstrated what she wanted him to do. He kneeled beside her and attempted to follow her instructions, but kept restarting. "It doesn't need to be perfect. We won't be attending any balls tonight."

It certainly wasn't perfect, but Larry improved as he went along. There was more than enough hair to practice with. Just as she handed him a ribbon to tie it off, Theodor returned.

"Shall we get moving?" asked Khay, finally clothed. "We all look pretty dry."

Theo opened his pack to reveal a collection of red and blue berries.

"Eat these," he said, "and get dressed. I want to show you something."

We each ate our share of the berries, remarking on the sweetness of some and the tartness of others, then washed our hands in the water. When Theodor's armor was all reattached, he led us into the woods for a surprise.

33

When One Doesn't Wake

Theo moved swiftly, perhaps retracing his steps, though I could see no evidence of his previous path through the scrub. He made no sound when he walked, and instructed us to try to do the same, demonstrating how to step on the sides of our feet, rolling from heel to toe while avoiding sticks and branches.

I had become accustomed to sidewalks and cobbled streets, so I was paranoid about snakes and other animals in the undergrowth. Every now and again, I was filled with panic when my face broke a spider web, as strong as dental floss, that somehow missed all the others and was saved just for me.

Theodor slowed, and we all slowed in kind to crouch behind a bunch of brambles. Staying as low as we could get without crawling on hands and knees, we moved behind a fallen tree. Theodor gave one final warning for us to be silent, then pointed over the log. We popped up to take a look, and I bit my lips to stop myself swearing. At a distance that felt entirely too close for comfort, a family of Wyverns were grouped in and around the trunk of an enormous hollow tree. The tree itself still seemed to be thriving; offering a canopy of soft green leaves to shelter the infant lizards that were taking, what seemed to be, their first tentative steps. All our mouths fell open in expressions of wonder, like children at a pet-store window.

"They're babies," mouthed Eileen, forgetting her usual cool demeanor.

The mother, curled up in the tree, was covered in bright red scales. Her two children were darker; whether that was to do with their age or their parentage, I wasn't sure. There were white flecks all over them, which I thought must have been some kind of disfigurement until the largest of the babies rubbed his head against the ground and wiped them away. They were bits of egg! The infants had hatched so recently that they hadn't completely shed their shells.

The mother, shaking off her exhaustion, came out of the hollow, and I was reminded that we weren't only being quiet to get a closer look at the creatures, but because they would rip us to pieces if they got the chance. The mother's maw was hanging open, and she had a restaurant's worth of steak knives tucked under her lips. As she walked, the talons at the end of her wings – which were also her forearms – ripped into the dirt like it was sponge cake. Her body was the size of a car and her wings, while too weak to fly, flapped open and closed as she moved.

Unlike the fire-breathing, four-legged Dragons that were created when animals merged with swamps of pure magic, Wyverns evolved over time. They are the descendants of the rock-skinned reptiles of the Northern Plains who ventured south eons ago and adapted to their new surroundings. There were different types, depending on their environment, but all had two hind legs and two wings with a set of talons at the end. Being smaller and less magical, Wyverns weathered the Coda far better than their Dragon cousins.

She stepped over her two little ones in a protective stance and sniffed the air. We all ducked down, listening to her taste the breeze. Then she made a kind of purring sound, deep in her throat, and received two chirping noises in return.

We couldn't resist peering over the log again. She shuffled away, the babies beneath her becoming a little sturdier with every step.

Then the mother stopped. Looked back. Not at us, but towards the hollow of the tree. She made a kind of long, low call, more of a word than a growl, so clear in its emotion that I felt like, if I'd heard it again, I would have known its meaning.

They moved away, leaving small and large scratch marks in the dirt, and disappeared into the trees. When it felt safe to speak, Eileen jumped in first.

"That was incredible!"

"Did we scare her off?" asked Larry. "When she smelled us?"

Theodor shook his head. "No, Wyverns change nests as soon as the babies hatch. Their scent will bring all kinds of predators hoping to attack while the mother is distracted and the young are weak: wolves, monitor lizards, large cats and the like. Right now, the children won't be able to fend off enemies that, in a week or two, would never stand a chance. So, they leave the nest behind. It would be wise for us to do the same."

"Wait." Khay was staring at the hollow of the tree. "What was she looking at?" She climbed up on the log, then over it, and peered across the clearing. "There's another egg."

The elation dipped down to despair as the mother's final call repeated in our ears.

Khay continued on.

"We should go," said Theo.

She paid him no mind and walked straight into the hollow tree.

We all followed.

Khay knelt beside the remaining egg. There was a thin crack and a small piece missing from the top, but it was mostly intact. From my wary position behind Khay, I could see black scales inside.

"What happened to it?" Larry asked, vaguely directing his question to Theo.

"Nothing. It just happens sometimes."

"It's the magic," said Khay, her hands on the crack of the shell. "This one had more of his father in him." She peeled away a piece of the shell and a leathery black wing slid out. "In the old world, he might have grown to be twice the size of the others." She pulled away another piece of shell, revealing the top of its head, ridged with stumpy red horns. Below that, a heavy brow and eyelid.

Theodor tried, again, to warn us.

"We should—"

The eye opened.

Eileen, Larry and I gasped. Neither Theo nor Khay seemed surprised.

"He's alive?" whispered Larry. "Then why did she leave him?"

Theodor unhooked the crossbow from his belt.

"Because he's not going to make it, and it would have endangered the others to wait. We really must leave."

Khay, without looking back, raised a hand.

"Let me try."

She hadn't yet tied the intricate knots that pinned her robe to her body, so it fell easily from her shoulders. She peeled away the rest of the shell, and the baby Wyvern, like a puppet without strings, dropped into her arms. Through her back, in the space between her shoulder blades, I could just make out his open eye as it looked up at her, more tired than afraid. Only a few moments in this world and he was already exhausted by its cruelty.

With Khay's bare skin resting against the infant, the animal whined in its throat; surely confused by the burning sensation, and unaware that this stranger, adding more pain to its already painful existence, was trying to save its life.

Through Khay's body, I watched the infant's face until it disappeared. Khay was solid again.

WHOOSH!

Khay lost her grip as the animal's wings extended like an umbrella caught in an updraft, cracking like a whip and catching her across the chest. She screamed and dropped backwards as the baby Wyvern howled – its chest heaving and its mouth open wide – baring its baby fangs and forked tongue, ready to attack.

We got to our feet . . . but the spasm stopped, the wings went limp, and the creature's eyes rolled up and away from this world.

Even Larry, prone to blurting out obvious questions, didn't need to ask whether the creature was still alive. When something dies in front of you, you know about it. You feel it in that part of yourself that knows the things you try not to think about so you can find a way to get up in the morning. It was gone, and that was that.

Khay lifted the cloth back over her shoulders, wiped her eyes, and stood up.

"All right," she said, "let's go."

We all turned and screamed.

34

Instinct

The mother had returned: roaring, mouth open, her teeth bared and wet, and talons clawing at the dirt. She'd left her last child behind but, hearing it call out, could not have resisted coming back. Then she'd found us over its body, backed into the hollow of the tree.

"Use your crossbow!" said Larry in a panicked whine.

"Not if we don't have to," said Theo.

"Won't do much anyway," I added. "Their hides are like armor." I looked up at the inside of the tree. It was hollow right to the top, which would be higher than the Wyvern could reach, except there wasn't a clear way up. "Can we climb this?"

"We should try," said Eileen. She jumped up and grabbed a piece of wood with both hands. It crumbled into pieces and dropped her back on her feet. "Well, I tried."

The mother screamed and swiped at us, taking a chunk of bark out of the tree and sending us farther back into the hollow.

Theo's hand was in my jacket. He ripped the pistol from its holster and pointed it at the Wyvern.

"Whoa, Theo. Are you—"

CRACK!

He fired, high, sending the bullet over the mother's head. She jumped back from the opening in the tree. He stepped forward. Fired again.

CRACK!

She moved back, confused and scared, creating enough room for our escape.

"Go!" shouted Theodor. "NOW!"

He moved and we moved with him, out of the tree and back towards the log.

The Wyvern shook away her fear. She'd never seen a gun before, and though the noise had scared her, there was no pain to let her know why she needed to be afraid. It was just a sound, nothing more, and with that realization, she turned on us again.

I ran. So did the others. We jumped the log and scrambled through the path. As she followed us – snarling and screaming and snapping at our heels – her wings sent gusts of wind that battered our backs, blowing us off course. Branches snapped and stones rolled under our feet. As I turned to check on Eileen – a couple of steps behind me – I lost my footing and landed on my side, scraping my body across the roots and rocks of the forest floor.

"MOVE!"

I barely got onto my hands and knees before Eileen grabbed me by the collar and dragged me into dense underbrush as the Wyvern mother closed in. We scurried under the brambles and through gaps that we hoped were small and strong enough to impede the Wyvern's chase.

Hot breath blew through the bushes as the beast roared, shaking the whole thicket and trying to get her teeth or talons into us. Claws slashed at the foliage over Eileen's head, and she ducked down with nowhere else to go.

She screamed. It sounded like someone else's voice. Slaughtered leaves and twigs rained down on us as the Wyvern's wings attacked the barrier of branches.

A frustrated screech from above, and the shadow of the Wyvern pulled back. We heard the desperate flapping of its wings, and more furious grunting, before it stepped away from the patch of underbrush and span around in circles.

I lifted my head out of the savaged brush to see Larry atop the Wyvern's head, holding onto the spikes on the back of its skull.

It thrashed about, but was unable to reach him with either its talons or its teeth. The kid had a good grip, but the Wyvern became more desperate. It cracked its wings like it was trying to take off, then swung its head downward so that Larry was thrown over its face, still holding on, and rested over its maw.

Theo brought the crossbow from his back. I tried to push through the brambles, but before either of us could make a move, or the Wyvern could wrangle Larry into her jaws, there was an explosion of white dust out of Larry's left hand that engulfed the beast's face. A few seconds later, they both dropped to the ground, unconscious.

Khay moved towards them, but I got a whiff of the concoction that Larry had employed (luckily not enough to get the full effect).

"Wait!" I called. "Let it clear before you get too close or you'll end up like them."

"What happened?" asked Eileen, behind me. Her voice was shaky. Almost childlike.

"Sleeping powder. A Warlock in Sunder hit me with a dose of it a while back. Give it a moment, then we'll drag him out of there, because the Wyvern will wake up before he does."

As soon as it felt safe to do so, we picked up Larry and carried him from the mother Wyvern. High-pitched squeals announced the two infants moments before they crawled through the brush, desperate to be back beneath their mother's wings.

"Will they be all right?" asked Khay.

"I can't imagine it will last long on a beast her size," I said. "We just have to hope she wakes up before any other creatures arrive."

"We made enough of a ruckus to scare away any other animals for some time," said Theo. "Let's get him out of here."

We each took one of Larry's limbs, carried him back to the water hole, and placed him in the shade while we caught our breath. Eileen checked his pulse and his breathing, just to be safe.

"The kid did good," she said.

"Yeah," I conceded. "The kid did good."

Khay looked worried.

"You all right?" I asked. She nodded unconvincingly.

"I'm sorry. I just wanted to help."

We could still hear the infant Wyverns calling out, trying to rouse their mother, and I prayed for them to be quiet before another creature answered their call.

"Come on," said Theo, taking charge. "Let's get Lazarus into the car."

We carried Larry up the embankment and did out best to push the fate of the little ones from our minds.

35
Light in the Dark

"That was pretty brave, kid," said Eileen when Larry finally stirred. It was sunset, and we had him resting by the campfire while the rest of us prepared dinner.

"Not really," he replied, clearly chuffed with the attention. "The back of the beast's head was the only place it couldn't reach me with its claws or jaws. Safest spot imaginable, as far as I could see."

We ate more vegetables and small game, and Larry demolished his portion like he hadn't eaten in days.

"Woah, slow down there, hero," said Khay. "You've been out for hours."

"Sorry."

"Where did you get that stuff, anyway?" I asked.

"From headquarters. Sleeping powder is standard issue. I forgot that I had it at first." He looked up and, perhaps because we were all being so nice to him, was uncharacteristically honest. "I've never been in any kind of altercation like that before. Not even a fist fight. I'm afraid I somewhat panicked."

"You did great," said Theodor. "Saved our skins without injuring the creature at all. I'm sure The Bridge would be proud."

I knew he'd done well, and that Theodor was just humoring him, but it still annoyed me that he was keeping up the pretense of The Bridge being some continental organization rather than a club of one that he'd created in his bedroom.

After eating, the others peeled off into their tents, leaving Khay and me by the fire. Her hood was down, and she held her ungloved hands out to the flames. Not to warm them – the night wasn't cold – but to enjoy the sensation of the heat against her skin. I'd observed her in similar moments: running leaves and bark through her fingers, savoring the smell of the campfire coffee, and closing her eyes to sink into the flavors of everything she ate, always aware that it might be the last time that she'd be fully in possession of her senses.

Khay had been fading that day, down by the water. Now, she was as real as the rest of us. Back at the morgue, her experiment had been a success, and we'd left town riding high on Mora's recovery. The baby Wyvern had been a tragic reminder that Mora was the exception to the rule, and that, without the crown, it might never be repeated.

"You have to remember that this isn't a gift," she said, staring into the flames. "It's a punishment. The jewelry only keeps the wearer in this world if they meet the conditions of the curse. If they don't, it drags them away."

A reckless beetle, perhaps overexcited by its first experience with a campfire, flew too close to the flames and cooked itself with a gruesome pop and sizzle.

"Drags you where?"

"When this world was full of magic, the other side felt lighter than this one. Now it's . . . now it's something else."

I felt a chill, despite the fire and the spring air.

"Magic isn't like any other resource," she continued. "It isn't something you use. You dance with it. Even now, after the Coda, it still surprises."

"But . . ." I was going to say something obvious, like "it's gone", but I stopped myself. I knew what she meant. It was gone, but that didn't mean that there weren't still surprises waiting to be discovered. She was living proof of that.

"The way it left things, and the way things continue to change, it doesn't always make sense. You've seen it yourself, right? Most things haven't stopped. They've twisted. They've become puzzles that unlock themselves when you view them from a different angle."

She had a point. I'd seen it in Edmund Rye, the Vampire who found new power in the bones of his victims rather than the blood. I saw it in the bodies of Faeries whose hidden potential was still waiting to be set free; like Amari, who had escaped from her lifeless shell of a body and been reborn. Not like she once was. Of course not. But alive again, in a way.

"The Genie have always existed between the two worlds. When there was magic here, the other side felt like the lesser of these places. An empty space that was ready to welcome me. Now, when I open myself up to the other side, I feel the power rushing back in. It wants to get back, and it's using the curse to do it. When I bring a piece of that power back into this world, it rewards me, and allows me to stay here a little longer."

"Even if it kills someone?"

She nodded.

"It doesn't care. But I do. That's why they need to agree to it. That's my code, now. They need to know the risks and the rewards and decide for themselves if they want me to heal them."

I could hear the uncertainty in her voice. The familiar self-doubt that creeps in when you're halfway down a road and start to wonder whether you should ever have left home in the first place.

"But you're getting better, right? Look what happened with Mora."

"The jewelry helps. When I only had a few pieces, it was . . . unpredictable. But I could feel how close it was. I glimpsed the potential. You saw the Angel's wings afterwards but, brother, you should have seen him *fly*." She stared into the flames, remembering the night that she'd stuffed Brother Benjamin full of magic and sent him soaring into the skies above Sunder City. "Maybe the crown will be the last piece. With that, and a bit of practice, it might be enough."

A cold breeze blew from the south, billowing the fire.

"Then we'll get it. Soon. I promise."

She looked at me, and I expected some kind eye roll or chuckle at my sudden seriousness, but she just said, "Thank you."

We said goodnight and I went back to a tent that, despite the warmth of the night, still smelled quite a bit like wet dog.

36

Kindred

As soon as the sun rose, it became too hot to sleep so we piled back into the car and continued on. The funk of the previous afternoon had lifted, and whether it was the heat, the amount of time spent together, or the fact that we'd all seen each other naked the previous day, a sense of relaxed familiarity fell over us. Eileen put her legs across Khay while she rested, Larry actually sounded his age when he joined in the conversation, and Theodor even treated us to a traveling song.

> Gather your memories, your tokens and time,
> For the roamers must roam as the poet must rhyme
> But when we walk together
> The sun always shines
> So roam on, my Kindred, roam on.

He sang it several times, until we all knew the words and could sing along with him.

> Keep your feet free from blisters, your boots free from stone
> And your soul free as ships soaring over the foam
> As my kin is my kingdom
> The world is my home
> So roam on, my Kindred, roam on.

The car had seemed so cramped on the way out of Sunder but started to feel more spacious every day.

Khay kept herself fully wrapped up, always wearing her gloves and keeping only her head poking out from her hood, but she was more tactile than she'd been the previous days, resting her shoulder against mine and gripping my leg whenever she said something especially impassioned.

It was strange, after spending so much time alone, to feel so close to these people; bound together by purpose and a growing number of memories, stories and jokes that only the five of us would understand.

I'd never been good at this. I was always better when it was one on one. In groups, I felt like the others had some connection that I wasn't really a part of, no matter how much time we spent together. I don't know what was different about that car. Maybe it was me, more sure of myself as I'd gotten older. Maybe it was the company. Khay, in particular, put me at ease. Why, I wasn't sure. Either we were just similar people – who would have always connected, even if we'd met each other at another time, in another place – or it was because we were bound together by a mutual desire and determination. I'd spent the last year feeling like I was the one man working against a world that wanted to move in the opposite direction. Now, we were rushing forward with what felt like an unstoppable force at our backs.

We didn't stop all morning and made good time down the highway. When we finally entered the tall redwood trees of Jallimar Forest, the temperature outside the car went from hot to cool to cold in a few minutes. Khay stuck her head out the window and took a deep breath.

"Smell that," she said.

The rest of us joined her, inhaling the damp air: rich with moss, pine and the wet, sawdusty smell of decomposing wood. I was halfway through a breath when she popped her head back into the car, grinning wide.

"Larry, turn off the engine."

He pulled over and did as he was told.

"Shhh," said Khay, and we all hushed. It was quiet at first. Still. But before long, a cacophony of birds screeched, sung, cawed, trilled and chirped over our heads. They became louder by the second, perhaps feeling safer now that the car had quieted. When we moved again, we kept the windows down, and listened to the chorus of diverse, contrasting voices carry us along.

The road was new and smooth, so, despite the dense woodland off to either side, we wound our way through the trees without trouble. Any fallen branches had already been cleared or pulverized by the wheels of the heavy trucks who'd come before us.

When we reached the other end of the woods and set up camp on high ground over a narrow valley, Eileen's bag made a clinking sound as she dragged it from the trunk.

"What was that?" asked Larry, having quite a good idea of what it might be.

Eileen revealed two large bottles of red wine.

"Took them from the Roost. Didn't want them to spoil while I was away. Why? Are you thirsty?"

Once the food was on the fire, the first bottle was opened and Theodor, Eileen and Larry each had a glass. I was quite happy to go without until Khay, who wasn't apparently much of a drinker, joined in. Not wanting to be the only one of our merry band not partaking, I caved, and held out my cup.

"You sure?" Eileen asked.

"Just the one. It'll be fine."

We opened the second bottle the same time as we opened Portemus's book of anatomy – the one he'd given to Khay after Mora's magical surgery.

"Here!" shouted Eileen, unnecessarily loud. "The Minotaur!"

Khay and I leaned over her shoulders while Theo and Larry portioned out the remaining vegetables between them.

"Each Minotaur is made differently," Eileen read, "as they were each created from the hides and pelts of different animals, worn on different areas of their body. It is useful to think of the Minotaur as men who have had armor fused to their flesh. Though they are now one creature, a surgeon should favor the Humanoid parts of their body for an easier approach. If the fur of the creature makes this difficult to determine, imagine it is wearing an outfit and select the areas where the seams would naturally be."

"Helpful?" asked Larry, his mouth full of pumpkin.

"It's talking about surgical incisions," I said. "I'm hoping we won't have to get that close."

"Indeed," agreed Theodor. "We should avoid the beast entirely. Attack it from a distance only as a last resort."

As he spoke, he leaned into his pack and pulled out another bottle. This one had no label and was full of pitch-black liquid.

"What the fuck is that?" asked Khay.

"Ansidium. A Lycum treat. Who wants some?"

I didn't pause.

"Just the one."

37
Over

I woke up in the tent. No Theodor. It was light outside. Still daytime? How long had I been asleep? Flashes of memories, indiscernible from dreams, brought no clarity; just that familiar sense of regret.

Voices. The rest of them were outside. What are they saying? My head hurt too much to focus. I should just go back to sleep. *No. Get up.*

Get the fuck up, Fetch.

I sat up, and everything hurt even more. I stank. My tongue felt rough and furry like a dried-out mango seed. There was dirt on my knees. Cuts on my hands. A fight or a stumble? I was wearing the same clothes as yesterday, my shirt unbuttoned. I started to do them up before a kettle boiled over in my stomach and I threw open the flaps of the tent to hurl into the grass.

"There he is!" Eileen was leading the celebration and everyone joined her in a round of applause. "I thought you were an old hat at this."

"It's been a while."

"Well, there's a small creek down there," said Theodor, pointing towards a line of trees. "I suggest you get cleaned up."

I did as I was told. There was a dark cloud over everything. Was it just the effects of our overzealous drinking, or had I said or done something offensive that I could no longer remember? Probably both.

The creek was just a few inches of freezing spring water, but it was clear and clean. I stripped off and stepped carefully over the stones, still nauseous and fragile, with a rising darkness that the cool water did little to deter.

When I got back, everything had already been cleaned up and I was looking forward to crawling into my seat and nodding off.

"Maybe Fetch shouldn't be in the middle," said Khay.

"That would put three magic folk in the back," said Eileen, trying not to appear too fearful of Khay's powers.

"I can drive," suggested Theodor.

Larry seemed affronted.

"You know how?"

"I drove you the other day, while you were asleep. I'll take the wheel and you can sit between Ms Khay and Ms Tide."

Larry tried to look reluctant as he handed over the keys. I slumped into the passenger seat as Theodor got himself comfortable behind the wheel. I wrapped up my jacket, stuffed it under my head, and closed my eyes.

It wasn't quite sleep, but I wasn't properly conscious either. I was in the foggy place that's full of shame and a growing fear that I'd done something terrible but couldn't recall it. That's one of alcohol's cruelest effects: being unable to remember moments that can be our most defining in the eyes of others.

The back seat was excitable, more vibrant than when I'd been back there. It was like the women had absorbed some of Larry's youthfulness. Or perhaps he just brought out a lighter side of them than I did. I fell into a funk, one of those moods where you think everyone hates you so you just get on with hating yourself too. I felt like I could open the door, fall out onto the road, and they would just keep on driving without looking back. Someone made a crack. I wasn't listening, but laughter erupted from both the back seat and Theodor as well. Whatever was said, I sensed that I was the subject of the joke.

"I can see why you gave up the drink, Mr Phillips," said Larry, with his trademark tendency to shine a light on a lantern.

"Go fuck yourself," I growled, not opening my eyes.

The car went silent. Stayed silent for a while. Eventually, Khay dared to break it.

"Sorry. You thought it was funny last night. We didn't mean anything."

I was too angry to apologize. Too ashamed to argue. I kept my eyes closed. That was a shame. If I'd opened them, I might have noticed the spikes that were strung across the bridge. Theo had his eyes on the map and didn't swerve until the tires were already shredded and we were skidding over the edge.

38

Pitstop

The railing hit the windscreen – turning it into a web of cracks that obscured our vision – right as the front of the car dropped over the edge.

We all screamed. I gripped the headrest behind me. The world moved underneath us as the back of the car lifted up until the nose pointed straight down. The freefall, likely only a second or two long, was an eternity of panic. Water burst through the shattered windscreen, blasting me and Theodor in the face as the force of the fall drove us into the ground. My head and limbs connected with unknown objects. My eyes, nose and throat filled with dirty water. The river wasn't deep enough to sink us, but the car kept toppling, straight overhead, until we found ourselves upside down. The roof of the car was full of water and the engine screamed as it gargled the river. Those of us who had air in our lungs were crying out in panic.

I turned myself right side up so that my head was where my feet had just been. The car was tilted forward with the front window fully underwater. The water at the side window – which was also smashed out – only reached halfway up. I squeezed my way out and stood in the knee-high river, spluttering up a torrent of my own.

Khay opened her door and pulled Larry out with her. Eileen was wailing – her voice in a register that I'd never heard from her before – and Theodor was still in the car, trying to talk to her. I waded around to her door and tried to open it but the metal was jammed and it wouldn't budge. Steam shot up from the underside of the car, hot air blasting my face. It took some coaxing, but Theodor was able to direct Eileen out the other side where she fell into Larry's arms, sobbing.

Theodor crawled out of the car. Then, the Satyr spoke.

"Get yourselves safe there, you lucky but unlucky bastards," he said, the longbow pulled tight and aimed at Khay's back. "But don't be making any sudden moves or reaching for any weapons, now. You haven't made it out alive just yet."

We were instructed to come to the water's edge, get on our knees, put our hands in our laps, and stay that way until we were told any different.

The Satyr kept his distance. He was shirtless, except for leather cuffs, and three too many necklaces not to be a certified piece of shit. His hair and fur looked brown but most of that was mud. His goatee suggested he was actually blond. One of his horns had the tip snapped off it, and his nose had been broken more than once. We could probably take him, if we all rushed at once, but he'd get one shot off and I reckoned he knew how to make it count. So, we waited silently, except for Eileen who couldn't stop sobbing. It was probably just shock, but the fact that our captor didn't care at all made me eager to find a way to squeeze a couple of tears out of him in return.

"I want to be knowing where you came from, where you're going, and what your titles be," he asked, stuffing unnecessary words into every sentence. Khay and I looked sideways at each other, but nobody spoke. "Don't be looking at each other like that, all secretive and slimy. I want the truth and if I don't get it, I'm gonna be getting real shirty now. Don't waste my time because I can't be holding this bow all day. After a while, my fingers have the tendency to get a little slippy now."

"What do you mean *titles?*" I asked.

"Your jobs, you numpty. Your ranks and positions at Mortales and all that."

I groaned. Of course. That damn car.

"We're not with them," said Theodor. "Look at us."

"Oh, you think I don't know that there's more than Humans working with Mortales these days? That just because you're a wolf and Witch and a whatever else, that you can't be in cahoots? I'm not falling for that, you daft fuckers. They'll recruit anyone if the pay's right. I bet you're the guard, you furry bastard, and I guess you won't be getting your bonus this week. What about the rest of you?"

Eileen breathed deep, trying to get herself under control.

"Are you all right?" I asked her.

"Eyes on me, Prince Charming. She's fine for now. What's your job? Not dressed well enough to be the boss but not enough muscle to be the muscle. Mortales just pay you to carry the bags, do they?"

"He told you," I said. "We don't work for Mortales. We stole the car from—"

"Ooooh, yes, if I was going to steal a car from Mortales, the first place I'd drive it would be the main highway between two of their most visited cities. What ingenious criminals you must be."

We all fell silent as my attempted ruse was so quickly shot down.

"I'm gonna tie you up," said the Satyr, "so you're less likely to try anything stupid." He swung the point of the arrow at Eileen's head. "Grab one of those ropes and follow me. The rest of you, don't get excited. I'll be a little ways away, but I can hit you dead in the heart from five times the distance. Come on, missy."

Eileen got to her feet.

"It's mine!" shouted Larry. "The car. It's my dad's, he's—"

The Satyr kicked him in the face with one of his hooves. The kid, to his credit, took it well.

"Shush now. You'll get your chance in the hot seat, young man. Now, the rest of you, move apart. I see your lips wiggling or any sign that you're talking to each other, I'll have her throat cut and one of you shot before the rest of you get up off the ground."

Eileen followed the Satyr as he walked backwards, bow always at the ready, until he moved past a rock and told her to sit down on it. She did, and he stood behind her, eyes flicking between her and us, then put down the bow, took out his knife, and held it while he tied her wrists together.

What would the Satyr do when he discovered who Larry's father was? If this attack was all about Mortales, and he now had the son of a Mortales executive in his grasp, there was no telling what he'd do next.

Larry stared at the Satyr with an expression I'd never seen on him before. It was the look of a man who wanted to tear someone's throat out. I hoped he wouldn't try because I believed that the goat-legged bastard could fire an arrow and cut a throat as fast as he said he could.

I looked back at the ruined car, our belongings scattered everywhere. Thick metal spikes were stuck into the tires and the line they were attached to was strung tight between the front and back wheels.

It reminded me of another attack like this: when Hendricks, disguised as Mr Deamar, launched similar attacks on Niles company vehicles. Was it just a coincidence? Or had Hendricks and this Satyr crossed paths at some point? I always suspected that Eliah wasn't working alone all that time. If it was true, I could maybe convince the Satyr that I'd also been a trusted ally of Hendricks.

Khay, like the rest of us, was soaked. Her hood and eyes were down. The black robes clung to the skin of her torso and sat in the mud around her legs. She barely moved, as if she wasn't worried about the situation at all. Maybe she'd been close to death for so long it didn't really bother her anymore.

The Satyr directed Eileen back over to us. Her eyes were red, and she was shaking a little, but she'd managed to pull herself together. The Satyr followed her, bow in his hands and his eyes on Khay the whole way.

"You're next, Baldy. Up you pop."

Khay stood, and the Satyr stepped back. Her foot stepped on a loop of her robe and pulled it down.

The Satyr stopped.

Who knows what was going through his head; whether it was something lewd, or perhaps a moment of compassion before he stopped to let her redress herself? We never found out because Khay launched herself forward.

As soon as she was inside the point of the arrow, she pushed it away, spread her arms, and wrapped them around the Satyr's body. Having the bow only half-cocked, the arrow fired limply into the shrub. The Satyr dropped the weapon and tried to pull Khay off of him, but she gripped tight. He grabbed her waist and tried to push her away, then pulled his hands back and yelped.

Khay held on tight, her naked limbs wrapped around him and her head pressed against the side of his face.

Over the sound of the shallow river and the Satyr's increasing screams, we heard him sizzling. He spun around, screamed, and pummeled her with his fists, but Khay held on, her face calm, as if he was her father carrying her to bed after a long day. The Satyr fell into a seated position and tried to push her off despite the steam that came up from his palms.

He had his back to us. Khay's face pressed against his, turning the skin on his cheek bright red.

His horns grew and grew. We watched in wide-eyed horror as the unbroken one curled back around towards his muddy blond hair and kept going, until the sharp point drove itself into his scalp.

The Satyr's scream turned from panic to unbridled fear, then stopped.

Khay dropped him in the mud, not a mark on her other than the dirt and scratches she'd caught in the car accident. The Satyr's body shook in that unsettling way only the dying do when the last bits of life rattle loose.

Khay picked up her robe, wrapped it around her shoulders, and sat on the rock in silence. The rest of us were just as quiet, trying to absorb everything that had happened since the accident and what it would mean going forward.

I was thankful, once again, to have Theodor in our party because his practical nature eventually broke us out of our stupor.

"Let's collect our things," he said. "See what's still useful."

Eileen, Larry and I followed him into the river, happy to be told what to do rather than be forced to think on our own.

Khay stayed on her rock.

We dragged bedrolls, tents and cooking utensils onto the riverbank. Our main pot was broken, along with a good number of tent poles. I rocked the car so Larry could pull out the waterproof covering that was trapped underneath, but it was already pretty torn up.

Theodor had ignored most of these items; he'd been searching for one thing in particular: his crossbow. It had come loose in the crash and been thrown downstream, which was only slightly better than if it had ended up under the body of the totaled car. He sat down on the riverbank and fiddled with it: checking the strings, locks and gears. He fired it empty and grumbled to himself. Then he loaded a bolt, fired, and it shot out sideways, spinning past my head.

"Sorry," he said. "I'll need to replace some parts before it works again."

Once everything was out of the water, we hung things from trees to dry, then I bent over the Satyr and searched him. I had no desire to take any of his necklaces, and he had no pockets, but his longbow was finely made and his quiver was full of arrows. I tested the string and it was tight as hell.

"You used that before?" asked Theodor.

"Not since my Shepherd training in the Opus, and that was only target practice."

We dragged the Satyr away, trying not to dwell on the fact that one of our merry band had cooked him with her bare skin.

While the sun dried our belongings, we ate the damp leftovers of our remaining food and were forced to come to terms with the reality of our situation.

Theodor flattened out the faded map.

"We're here." He pointed to a spot two-thirds of the way between Sunder and Incava. "The car wouldn't have taken us much further anyway: the road ends in another day's drive. It's the journey back we need to consider. We're beat-up, we have no transportation, and we've lost a good portion of our supplies. If we turn back now, our safe return is far from assured, but it is possible. If we continue onward, our path will be tougher than expected and the journey home will be . . . challenging, to say the least."

"We can't turn around," said Khay, her first words since the accident.

"I'm not saying that we should, but we must consider all options. What will change if we do it in another month, or two?"

"I'll have faded from existence, never to return, taking the last of the Genie power with me."

"She's right," I added. "We're not turning back."

Eileen had composed herself, but she was quiet. Perhaps she was sheepish about her recent episode. I felt sheepish about the fact that I hadn't been able to help her when she'd been at her most fraught, and I imagined the others felt the same.

"Why do you need it?" she asked Khay. "You seem powerful enough as it is."

Khay looked down, frustrated.

"I can't control it yet. Not properly."

"But you're solid again," pressed Eileen.

"That's because she killed him," said Larry, with less tact than a two-year-old.

"Exactly," Khay said, deadpan. "So, unless our plan is to fry as many folks as we can before the curse drags me into the other world, I need the crown."

We were all quiet for a while. The air was heavy and the cloudy sky felt like it was pressing down on our shoulders.

"Let's camp here," I said. "Patch ourselves up and decide what we can carry with us. We'll start walking at first light." Nobody responded. Khay was impatient, the others uncertain. "Theodor, can you find something for us to eat around here?"

"Of course."

"Good. Khay, I know we need to get moving, but we can't set off ill-prepared. Taking our time today could save us trouble down the road. Let's go over everything we have and work out what we're taking, who's carrying what, and have it all ready so we can leave first thing in the morning. Sound good?" I waited. Eventually everyone managed a small nod. It would have to do. "Good. Thank you."

I moved off. I didn't know what I was about to do, I just wanted to create some momentum and hope it caught on with the others.

I went into the bushes to take a piss, wondering how our group had come apart so quickly and how I might be able to bring everyone together again. A bit of food and some sleep would be a good start. Once we got to the end of this terrible day, things would get better.

While I was relieving myself, I looked over at the Satyr's body, discarded in the long grass.

Khay's red imprint was burned onto his naked torso in shocking detail. The curves of her body were broken up by the harsh lines of her jewelry, which had made marks that were darker and redder than where she'd touched him with her skin.

I'd wondered why she undressed herself when she attempted

her spells. Why the contact between her body, the artefacts and her subject would be so crucial. I'd tried not to make uninformed guesses, knowing that I would be better educated by discussing it with her when the time was right, but the gruesome Satyr corpse forced the question back into my mind.

Khay spoke about her powers so confidently that I took her at her word. Who was I to question whether one more treasure might truly unlock the magic we were seeking? I'd watched what she'd done to Mora, and I'd seen the miraculous nature of even her failed attempts. But looking at the lethal self-portrait she'd burned into the Satyr's body, I wondered if it was the jewels themselves that contained the power, rather than Khay herself.

What if Khay wasn't using the artefacts to fulfill her desires, but rather the other way around?

Hell, what did I know? If Khay hadn't done what she'd done, it would be us lying in the grass instead of the Satyr.

I shook myself off and went back to the riverbank to review the map.

39
Party Lines

Theodor caught a couple of small fish and we paired them with some Sunder potatoes and wild radishes to make quite the satisfying meal. Not that you'd know it from the mood of the diners.

Eileen had injured her arm. It wasn't broken but it hurt when she lifted things, so we all agreed to carry a share of her belongings while she healed.

Larry, usually happy to talk his mouth off, was even quieter than Eileen. He moved the food around his plate, barely eating, and when any of us spoke, he just stared at us. He looked like he was about to jump in and start an argument, but never did.

I wasn't used to the tension that was coming from the two of them. Creating an uncomfortable mood was one of my specialties but I had no idea how to diffuse one. Still, as the unofficial leader of this cohort, it was my responsibility to try to make things better.

"I know this is shit," I said, "and I'm sorry. But we've been lucky so far. We would have tried to do this even if we'd never had the car at all. We could still be days behind, dealing with horses or mules or anything. Just because our luck has taken a turn, it doesn't mean that it's run out. We have to remember why we're doing this."

Nobody shouted me down, so I kept going.

"Back home, there's plenty of light and color coming into the city, but it's only covering up the reality of things. People are still sick. They're still dying. If we don't do something, future generations won't remember Dragons and Unicorns and the Fae.

They'll be forgotten, to make room for new cars, higher buildings, and more efficient killing machines. I've been looking for a way to turn things back ever since the Coda, and this is the best shot I've had to actually do some good. With the crown, Khay will be able to save people like she saved Mora. Beyond that, who knows? If we start with the impossible, anything might follow."

Theodor nodded slowly. Larry finally took a bite. Eileen rubbed her arm. My speech hadn't inspired cheers or a spontaneous change of mood, but they did start talking. Theodor gave the others a brief rundown of our planned route: we'd keep close enough to the highway to spy roadhouses and stores, but not so close that we'd be spotted by vehicles. Then, when the road turned west, we'd move through the forest into a valley on the north-west side of the city.

Theodor had traveled safely through some of this route, back before the Coda. He knew of no notable dangers in the area and was confident he'd find a clear path through the woods. There would still be angry Wizards and a rabid Minotaur at the other end of the journey, of course, plus the long walk home that followed, but we had to focus on one challenge at a time.

Eileen yawned.

"Sorry. I'm beat."

"The tea can make you tired," said Theodor, who had been serving her a medicinal blend of herbs all evening. "And you will heal faster if you sleep. We should all get to bed if we plan to start moving at dawn."

We put out the fire so as not to attract attention from the highway, and Eileen and Theodor moved off towards the tents. Larry, who had been sleeping in the car up until that point, shuffled towards the lean-to he'd strung from a nearby tree.

"Don't be silly, Lazarus," said Eileen. "There's room in my tent for two. You'll get bitten to pieces out here."

Larry was dumbstruck.

"Oh, uh . . . you sure?"

He looked between us, trying not to make it weird, and failed so fantastically that the rest of us cracked our first smiles since the accident.

We sent them on their way with sing-song goodnights that made Lazarus blush and restored some sense of normalcy to the group. Theodor cleaned the plates and packed them away. I felt bad that we'd come to rely on him for so many jobs that the rest of us didn't think of doing them ourselves. When someone is efficient, and the others are even a little lazy, they adopt certain roles by default. He didn't seem to mind, and he was the only one getting paid for coming on this adventure, but I told myself that I needed to pick up my game.

Tomorrow. It would all be different tomorrow.

It was not a good night's sleep. We'd set up our tents in the small trees, but the trucks that rumbled over the bridge came and went like earthquakes. Wild dogs howled all night, first distant, then disturbingly close. Theodor even went out and howled back in an attempt to scare them off, but they never stayed quiet for long.

I wasn't sure if I slept at all, and I heard enough grumbles, rustles and whispers to know that the others had a similar night. Despite my fatigue, as soon as the canvas of the tent began to glow, I stepped outside, filled the pot with river water, and put it over the fire. I had a small bag of coffee that I'd been saving for the harder days of the journey, but it had got soaked in the crash and wouldn't last much longer. Anyway, I hoped that there wouldn't be many harder days than this.

I stirred the pot, praying that it was just the remedy we needed to lift out spirits, and Eileen came and stood beside me.

"That from Georgio?" she asked.

"Yeah, but don't expect it to be as good. I might have the beans but he has the technique."

She smiled politely, then said, "I'm not going any further."

I stopped stirring. I could feel her nervousness, and her fear of my response.

"Eileen, you can't—"

She was crying.

"Fetch, I . . . I can't do it and . . . I've been thinking about it and I shouldn't have to. I lost enough when the Coda happened. I want to rebuild my life in this world, and if that makes me happy, then I should be able to do it. I shouldn't have to feel guilty about moving on or looking to the future. I should be proud of what I've done and how hard I've worked. I know that it means taking money from Thurston, but if it's for something positive then I don't see what the problem is. I can do more at the library than I can out here. It's important. I'm not saying this isn't but . . . but I don't think it's worth dying for."

Eileen registered my silence as anger and kept talking.

"I'm sorry. I know you think I should have thought this through before we left Sunder, and I did, but I wasn't strong enough to say it, and I thought at the time that maybe this was right, but . . . I'm going home, okay?"

There were too many things not to like about it. It was bad enough that she was going, but she wanted to blame it on the fact that I'd badgered her into coming along in the first place.

"I didn't mean to pressure you into doing something you didn't want to," I said. "I didn't even think that was possible. You're smarter than me, Eileen, and I thought we were doing this together."

My non-apology slapped the remorse out of her face. I wasn't angry. Not exactly. I just resented the way she was trying to throw this whole thing at my feet as soon as it had gone sour. I was disappointed in her lack of faith and her lack of ambition.

"I spoke with Lazarus," she said, "and he knows how to get us to Mira. There he can contact his father and organize another vehicle."

"You're taking him with you? Great. What happens to Theodor when our financier goes home?"

"I'm sure we can work that out. Lazarus doesn't want to jeopardize the mission any more than I do, but he's not cut out for this either. He's just a kid."

"A kid who can call in favors from Mortales any time he wants. He approached us, remember? He said he wanted to try to fix things. Take him if you want, but don't pretend you're doing it for his sake. He knew what he was signing up for."

The "and so did you" was left unsaid, but she heard it loud and clear. I knew I should have been more compassionate. We'd had a rough twenty-four hours and she was right about the fact that she didn't owe me anything, but I was too frustrated and tired to let those thoughts reach the surface.

"How far to Mira?" I asked.

Eileen had stopped looking apologetic. It was all business now. "Two days' hike."

"I suppose we should split up the gear."

Lazarus and Theodor made arrangements to meet back in Sunder to finalize payment. I was relieved that I'd hired such a seemingly trustworthy companion who would see the job through to the end, even when his employer was turning tail.

All morning, as we discussed our plans and separated out the supplies, I kept telling myself to be kind – to let them leave graciously, that they were my friends, that their choice was understandable, and that I wanted them to be safe – but I couldn't put those thoughts into my actions. I grumbled and made no eye contact. When I moved things, I yanked them and threw them down instead of placing them. I responded to questions with single-word answers. Essentially, I acted like a shitty teenager having a sulk.

Khay was more apologetic than Eileen was, perhaps thinking that this was her fault. She helped them prepare their packs and kept giving them things that I needed to take back, reminding everyone that we were marching into unknown lands while they'd soon be in a safe-haven city, living off Larry's credit.

We filled our canteens from the stream, and Theodor filled a huge water container and told me to stuff it into my pack.

"We're traveling on foot now," he said. "Water will be important."

Eileen and Larry took one of the tents and the few supplies I allowed them (we couldn't carry all their stuff anyway) and we all stood around awkwardly.

It was such a waste. All this way just to split our band down the middle. We should have recruited others instead. Fighters who would have been strong enough to stick it out. Hell, I'd never wanted Lazarus Q. Symes on the journey anyway, but now that he was leaving, it felt like a betrayal.

"Look after the kid," I said to Eileen. "Until you're in Mira, there are certain people who'll see a target on his head. If you see anyone out there, just be ready to run."

We shook hands and they turned and went back the way we'd come, leaving Theodor, Khay and me to venture on without them. Things were quiet and the road ahead was dark and winding.

We traveled in a straight line, just off from the road, over flat terrain between small trees. The morning was uneventful and, when it got close to noon, Theodor asked to take a look at the maps. I reached into my pack, and my fingers touched something wet.

"Shit."

The car accident had broken the bottom of the water container. The crack wasn't big enough to notice when we filled it in the stream, but after being jostled all morning, the container was empty and everything in my bag was soaked. Most of it wasn't critical. The maps were damaged but legible, and everything else would dry in time, but Theo was most concerned about the water.

"In the forest, most of the water will be stagnant. We may stumble across some streams, and we can salvage sap from some trees, but it's advisable to search for water before you need it."

Theodor was able to intuit where water sources might be from surveying the land, and he thought that there might be a creek up ahead. Before we got there, he spotted something else.

"Binoculars, please." I handed them over and he took some time peering through them. "It's a cottage with a sign out front. The Harpy House. Looks to be an inn. There's a garden out the back, and a well."

He chewed his lip.

"What are you thinking?" I asked.

"I'm weighing up the dangers of visiting the inn versus avoiding it all together."

Khay shared his reservations.

"Mortales uses this road, right? And we're close to Incava."

"True," I said. "But without the car, we don't have anything that raises too many questions. We're just travelers on a journey to . . ." I couldn't think of any other city nearby that made sense.

Theo shook his head.

"Out here without horses or an automobile, there won't be any other destinations that sound believable."

Khay nodded. The choice to avoid the inn was winning out, but with wet supplies and an empty stomach, I was drawn to the idea of having a proper meal by the fire before we committed ourselves to the woods.

I looked down, thinking, and the sun glistened off the silver badge pinned to my jacket.

"I think I have an angle."

I rang the bell, and the door was opened by a silver-haired woman with suspicious eyes, white pupils, and deep laugh-lines on her tanned cheeks.

"Hello," I said. "We're representatives of The Bridge: a group of community-minded individuals who have charged ourselves with guiding the world back to the magical existence we've left behind. Is your kitchen open?"

40

The Harpy House

The silver-haired woman looked from me to Theo to Khay, and her eyes squinted in distrust.

"You're not going to try and sell me anything, are you?"

"No, ma'am. We're in need of food and fresh water, and we have the bronze to pay for it."

The tip of her tongue ran from one side of her lips to the other as she gave us a final examination.

"All right. Come in and take a seat."

The interior was log-cabin walls with tiny windows, low ceilings, plenty of old photos on the walls, and lanternlight coming from every corner. We were led into a room with four tables and took our seats at the largest. There was only one other patron: a weathered Ogre with a wide-brimmed hat and dusty trousers. His bloodshot eyes looked us over as we entered, then fell back to the barely touched bowl of stew in front of him.

"What's on the menu?" I asked.

"Beef," said the innkeeper.

"Any vegetables?"

"Beans."

"Two servings of beef and a bowl of beans, please."

Theodor raised a hand.

"Is there any meat in these beans?"

"Nope. Just bacon." Theodor nodded slowly, as if he'd assumed as much. "We got some bread too, if that interests you."

"Please."

She squeezed through the tables, out of the room, and we heard her shout the order to the cook.

"Excuse me." The Ogre on the far table took off his hat and turned to us. There was an awkwardness to his expressions that spoke of a man who was used to spending time on his own, trying his best to adopt the perceived manners of an unfamiliar world. "Have you seen my son? He went missing several weeks ago. Traveling these parts."

He handed Theodor a small photograph with crumpled edges, and we all leaned over to look at it. It was a picture of an adolescent Ogre with narrow tusks, icy blue eyes, and a short-cropped mohawk. He was shirtless and laughing, with a silver chain necklace that had a skull pendant at the end.

"I'm sorry," said Khay. "We've only just arrived ourselves."

He nodded, took back the photo, and used the edge of his fist to flatten it against the table while his stew went cold.

"Look." Khay pointed to a framed black-and-white photo behind my head. It was larger than the others, faded and yellowing, and pictured two women standing in front of a carriage with no wheels. Instead, there were sails on either side, stretched over wings that stuck out like the paddles of a rowing boat. Along the side of the carriage, there was a pattern I'd seen somewhere before, though couldn't place it. Khay stood up to get a closer look and pointed to a black shape in the top-right corner. "That's it. Incava."

The patterned carriage was on the top of a hill. Behind the two women and the vehicle, you could see the looming black shape of the castle, like a nightmarish beast creeping up on the unsuspecting subjects. Most of it was lost out of frame, but the smooth black walls seemed to grow out of the rock like the base of a mighty tree, spreading its roots and splitting the earth. The only give-away that it wasn't an organic structure were the ornate windows cut into the stone at equal intervals.

"I was quite the looker, wasn't I?" The innkeeper dropped water and glasses on the table and smiled at the photo with a nostalgic look in her eye. "That was when I first arrived from Rakanesh. Youngest pilot to cross the continent."

Once she mentioned it, her resemblance to one of the women in the photo was unmistakable.

"Rakanesh?" I repeated. "You piloted their flying machines?"

The pattern on the flying carriage was the same as on the Rods of Rakanesh: the metal batons that the mask-maker had used to flip my inner-ears in his workshop.

"That's right. Penny and I spent ten years doing supply runs in and out of Incava."

I hoped that the pregnant silence – as Theo, Khay and I traded knowing looks – wasn't noticed by the host. She'd lived in Incava, and was a potential well of inside knowledge, but what would she think if we revealed our plans?

"Who's Penny?" I asked, to move the conversation on before she got suspicious.

"Only the best darn cook in Archetellos!" The voice came through the door, along with a big, feathered body wearing a thick, knitted coat. "You kids better be hungry."

It took some squeezing for Penny to fit through the door, though most of her bulk was feathers. They stuck out of her sleeves, around taloned hands that held a tray carrying two steaming bowls of stew and a plate of buttered beans and bacon.

"Penny flew solo," explained the other woman. "Mail and money, mostly. I moved people and supplies."

"Yeah, back when my wings were working and my waist was half the size. I didn't need any clunky contraption like Betty and her skymobile, neither." She dropped the food on the table and gave Betty a kiss on the cheek. "I'm only teasing you, my love."

"You're just angry you never beat my round-trip record!" the Mage called out, as the Harpy took her tray from the room. "They were wild days back then. Mad times. Look at the cheek on that young one's face." She pointed to the black-and-white version of herself. "Whole world beneath her feet."

"When did you leave?" asked Khay.

"Five, six years ago. The men went mad after the Coda. Didn't want to learn how to take care of themselves. I couldn't handle it anymore. The whining. The stink! Penny and I came out here instead. It's not much, but it's better than that dark shithole."

"Not much?" said Penny with faux hurt as she reentered with a loaf of bread and a pot of bright red jam. "You never ate so good, even when you were flying anywhere you wanted. You should be counting your blessings, girl."

We were the ones who needed to count our blessings. We had a better source of Incava information than any of Eileen's books. The stew was darn good as well.

"What was it like? Living there before the Coda," I asked, as Betty sliced a piece of bread for each of us, including herself.

"Depraved." She wiped jam from her chin and smiled like a kid caught with her hand in the cookie jar. "And glorious. After the madness of the Fifth War, they stopped thinking about expansion or combat. They just fortified their defenses and got to living life. They ran the city so well that nobody had to work, other than those flights in and out to trade goods. We read and danced and got drunk and fat. It was quite the time."

She closed her eyes and revisited some part of those glory days before Theo pulled her back to reality.

"How did you have goods to trade if nobody worked?"

"Ah, well—" She was interrupted by a rumbling sound that got louder and louder until the cutlery was dancing on the table. "One moment."

When the rumbling stopped, we heard Betty open the front door and call out, "Hello, gentlemen! Here for lunch, are we?"

I couldn't hear their response, only the sounds of car doors closing.

"We should get out of here," said Theo.

"Too late now," replied Khay. She was right. Betty came back in, leading two tall men to the table beside us.

"Busy today!" she exclaimed, before taking their orders.

One of the men hadn't taken his eyes off us since he entered the room. He was my height, in a black suit that he'd clearly been wearing for a while. His eyes were red and his hair was all kicked up on one side, like he'd just woken up from a nap. The other, a bald man with a mustache and cleft chin, was wearing sweaty coveralls and was much more concerned with the food on offer than our trio.

"Two beef, two beans, coming right up. Won't be a moment."

The suited man didn't even wait for her to leave the room.

"Who are you?"

Theodor and Khay looked to me, but Betty spoke first.

"They're from The Bridge. Off to find some magic or something, aren't you?"

The suited man squinted at us. Betty toddled out, and the man in coveralls watched her go.

"Where are you from?" came the next question. Keeping my eyes on the man, I addressed my table.

"Friends, fill our canteens and see if Betty and Penny have a container we can buy. I'll be out shortly."

Theo and Khay rose.

"Wait," said the suited man. He lifted his hand from the table and moved it towards the inside of his jacket, but my pistol was out before it got there.

"Hands back down before I spoil that lovely suit," I said. He obeyed.

Theo and Khay continued their exit, and I listened as they made their request and Betty responded enthusiastically.

"What do you want?" asked the suited man. The other looked perplexed, but not at all afraid.

"Nothing," I said. "I don't want to know who you are or where you're from or what you're up to. I don't want anything from you, because I don't want to give you any reason to follow us or think about us once we leave. We're travelers, nothing more."

He made a big show of not believing me.

"Then why all the melodrama?"

"Because you were asking a lot of questions – in fact, I'm not convinced you're capable of saying a sentence that isn't one – and you look like a guy who gets angry when he doesn't get answers." He sneered, suggesting that I was correct and that he wasn't ashamed to admit it. "I don't want to give you any answers. I'd love to give you a few slaps, or a hairbrush, or find out where you're headed and what your deal is, but I don't want to spend the next week looking over my shoulder or waste my day digging two shallow graves; yours wouldn't be much trouble but your buddy's would take all afternoon."

"You really believe we won't follow you?"

I shrugged. "Do what you want. Maybe I want you to follow me. Maybe I want an excuse to extract a few thoughts from your head and teeth from your mouth, but you look like an important guy. You've been driving through the night, trying to meet some deadline or make good time, so you won't wanna throw all that away to chase down three grubby hikers for no reason."

"Maybe I do."

"Look at that. A statement. I knew you had it in you."

"I—"

"HEAVENS!"

Penny stopped in the doorway with her overflowing tray.

"Sorry, ma'am. I was just about to be on my way."

She stepped back and I squeezed past, my pistol pointing at the suited man's heart the whole time.

I stepped outside into the line of Theo's crossbow.

"What the hell was that?" he asked. "Do you know them?"

"I know when someone's going to draw on me. Just wanted to get in first." I let him know what I'd told them. He didn't appear to approve, but he didn't admonish me either. "You check out their wheels?"

"Yeah."

"Learn anything?"

"It's a car. I can't tell them apart."

It was a simple model. Not as nice as either of the ones owned by Larry's family. More like the ones that Niles's goons liked to drive. If there were things to learn from it, I left them unlearned. We had grander discoveries ahead of us. "Where's Khay?"

Theo took me out the back, where Betty was filling a large flagon from the well.

"You better not be making any trouble in my home," she chided, equal parts joke and threat.

"Avoiding it, if we can."

"Where you lot off to?"

I pointed to the edge of the forest. Vine-covered trees stopped in a sharp line at the back of the property.

"In there. We ready?" Theo and Khay both nodded. "Then let's go."

41

A Walk in the Woods

The soundscape changed in a second. The southern wind that had been a constant on our travels was swallowed by the canopy, leaving a hushed vacuum. It was so still that every cracked twig or dry leaf beneath our boots became an obnoxious disturbance of the peace.

The trees were hundreds – perhaps thousands – of years old, and if the ground had ever been cleared by fire, it hadn't happened for an age. There were no paths here, not even those bashed into existence by the hooves of horses, Centaurs and Unicorns. You couldn't see the ground, just the impossibly thick trunks of trees that grew at all angles from the decaying corpses of the ones who'd come before them.

"Have you trekked these woods before?" I asked Theodor.

"I crossed them the other way, at a diagonal. I've never walked this direction, but I have a sense of the landscape and I believe we can reach the other side within a week."

There would be no respite till we reached the other side. No passing vehicles to hail or roadside taverns to rest our feet. We would live in the shade of those ancient trees until we made it to Incava, if we made it there at all. The forest appeared to be impenetrable, but, from what I knew of Theodor, I was curious to see how he would tackle the labyrinthine mess that lay before us.

"Step where I step," he said, and used a twisted branch to pull himself up onto a horizontal tree. I followed Theodor and Khay followed me. Only a few steps later, my foot slipped. I grabbed a branch for support, but it snapped under my weight and I tumbled off the tree into a bed of mulch that swallowed me up as if I'd plunged into a bubble bath.

I scrambled to my feet, frantically slapping debris from my body and shaking it out of my shirt. It was mostly leaves and bark, but there were enough bugs and spiders crawling through the undergrowth for me to shiver and squeal at every scratch against my skin.

"I told you to step where I step," chided Theodor.

"I did!"

"No, you stepped here." Theodor pointed to a clump of green moss. "*I* stepped here." He pointed to a slightly lighter clump of green moss right beside it. "Which is why you slipped. Come on."

He pulled me back up and we continued along the mighty trunk, then across a ridge of flat rocks. We went between two lines of trees whose roots created an elevated path that kept us out of the undergrowth but threatened to snap an ankle if we lost focus.

The birdsong started slowly. It seemed that they'd quieted down when we entered the woods, then had waited to get a sense of us before starting up again. When they did, their voices erupted like an excited party of sports fans in the final minute of a game, screaming and screeching in an endless wall of sound.

As we walked, my ear tuned in to the individual calls coming from all around us: chirps, trills, rasps, wheezes and peeps. Some seemed to be repeated from one bird to the next, down the line, in an ongoing call-and-response that traveled from one end of the forest to the other.

Theodor raised his hand.

Khay and I stopped. Theo looked around, searching over our heads, then in the gaps between the roots that made up our path.

With a hand signal that told us to stay back, he stepped forward, eyes scanning on both sides, below us and up above.

He froze, eyes staring straight up. He stayed that way for a while, took a careful step back, turned, and held out his hand in the shape of a pistol. I took the machine from its holster and handed it over. He raised it above his head, tilted one way, the other, and fired.

The birds shook the forest with their wings as they scattered. I couldn't see where the bullet had struck – it all just looked like a mass of leaves and branches – until I heard a scraping sound. A loop of green scales dropped down from the canopy, kept sliding, and then—

THUMP! A giant serpent landed in front of us, writhing around and twisting itself up in a knot that looked a lot like Eileen's hair.

Theodor shoved the smoking gun back in my hands so he could draw the largest of his knives, then launched himself onto the snake. I expected him to start madly hacking at it, but he took his time, searching, with the tip of the blade always pointed at the knotted mass, until the body of the beast unwound, and its terrifying face emerged: mouth open and ready to strike.

Theodor moved swiftly, stabbing his dagger into the pale neck of the snake, just below its maw, then twisting and dragging the blade towards him. The knife sliced through the scales and sent blue blood gushing onto his arms.

Theodor jumped back as the snake continued to twist itself up, tightening into a ball. It was the reaction of a dying nervous system, and no longer anything for us to be worried about. Theodor used the thick leaves of a nearby fern to clean his knife and his hands. Khay and I watched in wonder.

"How did you know it was there?" she asked.

"The birds," he replied, as if it was obvious. They were still screeching and flying in circles around us, and I couldn't imagine how he'd been able to distinguish one voice from the next, let alone interpret their meaning.

"How can you understand them?" I asked.

"Same as anything. It takes time. Warning sounds, contact calls, mating songs. You get to know them all after a while. Their language isn't like ours. As in, you don't hear specific words, but after enough time in the woods it starts to make sense. Same as the tracks and the smells and the lines of the trees. They all tell a story."

The serpent slipped down between the roots, and Theodor stepped over the spattering of blue blood. I followed, listening to the mad screams of the creatures over our heads.

"Firing the gun was unwise," said Theodor. "We should resist doing that again, if we can help it. It means you'll have to practice with the bow."

I didn't like the idea of bearing that responsibility, but I knew he was right. Something about the noise of the pistol in this quiet place had felt wrong. It took an hour for the birds to settle down again. When they did, Theodor began his first lesson.

"Hear that?" he asked. "The pigmy swallow?"

"Which one is it?"

Theodor whistled, and I listened intently until I could zero in on the correct sound: a three-burst call that started near us, then repeated itself a little further away, and then further away again. The tune was being passed from one bird to the next like a hot potato.

"What does it mean?" asked Khay.

Theodor whistled again.

"That's us. They're telling the rest of the forest that we're here and which direction we're going."

It made me feel self-conscious. That was silly, I know, but I never liked knowing I was being watched.

"Is that all they're saying?" I asked.

"What?" said Khay. "You think they're commenting on your haircut or something?"

Theodor laughed. "I have no idea. I can't translate them, or anything like that. Eventually, you just learn to feel it."

I almost said something, then stopped myself. What I was about to say was, *It feels like magic.* Because it did; being able to understand the animals and use their language to identify potential dangers on the road ahead. When I was back in the Opus, leaders would often use magic to commune with animals or reveal traps. Out here, in nature, with our Werewolf hunter leading the way, you could pretend, if you wanted to, that the Coda had never happened at all.

I followed Theodor's footsteps and listened to the song that the birds were singing about us like the fanfare that goes ahead of royalty before they enter town. While it was likely more of a warning to other creatures within the woods, I chose to think of it as a welcome, and I breathed the damp air deep into my lungs, becoming more confident of my footing with every step.

42

The Hunt

On Theodor's recommendation, we avoided the depths of the forest floor and made camp on the top of an old tree trunk whose branches splayed out in different directions, creating a kind of cradle in its center. The space wasn't perfectly level, but it was flat enough to put down our packs and sit comfortably to rest our feet.

I slapped a mosquito on the back of my hand, leaving a splatter of my own bright red blood.

"See this," said Theodor, pointing to a spiny, bulbous growth on an overhanging branch. "Go look for some more. Don't let them touch your skin – the toxin has an awful sting to it – but knock them into a bag and have them ready when I get back."

He gave Khay instructions on how to start a fire in the tree without setting the whole thing alight, and I searched for spiny balls while he went hunting.

It was cool in the woods, but the temperature hardly changed as night fell. I searched the nearby trees for more of those bluish, spiky growths, and used a stick to knock them into a canvas pack. Once the bag was full, I returned to the tree and found Khay over a small fire. Her gloves were off, and while she prodded the glowing embers with one hand, she held the other in front of her face, looking through it to the flames.

"Already?" I asked. "But you just . . . you know."

"Yeah, that's why I need more jewelry. The spell brings me back, but it doesn't last as long."

I sat down beside her and almost said some meaningless encouragement like "we'll be there soon" or "we'll get you that crown", but thought better of it.

"Do you think about death?" she asked.

For a change, I found it easy to be honest.

"All the time."

She nodded, like that made sense.

"What do you think about?"

"For a long time, I thought I wanted it. The release of it."

"And now?"

"Now . . . now I know it's coming. I meet it too often to forget it. Which means I have a limited amount of time to turn things around. My life, so far, has been one big mistake, so it's going to take something real big to even the score."

She looked at me – a curious expression on her face – then turned her attention back to the fire.

"You think about death?" I asked.

"Yeah. I'm terrified of it. Not because of the pain or what I think is waiting on the other side. I just don't want this to end. That's why I joined the Genie in the first place. I love every minute of being here. Being me. Curse or no curse, pre or post-Coda, I just . . . if I stop and just *feel*, I . . . I can become overwhelmed. On nothing. On the fact that we're here. That any of this exists. I mean, look at this place." Our eyes lifted up. The last beams of daylight blasted their way through the treetops, catching the thick, pollen-filled air in its golden fingers. Dropped leaves spiraled down around us, falling from the branches of prehistoric trees that had stood longer than some empires and had never done anything to hurt a single soul. They served the forest and its inhabitants in silence, without asking for so much as a thank-you. "The thought of this stopping, of losing it all . . . it breaks my heart."

The birds had gone quiet. Maybe they were listening too. If they were smart, they would have been.

"Look at that fire!" Theodor said proudly, as he landed back on the mighty stump with a sack of raspberries, mushrooms and hazelnuts, and a small furry creature that looked like a fat squirrel.

"You prepare the meal," he said, picking up the bag of spiky things, "and I'll take care of this. If anybody wants to use the bathroom in private, this is your last chance till morning."

While I gutted the squirrel and Khay chopped the vegetables, Theodor dipped the tip of his dagger into the first of those spiny growths stuck to the branch above our camp. When he removed the blade, a string of thick white liquid stretched between it and the cut in the fruit. As Theodor walked several paces away to wipe the dagger against the closest tree, the white string remained intact. He repeated the action, stretching another line of white alongside the first.

Soon, there was a fan of white spreading out from the growth in both directions, creating a netted wall on one side of our camp. Theodor stabbed another of the growths, lifted it out of the bag, wedged it into the fork of a tree on the other side, and repeated the process until we were surrounded by spiked balls and their web of stringy innards. I looked closer and saw that each string was covered in tiny tendrils. They were growing! Over time, they stretched long enough to reach a tendril from another string and latch themselves together.

"Theo, what is this stuff? It's creeping me out."

"A carnivorous plant we call spider-bush. At night, it seeps out the white liquid and waits for bugs to crawl over it. The concoction has a paralyzing effect, and in the morning, it sucks the liquid back in and devours its meal. No better bug protection anywhere in Archetellos."

When we sat down to eat – protected by Theodor's web, and eating the food that he'd single-handedly supplied – I found myself considering the skewered squirrel.

"How long does it take," I asked, "for the meat to leave your system, so that the prey won't smell your scent during a hunt?"

"Maybe a week," he replied, crunching into a hazelnut, "but as we're only hunting rodents right now, and we're such a small party, it isn't too much of a concern. Why? Would you like to try your hand?"

I looked over at the stolen longbow and was reminded of my ill-fated attempts to master it while being trained by the Opus.

"I'd like to watch, if that's all right with you. Maybe learn a few things."

He nodded, and I sensed the familiar pang of pride that came whenever a friend or mentor seemed pleased with me.

"Tomorrow night, then. We'll leave your bow for now, but you should try your hand at it when we find some space."

"Thank you." I looked down at my share of the meat – crispy, tender and dripping with fat – and halfheartedly pushed it away.

"Eat the bloody squirrel," growled Theodor. "It's not fair to let it go to waste. But tomorrow, we'll hunt for smaller game."

The meat was all the sweeter, knowing that it would be my last serving for a while. It felt like a good way to focus on the journey ahead. To solidify the seriousness of our mission. We were traveling through a wild forest to the city of Incava, to battle the Minotaur and steal the crown of the Wizard King. It sounded like something from a poem, and I dreamed that one day it would be.

The world was just starting to shake off the dark when I was jolted awake. Out there, somewhere, the sun was rising, but it struggled to penetrate the woods. Though the air was cold and damp, it was clean, and I woke feeling refreshed.

"We moving already?" I asked the Theodor-shaped shadow beside me.

"No. Let her sleep. I want to see what you remember." He handed me the bow and a single arrow. "Come on."

During the night, the tendrils of the spider-bush had continued to reach out and weave together, turning the web into a solid wall. I hadn't been disturbed by a single bug all night, but when Theodor sliced a hole in the white and we stepped outside, I saw that the exterior of the dome was painted black with flies and spiders of a dizzying variety and terrifying size.

Theodor led me through an archway of vines into a narrow clearing.

"That tree at the end is cork, so it won't damage the arrow when you fire into it. Let's see your draw. Don't shoot yet."

I set my feet in the way I remembered being taught, tensed my body to a position of military discipline, raised my bow arm, and drew the string.

"Ah, you're a good boy," said Theodor, though it certainly didn't sound like a compliment. I let the line go slack.

"What?"

"You're still trying to impress your teachers. It's all right, keep going." I drew again. "You're taller than the Satyr, so these arrows are too short for you to get a full draw. We'll need to make you some new ones."

"I'm never going to be a great archer. Can't we just make do?"

I felt his unblinking stare even though I couldn't see it.

"Whenever you learn anything, you must learn it the right way. Only then can you improve with practice. Only then can you ever hope to master it."

I kept the string drawn, already starting to shake.

"Theo, have you met me? I'll never master this anyway."

"But you want to get better, don't you? You want to be useful?"

"Well, yeah, but . . ."

"But what? You don't think you'll have the time? Your plan is to save the world in, what? A couple of weeks?"

"Well . . ." My fingers slipped and the arrow fired, missing the cork tree and glancing off a think pine instead.

"What happens after you save the world? You plan to just fade into dust as soon as someone makes a little magic again? You don't plan to grow old?"

That one stumped me.

"I haven't thought about it."

"You don't have to think about it, but don't treat it as an impossibility. You don't want to wake up one day with gray hair and sore bones, but no more knowledge than you have today. You're already past the point where ignorance is charming, and it becomes less attractive every year."

"Thanks, Theodor, but we both know I'm gonna step too far onto the wrong side of someone any day now. This will all be over soon, so I don't want you wasting your time."

"The world hasn't killed you yet, Mr Phillips. Maybe you should start building your days into weeks and months and years, instead of treating each of them like their own individual adventure, untethered from time. Draw again, don't fire."

I did as instructed: back straight, elbow high, hips tucked. I managed to hold the arrowhead against the bow without shaking at all; maybe I'd remembered more than I thought.

Theodor groaned.

"Blasted military men. Posture and position all dictated by how you look in a firing line, instead of what's effective. How's your off-handed draw?"

"Terrible, probably. I've never tried."

"Let's see it."

Somewhat dejected, I passed the bow into my right hand and strung the arrow with my left, already fumbling with the strangeness of it. When I pulled, I didn't have the strength to get a full draw, and the arrowhead swung away from the string.

"Much better," said Theo. "I can work with this."

"You're kidding."

"Unteaching bad habits takes as long as learning good ones. Nothing to unlearn on this side. It's a fresh start."

"But I'm so much weaker."

"Good. Then you can't use your strength to cheat. Your strength is different in the morning to what it is at night, but your shot must always be the same. You need to pull with your bones, not your muscles, if you want to be able to shoot in ten years, twenty, or more. You can pull with strength for a few good years, but you can pull correctly for a lifetime."

I heard his words, but I found it hard to be enthusiastic about them. The easiest thing would be to give me a few pointers on my right-handed draw and go from there. I just needed to be good enough to play along while he taught me his hunting techniques and all that useful stuff. After all, we had bigger things to worry about than perfecting my archery skills. But he'd made his speech, and he seemed so passionate about it, so I nodded and thanked him.

"I'll keep an eye out for the right tree to make you some new arrows," he said. "Olive might be nice." When we got back, the slice in the dome had reknitted itself, so Theodor cut our way back in. "Careful, the sap has paralyzing power. Always use your knife to move it."

Khay was awake, but more somber than she'd been the night before. She was thinner again; only a shade more transparent, but I'm sure she could feel the difference more than we could see it.

"How much longer?" she asked Theo.

"A week or so in the woods. Then we should come out right at the edge of the city."

She nodded. Surely not satisfied, but trying to come to terms with it. Time had flown by with the car beneath us. Now, the days would be longer, slower, and rely on constant effort if we wanted to make them count.

"Let's pick up the pace today," I offered. "I don't need to follow your footsteps so closely now, Theo. At the beginning, I couldn't tell the moss apart at all. Now the slippery stuff might as well be lit up with neon light. The soft dirt, too. Warn me about anything that I might miss, but we can afford to hurry along."

Khay gave an appreciative smile, and Theo seemed disposed

to the idea. We packed and balanced our packs and as soon as Theo started moving, I had to work hard to keep up, bouncing over rocks and constantly switching my hands between branches for support. It felt good. We had to make untold decisions every moment: how far was the step, how wet was the surface, how strong was the support, how sloped the rock, how decayed the tree. With my mind caught up in those questions, it had no space left for the usual second-guessing, overthinking and replaying of past blunders. It was, perhaps, the first real break I'd given my waking brain in years.

Theo picked up a long stick, cracked a couple of twigs from the end, and held it out in front of him. For the next hour, he swirled it around in circles, making shapes in the air as he walked. It reminded me of the way Wizards used to do spells: moving their fingers in the exact motions required to conjure magic. I deduced that Theo must have been performing some kind of spell of his own. Maybe a protection ward or a way of communicating with the spirits of the forest. That must be more superstition than magic these days, but if it made him feel safer it was fine by me.

"Shhh," warned Theo, holding up a hand. We stopped. Tensed. Beneath the sound of the birds, I heard the almost imperceptible sound of footsteps. Then, just ahead of us, a wolf with a healthy brown coat stepped onto the path. "Don't make eye contact," Theo whispered. "They see it as aggression. Or maybe an intent to mate, which will be even more worrying to them."

The whisper was heard by the wolf and it froze. I felt like he was looking in our direction, though I followed Theo's orders and kept my head down, only watching him from my periphery.

I moved a hand into my jacket, towards the pistol, but Theo shook his head.

"No," he said. Then his voice turned high, calm, and directed at the wolf. "We're just passing through. Is that all right with you?"

The wolf stepped back, slowly, and never took his eyes from us. Theodor barked, using the same non-confrontational tone that he'd spoken in, and the wolf growled in response.

"I don't speak his language," I whispered, "but that doesn't sound like welcoming."

Theodor barked again and stepped away from the animal, while still moving in the direction we were headed.

"He's just being cautious. Follow me slowly." He led us behind some small bushes, with the wolf watching us the whole way. "He just stumbled into our path. He's not hunting us. We have nothing he wants."

Sure enough, as soon as we had created enough distance, the canine bounced away in the opposite direction, and Khay and I gasped our first full breath in over a minute.

Theo pointed to the spot under my arm where the gun was holstered.

"That should only ever be a last resort," he said, without laying the admonishment on too thick. "That python was lying in wait, and would have no problem attacking creatures our size, but most animals just want to know you're not here to hurt them. They'll usually only attack if they see you as a threat."

"Copy that. Sorry."

"No apologies needed. We learn as we go."

He checked his compass and went to move on.

"One second," said Khay. "Look at your breath."

All of us were puffing out clouds of mist, and, now that I'd stopped, the sweat on my forehead started to chill.

"How is this happening?" she asked.

"We've been moving downhill, ever so slightly, all day," replied Theo. "This forest fills a valley, and we must be reaching the bottom. We should keep moving. Don't want to freeze up."

We took off, falling immediately back into our rhythm, but after a couple of minutes, Theo stopped again.

"Hmm. This is something I've never seen before."

He cut through a couple of overgrown vines and stepped one of his boots out onto a patch of snow.

"Where did this come from?" asked Khay. Neither of us answered. We stepped into the clearing, frost beneath our feet, and looked around in wonder. The circle of trees at the edge of the clearing had ice running down their trunks and frozen drips dangling from their branches.

"Is it just because of the valley?" I asked. "Has it been too cold down here to melt it?"

"Since the middle of winter?" Khay bent down, grabbed some snow, and let it run through her fingers. "That would mean it has been here for months, but this feels . . . fresh."

"No tracks. No dirt." Theodor scraped at the snow with his knife, treating it with the same caution he'd used with the spider-bush. "It's not natural."

We all stepped back onto the dry, warm forest floor.

"Listen," said Khay. We all did. I gasped.

"The birds. They're silent."

Since we'd entered the woods, it had never been so quiet. *Beyond* quiet. It was a silence so loud it chilled my bones more than the unnatural pocket of ice.

"Let's go," said Khay. "I don't like it."

Neither of us argued. We stepped away from the cold spot and, after a few minutes, our breath turned clear, and the birds went back to singing their songs. I knew the sounds so well by now that I could have filled in as a replacement if one of them came down sick.

But I felt unsettled, and the others clearly did too. We moved swiftly, but without the ease that we'd found that morning. There was a moment when, for the first time, Theodor lost his footing. It was only momentary – just one foot sliding a few inches on loose dirt – but it was such a new phenomenon that Khay and I looked at each other in shock as soon as it happened. It worried me as much as the snowy clearing had. Hell, more. Theodor could have told us anything about that snow and we would have believed it: that some trees use so much energy to grow that they freeze the air around them, or that it wasn't actually snow but some kind of pollen from a snowberry tree or some shit. Khay and I would have marveled at his explanation for a few minutes, then kept on moving. It was Theodor's reaction that had put us on edge. Theodor knew the forest, but he did not know this, so it made me more nervous than anything we'd encountered yet.

43

When Nightmares Come

"It's not a pause," said Theo, "it's a held note. In the moment between the pull and the release, you must check your aim, your balance and your intention. This moment is created out of the actions on either side of it. You must bind the entire movement with a single purpose. If you pause, lose focus or change your target, the entire action is diminished. It is one act made of many parts. The first part is the turning of the shoulder. That's what we will practice today."

"What? Like, *all* day?"

"Yes, and this is an expedited lesson because I know you are impatient. Good shoulder technique should take weeks of work."

"Right," I said, unconvinced, but I rolled my left shoulder the way he'd shown me.

"Good. Leave the bow here and keep practicing that while we head out for the hunt."

"How are we supposed to hunt without the bow?"

Theodor, often so serious, grinned mischievously and wagged his tail.

"Today, we're catching pelogliders."

"There's only one technique I know of to catch them," said Theodor quietly, "and it requires at least two strong hands."

He gave me the two largest of his knives, and unhooked a weapon from his back: a wooden stick with a heavy ball carved into the end. He gave it a couple of practice swings, stretched his good arm, and we ventured out.

"Pelogliders hide between the bark and trunk of syrup-producing trees, eating insects and drinking the nectar," he whispered, licking his lips, "that's why their meat is so sweet."

A little way down the path, he stopped. I thought he must have spotted something, until he then turned his attention to me.

"Look," he said, "you're not in Sunder anymore."

"Uh . . . yeah, thanks for pointing that out."

"You still walk like you're trying to pick a fight. It's scaring the birds."

I scoffed. There was some kind of thrush in our path, and I gestured to it.

"You think he cares about my—" The thrush shot away, chirping madly.

"Yes, he cares about how you walk. How you hold your shoulders. He cares about your footfall and your eyeline. If they see us as predators, they'll warn the other animals. The message will go out minutes ahead of us and we'll never have a chance to see what creatures inhabit the area. You must move like a herbivore. Like a disinterested, lazy, but respectful part of the forest. That's why we don't walk in a straight line. We meander. We move around obstacles, not trample over them. Understand?"

I nodded. It seemed like superstition, but, as we went forward, I forced the aggressive posture out of my body; the stance that kept me safe in dark alleys and stopped pickpockets and muggers from trying their luck. As I did, the forest responded. The birdsong dropped down to a relaxed, conversational exchange, like we'd walked into a dinner party of polite acquaintances. I heard more noises above: not just the birds, but the clicks and purrs of other creatures too camouflaged to see. The frogs and crickets that usually quieted before we got too close now continued their strange calls uninterrupted.

Theodor held up a hand. I couldn't see anything of note on the forest floor, but he followed the trail like it was drawn on a map.

He pointed to a tree, stepped forward, soundlessly, and cocked his ear to the trunk. He moved up and down and around, until that same mischievous grin crept up his face. When he beckoned me closer, I put my ear to the same spot.

There was a crunching sound. A scratching. Theodor nodded enthusiastically and mimed what I was supposed to do: he held both hands over his head, and brought them down, almost touching the bark in two places right above the spot where the noise was coming from. Then he made a ripping motion, pulling his hands back towards him.

I thought that I had the idea, so I stepped up to the striking spot, lifted the knives, took a deep breath, and stabbed them down into the tree.

"PULL!" yelled Theo, and I did, tearing off a chunk of the thick bark.

The piece wasn't big enough. I looked down into the hole and saw two beady yellow eyes stare back at me, before vanishing in a flash of fur.

"Shit," I said, and put the knife back in the hole to tear more of the bark away. Theodor put a hand on my back.

"Leave it," he said. "It's gone."

"No, we can get it. I can keep cutting."

"If you do that, you'll kill the tree. No. We'll take our time and try again."

"Sorry. I screwed that up."

"First time. No bother."

We left the little peloglider to scurry around inside the bark, and moved off. It took twenty minutes for Theodor to find another trail and set me back in position, knives raised, thinking carefully about the best striking angle to get the most leverage on the bark.

I leaned down to listen to the location of the creature, checked my stance, had a couple of test swings, then THWACK! As soon as the knives went in, I pulled and stepped back, ripping off a sizable square of bark that fell to the floor with the peloglider still gripped to the inside. The creature was a bundle of fur with leather wings tucked into its sides and two yellow eyes staring out in panic. Theo wasted no time. He stepped up and readied his stick for an underarm arc. The little bug-eyed creature looked so cute and so vulnerable that I felt a little sick. As a man who had put away enough bacon and sausage to fill a dozen farmyards, I knew that I was in no position to judge Theo's actions, but I couldn't help hoping that he'd stop.

Miraculously, he did.

"Don't. Move."

He was staring past my body with an intensity I'd never seen in his face before. I was about to ask him what he was looking at, when I heard a growl that sent sparks through my nervous system.

Theo growled back, curling his lips to expose his back teeth.

"I thought we weren't supposed to make eye contact," I stammered.

"That's when we just cross their path. This one already wants a fight. When I say go, I want you to turn, stand on your toes, put your hands over your head and clap and scream. All right?"

I was a hell of a lot closer to the thing than he was, so I didn't much like the idea of provoking it.

"Theo, I'm not—"

"GO!"

He stepped forward and barked, loud and aggressive, waving his hand over his head. I turned, clapped my hands over my head, and yelped out a manic squawk.

It was fucking huge. A mangy, gray dog with only one ear, barely three feet behind me. Hackles like jagged glass and thick spittle dripping from its jaw. The patches of furless skin under its neck and belly looked irritated and sore.

My voice cracked, but I clapped faster, sure that there couldn't be anything less intimidating than me giving an awkward applause while I was popped up on my tippy-toes, screeching like an alley cat on heat.

But Theo stood beside me, and the wolf looked between us, backed away, and bolted.

I swallowed, pushing my heart and balls out of my throat and back into my body, shaking like a wagon with loose screws. I heard the high-pitched laughter before I realized that it was coming from my own mouth.

"You all right?" asked Theo, with genuine concern.

"I am now. Just surprised. I was starting to feel at home in the woods. Safe."

"That wolf wasn't well. Some disease or injury has slowed him down. Probably can't catch his prey, so he's starving and desperate."

"He wanted to eat us?"

"Maybe, if we hadn't stood up to him. But he was likely after the peloglider."

I looked around.

"Oh, damn. Where did it go?"

"Scurried off in the commotion. It's all right. Another time. We'd best get back before it gets too dark."

Slap.

I was woken up by my own hand hitting myself in the face. There was enough moonlight to see the bits of squished bug on my fingers, the hole ripped in the spider-bush covering, and the fact that Khay wasn't there.

I got up.

"Theo." His eyes snapped open. "Khay's gone."

He immediately sprang to his feet.

"One of my knives is missing," he said. I moved to the gap in the white wall. "Put your boots on and grab your weapon. We don't know what's out there."

He took his other blades and I took the bow. Moving through the spider-bush, I brushed against the sap and it stuck to my jacket. As I pulled away, it stretched with me, and found more purchase every time I tried to twist out of it.

"Stop moving," said Theo. He cut me loose and used a stick to scrape the tendrils from his knife.

It was that awkward kind of darkness – top-lit by the full moon – where you could see just enough detail for your mind to fill in the gaps. Every tree looked like a standing figure and every bush like a snarling wolf. I didn't know whether to call out for Khay or remain quiet; it all depended on what had happened to her.

"What do we do?" I asked Theo.

"Shhh." He had his head turned to the side and an ear cocked. "Hear that?" The rustling of leaves. Scratching. "This way."

I followed his lead, as usual, letting his canine eyes find the path through the dangling leaves and fresh spiderwebs, toward the sound of frantic scrambling. I heard whimpers too. A pained cry. We moved faster.

Theodor broke through the foliage into a clearing. Khay was there, kneeling in front of a wide, vine-wrapped tree, slicing away the creepers and tearing them from the trunk. She was covered in dirt, with tears on her face and a cut on her hand that had smeared her skin with blood.

"Khay, what are you doing?"

She ignored me, digging deeper into the tree as if searching for something. She tore leaves and wet bark from behind the vines, cut through thin branches and wayward roots, muttering unintelligibly the whole time.

I looked at Theo. Lost.

"THERE!" Khay screamed and jumped back.

She sat, panting, and pointed at the hole she'd carved into the pillar. Carefully, I leaned down and looked in. It was so dark. I lifted up my lighter and flicked it on.

"Shit!" I stumbled back, tripped over, and fell beside Khay on the grass.

Amari.

No. But it looked just like her. Almost.

It was another Forest Sprite. A Fae who had been petrified when the Coda happened. She'd been left alone in the woods with her body growing out of control. Amari, when she was still in her frozen Fae body, had me to take care of her. To trim back the weeds. To get rid of the moss and the mites. To protect her. This Fae had been stuck here, alone, slowly overtaken by her own power.

Theodor looked into the hole, then back at us. Confused, I imagine, by my reaction and to Khay's knowledge that there had been the body of a Fae tucked inside the tree.

"How did you know?" asked Theodor.

"I could see her. I could see her face. Not in this world, but . . . in the other." She held her hand in front of Theodor's light and I could see her bones through her skin, the veins and arteries beneath her flesh. "I'm fading."

"We'll move faster," I said. "We'll get you the crown."

She turned her hand around, looking through it, then her eyes shifted out into the darkness, staring at things that neither Theodor nor I could see.

"Come on," said Theo. "Let's go back to camp."

She nodded, and we slowly walked back to base and slipped through the spider-bush. I linked the lines of sap up again, and we all lay down, but I didn't feel much like sleeping.

"Fuck," said Khay.

"What?" I asked.

"I can see through my eyelids." She pulled her hood down over her face and wrapped her robes and blanket tight around her. "Fetch, can you come here? My bones feel cold."

I slid next to her and put my blanket over both of us. Then, I put an arm around her, and pressed my chest against her back.

"Better?" I asked.

"Better."

44

Interruption

After Khay's freak-out, we should have woken up early and headed off to save her life with more determination than ever. Instead, we were all sluggish to get started. None of us had gotten much sleep, and we all had bug bites on our faces.

We didn't bother with my morning archery lessons, just packed our things and started walking. It got cold again, and we stumbled upon another field of snow. Khay stopped and looked down at it.

"That's another one of them," she said to me.

"Another Fae?"

"Similar."

"I guess that explains it," said Theodor, still walking. "An Ice Sprite."

"Don't!" Khay shouted, her face struck with the panicked expression she'd worn the night before. "You have to go around."

Theodor looked at the snow under his feet.

"Of course. I apologize."

We went around the icy area, and I thought I too could see the outline of the frozen body beneath the snow; some other miraculous creature cut down in the Coda, their old powers seeping out from beyond the grave.

"We need to go," said Khay, her hood pulled low across her face. "We need to get out of here. The forest has fingers. It has thoughts. You don't sleep on the corpses of gods."

She wasn't talking to me, it seemed. To herself. To her hands. I quickened my pace and caught up to Theo.

"How much longer till we're out of here?"

"Days."

"What if we just go east or west? Just clear the forest and go around?"

"Then it will take longer to reach Incava."

"She sees things that we can't. Maybe she knows something we don't."

"This forest is dangerous, but it has no malevolence, no will of its own. If we respect it, it will respect us, and we will get out of here. Safe. Soon."

I looked back at Khay – her eyes flicking furtively in all directions – and I wanted to tell Theodor he was wrong. Just because he knew how to navigate the forest, he thought that he was master of this place, but Khay was walking between worlds, one foot on the other side of existence. The stronger her conviction that we needed to leave here, the more I believed her.

We collected food as we walked so that we wouldn't have to go hunting. We found nuts and berries and a large, savory fruit that Theodor told us was good for energy. It started raining, so we made camp under a thick part of the canopy. The raindrops put holes in the spider-bush but also quieted down the bugs.

"You know you don't have to follow me," said Theodor at dinner, seemingly out of nowhere. "In fact, you probably shouldn't."

I wiped juice from my chin.

"What do you mean?"

"I know I come across as some kind of expert, but I'm not. I have some skills, and a little experience, but I've made as many mistakes as anyone. You can listen to me if you like, but you don't have to do as I say."

"But you make so much sense," I said. Theo didn't respond. He just shelled his serving of hazelnuts with his good hand, and put an extra dose of seriousness into his already serious expression.

"I take the role too lightly," he growled. "I get caught up in my own ideas and forget what's at stake. We could have died in that car crash. We could still die out here. I ask you to take risks, and I have no right."

"This is our screwball plan, not yours. I'm sorry that decisions keep falling on your head, but that's the burden you bear for being someone worth listening to." He chewed his cold dinner, and his spirits didn't lift in the slightest.

Khay pushed away her food.

"Something wrong?" Theo asked her, shaking off the heaviest layer of his dark mood.

"I can't taste it," she explained. "You two can have my share."

It was quiet for a while, so I finally asked Theodor the question I'd been wondering about for days.

"Theo, what are you doing with that stick? Those shapes you're making in the air, are they an enchantment? Some kind of protection?"

Theo stared at me. Blinked a few times. Then I saw an unintended smile creep up his face before he managed to swallow it.

"I'm clearing spiderwebs," he said, doing his best not to sound too condescending. "You don't know you've walked into them until it's too late. I hate spiders."

"Oh," I said.

Khay burst out laughing.

When I got into my bedroll, Khay curled up against me without saying a word. Even though she was all wrapped up in her robes, with both our blankets and my body heat, I woke several times to feel her shaking. I held her tighter and, either consciously or in her sleep, she moved her body into mine, sighed and, after a while, the shaking stopped.

So many years trying to work out ways to help people. I'd dished out countless punches and taken many more in return. I'd sacrificed friends, bronze, and my body to the cause. I'd embarrassed myself a million times over, and given up any chance of having peace, love or a long life. All that effort. All those earnest actions. And for what? For next to nothing. Most of the time, to leave things worse off than if I'd never got involved. But here, without a word, without a tensed muscle or an ounce of pain, I brought someone comfort with the simple act of being by their side.

Khay disturbed my sleep, occasionally, but I dropped back into slumber more easily with her there. When I did sleep, it was deeper than those nights when I'd used half a bottle of whiskey to send me on my way.

If only I'd been a little more restless.

There are plenty of bad ways to wake up, and I've ticked off most of them.

Back in Weatherly, I remember advertisements for toasters that pictured a well-groomed man sitting up in bed as his doting wife delivered a full breakfast onto his lap. I've read books that feature a young woman roused by the lips of her lover. I've never had anything like that. I get glasses of water thrown in my face or goons dragging me out of bed by my legs. There have been countless hangovers with unremembered origins and even worse remembered ones.

Being dunked into a river had taken top spot until that night in the woods, when I woke up to a gag being shoved into my mouth, and hands holding down my feet and arms.

Pre-dawn light barely illuminated the bearded faces above me. My mouth was full of cloth and I snorted snotty, desperate breaths out of my nose.

I was snatched up off the ground, every one of my limbs in the hands of some brute. I attempted to kick myself free – which was never going to happen – but managed to turn my head. Theodor was in much the same position that I was in but fighting harder and getting a few punches for his trouble, and Khay . . . Khay was nowhere to be seen. Perhaps she'd already been taken away.

A punch to my stomach slowed my struggling. Hands reached into my pockets, took my knife and my knuckles, and grabbed the machine from its holster. Rope was wrapped around my wrists and ankles, and whenever I resisted, another strike made me reconsider resisting again.

My head tipped back. In my upside-down view of the world, I saw Theodor take more hits from our seven-foot assailants as they hogtied him and dragged him by his legs. We were outnumbered and overwhelmed, but perhaps Khay had gotten away. That was something. I stopped fighting and let them carry me deeper into the woods.

45

The Scrappers

"This is quite convenient, ain't it, fellas? Products are delivering themselves right to our door."

He was more beard than man: a hulking mass of hair and flesh with a double-edged axe in his gigantic hands, covered all over in crimson leather armor. He was an Amalgam – half Orc and half Elf – but the biggest Amalgam I'd ever seen. Over the top of his bushy black mustache, he had the full cheeks and twinkling eyes of a kindly grandfather, which only made the situation more unsettling.

I was on my knees with Theodor beside me. His head was bleeding, and his bung arm was out of its sling and tied to the other. It was the only part of his body not covered by black fur, just smooth human skin over shrunken muscles.

The big man was flanked by half a dozen other woodsmen, all wearing the same red shoulder-pads and breastplates. A couple were smaller than him, Humans; then there were a few burly Half-Ogres and another Amalgam who was the biggest of the lot. It was like facing down a family of monsters made from the offcuts of a butcher and the sweepings of a barbershop floor.

The ground had been cleared of trees and rocks and filled with rows of canvas tents. Crates had been stacked around the edge of the camp like a half-assed barricade. Several automobiles were sitting at the back, but the pile of scrap metal suggested that there had once been many more.

The big man pulled the gag from my mouth with his fat fingers.

"You from Mortales, are ya? Come out here to try and get your goods back?"

"We're not with Mortales," I grunted. "Not with anyone."

"Then what *are* you doing?" I didn't want to mention Khay, which meant that I had no good answer. He didn't wait for me to make one up. "And if you're not with Mortales, then how do you have this?" He pulled my pistol from his duster. It looked small in his hands. He held it sideways, gripping it across the barrel, like he didn't know what to do with it. "We haven't seen one of these before. You must be real special to be carrying something we ain't seen yet. So, what is it?"

His voice was friendly, and his eyes were warm, but there was no way to ignore the threat of deadly violence in every question. If he didn't know what the machine was, it felt like a really bad idea to tell him.

"It's . . . it's nothing. Just a . . . a tool. A prototype."

"A pro-to-type?" He sounded the word out, mockingly, as if I'd spouted some highfalutin jargon from the upper class. "Well, we don't know what that is, and you're not being the most helpful of fellows, but I reckon we can work it out on our own."

He twirled the pistol around, looking at it from all sides. When his finger brushed over the trigger, Theo flinched a little, but the big man didn't seem to notice. He looked at me down his nose and gave me another of those dangerous grins.

"I worked it out," he declared proudly. "It's a pipe, isn't it? A sort of automatic smoking device. Ha! And you didn't want to share your treats with the rest of us. After all our hospitality." The other big men chuckled. "Now, I suppose this goes in here . . ." He turned the pistol upside down and put the end of the barrel in his lips. "And I bet this," he mumbled, mouth full of metal, "is how you light it."

He squinted down at the pistol, barrel in his mouth. Then he put his hand around the butt and rested his finger on the trigger.

Theodor looked sideways at me. If this happened the way it

looked like it was going to, we'd have to move quick to get a jump on the others.

The big man breathed out in anticipation of a big breath in, then put his eyes on me; his lips locked in place and his finger primed to flick the switch.

Then . . . he winked.

All the men burst out laughing, the big man hardest of all.

"You were gonna let me do it! You little shit!" He punched me, hard, and the left side of my head hit the dirt. "Oh, we know what these bloody boom-sticks are. We've been nabbing crateloads of them every week for the last year. We don't like them much, though." He threw the pistol off into the bushes like it was a leftover bone from dinner. "We prefer the kind of weapons that take a real man to swing 'em." He dropped the axe in the dirt, right by my head. It landed with a dull thump, the sharp blade sticking it in place. "Ammoth, take the Dog-man. I don't think they've had one of these yet." One of the smaller big men – a blond-haired bastard – grabbed Theodor by his collar and heaved him away towards the far side of the camp where all the cars were. Three of the others followed him, leaving two with me. "And make sure you get paid proper this time!"

"Theo!" I called out, unable to do anything else, and the big man with the twinkling eyes pulled me back onto my knees.

"So, tell me, truthfully, what you're doing in my woods."

My head hurt, inside and out. I racked my brain for a convincing story.

WHACK!

He hit me again. Same spot. The same patch of wet dirt caught the same side of my face, and I felt the same jerk to my neck as he dragged me back up.

"Why are you here?" he repeated.

I was dazed. Scared. Too rattled to come up with a good lie, and the more time I took to answer, the longer the others would have to take Theo wherever they were taking him.

He raised his hand to hit me again.

"To steal the crown of the Wizard King."

The creases around his eyes deepened. He laughed. The men around him laughed too.

"Now that is ballsy. Very bloody ballsy. And why would you want to do that?"

I only paused for a moment before he hit me again. The other side. Dirt painted the other half of my face, completing the picture. He dragged me up.

"Thanks for evening me out," I said.

"Don't be a smart ass or I'll start taking teeth. Why do you want the crown? And I want the truth straight out of your mouth, right now, or I get the pliers."

Fuck it.

"Because I'm working for a Genie who wants to get her hands on it. She thinks it will bring her powers back. Then she can use those powers to heal the magic creatures who are dying without them."

He sat back for a bit.

"If you made that up, I'm quite impressed. If you didn't, I might be even more impressed. What's your plan for getting the crown? Attacking the Wizards head-on?"

"We haven't thought that far ahead."

"Hmmm." He reached through his wiry beard hairs to scratch his chin. "You're ready for a fight if it comes to it, aren't you? You'll kill them if need be?"

He seemed so amiable, I couldn't tell what answer he was hoping for. Maybe these woodsmen had a problem with the Wizards. Maybe they wanted allies to help them attack the city. Maybe we had a way out after all.

"Uh, I guess so."

He clicked his tongue, like I'd failed the test.

"Here's the thing, city boy: we've got a deal going with those Wizards. We deliver them magical creatures to experiment on.

Sell them the machines we steal from Mortales trucks too. It's a good little business, it is. So, the idea of you running in with your bows and arrows and boom-sticks isn't something we like the sound of, do we, Chappa?"

The other, bald woodsman shook his head.

Shit.

"Good thing we found you when we did. Would have hated you to stumble into Incava and kill our best customers. You could have made a real mess of our operation."

A cold, cruel chuckle came from the woodsmen. The other one's smile lacked the humor of his leader; just the dead-eyed grin of a man who'd long ago stopped worrying about what was right and wrong.

"But that doesn't mean we're single-minded brutes. We know how to pivot our enterprise when the right opportunity presents itself. So . . ." He grabbed my face in his hands, and they stank of blood and shit. "Where's this Genie of yours? Sounds like a power that could be worth a little something. *If* you're telling the truth."

An engine roared and headlights lit up the trees at the other end of the camp. They were taking Theodor away, and I had no chance of slowing them down. But Khay must have escaped the camp before they found us. If Theo was kidnapped and I was about to be dead, I wasn't going to let them know that she was somewhere in these woods.

"Sunder City," I said. "That's where I came from. She's waiting there for me to bring the crown back to her."

The leader looked to the bald man, a disappointed expression on his face.

"Sunder? Well, I can't be fucked going that far. Not for a silly story like this. Anything else you want to ask? I reckon we're done."

I didn't like the way he said that. The finality to it. There was only the two of them near me now – the leader and the bald one – so I wouldn't get a better chance than this.

I sprung forward and drove the top of my head into the big man's face. He howled in pain, which made me feel better about the fact that it had also hurt me a whole lot. With my ankles and wrists still tied, it was impossible to get my balance in the wet mud. The hairy one kicked me in the stomach and knocked me onto my back. The big one was laughing again, blood all over his face.

"You city slickers have some guts in you after all! Why don't we take a look at them?"

There was a CRACK from the bushes, and the side of the bald one's head exploded. His body fell to the ground with a loud thud. The leader spun on the spot, searching in the dark.

"You crafty bastards. Who's out ther—"

He took the hit to the chest and fell backwards. I spun around on my ass, lifted my feet, and pushed the rope that tied them against the blade of the great axe. It was sharp enough to cut through after a little sawing.

The leader groaned, eyes open, staring up at me. His duster and heavy build must have slowed the bullet, and he looked as if he might still be able to recover. I didn't wait to give him a chance. I grabbed the handle of the axe in my bound hands and yanked it from the dirt. It was damn heavy, but I swung it back and found the momentum to lift it overhead.

The big man saw it coming and rolled out of the way, screaming in pain. He was hurt but he still had some fight in him. My second swing was an underarm attack and, though he rolled away, it hit him across the shoulder, slicing deep enough to make blood gush from a cut in his duster. He howled again, and Khay stepped out of the bushes with my pistol aimed at his head.

"NO!" I yelled. She looked at me, surprised. "It's our last bullet. Save it."

I lifted the axe in the air, held it until I was sure the strike would connect, then brought it down hard, across his jaw, cracking the big man's face in half.

Khay fired. I turned to see another hairy woodsman drop, blood gushing from a hole in his throat. The car had taken off, but not all of the woodsmen had left because there was shouting and movement in the shadows at the other end of the camp.

Khay dropped the gun. I dragged the axe from its bed of blood, flesh and teeth, knowing that I'd be too slow to wield it against anyone who wasn't already injured. Then Khay called out.

"Our stuff! Here!" I took my brass knuckles and my bow from the pile. The arrows were apparently too short, and I hadn't done enough practice, but we were all out of ammo so I didn't have much choice. I certainly didn't feel comfortable shooting with my left hand like Theo wanted, so I set myself up in my clumsy right-handed style and moved forward. Khay gripped her two knives; the blades pointing behind her as the remaining woodsmen approached.

The size of the two men made them easy targets. Khay moved away from me, circling to the left. I pulled the bow string, steadied my breath as best I could, and fired.

The arrow lodged in the chest of the biggest one, but his flesh was so thick that it barely bothered him. I nocked another arrow, pulled in panic and shot wide.

I fumbled the next arrow as the huge man charged, an already bloodied short sword in his grasp. There was no time to aim and fire, so I threw the bow at him instead. It never would have hurt him, but it distracted him long enough for Khay to jump onto his back and drive a knife into his neck.

She kept it embedded in his flesh, and used it as an anchor point, while she stabbed him over and over with her other hand. He was surprised for a moment, dead the next; his head dangling from his neck as he collapsed to the ground.

The final woodsman, a slow but sturdy Half-Ogre with a severe underbite, charged at her undefended back, swinging a hammer that was made for bashing brains, not nails.

I grabbed the short sword – still heavy, but easier to wield than the axe — and intercepted him with a slash that didn't hit, but gave Khay time to tear the daggers from her victim and spin around.

"Spread out," she said.

The woodsman snarled like an animal, trying to keep an eye on both sides as we flanked him. The flat end of his weapon was mean enough, but the hooked spike on the other side made me shiver as it caught the moonlight, swinging back and forth; a lethal pendulum counting down to the attack. With his long arms, his reach was greater than mine or Khay's. One good hit would take either of us out and, if that happened, the other would surely follow.

I glanced back towards the discarded bow, and as soon as my eyes looked away, the woodsman used his advantage. He stepped forward and swung the hammer in a wide arc. I stumbled back and felt the whoosh of air as it passed my chest. He pivoted and went into a backhand that anticipated Khay's attack. She ducked, messily, but just in time, then scurried away as the woodsman closed in. The hammer swung, missed, but left her no time or space to respond. If I didn't move, he'd have her on the next swing.

As soon as I stepped forward, he kicked me hard in the chest and sent me tumbling. Without a moment's pause, he closed in on Khay who had her back against a tent. I rolled onto my feet and screamed as I ran, demanding his attention. I committed to the charge with so much forward momentum that I wouldn't be able to retreat from this attack: it was duck, block or die.

The hammer came around in a horizontal sweep. I fell to my knees, deflected it with the sword, and it passed over my head. The force of the hit slowed both of us, but it gave Khay the moment she needed to get back on her feet.

I lashed out at his legs. He jumped back, raised the hammer, and brought it straight down. I skidded to the side, got my front foot under me, and kicked myself back to standing. I hadn't managed to touch him, but Khay had got herself off the ground, so I chose to count that as a win.

I moved the grip of the sword around in my hands. There was so much blood and dirt on my fingers that it never felt comfortable. Khay looked exhausted. Hell, she was struggling to get through the night even before the burly men tried to cut her into pieces. We both shuffled on the balls of our feet as the woodsman looked between us, deciding which dessert to eat first.

"Together?" I asked.

"Sure," said Khay. Then, rapidly, "Three, two, one, go."

I hoped that my attack would force him to defend himself, but he was more interested in getting his swift revenge. He stepped backwards but, rather than blocking, he swung out. It was another backhand, meaning that I was first in the line of fire. The hammer struck me in the shoulder before my blade could find his chest, twisting my body and sending my back to the ground.

His boot, as heavy as if it had been full of Hyluna rocks, landed on my already pained arm. I was pinned, but I'd served my purpose, because Khay plunged both knives into his chest. The Amalgam dropped his hammer and grabbed at Khay. He pulled the hood from her head and, finding no hair to grab onto, clasped her skull so tight that he made her scream.

He screamed too. Pain from his various wounds and the sizzling burn of having his palms against Khay's bare skin. He would die, soon, but he was set on taking Khay out with him.

I leaned forward and plunged the sword into the woodsman's side, where it slipped beneath his ribs and into his bowels. I twisted. The villain coughed blood onto Khay as he let her go, spluttering and gasping.

He collapsed. Khay was on top of him, whispering, "Not yet, you fucker," as she put both her hands around his throat, hoping to grant him a dying wish that would bring her back from the fade, but it was too late. "Shit."

We fell onto the blood-soaked dirt beside each other, listening to our heaving breaths and the trickle of blood as it hit the ground.

"You all right?" I asked.

Khay coughed, gave a pained groan, and nodded.

"I think so."

"Good. Because we need to get moving."

46

And Then There Were Two

There was only the waxing moonlight and a couple of lanterns around the camp, but it was enough to search the cars and see that none of the ones remaining were in any state to take us anywhere. They were all busted up: either damaged when they were stolen or broken down for parts. The whole camp was full of scrap and other stolen cargo, some of it being turned into bizarre contraptions that were beyond my comprehension.

"So, what do we do?" asked Khay. "We'll never catch up with them on foot."

"They're taking him to the castle. Apparently, the Wizards perform experiments on magical creatures. So, we keep going. Fast."

She nodded, but I saw the exhaustion in her face.

"All right," I said. "Lie down for a bit. No use marching off till dawn. I'll check the place out, see if there's anything useful."

I counted the tents around the camp. There were at least ten of them, and we'd only killed five woodsmen. That must mean that there were others, maybe close enough to have heard the shots.

"Fetch, you need to rest too."

"I will. Later. This place probably isn't safe. You sleep, and I'll keep watch for a while."

She went into the closest tent. I picked up my pistol and put it back in its holster, then opened up the crates. Most of them were full of appliances: toasters, hairdryers, heaters, and stuff like that. All stolen from the back of Mortales trucks. One had quite a bit of ammo in it, so I loaded the chambers of the gun and filled my pockets with so many bullets that when I walked I jangled as much as Khay did.

Theodor's belt was with our belongings, and it held three beautiful daggers in leather sheathes. I wrapped the belt around my waist and searched the tents, where I found a few lighters and a traveling lamp. There was a vat of red dye where they clearly stained their signature armor. Most of the weapons were too big for either of us to wield effectively, but despite the leader's proclamations about not using the guns, I found a selection of firearms that rivaled anything we had in Sunder.

I picked out one for Khay and, to my surprise, it held six bullets. If I'd been smart, I would have swapped my three-shooter for one of the newer models, but I always was sentimental about the stupidest things. There were arrows. Longer that my last ones, just like Theodor had wanted. I'd been looking forward to having Theo teach me how to make them. How to find the right trees, select and prepare the branches, and shape the arrow heads. I'd learned a lot from our guide in such a short time, and wondered if he'd ever have the chance to teach me anything again. Not if we didn't save him, he wouldn't. I filled my quiver and kept searching the camp until the eastern sky turned pale gold, with the first hint of dawn coming over the hills. I went into Khay's tent and put a tankard of water and the new pistol down beside her.

"Time to get moving."

Her eyes blinked open. She looked up. Smiled. Maybe she'd been dreaming about some other kind of adventure, far away from here.

"I know it's early, but it's not safe to stay, and we need to get to Incava before you fade."

She bit the fingertip of one of her gloves and pulled it off. When she held up her hand, the morning light filled her translucent flesh.

"It's all right," I said. "We'll get the crown. We'll get Theo. We'll get you sorted out."

She nodded sleepily and smiled. "You're all glittery."

"What?"

She slapped me on my ass, and a cloud of shiny color billowed out of my trousers.

"Oh, must have leaned on something in one of the workshops."

"It suits you."

We took what we could carry back to our old camp, packed the best mix of our old equipment and new loot, then headed off in the direction of the rising sun.

"I thought there were no roads to Incava."

I'd unfolded one of Eileen's maps and taken out a compass. Though I wasn't adept at reading them, it was clear that the wide path leading out the back of the woodsmen's camp went in the direction of the Wizard city.

"Not before the Coda," said Khay. "But if they can't fly in and out, they'll have had to adapt. This must be the way they took Theo."

The path was all dirt and dead leaves, flattened by feet and wheels in a perfectly straight line.

"We can follow the road, but we should do it from a distance. It's too exposed."

"That'll slow us down," she warned.

"Yeah, but that camp was home to more men than the ones we took care of. If any more of them are out there, we want to see them before they see us."

She nodded, but I saw her reluctance. She was impatient to get to our destination, and so she took off through the woods at a cracking pace, moving through the scrub in a path that was parallel to the road but covered by branches.

Though Theodor was gone, his lessons remained, and I didn't need to think too hard about where I placed my feet or which path to take. Until a few hours into the day, when my lack of sleep caught up with me.

"Shit." My foot caught an exposed root and I fell onto my bruised knees and cut hands. "Goddamnit."

"You okay?"

I dusted myself off and gathered my weapons, but there was no hiding the fact that I was feeling woozy.

"Yeah. Just . . . just lost my footing."

I managed another hour, until a stumble left a rough graze on the palm of my left hand.

"Fetch, you're dead on your feet. Let's stop for the night."

"No. We can keep going. I'll just—"

She clamped her gloved hands on the sides of my head and put her face in front of mine.

"Listen. You're all I have left, and I need your help to get this done. You're my Man for Hire, remember? I can't have you falling apart before you finish the job. Let's find a place to lie down and I'll get us something to eat. It's about time I pulled my weight."

I was too tired to argue, so we made camp beneath a healthy-looking pine tree, and I peeled the pack from my back to rest against it. My Clayfields were running low but I took a double dose and closed my eyes to savor them.

I woke alone, sometime later. The sun was only starting to set. Khay had evidently left and come back at least once, because there was a pile of spider-bush buds beside me. I wiped my eyes and got to work stringing them up. I'd only done a few strings before my sore fingers slipped and a thread got wrapped around my hand, immediately sticking to the skin. It took me more than a minute to scrape it off and by that time, the fingers on my right hand had already gone numb, so I sat back down and waited to see how long it would take to get the feeling back into them.

When Khay returned, her arms full of bright yellow fruit, she immediately noticed the mess of web hanging over my head.

"What have you done now?"

"Just slipped a little. Paralyzed my fingers, but they're working again now, I think."

"I told you to rest. No meat tonight, I'm afraid, but I found some of those juicy stone fruit you like, and a few chestnuts to throw in the fire." I went to get up, but she put a foot on my chest. "No. Stay. Don't want you knocking yourself out or chopping off any fingers while you're all dopey like this. Let me do it."

I agreed, but it wasn't easy. She finished my botched attempt at the webbing and then got the fire going. The chestnuts went in and she chopped up the fruit, which was delicious but so full of juice that everything became sticky after we ate it.

We ate the chestnuts for dessert and, as the night wasn't too cold, let the fire go out so as not to attract any attention like we had the previous night. I could barely keep my eyes open, so I lay down under the blanket and was about to fall asleep when Khay crawled in behind me and put her arms around my chest.

"Goodnight, Khay."

She took a while to respond.

"Thank you," she said. "For staying with me."

"Of course."

I took one of her hands in mine, feeling the soft material of her gloves. It had gone hard in places, due to blood or fruit juice or some other mess we'd acquired on our adventure. Her breath was warm against the back of my neck.

"I'm probably due for a bath," I said. "We should look for a swimming hole tomorrow."

"Nah, you're good."

She tightened her hold around me and I forgot how sore I was.

"Those Fae you saw, in the tree and under the snow. Are they still alive?"

"No," she said. "Of course not."

"But if the magic came back, do you think they would too?"
She was quiet for a while.

"Honestly, I don't have any more idea than you do. I don't even know why it went away in the first place."

"You don't believe what they say?"

"What do they say?"

"That it was because us Humans put our machines in the sacred river. When we invaded the surface and contaminated its power, it froze. We just need to find some way to get it flowing again."

"You think that's all it took? Just somebody sticking their finger into the flow? I don't know about that. And I don't know what happens to those Fae if it ever gets going again. I'm sorry."

"Nah, that's all right. I was just wondering."

She took my hand and linked her fingers through mine. Despite the gloves, robes and other material between us, it felt good to be close to someone, and be silent, knowing we were on the same side.

The birds were screeching but I couldn't make sense of them. No. Not birds. Voices. Not screeching either. Screaming. I dropped the sword. My hands were covered in blood. Fresh. Glistening. Not mine, though. No. The blood belonged to the body at my feet. I'd killed them. More screaming. Louder. I killed it all. The world was already breaking. Blood thick on my fingers. On my soul. A scream, louder than the others, cuts me. A woman. Eyes of accusation. Of hate. She readies her attack.

Do it. I think. *Kill me. I deserve it for what I've done.*

She screams again. I don't stop her. She pushes the pain into my heart.

"AAAAH!"

I jumped up, tore away Khay's arms, and slapped at the back of my neck like I was trying to put out a fire.

"What is it?" she asked. "What's wrong?"

"A bug or something. I don't know. Did you bite me?"

"No, I didn't bite you!"

"Well, something did."

"Let me look."

I turned around. She lifted up my hair to take a look.

"Uhhh." She ran her thumb over the sore spot. "Interesting."

"Is it bad?"

"No. Look, I promise I didn't mean to."

"Mean to what?"

"I'll get you a mirror."

She gave me the small square mirror from her pack and held up the light so I could take a look. It wasn't easy, but, out of the corner of my eye, I could just see the mark on the side of my neck.

"You kissed me?"

"I didn't kiss you!"

"It *looks* like you kissed me."

"I didn't! I wouldn't kiss you in your sleep, you idiot. My mouth must have just rested against your skin or something, that's all."

"Right."

"Fuck you. If I was going to kiss you, I'd at least wait till you were awake."

"Sure."

"You're not really encouraging me to give that a go either."

"Good."

"Good?"

She gave me a look that would strike fear into the heart of any man.

"Yeah, if it's going to hurt like that! I thought you only burned magical creatures."

"I do."

We finally paused. She looked me up and down.

"I'm Human," I said emphatically.

"So you say."

"I know I am!"

"How?"

"I just . . . I just know! I grew up in Weatherly. People would have known. The Opus would have known, I . . . This is crazy. I'm Human!"

She sighed. "You're right. You're the most human Human I've ever met."

It was a relief to hear her say that. I'd been close to having a panic attack.

"So, what is it, then?" I asked, forcing my voice back to an acceptable timbre. "Something to do with your powers? Do they get stronger as you get more artefacts? Maybe they react to Humans now."

"Maybe."

Another long pause. We both had plenty of questions but neither of us had answers.

"Let's go back to sleep," she offered. "If you think you can."

I rubbed by hand over the mark. It was warm but it didn't hurt too bad.

"Yeah, sure."

Another pause.

"You want me to make another bed?" she asked.

She tried to play it off as a joke, but I knew that the question was real enough. I felt the weight of it because I knew how nice it felt to hold someone when you hadn't in a while. She was another lone soldier. One of the few of us willing to wander. To venture out into the darkness in search of the light. We'd done it alone before. We could do it alone again. But there was no denying that it was better to do it together.

"No," I said. "But I'm the big spoon."

"Fine." She got back under the covers. "Just don't you dare try to kiss me."

"Are you kidding? I'd melt my fucking lips off."

Her laughter shook both of us. It took us a few adjustments to get comfortable, but I could soon tell from her breathing that she was asleep in my arms. It took me a long time to join her. My mind had broken into pieces that didn't know how to fit back together, and I was scared to go back to sleep in case the same nightmare was waiting for me.

I didn't know enough about Khay's powers to know if they could change or not. Maybe, if we met another Human on our journey, we could run a little test. See if he reacted the same way I did. Until then, it was a mystery.

As I fell asleep, I heard wolves howling in the distance, but I didn't know if they were coming from the forest or my dreams.

47

Ambush

Khay lowered the binoculars.

"No movement. Nothing. They just left it there."

The dirt road ended in a dense thicket, and sitting off to the side was the car that surely belonged to the woodsmen.

"The road mustn't be finished," I said. "They had to go the rest of the way on foot."

"Poor Theo."

I was refreshed after a good night's sleep, but guilty for the fact that it had slowed our progress. We'd be no use to Theo if we stumbled into Incava without our wits, but they had such a head start, I hated to imagine what might be happening to him.

"Let's get moving," I said. "But stay alert."

It was slower moving through the thick forest, and we spent most of the day in near silence, keeping our focus on the careful placement of our feet.

"You're an orphan, right?"

The canopy had thinned out overhead and the noon sun beat down on us as we walked through the short grass.

"Yeah," I replied.

"Well . . .?" Khay did that annoying thing with her eyebrows.

"I'm Human."

"You *think* you're Human."

"I know I am. Everyone knows I am. You said it yourself."

"That's just because we don't know all the possibilities! What if there are other species out there? Maybe you're some as-yet-undiscovered creature."

"Nothing changed in me when the Coda happened. I'm as useless as I was before."

"Maybe you just never worked out what your powers were."

"I don't have powers!"

"Of course not. Because of the Coda. But maybe you did before, and you just never tried."

By the afternoon, the heat was making me surly. The conversation didn't help. Khay kept teasing me about the mark she'd left on my neck, but it cut too close to old wounds for me to enjoy the joke. The truth is I would have loved her hypothesis to be true. I'd entertained that very idea during my first years out of Weatherly, always waiting for the moment when I'd hear about some new kind of magical creature that was indiscernible to Humans. I would research their talents, hoping to find out that they were only unlocked at a certain age or with certain information. I tried moving candle flames and cups of water with my mind, and pushing pens along a desk without touching them, in case it turned out that I was an as-yet-unidentified Sorcerer, but my attempts never yielded any outcome.

Even if I'd been secretly hoping for some wild revelation, those around me never questioned my species. It was just like Khay had said: I was the most human Human there ever was, and magical creatures could sense it the moment I walked into the room.

"Believe me, I tried. I just—"

"Shhh."

She turned east. I couldn't see anything, but when I stopped and listened, I heard it too.

"The birds," I said.

"Yeah." It was just like Theodor had said. We couldn't understand their language, but I could feel the change in their energy, and it sounded like a warning. "Hide."

We moved fast – not so fast as to disturb the birds and send a warning back the other way – and crouched behind the longer grass in the shade of the trees.

We waited, listened, and finally heard the voices. They had none of Theodor's skills, or were choosing not to bother using them: talking so loudly that we could make out what they were saying before we could see them.

"Fuck what the boss said. We can't do anything with that crystal. We need bronze."

"He's not gonna like it."

"Then he can take the next prisoner, and get *his* arms chewed up and spat in his eyes."

"When we want quartz, we can come back for it," said a third, more measured voice. "They've got plenty."

We didn't dare raise our heads, but through the gaps in the grass we saw the three woodsmen who had taken Theo from the camp. One was an Amalgam, as large as the leader, but the other two looked Human; they were all wearing the same red armor.

Khay drew her pistol. I gave a look of admonishment but she didn't put it away.

I wanted to get to Incava. Find Theo. These assholes were to blame, but I didn't want to risk fighting them just for a little revenge. The fight in the camp had almost ended me.

"They've come from Incava," whispered Khay. "We kill two, question the other."

It shocked me, sure, but it emboldened me as well. I admired the directness of it – it was like an order – but, as they passed us, oblivious, I couldn't bring myself to shoot those men in the back.

Theo, she mouthed, hoping to turn my anger against my better judgment. It almost worked, but it still felt like too big of a step. I fought when I had to. I'd used the gun on plenty of people – people I wished I hadn't – but it had always been in combat. I didn't like the idea of executing someone just because they'd crossed me.

"Hold up," said the older woodsman with the calmer voice, and got down on his haunches. Perhaps he was in possession of some of Theodor's skills after all. He was examining the grass where Khay and I had changed course to move around an obelisk, which was all the encouragement she needed to act.

She stood up. Their backs were still turned to us, so there was no reaction from them until she fired. The man on his haunches gained a hole between his shoulder blades and slumped forward. One of the others turned his attention to the injured party while the third turned on us. His crossbow was hanging from a hook at his side. He fumbled for it, but I moved faster and shot him in the chest, forcing him backwards over his friend.

The last man screamed. Not like a warrior. Like someone who had just seen his friends – perhaps his family – slaughtered in front of him. He drew his sword. Khay and I pulled back the hammers of our pistols to ready our next shots.

"Don't move," she demanded, but the man was filled with too much rage and grief to hear her. "I said stop!"

He charged. She fired low. It clipped the side of his abdomen, making him flinch but also run faster. Khay and I backed away but there was no time to wait if we wanted to live.

He was only a few steps from us when I shot out the kneecap of his right leg. He went down with a fleshy cracking sound as his face connected with a buried stone.

I kicked the sword away, which was likely unnecessary.

"Hey." Khay put the barrel of her gun to the back of his head. "We have questions."

"FUCK YOU!" He thrashed out. There was no convincing him of anything. Right now, he'd rather die seeking vengeance than start coughing up information. "FUCK YOU!"

She kicked him in the face.

"You think this is as bad as it gets? You've got no friends here. Nobody is going to save you. Where did you take the Werewolf?"

He turned his head. Not to her, or me, but to the bodies beside him. The reality hit him for a second time, and he broke down, wailing through bloody tears and a face full of dirt.

"I'm talking to you!" yelled Khay.

"Hey," I said, trying to get her attention. "Give him a second."

Khay looked between us, seemed to come to her senses, then nodded and stepped back.

We let him cry himself out. Waited for his adrenaline to fade and the pain seep in. It was fucking miserable. Khay noticed my expression.

"We couldn't take any chances, Fetch. You want to go through another night like you did back at their camp?"

"I know."

"You might be fond of taking punches, but what do you think would have happened if they'd got hold of me?"

I met her eyes. She wasn't admonishing me, she was sharing something real. Something known through hard experience. There was no arguing with that.

The woodsman finally went quiet.

"Hey, you still awake?" Khay went over to him, treading carefully, her gun raised in case it was a ruse. "You ready to talk yet?" She knelt down, and I backed her up, ready to fire if he got even a finger on her.

"I know it hurts," said Khay, a hint of compassion finally finding its way into her voice. "You tell us what we need to know, and it's all over." His eyes fluttered open. He gave her a look of pure hatred but didn't say anything. "Why are you selling prisoners to the Wizards?"

His face was so full of pain that it hurt to look at him.

"I don't know. We started selling them machines. Stuff we stole from trucks. Then they asked for . . . they said they needed subjects."

"Subjects?"

"To experiment on. That's all I know."

Khay sneered, and I pushed down the urge to give him a beating of my own.

"Where's the Minotaur?"

"Fucked if I know. We do the handover at the castle gate and get out. It's probably bollocks anyway. A story to stop people from raiding them."

"If we did want to raid them, where would we enter the city?"

He coughed up blood.

"Fucking kill me, you bitch."

"In a moment. How do we sneak into the city?"

"Just stroll on in. They're lazy pricks. They have no servants now. They barely wipe their own asses, let alone stand guard in town."

"But the castle?" I asked. "They keep the front gates locked?"

His eyes lolled in his head. Khay slapped him.

"Answer the question, and we let you rest. Is the castle locked up?"

"Yeah. Yeah, it is. But . . . there's a crack in the north wall. They chuck waste out of it. Lazy fucks. I always said that we should . . . we should get in that way. Take the castle for ourselves. Now, just let me—" He tried to cough again, but the blood got caught in his throat. "Let me die."

"One more thing." She used her teeth to remove her glove, and put her hand around his neck. "You're Human, aren't you, sir?"

He snarled.

"Fuck you."

"Aren't you?"

"Yeah, I'm fucking Human, you cunt."

Khay removed her hand from his throat, looked up at me, and wiggled her fingers.

There was no handprint on his skin.

She gave me a playful smile.

I shot the woodsman in the face.

48

When You Get There

"Are you mad at me?"

"No," I said, sounding pretty mad.

By the time we'd searched the woodsmen and dragged their bodies into the scrub, the sun had already set. If anyone discovered the ambush, they'd surely search the nearby area, so we marched in near darkness, looking for a place to camp that felt far enough away.

"Fetch, we didn't have a choice."

I had plenty of arguments I could have made about what we did, the way we did it, and how we could have got information out of the woodsmen without going in guns-first, but I knew she'd have just as many arguments of her own, and that most of them would be convincing.

I marched ahead, forgetting all Theodor's lessons, cracking twigs under my boots and sending flocks of birds scattering away like old-world Banshees.

"Can I get some more ammo, then?" she asked. I tried to ignore her, but she wouldn't have it. "What? You're taking away my pistol privileges?"

I pulled a handful of loose bullets out of my pocket, turned, and held them out.

"Here." My fist hovered between us. She just stood there, waiting for me to meet her eyes.

"Fetch, what do you think happens when we get to Incava? You think the Wizards are just going to hand the crown over?"

"We're going to steal it, right? Not go on some kind of murder spree."

"Yes, we're going to steal it, but the stakes are high. If you believe, like I do, that getting the crown can save countless lives, then aren't a few dead assholes worth it? Especially fucks like those woodsmen we took out. They'd spotted our tracks. If we'd acted too late, we'd be the ones lying dead back there and, if you hesitate again, there's a good chance that it *will* be us next time."

She was right. More than that, she didn't yell or scold me like a child. If she had, my petulant side would have pushed back. Instead, she spoke to me like a friend, which helped me let the frustrations fade away.

"Sorry. I think it's just the guns. They feel so . . . cheap."

"They are. But so are you; and we need to do whatever it takes to get this done. At the end of it all, I'll find a proper bad guy for you to swordfight so you can feel like a real hero. Until then, we won't try to hurt anyone we don't have to, obviously, but if pricks like those woodsmen get in our way, we put them down. We don't have to like it, but it's the price we pay for trying to change the world. Does that work for you?"

"Yeah, it does."

"Good." She grabbed the top of my shoulders and gave them a squeeze. "And thanks."

Khay held out her hand and I dropped the ammo into it. We both emptied out our spent cartridges, refilled the chambers with fresh ones, and stumbled through the woods for a few more minutes before we found a patch of level ground that felt like a suitable place to camp.

There had been no time to gather spider-bush or firewood, so we clumsily set up a tent, crawled into it together, and prepared for the nightmares likely to come.

"What will we do if this works?" I said to the back of Khay's head.

"If what works?"

"The crown. If you can make people magic again, then what's the plan? Wander from place to place putting it all back like it was?"

"Maybe. Eventually. But it takes it out of me, so it will take time. Best to stay somewhere well-populated and let people come to me. Sunder makes sense."

I thought about that. It did, in some ways. But what about Niles, and everyone else who'd invested in a world where magic was gone for good? What would they do when a Genie set up shop on Main Street and started turning back the clock? How would they feel when automobile sales dropped because folks were flying again? When Wizards and Witches made their electric appliances obsolete?

It wasn't something Niles would take in his stride, I knew that. If he still held power there, then Sunder would be the last place she should think about staying.

I didn't tell her that, though. No need to get ahead of ourselves.

"I hope I'll be able to control my powers completely," she said. "Stop this whole 'burning hands' thing. It wasn't an issue before the Coda."

We were both quiet for a while. The idea hung over our heads, along with the implications of what would happen if her wish didn't come true. She wouldn't be able to touch a magical creature ever again.

"Roll over," she said.

Her gloved fingers pulled back my collar and touched the burn that looked like a lipstick mark left on the envelope of a salacious love letter.

"Have you thought about why?" she asked.

"I've thought about it. Haven't come up with much."

"You don't think it's your bloodline?"

"I don't remember much about my parents, but I know they were Human."

"What about their parents? One of them might have had a Half-Elf mother or something like that. It happens." She rubbed the tips of my round ears between her thumb and fingers. "Which would make you an Eighth-Elf. Or an Eighth-Ogre or something. Maybe a sixteenth. Who knows?"

I had to admit that it made sense, and I found it kind of comforting. I knew nothing of my family tree, but the idea that some kind of magical creature had been a part of it, somewhere along the line, made me feel . . . good.

I held her gloved hand in mine and took a deep, relaxing breath, letting the idea sink into my body. It didn't really change anything, of course. Not in the scheme of things. But it shifted something inside me. I'd spent my adult life obsessed with the dividing line between my species and all the others. There always seemed to be some expansive gap between what I was and what *they* were. I'd forgotten that, if you went back far enough, history bound all of us together. Hell, a lot of magical creatures had been fully Human before the great river reached out and touched them, like Reptilia, Werewolves, and even some of the Genie. Maybe we all started out the same, way back when. It's the kind of thing Eileen would know about. Baxter for sure. They'd have some stories. Thinking of them made me miss Sunder a little.

But only a little.

Khay's breathing slowed as she drifted off to sleep, and I was quite happy to be exactly where I was.

When we woke up, we were surrounded.

49
Out of the Mud

I poked my head out of the flap, spotted the silhouetted figures in the dawn light, and immediately pulled my head back inside the tent.

"Khay," I whispered, "get your gun."

There was no way they hadn't seen me, so I waited for the sound of swords, orders or gunfire, but the world outside was silent.

Khay lifted her six-shooter and used her eyebrows to ask me for more information. I leaned into her ear.

"A dozen of them. At least."

"Who?"

"No idea."

We waited. Listened. None of them moved. If they did, it was inaudible. Even the birds weren't disturbed by the crowd that had gathered outside, singing their morning songs the same as they had every sunrise since we'd entered the woods.

Khay shrugged, suggesting that I must have been mistaken, and poked her head out the tent.

"Khay, wait—"

I held my pistol tight, in case I needed to start a shootout with the unseen battalion on the other side of the canvas.

Khay laughed and crawled out of the tent.

"Come on out, Fetch, and meet the creatures who built Incava."

We'd pitched our tent in a small clearing, and the men were standing at the edge, blending in with the boulders and trees. I approached the closest figure. He was leaning back with his hands close together, like a sailor heaving on a rope, except there was nothing in his hands. Whatever he'd been pulling when the Coda hit had crumbled from his grasp.

The man was naked and his flesh was a uniform mass of red rock, featureless save for two eyes made from dull white stones. There were cracks around his joints and a few clumps of his body had broken away, but his thick legs and arms looked like they could weather a few decades out in the elements before completely breaking down.

He had an extended family of identical brothers, all posed mid-action in some kind of manual task: hauling rocks, wielding axes or dragging logs.

"These are the workers who served the Wizards of Incava," said Khay. "Constructs who were created from magic-infused clay, enchanted with powerful spells to perform any task the Wizards required. Whatever they couldn't accomplish with pure magic, they had the stone statues do for them, from working the land to spoon-feeding them their meals. It was a point of pride for them never to lift a finger except to cast a spell."

We followed the faceless servants through the scrub until beams of morning sunlight shone through the last line of trees.

"Fetch, we made it."

Crouched and careful, we made our way to the edge of the pines and peered out at the valley floor. There was no more green, only dead grass and weeds under the feet of hundreds more clay figures in pantomime poses, working fields that had died long ago. The rough tracks left by the woodsmen came out of the trees to the south and went through the valley, weaving between frozen Constructs, and ended at the point where the two hills converged at the base of a monumental cliff. From beneath the shadows of the bluff, the black stone castle of Incava lurked like some nocturnal monster waiting in the dark.

"There it is," said Khay: "the Wizard city."

I was already anticipating the torture of having to step out of the forest. I'd become accustomed to the safety of the woods, and the idea of leaving them felt like stripping naked in front of a crowd. Khay had no such reservations.

"We should approach from the high ground," she said. "The southern ridge is nothing but jagged cliffs, so we take the north. Move along in the trees until we get behind the hills, then make our way from there."

We hid the camping supplies and prepared ourselves for the task ahead. I had my pistol, my knuckles, the bow and arrows and Theodor's knives. Khay had her six-shooter and her two daggers.

It was overcast and muggy, but we traveled lighter, having left most of our stuff back at camp. No point trying to storm a city with a bedroll on your back.

The hike was uncomfortable because we were always at an angle, moving slowly along the side of the hill to stay hidden from the two guard towers. We took Theodor's lessons seriously, keeping to a meandering pace with feather-light footsteps, wandering like two woodland creatures out for a stroll. Sometimes we'd stop and stretch out, facing back the way we'd come to realign our legs on the incline, then wander on, always waiting for the telltale change in birdsong to let us know if someone else was up ahead.

It was tiring and tedious, but there were no signs of scouts or patrols. In fact, it looked like these woods hadn't been entered in years. Overgrown grass and weeds sprouted around piles of mulch and dead branches.

"We're close," said Khay. "I'll go take a look." I waited in the scrub while she crept up to the ridge, returning a little later with a wide smile. "Not far. The guard tower is right here but there's nobody manning it."

I followed her back to her vantage point. From behind a boulder, we could see the guard tower, and though some of the platform was hidden behind a barrier, it looked empty. We watched for ten minutes but heard no sound nor saw any movement.

"Well," said Khay, "let's get up there."

I took out my bow and nocked an arrow. I wasn't the greatest shot, but it was better than alerting the whole city with the pistol. I was, of course, ready to drop the bow and go for the gun as soon as things escalated.

Khay tested the ladder. It took her weight without shaking or making any noise that would alert someone at the top. She climbed silently, and I circled around, scoping out as much of the tower as I could without putting myself in full view of the city. Khay was exposed. If anyone in the city was watching the tower, they'd have a good chance of seeing her, but with the setting sun and her dark robes, hopefully a little luck would allow her to climb unnoticed. I watched her in my periphery, keeping my focus on the platform in case there were any signs of life, but the first movement up top was Khay's beckoning hand.

Wearing the bow on my back, I climbed up and joined her. It was only two stories high but, with the hill beneath us and the city in the valley, we had an extensive view of Incava.

You can tell a lot about a city by looking at it from above. Sunder's grid center, surrounded by a twisted mess of winding streets, spoke of a place that had quickly grown out of control. Weatherly's wide roads and rows of perfect houses showed that they had never lost sight of their plan. Incava was not a city. It was a fortress. The castle was all that mattered, and everything else was created to give it protection, supplies or support.

Like a giant black squid, tentacles wrapped around everything in its vicinity, each part of Incava was linked to the castle. If the Wizards lived up there, then the rest of the city was only inhabited by their Construct servants – a population that needed no housing, food, entertainment, sanitation or energy.

The fields in the valley were connected to the castle by a chain of statues pushing rusted wheelbarrows and dragging rotten wooden carts. The buildings included mills, forges, stables, masonries and a huge cage that I hoped had been for livestock and not for prisoners. Statues filled every street and doorway, frozen in time, but there was movement around them, as hundreds of goats roamed the abandoned buildings, munching on the weeds that sprouted out of the cracks in the stone paths. Others wandered out of the city walls, climbed the rocky cliffs of the valley or bounced through the longer grass of the overgrown and untended fields.

"It's filthy," said Khay, wrinkling up her nose. She was right. The whole city had a sooty, dust-covered quality like it had been dug out of the trash and never been cleaned. Even at a distance, you could see the potholes, the caved-in roofs and the crumbled walls. Dust, the same color as the cliffs above, was sprinkled over everything. Either there had been some kind of earthquake or it had slowly built up over time without anyone bothering to do anything about it.

"The crown will be in the castle," said Khay, and I waited for her to continue.

"And?"

"And we go in and get it."

"*That's* the plan?"

"Till we come up with a better one. What? Did you want me to come up here and scout it out before I brought you along? I would have faded to nothing before I ever got back to Sunder."

"So, what are our options?"

"The side wall of the city is broken." She pointed to the northern wall, closest to us, where there was easy access into the city. The row of cottages just inside the gap looked uninhabitable. "I say we enter through there, move up towards the palace, and find that crack in the castle that the woodsman talked about."

"Maybe we should watch a little longer. See if anyone comes in or out."

"Fetch, they're old men without magic. The Minotaur is the only enemy we need to worry about, and he won't be wandering around out here."

I felt resistance rise up in me and couldn't work out if it was fear or my old habit of putting things off for as long as possible.

"What do we do about the Wizards?"

"Hopefully nothing. Ideally, we find Theo and take the crown without being seen. If we're spotted, we'll try to threaten or negotiate before getting into any kind of fight. You think they're ready for a battle? Look at them: they don't even clean their streets."

It didn't look like they'd be able to launch any kind of organized defense. We could probably scare them into submission the first time we fired a pistol.

The palace itself was built from a kind of black glass. The material was smooth, but the construction was imperfect. Every turret reached a different height, and they all leaned at slightly different angles. The windows looked like they'd been blown out by cannons as an afterthought. Metal balconies had been built onto the upper levels, and there was a platform full of derelict weapons crammed on the roof between misshapen turrets and forked spires.

"How do you build something like that?" I asked. "It looks like it exploded out of the earth."

"It did. The Wizards of old shaped it with their powers, drawing huge streams of sand and mud up into the air and casting fire spells to set them. It really is an explosion frozen in place."

"But why build it at the base of the mountain like that?" I asked. "It's so dark."

I'd always thought that high ground was the ideal place for a castle. This one was dug into the cliffs like a skulking animal that didn't want to be seen. I suppose it gave it protection, but it looked like a miserable place to live.

"Don't ask me why Wizards do anything," said Khay. "It's an awful fucking place, so let's get in and get out."

I took one last moment to memorize the path from the hole

in the wall to the front of the castle, planning a route that had the most chance of keeping us hidden.

"All right," I said, "let's go."

Khay climbed down the ladder. I followed after her, glancing around to make sure nobody from the city happened to be looking up.

"Shit."

I pulled my body tight into the ladder, as if it would make me invisible.

"What?" asked Khay.

Across the valley, at the top of the other guard tower, I'd just seen somebody move. At least, I thought I had.

I squinted. There seemed to be a shadow peering over the ledge. I held onto the ladder with one hand and searched for the binoculars, but by the time I held them up, the shadow was gone – if it had ever been there at all.

"Come on," hissed Khay, already at the bottom. "You stand out like a Troll in a tea house."

I hurried down to join her.

"Looked like someone on the other guard tower. Looking at us."

Khay took the binoculars and looked over.

"Can't see anyone now, and they haven't raised the alarm."

"Not yet. Maybe we should wait and see what they do."

But she was getting impatient.

"If they haven't alerted the others, they mustn't have seen you. We'll keep out of their line of sight, but the quicker we get moving, the better."

We went down the hill, staying mostly on the side that faced away from the city, then made a direct line for the broken part of the wall. I could hear the dull whir of machinery, but no voices or other noise.

The wall had been damaged years ago, because grass had sprouted between the rubble. We peered in at an alley piled high with bricks and fallen tiles.

"Do you smell that?" asked Khay.

"Yeah, it stinks."

Had we been in the forest long enough to make the aroma of any urban environment offensive, or did the whole place really smell like garbage, piss and shit? Sunder probably had a similar smell, especially in the heat of summer, but I didn't think it was ever as strong as this, and we weren't even inside the walls yet.

Despite the odor, we climbed through the crack, my bow at the ready.

The narrow streets were about a quarter of the width of an average road back home. When they weren't covered in debris, they were mostly just bare dirt, with gutters full of rancid water. It was quiet but not abandoned. There were fresh-looking footsteps in the dust and goat shit, along with small tire tracks that must have been made by those machines that the woodsmen were selling them. There were trails of sawdust and pieces of shiny scrap metal, but nothing that spoke of any community. No sounds of music or conversation, no food scraps or kitchen smoke. It became clear that we wouldn't be facing off with a thriving Wizard population, but only the sad remnants of a society left to die. That didn't mean they'd be any less dangerous. In fact, as we moved through the crumbled streets, I became more terrified of what the feral Wizard city was going to throw at us.

I counted the buildings, leading Khay along the route that, from the guard house, had seemed the safest. We scrambled over a broken-down stall to reach the next road, higher up the hill. From here, I could see the southern guard tower, but there was no shadow. No movement.

Water trickled between our feet, stinking like sewerage, and I poked my head around the corner of a storehouse to search for anyone who might give us away.

"There's nobody here," said Khay. "They must all be inside the—"

"Look!"

Blocking off the end of the alley there was a crumple of metal, wood and faded canvas. It looked like a bloated tropical fish, its skeleton exposed and its webbed fins full of holes. The paint on the object matched the swirling pattern of the Rods of Rakanesh, and the photo on the wall of The Harpy House.

"That's one of the flying machines," said Khay, "like Betty used to pilot."

Though its wings were shredded and its hull a mess, there was still something wonderful about it. A kind of old-world contraption I'd never seen before that, despite its magical origins, no longer seemed so alien. We were driving high-speed automobiles and firing deadly weapons. If those things could exist in a non-magical world, why not something like this?

I mentally kicked myself for allowing my imagination to betray me. We would get the river flowing again, somehow, and when that happened, there would be no need for Mortales motors or Niles Company contraptions. The Rakaneshian airships would fly again, along with Angels like Benjamin and families of Wyverns. We'd start with Khay, and we'd keep going, until the magic of the sacred river was moving through every creature once more.

"There," said Khay, climbing up on the shattered airship, "I can see the crack in the castle that the woodsman told us about. Follow me."

I followed, quickly, and left thoughts of flight behind. I wish I'd held onto my hopes a little longer, because inside the castle of Incava, they all came crashing down.

50

Storming the Castle

"Oh good," said Khay, "I thought 'waste' was going to be . . . you know."

The crack was a lightning-bolt crevice that split the northern wall from the foundations to the battlements, with an open chasm about halfway up. The ground outside was covered in bits of rubble, broken wood, old books, some smashed crockery, and more of that glittery dust that had rubbed off on my coat back at the woodsmen's camp.

"What is this stuff?" I asked, running my finger over the back of a smashed bookcase, collecting the sparkling dust. Something about the color was familiar: kind of purple and silver but not really either of them.

"Must be some kind of residue from . . . I don't know. One of those machines the woodsmen were making?"

"Maybe." I wiped my fingers on my trousers and looked up at the crack in the castle. The jagged shards that jutted out from the gap gave us plenty of hand- and footholds, but a wrong move could dice us into deli meat.

Khay put a gloved hand on one of the shards.

"Not as sharp as it looks, but it's strong," she said. "We should be able to climb them."

"It's the falling on them that worries me. You want me to go first?"

"Nah, I don't want you slowing me down."

She grabbed two of the spikes and used them to pull her legs up into the gap. I looked around. There wasn't anything between the northern end of the castle and the stone wall, other than a dead garden that was as dry as Dragon's breath. As we got higher, we'd be more visible, but hopefully the depth of the crevice would offer us some cover.

Once Khay was well above my head height, I climbed after her. She was right; the edges of the spikes weren't too sharp, but the points certainly were. It only took a few seconds for me to scrape my knee against the end of one and set it bleeding. I was more careful after that. I moved slowly, keeping my body back from the glass daggers even if it meant sticking my ass out into the open where someone could spot it.

Crack!

A piece of wood landed on my head, corner first.

"Argh!"

"Shhh."

"Shhh?" I whispered, still louder than I should have been. "Stop dropping things on me."

"I didn't mean to. We're in a garbage chute, remember?"

There were all kinds of crap caught on in the gap: papers, burnt bits of rope, chicken bones and tufts of fur. To break up all the rubbish, there was an owl's nest built into one of the deeper nooks, and the owner stared at me with her twin eclipses.

I was so focused on not slicing off my fingers that I didn't notice Khay had stopped climbing. My head hit her foot, dangling freely in the air, and she let go with one hand to put a finger to her lips.

A rattling sound above. Hushed voices. We both tried to tuck ourselves into the gap, but we were at a precarious point without much room to move.

Whoosh!

A cloud of shining powder shot out of the hole above us, along with more random trash. We tucked our heads as pieces of tin, and a couple of apple cores bounced past. Then I heard Khay yelp, and there was a scraping sound before her weight came down on top of me. I kept one hand tight on a spike but twisted around and grabbed her with the other before she could fall too far. She wrapped her arm around my neck, and her head was close enough to mine to whisper.

"Sorry. Caught something on the back of my head."

I helped her climb around me. She put her back into the crevice and I leaned over her to cop the brunt of the debris that continued to fall. Her hood had been knocked back and was filling up with pieces of garbage. The cut on her head didn't look big, but it could have been deep. Blood trickled down the side of her face, near her left eye, and she grimaced to suggest that it was irritating her. Despite the pain, she kept one hand on the wall and the other around me, in case another heavy delivery dropped from above.

There were a couple of drum-like sounds – likely a hand slapping the bottom of a bucket – and a final celebration of sparkles drifted over us.

"Close your eyes," I said. She did, and I blew a puff of air over her face to clear the dust away.

"Thanks," she whispered. "I'm really, really glad it wasn't the other kind of waste."

She opened her eyes. Only inches away.

"You all right?" I asked.

"I think so. How does it look?"

"Not like it'll kill ya."

"What a shame. You almost got yourself out of this mess at the last second." She gave a little smirk. "Weird to see your face this close. I'm used to staring at the back of your head."

I tried on a smirk myself.

"That's my better angle anyway."

She laughed, and her big eyes gave that owl a run for its money.

"This side ain't so bad."

She stared at me for a while to watch the words sink in, then shook the dirt from her shoulders. Once she'd emptied the debris from her hood and pulled it back over her head, she tapped the side of my body like I was a horse she was coaxing into a canter.

"Up you pop. Your hard head can handle more hits than mine."

As instructed, I climbed on up, but we were spared any further dumps of debris.

The crack opened on a long hallway with walls the same color as the outside, and lamplight flickering off every surface. Distant voices ricocheted back and forth, making their origin impossible to determine.

I climbed inside and helped Khay in after me.

She immediately drew her pistol and lowered her stance.

It was cold, musty, and there was something strange about the building. I popped my ears but couldn't clear the foggy feeling of being underwater. I really wanted to get out my gun, but I stuck with the bow. If possible, I wanted to avoid bringing every Wizard in the place down on our heads.

There was a statue of a bull at the end of the room, and corridors leading left and right.

"Stay together?" Khay asked. "Or split up?"

"Together. The Wizards might not put up much of a struggle, but neither of us wants to encounter the Minotaur on our own."

"Left, then. Maybe it circles around."

We turned left into another hallway with high ceilings and walls full of faded tapestries. There were disused rooms off to each side.

Footsteps, moving fast, from back the way we came.

I grabbed Khay by her robes and pulled her into a doorway. We held our breath. The footsteps came closer. Slowed. Closer. Slower.

Stopped.

I pulled back the bowstring. Khay readied her gun.

A figure moved past the doorway. They were wearing a dark-green hood and cloak, and I heard the tinkling of weapons on their belt. They kept moving, deeper into the castle, the same way we'd been traveling.

"That's who I saw on the guard tower," I whispered. "They've followed us."

"Then we go the other way. Come on."

Khay led us back past the crack and the statue of the bull, straight down a hallway on the other side, and eventually we came to the entrance chamber.

We were on a balcony, looking down a flight of stairs to an open archway. The last light of the day stumbled in and tripped over a clutter of crates, machinery and metal scraps. They must have been the items delivered by those woodsmen we'd met on the road; dumped into the entrance hall, and nobody had bothered to clear them up. The ground was littered with huge brown footprints. I guessed that this must have been where Constructs had frozen, then been knocked down by the Wizards to clear the way.

There were three hallways leading off from the balcony: the one we'd just came out of, a middle one, and one on the opposite side.

"Let's take the far one," I suggested. "Get as far away from that scout as possible."

Khay agreed, and we went down the far hallway.

It was much like the first – empty rooms and tapestries, mostly silent – but as we went further along, a faint humming sound vibrated through the floor and walls.

"Sounds like machinery," I said.

The hum got louder, and the stink of the city combined with a metallic burning smell that would have made me cough if I wasn't scared of alerting anyone. The darkness strained my eyes and, together with the droning hum, made me sleepy despite the adrenaline. It was an awful fucking place. Can't have been much better back when there was magic, but now it was truly horrible. We looked in at abandoned libraries, filthy kitchens, and someone's bedroom that would have put an alcoholic Centaur to shame. As the hallway opened up, and we saw light coming from a room on the right, there was a noise behind us.

"AAAH!"

We turned. A short, stumpy Wizard stepped out from a side door. He screamed again, and ran back the way he'd come before either of us could get off a shot.

Without needing to say anything, Khay and I crept closer, weapons raised. The door was swinging slowly on its hinges, squealing like a swine. I approached the threshold, and the torches inside, having been disturbed by the panicked Wizard, made every shadow a dancing decoy.

The opposite door slammed. There was nothing else in the room but tables, bookcases, and a petrified Construct.

"He's running," I said. "Let's get him before he alerts the others."

I was halfway across the room when the statue punched me in the chest.

51

Meeting the Shadow

The wind shot out of my lungs and I fell backwards over a cluttered table into a pile of books. Gasping, waiting for the familiar pain of cracked ribs, I heard Khay fire twice. There were two dull thuds as the shots found their target, but no scream, no groan, no fall. I righted myself and saw that the bullets had put a couple of shallow divots in the Construct's clay chest, without affecting it in any other way.

The monster was identical to all the others, except for a crater on its forehead where a dark crystal the size of an acorn had been embedded. The clay carving lumbered toward Khay, its tree-trunk arms outstretched, and its dull eyes devoid of mercy. When it tried to grab her, she ducked around it and shot it in the back of its knee, hoping to find a weak spot, but it only created a puff of dust and another inconsequential cavity.

I'd had some practice fighting impossible enemies and it never got easier. They'll break your bones before your brain catches up. My mind was still telling itself that these Constructs weren't supposed to move, when the one in front of me pressed the table in my direction and forced my back against the wall.

The table flipped up and the top of it slapped me in the face and pinned my arms, creating a Man for Hire sandwich with the table and bookcase as the bread. He would have succeeded in turning me into chunky jelly if there had been a solid wall behind me. Instead, the bookcase had been used as a divider between two rooms, and the force of the attack sent the whole thing tumbling backwards.

The shelves bruised my back like grill marks on a burger, and the table bounced against my face a few times, but at least the Construct hadn't tumbled down on top of me. I pushed the table aside and saw one of his two-ton feet moving in my direction, ready to stomp a hole through my chest.

I rolled to the side, back onto solid ground, and the sound of splintering wood gave a good idea of what would have been done to my bones if I hadn't. I reached for my gun but neither it nor the brass knuckles nor the dropped bow would be any use against a solid statue brought to life.

I backed away into a curtained wall. Khay kept her distance too. The Construct turned his head left and right, no features on his face except for those unchanging bits of gravel. However the slave was powered, he still used his eyes like anyone else, and kept looking between us to track our positions.

When the Construct chose Khay as his next target, I grabbed the curtain and yanked it loose. Khay fired again – more from a lack of other options than any hope of its effectiveness – and I took the opportunity to throw the curtain over the creature's head.

It wasn't much of a plan, but it worked better than I'd hoped. The Construct's simple mind and limited senses meant that he didn't react to the blinding the way an animal or Humanoid would. Rather than thrash about, it spun on the spot, jerking around, in a state of confusion. Each time it moved, I thought my shoulders would be ripped from their sockets, and I was wrenched off my feet, over pieces of the broken bookcase.

Khay dropped the gun, grabbed the other side of the curtain, and attempted to keep it taut so it wouldn't come loose from the Construct's eyes.

"What now?" I asked. The clay head turned when I spoke. Apparently, he could hear too.

Khay cocked her head towards the wall I'd ripped the curtain from, which wasn't a wall at all, but a huge window overlooking a circular room that must have made up a quarter of the castle.

The ceiling was too high to see from my vantage point, and the ground was several floors below. A nice drop, if we could convince the Construct to take the step.

A nod communicated our mutual understanding, and we heaved with our collective might . . . making absolutely no difference to the stone figure's position.

"Well, this is entertaining."

The runaway Wizard had returned. He stepped over the fallen bookcase and picked up Khay's pistol, both his thumbless hands tight on the grip.

"I was looking forward to seeing my servant pull your limbs from your body, but . . ." He pointed the barrel at my face. "I've always wanted to give one of these things a try."

He smiled, tightened his fingers . . . and a piece of red-stained silver burst out of his belly.

The pistol fired wide and dropped from his fingers. His body crumpled, revealing the figure in the green outfit standing behind him, blood dripping from the end of their short sword.

"Uh . . . thanks," said Khay.

The shadow pulled back their hood and a mane of locks tumbled out, revealing the fearsome face of a dark-furred feline with a self-satisfied smile.

"My pleasure," said Linda Rosemary. "Now, pull!"

Khay and I did as we were told. It felt as futile as ever, but we both strained ourselves against the twisting Construct, our muscles stretching and tearing along with the curtain.

Linda pulled a leather pouch from her pocket.

Surely not, I thought. *She wouldn't.*

I'd seen similar pouches a year ago, wielded by that homicidal Warlock Rick Tippity. Those pouches had contained the essence of a Faery corpse, and were primed to unleash a burst of elemental power. I wanted it to be a coincidence – a leather pouch could contain just about anything – but when she launched it into the Construct's chest, it exploded in a maelstrom of fire and wind.

The sentinel teetered, Khay and I pulled the curtain tight, and Linda ran forward, pounced, and put all her weight onto the creature's rocky chest.

It toppled into the window and went straight through it. We let go of the curtain as it was torn to pieces, and Linda sprang back to land between us. Shattered glass filled the air like a celebratory farewell to the falling monstrosity who, his vision cleared, stopped fighting and relinquished himself to his fate. There was a booming collision that shook the foundations, and the walls were still rumbling when I turned on Linda.

"Tell me that wasn't what it looked like."

"It looked to me like I saved your ass, Sunshine. What did it look like to you?"

"It looked like Rick Tippity's Fae magic."

"Lucky for you, it was."

"You're cutting up Faery corpses?"

"I'd say I put them to good use. Why are you so shitty?"

"Because what happens when the river starts flowing again and all the magical creatures come back, except the poor Faeries whose faces you cut up?"

"Fetch—"

"Decimated, just so you could make one-off little weapons like this?"

"Fetch."

"I thought we saw eye to eye on this stuff, Linda. I thought we were on the same side."

"FETCH! Turn the fuck around."

I did, and a shimmering light drew my eye down, past the pieces of crumbled clay, to the pit beyond; a chasm that went straight down into the earth, ending in a luminous pool of silver and purple light. There were Constructs moving around in the pit, lumbering up ramps and climbing ladders, even stepping off the light itself: a frozen, glowing lake. The Constructs carried picks and buckets. The buckets were full of rocks. Rocks that were the same color as the pool at the bottom.

"Linda," I said, breathless at the audacity of what I was seeing. "What is that?"

She stepped up beside me, and put a comforting hand on my shoulder.

"That's magic, Fetch. They're mining it. These pricks are digging into the sacred river."

52

What the Cat Dragged In

Seven years ago, when the Human Army pierced the surface of the sacred river with their machines, the soul of the planet responded by turning into crystal. Fae became petrified. Dragons crashed through rooftops. Lycum were trapped between two forms. Angels' wings could no longer hold their weight. Spells vanished from Wizards' fingers. Genie wishes could no longer keep them from the fade.

We lost life, loved ones, friends, and the future.

I thought I could bring it all back. If one small mistake had started this mess, maybe one uncovered secret could end it. One of my cases, when cracked, would make the river flow again. All it needed was a little encouragement. A way to undo what was done.

But now a quarry had been dug into the river's surface. Now there were chunks of the divine being dragged away in mine carts. If all it took was a single intrusion into the river to stop it flowing, then how could it restart after an assault like this?

This pit must have been made back before the Coda – just the kind of thing a kingdom of power-hungry Wizards might create if they wanted to increase their connection to the source of all magic – and that meant that it was all ready to be exploited once the river froze up.

There were no words for my rage. My heartache. No sound that could express my dying hope. There would be no big fix. No turning back the clock. No undoing the damage I'd done. If we couldn't fix it all, then why was any of this worth it? What were we doing here? Why had we come all this way?

I had no big answers to those big questions, so I pushed them aside and focused on the simple ones.

Theo. The crown.

That's what we were here for. Save your friend. Give Khay her power.

Find a way to punish these fucks later.

Linda, Khay and I stared out the broken window. The Constructs continued their work, unaffected by the commotion we'd made when we turned their brother to rocky debris.

"Why haven't they noticed?" asked Khay.

"They're automatons," replied Linda. "They have no mind of their own, but just follow the orders of whoever enchanted them."

Khay turned to Linda.

"Sorry, sister. Thanks for saving our asses and all, but who the hell are you?"

"Khay, this is Linda Rosemary, the friend I sent a telegram to before we left. Linda, I'm surprised you made it."

There was a short pause before she answered. Like she was distracted. Maybe her keen feline senses were picking up something I couldn't hear.

"Oh, right. Yeah. You know me, always up for an adventure." She looked Khay up and down, not offering her hand. "So, Khay, are you the . . . uh . . .?"

"Last of the Genies?"

"Yeah."

"That's me. Hope you're ready to make a wish."

Khay reclaimed her pistol from the fallen Wizard and reached into my pocket for more ammo.

"Where are we going to find this crown, then?" she asked. "You haven't seen it, have you, Ms Rosemary?"

Linda shook her head, but I pointed to the trail of Constructs moving mine carts down below. The ones who were loaded up with crystal disappeared down a tunnel on the opposite side.

"That's where they're taking the pieces of the river. I want to know what they're doing with it."

"I saw a stairwell back there," said Linda. "I'll show you the way."

Khay looked to me.

"You trust her?"

"I wouldn't go that far, but we have mutual interests."

There was movement below. A few Wizards emerged from entrances around the pit, looked up at us, and started shouting.

"Let's go," said Linda. "I'll fill you in on the way down."

She wiped her sword on her cloak and led us out the door and down the twisting halls of the castle, telling us her story in bursts whenever she felt it was safe to talk.

"I left Sunder in search of returning magic, and my quest led me to the Island of Mizunrum. I'd heard that the few remaining staff members of Keats University were compiling rumors of rekindled powers, unexplainable anomalies or historical artefacts that had been kept secret. I crossed the continent looking for answers, but when I got to Keats, all I found were dreamers. Dreamers with potential but no knowledge or plan of their own; just overly optimistic creatures stitching whispers into stories."

Loud footsteps from behind made us duck into an alcove for cover. We waited, holding our breath, as two Constructs walked past. They both carried dead goats in each hand; necks snapped, and their limp heads dragging along the stone floor.

When they were out of earshot, Linda carried on.

"I'd gone to Keats seeking knowledge, but I turned out to be the one with the most information to share. I'd seen Rick Tippity unleash his Fae magic, and witnessed you use the Unicorn horn in response. I could reaffirm the tales they'd heard about the Vampire who drank the marrow from his victims' bones. I told them of the fires returning to Sunder, and the exploding desert dust being used to create new, deadly weapons. It was those stories that galvanized the group, giving them direction and purpose."

Whether she was aware of it or not, all the stories she'd told the folks at Keats were things that she'd discovered because of my haphazard cases in Sunder. Perhaps the last few years hadn't been such a waste after all.

"My stories launched our organization," she said, after peering around a corner to make sure the coast was clear. "When I told them about the Unicorn horn – and the fact that pieces of pure magic could be weaponized – the Wizards I was working with soon turned their minds to Incava. They knew of the chasm that had been created here. How the Wizards here had spent years digging down into the rock, hoping to draw their magic directly from below to make their spells more powerful than ever before. It was a secret endeavor, rarely spoken of outside those in the castle."

"Right," said Khay. "So it was their idea to start mining this place?"

"No. Well, not really. We surmised that if a shard of Unicorn horn was able to unleash unlocked magical power, then a piece of the river itself would have the same effect. We'd merely suggested the possibility when one of our younger members – an adolescent Wizard who had barely begun to test his powers before the Coda killed them – volunteered to go on an expedition."

Linda led us to a winding stairwell. So as not to get trapped in the tight quarters, she went down first, checked that nobody was around, then signaled for us to join her.

"What happened to the young Wizard you sent out?" I asked.

"He never came back. We feared that our member, rather than being our informant, had handed the information about the Unicorn horn to the Wizards still here." The tunnel ended in the huge room where the Construct had landed. In front of us, past the scattering of shattered clay, there was the pit. "Judging by what's happening down there, it seems that we were right to be afraid."

The Wizards had vanished. There were only the Constructs, marching in unison, pushing carts of pure magic from the top of the pit to one of the tunnels on the other side of the room.

Looking up, I saw that the room had no ceiling. It was a mighty chasm that went all the way from the sacred river up into the night sky.

"We following?" asked Khay.

"Let me go first," I said. "If they're waiting for us to show ourselves, we shouldn't all walk into the trap."

I stepped out, boots tapping against the smooth black floor and echoing off the curved walls. It must have been wild to be here when it was made: a whole city of Wizards shooting earth into the air and firing it solid before it fell. There were irregularities and cracks in the surface, but as that was evidence of its unique creation, it only made the whole structure more impressive.

I stopped by the railing that surrounded the pit. No alarms yet. Nobody yelling. How many Wizards were living here? A few dozen, maybe. Perhaps only a handful.

There were windows up above. Some curtained, some clear. Nobody behind any of them, as far as I could see. Plenty of noise, though. Clanging from down below. Voices, somewhere, bouncing in from the many tunnels that split off from this room. Beneath it all, there was a humming: some machinery somewhere, or maybe drills grinding against the crystal. For some reason, I imagined it to be the sound of the river itself, groaning in pain as the Constructs broke it into pieces.

I looked over the edge and stared down at the petrified river. Its surface was shining silver, but translucent, so I could see all the way down into its endless purple depths. The places where it had been damaged were outlined in white with glittery powder, scattered over the surface like dropped stars. The droning got louder, and my body went tight. Old injuries came back to visit, like the pain in my heart that comes and goes at the worst times. I fumbled for the Clayfields and only found a crumpled twig in the bottom of my pocket. I shoved it between my teeth and turned back to face the others.

They were gone. The tunnel I'd come from was empty. At least, it looked like the one I'd come from. They were all alike, so I couldn't be sure.

A gunshot. Another, and I couldn't tell if it came from the same direction or somewhere behind me. Sound was too strange in that cylindrical glass room.

I ran back to the place I'd come from – thought I'd come from – and listened. Nothing. Silence now. I searched for footprints, or any way to determine if I was in the right place. I wasn't sure, but I had to go somewhere, so I went down the hall, hoping to find Khay and Linda waiting in some side room.

It was the wrong tunnel. I discovered that soon enough, because I went around a corner and found the madman's door.

53

The Sculptor

The laboratory was aglow with lanternlight, flickering as though every unsettling object was buzzing with life. They may well have been. If those Wizards could grant sentience to a once-dead lump of clay, then why not imbue a bedhead or armchair with purpose.

There was one occupant who required no magic to move. He had his back to me and was absorbed in his work, which appeared to be drilling a hole into the forehead of one of his monolithic puppets. Would you call it surgery or sculpture? I wasn't sure, but I was glad that it held his attention long enough for me to step right up behind him and put the pistol to the back of his head.

"Don't say a word unless it's to answer my questions. If you try to give that thing an order, I'll give you a matching hole in your head. Understood?" He nodded. "Stand up and turn around."

I stepped back to let him get to his feet. He moved slowly, with his hands where I could see them, so I was hoping that this fellow might not give me too much trouble after all.

One look into his eyes told quite the opposite story.

He had white pupils, white hair, a nose full of busted capillaries, jowls like empty grocery bags, chapped lips, a mustache-less beard, and a smile so ecstatic, so elated, so rapturous, that it struck terror into my heart. The rest of him was just as worrying. He was thumbless, hunchbacked and twitching. His hands and face – the only parts of his body outside his robe – were sunken and pale. The robes themselves were ragged, faded and covered in dust, dirt and feces.

He noticed my revulsion.

"Please accept my apologies for my current state, friend. We have not yet taught the servants to launder." He looked down at his clay patient. "Have no fear; this one isn't able to follow orders yet. Look! Chalky, pull this man's arms off!" I aimed my pistol at the Wizard's face and prepared to fire. "Woah, woah. Look, friend. He's not moving. No life. No magic. Not yet."

He leaned down and twiddled his finger around in the statue's third eye.

"One more gag like that and I'll shoot you for the hell of it," I snarled.

"Ohhh, but then I won't be able to do my work."

"You mean digging into the sacred river so you have someone to wipe your ass for you?"

He giggled at that. The ground shook. The castle rattled. Somewhere nearby a battering ram was breaking down walls, dynamite was smashing the sacred river apart or the fabled monster was raging in his cell.

"There's no time for trivialities in the face of progress. We've been crumbling for seven years. Too many legends of the old world have already wasted away. Great minds lost to the Coda. Miraculous beings reduced to miscreants and cripples. Until now. Until me. Do not take up my time for too long, friend. Every minute you waste may cost us a miracle."

A small purple crystal was resting on the Construct's chest. Likely the piece he was about to place into its cranium. I picked it up.

"This is your miracle?" I asked. "Carving up the soul of the planet to power a few stone minions?"

He laughed on the inhale, making an unsettling squeaking sound.

"Oh, the Constructs are nothing. A means to an end. Mere assistants to my master work."

"Which is?"

He grinned wide. Yellowed teeth with infected gums.

"Bringing the magic back, of course. I'm going to fix everything."

It made me sick to look at him. Something in the gray whiskers, unwashed hair and desperate, manic determination felt too familiar.

I dropped the piece of crystal into my pocket. It felt good. Like I was reclaiming a piece of pure magic from someone who wished it harm.

"How do you plan to fix things if you destroy the source of magic itself?"

"I'm not destroying it! I'm harvesting it. Using it the way it was meant to be used. How it *wants* to be used. It wants to be inside us. To power us. I'm just helping it find its way."

My nausea increased. The hammering on the walls got louder.

"The prisoner," I said, and spat my chewed-up Clayfield onto the floor. "The one the woodsmen delivered. Where is he?"

"Ahhhhh, yes. I knew that you wanted to see my true work. Of course you do. Who wouldn't wish to behold a miracle for themselves? The question is: will you appreciate it?" He looked me up and down, and performed a parody of a dubious buyer examining a potential purchase. "You don't seem to appreciate my servants. That hurts my feelings. They are very helpful, after all." His eyes flicked over my shoulder, and I reacted too late. "Grab him."

I fired, just before the unbreakable arms of the Construct wrapped around my torso. All that noise had obscured his footsteps. He must have come with some delivery, or returned after completing his previous task, and the Wizard had waited till he was right behind my back to give the order. The bastard. He deserved the bullet in his belly.

The thumbless prick leaned against his other sleeping sentinel, watched the blood soak through his shit-stained robes, lifted his head, and screamed with every bit of breath left in him.

"TAKE HIM TO THE MINOTAUR!"

54
The Minotaur

It was no use fighting the Construct. I was a helpless infant in his stony grip, which tightened every time I even thought about wriggling loose. The Wizard's manic laughter followed us through the tunnels, down a twisting ramp, until the air grew cold and smelled like an abattoir.

"Drop me. Let go. Stop. Cease this!" I tried numerous commands, attempting to trick the Construct into unhanding me, but the spell had been tied to its enchanter.

There was light up ahead. A square doorway that already had one stone sentinel standing in it, with just enough room for the second to fill the gap. I contemplated throwing my legs up to push me back from the entrance, but feared that the Construct's strength would press on until my legs split from my body like twigs from a tree.

The huge room had no other exits. The floor was white tile with blood-red grouting. The walls, smooth as glass, went a whole story high before they hit a wraparound balcony behind bars. No furniture. No fixtures. The only thing in the room was a great stone statue of a furious Wizard seated on a glass throne. He was made to scale with one hand holding a glimmering staff, the other a crystal ball, and a golden ring balanced on his head.

The crown of the Wizard King.

There were bones scattered around the corners of the room. Tufts of hair. Hooves without legs to hold them. A whole goat head was dropped in the center of the room as if he was the host who had summoned me here.

There was one filthy Wizard waiting up on the balcony with his hand resting on a large lever. Rather than screaming for others or preparing a weapon, he just looked down on me with a sickening grin, and pulled the crank.

A piece of the far wall opened up, becoming a doorway that was twice my height. Even at that size, the beast that came through it still had to duck his head to enter, and his horns scraped both the sides.

Whatever this Minotaur was before the Coda, he couldn't have been any more monstrous: a hulking mass of muscle and fur with a double axe in his hands and a brass ring through his nose. His horns were the size of my arms and sharpened to deadly points. The slobbering, bloody mouth and bulging black eyes were that of a wild animal, but its movements were considered, thoughtful and intelligent.

The Minotaur stepped into the room, its cold eyes locked me in their sights, and the door closed behind it, trapping us together.

The beast stretched its neck like it had got up from a long nap, wiped its drooling mouth on the back of its hand, took a deep, husky breath, and laughed. The sound was a gargled, muffled chuckle, like it was coming from a voice beneath the bull's head instead of from the beast itself. It twirled the axe in its fingers – as if the man-sized hunk of metal weighed less than a walking stick – and stepped forward.

"HEY!" I yelled, hoping to, I don't know, talk him out of trying to squash me, but it didn't slow him down at all. Rather than wait to listen to whatever scintillating conversation I might offer to his clearly lonely existence, the beast charged.

I backed away and immediately felt the hands of a Construct on my shoulders. It kicked a clay foot into my back, shoved me forward – I guess I wasn't getting out that way – and I landed on my knees. The Minotaur roared.

From one knee, I fired the pistol into his fur-covered chest. His hide must have been made from the thickest leather armor imaginable, because the bullet dropped to the floor without even breaking the skin. He crossed the room in a few lumbering strides and swung the axe in a backhand arc. Having nowhere else to go, I ducked low and jumped forward. His massive knee clipped my side and sent me spinning, but at least I was away from the Constructs and my back wasn't against the wall.

I searched for a way out, but the room had been designed to keep the monster, and anyone else, locked in. If this gigantic beast couldn't climb out of this place, then a tiny gumshoe had no hope.

I backed away. The Minotaur followed. He walked now – a menacing saunter – so I lifted up the pistol to fire again, hoping I might get lucky and hit him in the eye or some other vital area. Before I pulled the trigger, he threw his axe right at me.

There was no time to dodge. If he'd had better aim, I would have become two halves of one very dead man, but it cut the air and collided with the glass wall in a clanging shower of sparks.

He moved to pick it up, so I backed towards the Constructs guarding the only exit. They were motionless as I approached – not even a shift of their stone heads – so I jumped through the narrow space between them. My head went past them. My shoulders. My waist. My—

Clay hands gripped both my legs. I stopped so fast I felt my brain smack the inside of my skull.

"HEEEEELLP!" I screamed, and the echoing tunnels screamed back. The Constructs yanked, and I was thrown into the arena, on my stomach, which vibrated with the footsteps of the incoming beast.

I rolled, and the axe hit the floor, skidding off the tiles. Close up, I could see the grouting wasn't truly red, but stained in uneven pools. So much blood had been spilled in this room that it had become a part of the decor.

I rolled again, which didn't avoid, but lessened the impact of, the Minotaur's kick. I fell onto my side and watched him laugh, likely enjoying a bit of recreation after being trapped in the depths of this castle all alone.

Alone. Well, that made two of us.

Didn't it?

A metallic scraping sound caught my attention, then a flash of silver slid past me. I stopped it with my boot.

It was a short sword with a smear of blood down the side.

Linda Rosemary's face was peeking in through the legs of the Constructs.

"Stay alive, Phillips!" she called, and pulled back to avoid the swiping hand of one of the stone soldiers. "We'll get in there as soon as we can!"

I snatched up the sword and got to my feet before the Minotaur could kick it away. I was still woefully outmatched, already injured, and the odds against me were stacked as high as a happy Harpy, but the words of my old pal Richie Kites were ringing in my ears.

You're never fighting alone, Fetch. Even when you think you are.

I adjusted my feet to the positions I'd been taught by my mentor Eliah Hendricks: the first person outside Weatherly who had ever shown faith in me, and the first friend who saw past my naivety to my passion and potential. I wasn't much of a swordsman, but I had been trained. I'd fought practice duels in the Opus: once the most highly regarded organization on the continent. I'd fought Wyverns and Wolves when I was a leader in the Human Army. Sure, too much alcohol and too little exercise had made me soft, but I didn't have to kill this thing, I just had to stay alive long enough for Linda and Khay to find me a way out.

The sword was heavy but well-balanced, with a circular silver emblem on the handle that looked familiar. I didn't have time to inspect it because the bull, having retrieved his axe, came at me, his black eyes squinted into angry slits.

I circled around him and tried to keep my distance without

getting trapped in a corner, but every one of his steps equaled several of mine.

The Minotaur ran out of patience. He jumped forward to close the gap and swung his axe upwards so I couldn't roll under it. It sent me stumbling backwards. Another upward swing forced me against the wall.

Shit.

I might have been trained by the best, but that was a long time ago. The only recent fight I'd had was with Thurston Niles, and it wasn't so much a fight as a humiliation. Particularly easy because his flash new armor wasn't up to scratch.

The Minotaur raised his arm – ready to cave in my skull – and I saw that the skin underneath was hairless. Pinker than the rest of him. Before his arm could begin its descent, I closed the distance and slashed upward.

The sword didn't go in deep, but it didn't bounce off either. I ran the blade over his skin as I slid under him and back into open space. When I turned around, he was trying to get a look at the small cut I'd sliced into his armpit.

So, the beast does bleed after all.

Thurston had asked me why I visited his place, and I'd told him it was because I hated him. That wasn't quite the truth. We were alike – too alike for my liking – so he made for good, though frustrating, company. There was no doubt that he was the enemy – he was fighting for a world I wanted to destroy, and I was fighting for a world he wanted to stay extinct – but he kept my mind sharp. He understood me – though I hated to admit it – and he was therefore a better friend than most of the people I wished I was closer to.

And, quite by accident, he'd given me a chance to save my life.

The bull howled, kicked, and swung his axe again. I span around him, cut the back of his underarm, and jumped away before his next swing went through my neck. The axe whipped past me with such fury that the gust of wind threatened to put me into flight.

I backed away, and the Minotaur approached slower this time. More considered. I may have scored a point, but I'd put him on edge. He hadn't thought me much of a challenge – in truth, I wasn't – but now he was wary enough to keep his shoulders down and his eyes always on me, refusing to allow another easy shot.

At least he'd slowed down, and that was something.

Just buy some time, Fetch. They'll come for you.

The drops from the Minotaur's arm left bloody splatters on the white tiles. His mouth was full of foam and when he snorted, a goober of pink snot caught on the ring that dangled from his nostrils.

The murals never bother to include the boogers, do they? The pus? The infections and the bile? I never worried about where I might die, but I'd given the *how* some thought, and I'd never dreamed of going down while covered in a mythical creature's bodily fluids.

I tightened my grip on the sword and circled to my right. He turned with me, waiting for my next attack. What was he expecting? I wasn't the aggressor here. All I wanted to do was survive until someone else found a way to save me. What was it that Baxter had said?

Nothing worth doing can be done on your own.

Well, there's no fighting a Minotaur on your own either. I should have brought a larger party. I should have convinced Eileen to stay. She knew about creatures like this. She might know how to defeat them. All she'd managed to tell me was . . . what? That Longhorn had worn a bull's hide over his head and shoulders?

Maybe that was something. If his top half was more animal than man, it may serve to keep my attacks low.

Longhorn swung the axe back and forth, pivoting to either side, but always keeping his weaker parts protected. That meant that he wasn't extending his arms all the way, and his reach was shorter.

When I stepped back and felt my heel hit the wall, I reacted quickly, unwilling to be trapped against it. I kicked off the glass, launched low, and pointed the end of the blade at the toes of his tattered boot. The tip of the sword was sharp, and he had nothing but loose leather for protection. I put all my weight behind the attack, and it went in deeper than I'd expected.

As soon as I had my feet under me, I rolled through the Minotaur's legs. He howled, kicked, and left a bloody smear across the tiles.

More of Eileen's insight might have been useful, but I was glad she wasn't here. I remembered her face outside the mask-maker's workshop after he fired on us. That had shaken her up, but I'd pretended not to notice because it didn't serve my purposes. Then I'd dragged her out of town, almost gotten her killed several times over, and after all that, I was the one with the audacity to be angry. Thank the heavens she hadn't been thrown in here with me. I might well deserve to be trampled by a monster, but Eileen Tide certainly didn't.

The Minotaur growled. Blood seeped from his boot. He'd naturally defend his wound, and he knew that I knew his bottom half was weaker than the rest of him. The smart tactic would be to aim for somewhere else, but what were my options? I couldn't reach most of him, and a slash at that fur wouldn't be worth the effort. I'd only managed to puncture his foot because I could put my whole weight down on it, and he wouldn't let me get away with that trick twice. If I could jump off a ledge or something, then I might have a chance, otherwise my only options were below the waist.

He swung out, keeping his distance, and making sure that he stayed balanced and always ready to parry my attacks. My only hope had been cheap shots, and each time one landed, he knew to be ready for it if I tried that trick again. Worst of all, he only needed to land one good hit to kill me, while I might need a hundred.

And where were Linda and Khay? Was I actually going to fight the bastard?

There was noise above. I looked up, hopeful, but there was no green cloak or dark robes, just more bearded men in dirty rags filing onto the balcony to watch the ensuing chaos, imminent bloodbath and eventual execution.

The Minotaur swung again and, this time, the crowd cheered. Buoyed by the audience, he closed in and committed to a horizontal slash. Without time to step back, I attempted to block the axe with my sword.

There was a CLANG as our weapons collided and then a THWACK as the flat edge of my sword smacked against my forehead.

Blinding pain. Blood. If the edge of the blade had hit me, I would have been dead. Instead, I was wounded and dazed, stumbling along the wall in search of open space.

I slid across the polished stone, and my horrific, blood-covered reflection stared back at me. The cheers and laughter continued, and they mixed with the blood and the pain and my disgust at this whole place. These Wizards were just like Niles: hacking up the old world to make way for the new. Burning the bridges to any way back. The whole stinking lot of them had given up. If Khay, Linda and I were the only ones left willing to fight for the old world, then I was going to fight till my last fucking breath.

The Minotaur closed in. I span and slashed at his thigh, but he anticipated the attack and used the axe to smash away my sword, almost wrenching my shoulder from its socket. I moved back the other way, not fast enough, and he grabbed the back of my coat.

Think quick.

I drop the sword, lean forward, and let my arms fall through the sleeves. The coat peels off my back. I hit the ground. Grab the sword. Roll away. Turn.

He's on me. He undercuts again. I hold the sword in my right hand, press my left against the flat of the blade. I block the axe but it feels like I've been hit by that goddamn car all over again. I spin around. Slash desperately. Make contact. Blood.

His right calf. Not deep, but it's something. He attacks in anger. Messy. I duck and cut again. Same place. I get him once more in the same spot, then I back off. Smart, because he turns on me and roars. Real fury now. The audacity of a lump like me daring to match myself up against a legend like him.

But I dare do more than he can imagine.

He charges. I back away. I wait for the swing of the axe but it doesn't come. He charges shoulder first. I hold out the sword but it glides off his thick hide. He pins me. I'm winded. He only needs one hand to hold me still. That snotty ring is right over my face, and his breath smells like a body dragged out of a river. Death in his eyes. My death. I jab at him. Useless. I'm too close. He bats the sword away. It skitters. The crowd cheers for blood. My blood.

Who thought anyone would ever cheer for me?

A giant fist collides with my face. Can't call it a punch; that would be too kind to every other punch that has ever been thrown. I try to find some new word for it, but I can't. My brains are mush. The world is fuzzy and wet. Cold. Cold metal in my hand. The knife from my belt. Theo's knife. My latest mentor. Kind eyes and enduring patience. He's been teaching me to hunt. To walk through the world without disturbing it. He's here somewhere. He needs me. Needs me to live. I pull the knife from its sheath. Small, sure. But at this distance, what does it matter?

The Minotaur turns his head to the crowd and roars. I wonder why; pure bloodlust, or do they feed him better if he puts on a show? No time to ask him. I'll ponder it later.

My arms move faster than they ever have before: snick, snick,

snick, snick. No time to aim, just strike. He lets go of me but I don't let go of him. I hold his fur in my left hand and stab with my right. Fingers. Flesh. Wrist. I slice. The blood spurts out like a busted garden hose. He screams. Not a roar this time. All fear. I let go of his fur, hit the ground, move in. The flesh is soft inside his thighs and the knife goes in easy. Not deep. Doesn't need to be. Stab then slice. Stab then slice. Like the bark of a tree where a peloglider hides. He steps back, hits me with his unharmed hand. I roll with the punch. He doesn't follow. Turns away. His mistake.

I picture Lazarus jumping on that Wyvern.

The back of the beast's head was the only place it couldn't reach me. Safest spot imaginable, as far as I could see.

He's not all bad. Just reminds me of myself when I was his age. Not the rich folks and fancy cars, of course, just the over-eager, under-informed, misguided sense of importance. But he'd been a good sport – he helped us out when we were clearly using him for his car and cash – and he had at least one decent trick up his sleeve.

I jump onto the Minotaur, as high as I can reach, and grab a hold of his matted fur. Portemus's anatomy book showed a dotted line across the Minotaur's back, between the shoulder-blades. Beside my fist, there's a similar line where the fur changes from dark brown to burnt red. Portemus has helped me solve many cases. He likes putting together a puzzle as much as I do. Let's see if he can help me solve this one.

The shorter blade keeps the strike on line, and it finds its mark. The blade slips through the fur, between two pieces of leather, and into flesh. I let go with my other hand, put all my weight on the hilt, and the knife cuts downward, slicing him open.

The beast howls. The balcony screams. The knife lodges.

I let go. Hit the floor. Blood rains down.

No knife. No bother. I see the sword. I reach for it and the world goes black for a moment: the force of the Minotaur's kick must have momentarily disconnected my eyes from my brain. My vision comes back blurred and red. I'm face down on the white tiles leaking lifeforce from my nose. I want to roll away but I don't know which way to roll. Another kick in the ribs sends me spinning on my back. The bull stands over me. Lifts his boot.

Gunfire. Screams. The Minotaur turns his head to the balcony. I scramble away. Look where he's looking. See a Wizard's face turn into mincemeat and confetti.

Khay.

I gather my wits before the Minotaur does. I slice the back of his knee. Weak spot. He doesn't go down but it shocks him. I cut up, and find the soft joint underneath his shoulder. His skin splits apart like the flesh of the rabbit. I slice again and—

He catches me by the head. Tightens around my hair; I've let it grow too long. He lifts me up. Screams into my face and I'm showered in spit, snot and blood. Not like this.

His hand tightens. The rough skin of his palm slides over my ears. I think I hear my skull cracking. Lights. My own screaming voice.

Explosions.

The Minotaur's face erupts. An eye first. Goes off like a rock dropped in a pond. A hole in his cheek flaps open like a clam. Bullet after bullet – from Khay's six-shooter, and whatever Linda is packing – rip him to pieces. Enough force to break the surface and damage the tender flesh beneath.

He releases the vice from my skull. Drops me. Bends over to cover his face.

His mistake.

I run up the Minotaur's back, point the sword at his neck, and fall on it with all my weight. It goes in – not easily, I have to force it – but I lean over and press it into him. Deeper. The beast screams. His arms go out from under him. His face hits the tiles. The blade rumbles in my hands.

Then, it doesn't.

He's dead.

I'm alive.

Unbelievable.

I'm hurt and I'm tired but I'm determined to claim my prize. I fall from the beast's back, stumble to the statue, climb the stone Wizard, and take the crown from atop its head.

55
Rubble

The crown was solid gold with sixteen horns along the top, each the size and shape of an eagle's talon. It was lighter than I'd expected, sturdy, and it felt like magic. I mean, it *was* magic – at least, I hoped it was – but it was more than just its potential Genie power. I was holding a piece of history. The crown had been forged in Incava four thousand years ago. Stolen by the followers of the Wizard Queen Riverna a thousand years after that. Cursed. Stolen again. Who knows where it traveled before it was finally returned to this place? I didn't need to see it grant power to know that it was special. Sometimes history is magical enough.

There were runes cut through the metal. The lines of each letter corresponded to the hand movements of a spell, a hundred tiny instructions etched into the gold, each representing some ancient feat of Wizardry.

Khay had her face pressed against the bars of the balcony. Her hood was back and, even from here, her eyes glistened. I held up the crown in triumph, and she reached her hand through the bars, beckoning me to throw it to her.

"I don't think I should," I called, worried that we'd come all this way just for me shatter the treasure because of a clumsy throw.

"I'll show you the way down," said Linda, at her side. "Come with me."

Khay, with some frustration, eventually followed, and I went about reclaiming my weapons. The sword took some yanking before it came loose. It was covered in blood, but as I was equally tainted, I didn't mind stuffing it into my belt the way it was. The Minotaur had crumpled at an awkward angle, swallowing Theodor's blade with its body. Unless I could find a way to lift the weight of the Minotaur's torso from it, the knife was gone for good. I was fine to leave it, being far more concerned with finding Theo himself.

I picked up my jacket. It was torn and damp, but the pockets were still full of bullets so I reloaded the pistol and faced the door.

The two Constructs were still there. Waiting. They'd been ordered to block the way, but clearly nothing beyond that. They wouldn't harm me if I didn't try to pass them, so I stepped closer and closer, careful not to trigger their directive. Even when I was a foot in front of them, they didn't react. They just stared straight ahead with their three eyes: two white and one full of purple crystal.

That gave me an idea.

I pointed the barrel of the pistol at the shimmering third eye of the Construct on the left. Even at point-blank range, there was no response. I didn't want to do it – shoot a piece of the sacred river that I was so set on restoring to its proper state – but the Wizards had already done most of the damage. I was just playing along.

CRACK!

I closed my eyes as pieces of clay exploded over my face. When I opened them, a dusty cloud had enveloped the Construct's head. It made a sound like it was groaning – impossible with no mouth – but that was just the creaking of its clay body as it tumbled backwards, hit the deck, and broke into several pieces.

The other clay soldier didn't even flinch. Not until I made a move to step through the gap. When it turned its head in my direction, I repeated the process and cleared the way, happy that these rocky slaves would no longer be a problem.

I followed the tunnel upwards and met Khay and Linda near the entrance to the room with the pit.

"Where the hell did you go?" demanded Linda.

"What do you mean? I turned back and you were gone."

"We ducked back for a minute because there were voices in the—"

"Hey!" Khay cut us off. "Can I . . . can I take a look at that, please?"

She was staring feverishly at the crown.

"Oh, yeah." I held it out to her. "Uh . . . here you go."

Khay reached out slowly, as if it might be some kind of trap. As if touching the crown might burn her, the way her hands had burned every other creature she touched. First, she tapped it with her fingertip, then she stroked the edge, then, when nothing happened, she took it in both her hands.

"Thank you," she said, her eyes wet and pink, and raised it toward her head.

"Wait!" said Linda. Her arms were tense, as if she was considering snatching it herself. "Are you sure you should do this now?"

Khay didn't take her eyes off the crown.

"Yes," she said, and placed it on her head.

She closed her eyes. Opened them. Nothing changed.

"How do you feel?" I asked.

She shrugged. "I don't know yet."

"We should get out of here," said Linda, looking around at the many tunnels, wondering which might be the exit.

"Not yet," I said. "Linda, we have a friend here. Delivered as a hostage. We have to find him."

"Fetch, we don't know how many stone servants they have here. How many Wizards are waiting to send them after us. You have your crown, we've seen the river, now let's go."

I wasn't sure what seeing the river had to do with it, and Linda's whole demeanor made me feel uncomfortable. She was hiding something – I was sure of it – but I didn't care, as long as she helped us track Theo down.

"The Constructs don't scare me anymore, and the Wizards are useless; you killed a whole bunch of them up on the balcony, and I put a bullet in the only one I've met. We—" Behind Linda, there were more tunnels. Two of those tunnels were connected by a dotted line of blood, smeared across the floor. The kind of mark you might leave if you were limping along with a bullet hole in your side.

Linda pounced on my pause.

"You've taken their crown, Fetch. They'll do anything to stop us leaving with—"

"This way."

I followed the bloody footprints into the dark.

You know some places are bad before you enter them. It's not a smell or a sound, it's a feeling somewhere down your throat, lying heavy on your heart. A knowing, as if ghosts are whispering a warning in your ears, letting you know of the horrors up ahead. The room at the end of the tunnel was one of those places. It made my mouth dry as I ran for it, ahead of the others, pistol at the ready.

I slowed at the entrance. I could see Constructs inside, spread out around the circular wall, waiting patiently. A different kind of light glowed from above. It was the same color as the river crystals; perhaps they'd found another way of abusing its power.

The Wizard I'd shot in the belly was sitting in a chair, his eyes closed. He was talking to himself, quick and quiet, interspersed with sobs and laughter. In front of him there was the body of an Ogre strapped to a wooden panel, tied at the forehead, neck, wrists and waist. He looked young. He wore a mohawk and a silver skull on a pendant: clearly the son of that sad fellow at The Harpy

House. I moved into the room and heard the footsteps of the others behind me.

Shoot him. I thought. *Now. Before it's too late. Shoot him.*

But where was Theo? I looked around. There were more bodies, all on panels, lying horizontal. A Dwarf. A Harpy. Some other creature, hidden under a sheet.

I moved toward the covered one. A human arm jutted out. Could be good, or could mean . . .

I lifted the sheet.

Black fur. Blood.

I span. Aimed.

"Servant," coughed the Wizard, "pull their arms off."

I was dying to shoot him, but it was too late, and now I couldn't risk wasting the bullet. I turned to the closest Construct – he was already closing in – and put the pistol to his forehead and fired.

"Shoot the crystals!" I screamed. "It's the only way!"

A clay fist grabbed my left forearm. Yanked it. The statue went for my right, but I dropped away, out of reach. It leaned down, chasing its target, and I shot from the hip. A chunk was blasted out of its scalp. Didn't care at all. I tried to pull away but he had me tight. Only one chance. I shoved my arm up close. The barrel made contact. He grabbed my wrist.

I fired.

Sand and sparks filled my eyes. The stone fingers let me go.

I put my hand in my pocket, fumbled for ammo as another Construct approached. I tripped, fell backwards. I had vague awareness of Khay and Linda struggling beside me, but I wouldn't be any help without ammo or arms. I cracked open the chamber. Got one bullet in. The Construct grabbed my leg. Second bullet. Dragged me close. Third bullet. Reached for my shoulders. I avoided him. Cracked the chamber closed. It grabbed the back of my jacket. Couldn't wriggle free. He found my right elbow. Held it so tight it spasmed in pain. I dropped the pistol. Grabbed it with my left hand. Heard gunfire from the others. Shouts of fear or triumph. Twisted around. Thought something was about to snap. Saw the statue's mouthless face. My left arm was awkward but I forced it to find its target. Fired.

The pain in my elbow dissipated.

"AAAHHH!"

Linda had one Construct holding one of her arms, while a second was fighting for the second. They were stronger than us, but they were slow. Small blessings. The second sentinel found her forearm just before my pistol found its friend. I shattered the crystal, sent it toppling. With her arm free, Linda finished off the other herself.

Khay was on the other side of the room. A Construct had one of her arms, and she was holding the other away from him as he snatched at it. Lucky for us, they weren't much for lateral thinking, and they only tried to harm us in the way they'd been directed. I went to help her, ducked under the swooping arms of another figure, and moved to execute her captor. Before I could get to Khay, the clay hand that was holding her shattered into pieces.

The shock of it stopped Khay but didn't bother the Construct, who used the opportunity to grab her other wrist. Without a second hand to complete his task, he dragged her towards his brothers. I found him first and expanded the crater between his eyes.

"Duck," said Khay, and I obeyed without question. Two terracotta arms swung through the air over my head. Before they could line up their next attack, Khay leaned over and executed their owner.

The clay foes were finished. The Wizard, on the other hand, was babbling.

"Leave them. Leave us. You don't know what you're doing. We are the future. You—"

"Gag him," I said to Khay, who was closest. She obliged with relish.

As he made muffled mumbles through a mouthful of her sleeve, I went over to Theodor and pulled back the sheet.

56

Rescue

Theodor was alive, though I'm stretching that word as thin as it will go. He'd been beaten up. Tortured. One eye was swollen shut and his jaw was hanging open. Blood seeped from his gums, around his fangs, and his tongue fell limp from his lips.

I listened for breathing. It was there, but only just: a rattled, wheezing sound that didn't come as often as it should. I put a hand on his head. It was wet. Soft. Something was broken inside.

That wasn't all.

There were cuts all over his body. Some sewn up, others still open, all filled with silvery purple power.

Khay dragged the Wizard over to us.

"What have you done to him?" she asked, and pulled the sleeve from his mouth.

I put my gun to his temple and warned him that if he said anything that didn't sound like an answer, I would end his life, but he couldn't have been more excited to explain himself. He looked up at me with steady indignation and said, "I'm saving the world, you fool!

"The world is dying, and nobody else is daring enough to rescue it. Only us. Only me. By coming here, you have killed the future."

"This is the future you're creating?" I asked, and forced him to look at Theo. "Linda, check the others. See if anyone else is alive."

"A small sacrifice," said the Wizard, his mouth drooling

red-tinted spit. "A necessary price to pay to bring magic back to the world."

I was furious and frustrated. I wanted to blow his head off, but I hated the way his words rang familiar in my head. It didn't take much imagination to picture Brother Benjamin in this room. An electrified Mage. A brain-dead Satyr. A bullet-ridden woodsman.

Not worth imagining. Not now. We had the crown. It would all be worth it.

"Nope," said Linda, after circling the room. "He's the only one left."

"Tie up the Wizard," I said to Khay, "and let's get Theo out of here."

I got questioning looks from both of them, but they didn't argue. We wrapped up Theodor's wounds as best we could, undid the straps from his wrist and ankles, and maneuvered him into a more comfortable position. I tied his arms to his body so they wouldn't fall away from him, and disconnected the panel from the table it was balanced on.

"I'll take this end," I said. "You two take the other."

We reloaded our guns before setting off. I asked Linda if she needed ammo, but she'd already reloaded her weapon from a pouch on her belt. Wherever she'd been for the last year, she'd managed to keep herself well-armed.

The wooden panel was heavy, but Theo was too injured to risk moving him without it. Khay and Linda led the way, sharing the weight of his feet, and I carried his head. We left the writhing Wizard behind and went back up the tunnel. I was sore, and I knew they were too, but we had to get Theo out of there. Once we were away from the castle, we could tend to him properly, but I could hear echoing footsteps and shouted orders bouncing around us.

We reached the end of the tunnel, which meant that we were no longer moving uphill, but there was no way to tell if anyone was watching. We scanned the many passages before us and the countless windows above.

"Which way?" I asked.

"I think I know," said Linda. "Come on."

She pulled us out of the tunnel and past the pit. Our tired footsteps bounced loudly off the shining surface, but, beneath that and my heavy breathing, I heard Theodor say something.

"Stop!" I called out. Then, "Theo, what did you say?"

He made a gargling noise before he found the strength to speak.

"Look," he said, ". . . up."

We were beside the pit. The open roof was above us, dropping moonlight on our heads.

"Khay, it's a full moon."

She looked up, then down at Theodor, who craned his neck to give her his good eye.

"I wish . . . I wish for you . . . to make me whole again."

He barely got the words out. Death was so close, I could feel its icy breath. Theo wouldn't make it out of the castle, let alone the woods. Not without a miracle.

I nodded to Khay, and we tried to lower the panel, but Linda held it up.

"We don't have time," she said. "They'll send more of those things after us."

"Then we have to move quick. Khay, get to work. We'll cover you."

We knelt to lower him. Linda didn't like it, but she couldn't risk fighting us when the real enemies were about to be upon us.

There was commotion somewhere. Doors opening and closing. Shouts. I couldn't tell what tunnel they were coming from.

Khay leaned over Theo so he could see her face.

"Are you sure?" she asked. "It might not work."

"I know, but . . . please . . . please try."

Khay closed her eyes, nodded, then removed her gloves. She put her hands on his cheeks and rubbed her fingers into his fur. If her hands were burning him, it paled in comparison to his other injuries. His eyes closed and his breath quickened. She whispered to him, her forehead against his, the crown between their skin, until he went rigid, and her body began to glow.

Moonlight filled Khay's body. The energy inside her rolled like an ocean reflecting faraway light.

"Argh!" Theodor thrashed so hard he knocked Khay over, and her daggers and pistol scattered to the floor. She tried to climb back on, but he lurched to the side and his Human arm shot straight out in front of him, tense as steel.

Khay swore and wrapped her hands around his neck from behind.

"I can't stop," she said. "Not yet."

The shouting grew louder. Shadows moved in the tunnel opposite.

"Khay," I said, "we're running out of time."

Theodor snarled and kicked out, fighting invisible enemies. Khay wrapped her legs around him, struggling to keep contact as he writhed and jerked around. Black fur sprouted from the skin of his Human arm. His existing coat grew thicker and longer, burying Khay in his fur as she continued to whisper into his ear. Theodor hissed through his already bloody gums as his fangs grew larger, cutting his lips and tongue.

Theo thrashed while Khay, glowing like the moon, held on for dear life, shouting her unintelligible words into his pointed ear. His weak arm was now covered in fur, and it thrashed like the rest of him, flinging blood into the air.

He howled, and the animals of the castle called back: owls, ravens and high-pitched bleating goats. Bats flew from the craggy alcoves and took to the air, swirling in circles over our heads.

Theo shook Khay from his back, and I caught her before she tumbled over the edge of the pit.

"Khay, what did you do?"

We stared at our friend – now a wild beast – as he stood up on his hind legs and roared into the night.

The wounds, stuffed with pieces of the river, were bulbous growths sticking out of his flesh. They looked raw and painful and, though his once-Human arm was now covered in fur, he carried it in front of him like it was still in a sling.

The Werewolf looked down at us with one open, glowing red eye. I fought to see the Theodor I knew in his face, but there was only the faintest glimpse of it behind the mangy black hair and bloody maw.

Did he recognize us? His wild, predatory energy was so different to the mild-mannered hunter we'd traveled with. He snarled, and his cut lip curled up the side of his face.

"Theodor, don't." I stepped back from him with my hands up. "It's us." Linda turned her gun on him. "No!" I drew Linda's sword from my belt and pointed it at her.

"Fetch," she said, not lowering her aim, "there's no time for this." A trio of Constructs emerged from the far tunnel. "Shit."

Linda spun towards the statues. I turned to Theo.

"Theodor, please." He snapped his jaws at my face. I avoided him, but only because it had been more of a threat than an attack. Something primal. When he wanted to hurt me, he'd have no problem.

He growled, and it sounded just like that starved wolf we'd seen while hunting the peloglider.

Khay raised her arms, turned her palms out, and took a step towards him.

"Theo . . ."

He span like lightning, slashed, caught her across the shoulder, and she collapsed to the ground.

I acted on instinct, informed by the lesson Theo had given me himself. I held the sword in one hand, and picked up one of Khay's daggers with the other.

"Hey!" I smashed the blades together over my head as hard as I could.

The Werewolf stepped back, growling but wary. I stepped forward and clanged again.

"Help!" screamed Linda. The Constructs were within reach. Khay went to her aid, picking up her pistol and firing it into the face of the closest clay soldier.

I smashed the blades together and shouted at Theodor. It was working. The animal in him cowed and backed off. The Human side of him was buried too deep to reason with the animal, but I could see a glimpse of it in his one working eye. As his shoulders hunched and he began to turn away, I swear I saw Theo look up at me, with betrayal in his eyes.

Then he turned and ran.

Khay's pistol clicked empty, so she pulled mine from its holster in order to fight the next wave. There were more figures behind them. Wizards. Men of all ages, all in filthy robes, coming for vengeance.

Two young Wizards emerged from a tunnel on the far side, and Theodor launched himself over their heads to make his escape. The rest of us wouldn't find it so easy. There were ten Constructs left, twice as many Wizards, and I was almost out of ammo. Even if we managed to clear this room, it wouldn't be enough. There were more explosions off in the tunnels. More shouts and screams. More enemies incoming.

They had us trapped.

On our left side, the Wizards turned to look back the way they'd come. Ahead of us, they did the same. For a moment, things went quiet – a held note – before a wave of roaring fire exploded out of a tunnel and barbequed a batch of Wizards where they stood.

Those who were unscorched attempted to flee down another exit, but a fearsome Ogre in plate armor stepped in their way and decapitated the first with a shining broadsword. The others scattered in all directions, searching for a way out that wasn't blocked by fire or brute. When one came in our direction, Linda fired a shot into his chest, and another at the one who followed.

More gunshots from overhead took out a panicked Wizard who couldn't decide which way to go. It took some searching to find the shooter, but when I spotted him in a window two floors up, I was even more bewildered.

"Larry?"

Lazarus Quintin Symes. What the hell was he doing in the castle of Incava? And apparently joined by some band of warriors who had arrived to save our asses?

I was too stunned to fight, but I didn't even need to. It was a slaughter. The Ogre moved through the Wizards, slicing them down like a farmer reaping corn. A Half-Elf entered the fight and fired pistol shot into the lumbering Constructs.

"Hit them between the eyes!" cried Linda. "In the crystal!"

It wasn't just helpful information she was shouting out. It was an order.

Linda knew these creatures.

The remaining Wizards attempted to flee through the far tunnel, but Larry wasn't about to allow that. He threw a leather pouch over their heads and it exploded at the exit, blocking their way with a fiery tornado. The flames caught the robes of the leading Wizard and he was forced to undress himself rather than be incinerated.

What the hell was going on? How could Larry be caught up with warriors like this? Unless . . .

Surely not.

Linda's sword was in my hands — sticky with Wizard and Minotaur blood — and I used my palm to wipe the gore from the silver emblem embedded in the hilt: a bridge over a river, reflected in the water.

Connecting one world to the other. Returning to the original.

No fucking way.

I'd thought The Bridge was nothing but the side project of some rich kid with too much time on his hands. But Linda was part of their ranks? Along with these actual fighters?

The Bridge was real?

The remaining Constructs stopped moving. Either their directions died when their master did or one of the Wizards had ordered them to stop as a way of ending the battle before they were exterminated. More members of The Bridge emerged from the shadows, and the Wizards were on their knees: pathetic, defeated – one of them naked – all begging the slaughter to stop.

The armored Ogre ignored them and marched in our direction.

"This her?" he asked loudly, pointing his bloody broadsword at Khay.

I moved between them.

"Get back," I growled as Linda joined us.

"That's her," she answered. "The last Genie."

Khay's hood was back, her robes were loose, she held a dagger in one hand and her six-shooter in the other. She was whole again, her body as real as anyone else in the room. All eyes were on her. The Bridge members were regarding her with fear and aggression, and she looked at me like I might have had something to do with it.

I turned on Linda, and my blood boiled with the dawning betrayal.

"Linda, what the hell is this?"

The Ogre stepped forward. I smashed his sword away, and the weapons of every Bridge member turned in my direction.

"FETCH!" warned Linda. "Step aside."

"No way. Did that dip-shit kid put you up to this? Hey, Larry! I've missed you! How about you come down here so I can give you a proper greeting?"

The Half-Elf came closer. Linda looked at the Ogre, and an unspoken agreement passed between them. They all stepped back.

"Linda," I said, "tell me what's going on, because you're not getting to Khay unless you go through me."

"Fair enough," said the Half-Elf, and threw something in my direction. I swung at it with the sword and, when it connected, an explosion of white powder engulfed me.

I knew the smell. It was the same kind of sleeping powder that I'd found in the pack of a maniacal Warlock pharmacist. The same stuff Larry had used to take down the Wyvern. Linda must have told The Bridge all about it, along with how to make those profane Faery pouches. She really had taken plenty of souvenirs from her time in Sunder.

I had just enough time to curse her before I crumbled to the floor.

57

Rise, Shine and Shudder

When I woke, the world was rattling. I was in my underwear with bandages and patches covering my cuts. My head was groggy, like it got when I had too many Clayfields; they must have given me some kind of painkiller while I'd been knocked out.

I was lying on a thin mattress in the back of a carriage. I wasn't tied up, which surprised me, so I got to my wobbly feet on the wobbly floor, and pulled open a small panel at the front of the compartment.

I could see the back of Linda's head, the Ogre holding the reins, and the two horses that were pulling us along. Ahead of that, a car led the way, kicking up dust.

All my clothes were gone, except for the Shepherd jacket that was dumped beside me. I put it on, opened up the side door, and climbed the thin platform around to the front.

"Where we headed?"

The Ogre glared over his shoulder; from his look to Linda, I could tell he didn't approve of leaving me unrestrained.

"Keats," said Linda. "Back to the University."

"Why?"

Linda had her own collection of patches and bandages. She looked tired, but she got up from her seat and moved to the bench beside me.

"After our member didn't return – that young Wizard who we'd sent to Incava – we assumed the worst: that he'd fed the Incarites our intelligence and they would be attempting to harvest the river's power. We spent weeks discussing our next steps:

arguing internally about whether we should stop them, help them, or whether it was our right to get involved at all. We were still arguing when we set off on our journey."

"You never received my telegram, did you?"

"Nope. Didn't know anything about it till you mentioned it yourself."

"But you bumped into Larry."

"I didn't 'bump into' him. He knew we were heading to Mira, and was waiting for us when we arrived."

I looked at the car in front of our carriage, and another car that drove in front of that. Larry would likely be in one of them, back behind the wheel. I was already dreaming about the things I would do to him when we came to a stop.

"I thought the kid was making this whole thing up," I admitted. "I thought The Bridge was something he created on his own."

"No, he's just overzealous. He met one of our members a few months ago. I believe he was accompanying his father on one of his business trips. He was given a badge and added to our basic correspondence, but we hadn't really vetted him yet. I suppose he saw this as a way to prove his worth."

Apparently The Bridge had already established a system of messengers and drop boxes, so it wasn't hard for Larry to anticipate their movements once he arrived in Mira.

"He sold us out," I grumbled.

"He merely told us what you'd found: a Genie with the ability to put magic back into creatures who had lost it. A real chance at redemption – if it was true – and that you were heading to Incava, no less. We could investigate the Wizard city and the Genie at the same time, as long as we left at once. On our way to the castle, he detailed the full extent of what you've been up to.

"He told us that this Genie of yours has killed several creatures on this trip, and an unknown number over the last seven years. He has only heard one account of these so-called miracles where the subject survived the experience, and fears that even with the crown she will bring more death than salvation.

"He also warned us that the two of you may be too obsessed to acknowledge this fact, and suggested that it might be wise to intervene in your attempted heist before anyone else could get hurt."

"So you came to stop us?"

"Not exactly. While we had planned to intercept you before you entered Incava, I must admit that I am curious to see what the effects of the crown might be."

"You saw what happened to Theo, didn't you?"

"Your Werewolf friend? I wouldn't count that as a ringing endorsement. We didn't find his body on the way out, but from what Lazarus told us, it can take a while for the side effects to set in. If the crown truly is the final piece to unlocking her powers, then we are now in possession of the greatest treasure of the new world. If it isn't, and her powers are unchanged – so that she must kill magical creatures to ensure her own survival – then I'm glad we captured her before she can harm anyone else."

My frustration spilled over.

"So that's what you lot are? Some kind of magic police? Deciding whether to lock up Khay, or stop the Wizards, or tell folks which way the world turns? Why should it have anything to do with you at all?"

I thought she might get angry. She didn't. She just nodded and looked tired.

"I don't know, Fetch. You should have been there when we started. They all thought they were playing some game, excited about the idea of helping people out. High on the idea of uncovering some secret. But once you decide to play with the fates of the people around you, do you get to choose what battles you opt out of? I imagine you ponder that question more than anyone. You made the call with Hendricks. You made the call with that Vampire. What makes Rye any different to this Genie of yours?"

"She's trying to put magic back into people, not suck the marrow out of them."

"A convenient excuse, perhaps. A way to justify the fact that if she doesn't do her little trick, she fades away for good."

"She's doing it to save people. That's why we needed the crown," I said, doing my best not to bark at her.

"Perhaps. When we get back to Keats, and run some tests, I suppose we'll find out."

58
The Bridge

"There's a river up ahead," said Linda, "we should give the horses a break."

She waved a piece of cloth for a few moments, then the automobile ahead of us honked its horn in recognition. We slowed as we approached a clear-water river with a far healthier flow than the one we'd driven Larry's car into.

The cars pulled off the road and we followed. The vehicle at the front was different to the ones I'd seen in Sunder: halfway between a car and a truck, with a section at the back that I couldn't see into. Khay must have been inside.

Lazarus got out of the second car. I couldn't hide my anger, so I didn't bother trying. When I took a step towards him, Linda moved between us.

"Fetch, do I need to restrain you?" She opened her cloak to show me more vials of white powder dangling off her bandolier. "I have no problem putting you back to sleep."

Play it safe, Fetch. Don't do anything rash till you get the size of things.

"Nah, I'll be good."

"If he's not," said the Ogre, pulling a crossbow up from beside his seat, "I'll take care of him."

I turned to Linda.

"What about Khay?"

"Let's talk a little first. We're not convinced she'll cooperate, and she'll be more dangerous than you if she decides to make trouble."

"Linda, you underestimate me. Trouble's my business, and I've had years of practice."

That's it. Keep it light. We're old friends.

The Half-Elf from the battle was there, as well as a Werewolf I hadn't noticed before. They all kept their eyes on me, and the Ogre's crossbow stayed trained on my back. Linda was giving me a chance to ingratiate myself with the members of The Bridge. Either because she wanted my help or because she just wanted to be a good friend. I suppose it made sense. In her mind, we were after the same things. I could be useful. After all, I was the one who'd given her all the information she'd brought to The Bridge in the first place.

She pointed to Larry.

"I believe you already know Lazarus."

The young man had never looked more slappable: a face full of bashful guilt covered by indignant self-righteousness.

"Where's Eileen?" I asked him.

"Back in Sunder. I put her on a Mortales delivery truck."

"Another favor from Daddy's friends?" He didn't answer. "You shouldn't have let her go on her own."

"She understood what was at stake," he snapped.

So earnest. People get like that when they know they're guilty. A problem I've always had myself.

"Larry, you know that Khay never tried to hurt anyone."

"I saw her hurt plenty of people," said Linda.

"You mean back at the castle? That's different. And we all delivered our fair share of pain, didn't we?"

"Unfortunately, we did," she said, sounding like she'd never regretted a thing, "but I never would have gone in if you two hadn't already tried to run the gauntlet. We only wanted to find out what was happening inside. You two wanted to steal and stayed long enough to turn it into a bloodbath."

"They had Theo and we needed the crown. You brought it, didn't you?"

No answers, but Larry couldn't help glancing at his parked car.

"Why was it so important to you?" pressed Linda.

"Khay needs it to get her powers back."

"No, she needs it to survive."

"Yeah, but she needs it to save people too."

"You mean *kill* people," grunted the Ogre.

Keep your cool, Fetch.

"That was before. The crown changes everything."

"Does it?" interrupted Larry. "Why? Because she said so?"

I didn't have a fast answer for that, other than to agree, and I didn't feel much like agreeing with any of them.

"Isn't this your whole business?" I asked. "The Bridge? Don't you want to fix things?"

"We're working to make things better," growled the Ogre.

"So am I!"

"She's killing people to save herself," said the Werewolf.

"Not now we have the crown. Let her show you."

"How?" asked Linda, doing her best to pretend it was a conversation and not an inquisition. "By letting her try her magic on someone else?"

"Well . . ." I waited for clever words to arrive on my tongue but, as always, they got lost somewhere along the way. Larry had a similar problem, but it didn't stop him speaking anyway.

"You know it will kill them if it doesn't work!"

As angry as I was, I still enjoyed watching Linda twitch with annoyance when Larry interjected.

"We just need to find someone who's willing to give it a try," I said, as calmly as I could. "Someone who's sick. Dying. That's what she's always done."

"Always?" asked the Werewolf with a sneer.

Linda and I kept our eyes on each other, and she tried to keep the conversation civil.

"Fetch, she promises them something she can't give. That she's *never* given. You think one more piece of jewelry will change things?"

I was about to start shouting. I wanted to ramble about the power of the crown, and what Khay had done for Mora, and how she only used her powers when someone asked her to – except if someone attacked her, or by accident – but I knew I wouldn't get anywhere. The safest thing I could do was shut up and find a way for them to trust me.

"What's your plan, then?" I asked, trying to throw the attention back their way.

"We take her to Keats and find a way to test her powers safely," said Linda. "Hopefully, you're right about her powers returning."

"Otherwise, what? You just let her fade away?"

"A lot of good people have faded away," said the Ogre. "They didn't try to take others with them."

All of them nodded, like the brute had said something fucking profound. All four of them in their green outfits with their shitty little badges and their ugly fucking logo stamped on their weapons. Larry hadn't got his uniform yet, which he surely thought was a huge injustice, but he still had his bloody badge. Everyone loves being in a club, don't they? You get yourself a costume and a title and a pre-packaged serving of agreeable friends who all have the same ideas and same goals and laugh at the same stupid jokes.

I thought Linda would be above all this. I suppose none of us are. I'd worn enough uniforms in my time. Hell, I've never taken mine off.

"Fine," I threw up my hands. "To Keats it is." The Ogre looked to Linda.

"He's a liability," he said. "I say we leave him."

"Fuck that!" I yelled, not helping my case. "I'm your goddamn prophet. It was all my cases and all my work that got you lot started in the first place. You should have a portrait of me hanging on your fucking wall, but I can't even come for a visit?"

"We'll talk it over," said Linda, and turned to the Werewolf. "Angie, bring the horses. Jasmine, come with us." That was the

Half-Elf. The Ogre, Mawrum, stayed to watch over me while Larry took care of the vehicles.

He went to the sedan first. It was similar to the one we'd crashed on the way out, though it was missing the more luxurious features. He got fuel from the trunk, opened up the plug on the side, and filled it up. I followed, keeping enough distance not to give the Ogre an excuse to stick a bolt in my back.

"So, young Lazarus, you've got a real band of brothers here, don't you?"

He scowled down at the canister.

"They're good people."

"Oh, yeah, I can tell. You see what happened to one of the members of the last group you went traveling with?"

He frowned.

"You mean Theo?" I nodded. "What happened to him?"

"We were surprised in the night. Could have done with a couple more sets of eyes and ears, I reckon. A few more bodies to push them back. If it wasn't for Khay, they'd have had me too. I count myself lucky to have a friend like her. Someone loyal, you know?"

The fuel spilled out of the hole, so Larry put the cap on and headed to the truck.

"Why did you come on the trip in the first place?" I asked. "To spy on us? So you could sell us out to your special little gang of do-gooders?"

"I came to get the crown, just like you!" He was more emotional than I'd thought. I almost felt bad about it. Almost. "But after the accident, Eileen and I got talking, and we realized there was no reason to believe that the crown would make any difference. She killed people. You saw it up close. We all did. We almost died, and we were doing it to help . . ." he lowered his voice. ". . . a killer. And we had no way of knowing if it would really work."

We stood near the back of the truck to refuel it, and it pained me to know that Khay was just inside. Could she hear us? Or was she knocked out, tied up, or worse? The Ogre followed me, tense and glowering, waiting for an excuse to pull the trigger.

"This is the way things need to be done," Larry continued. "Safely. With a group of educated minds all working together to make sure we do things right."

"And you decide what's *right*, do you? Bullshit. You felt guilty enough about being Human to come out on the adventure, but you don't really want anything to change, do you? Maybe for others – you like the idea of helping a few poor souls – as long as your dad and your friends at Mortales don't lose anything in the process. You wear your little badge to let people know you care, but you can't gain anything real if you aren't willing to risk what you've got. You don't really want to give up your nice cars and big home and fat allowance that lets you play hero. Hell, if I had what you have, I might not want things to change, either."

He hauled the canister back to the trunk of the sedan. I went to the side of the car to hold his eye. As I passed the open trunk, I saw the crown stuck between bedrolls and more containers of fuel.

"We *are* trying to change things," he said through gritted teeth.

"No, you're trying to control things. There's a difference. You want to find a way to do enough good to make yourself feel important, while not ending up anywhere unexpected. Khay isn't killing people; she's failing to save them. But at least she's trying."

Larry slammed the trunk shut.

"I wanted it to be true, Fetch. I did. And maybe it will be, but she can't be the one to decide if it's worth it to try. Because she *needs* it to be worth it. She needs this to be true or . . ."

Or she dies. He didn't need to say it, and I didn't need to argue with him. He locked eyes with me, and I could feel that he was truly asking for my understanding. For my forgiveness.

I locked eyes right back and gave him a meaningful look of my own: some kind of furrowed brow, lip-biting, concerned expression that would hold his attention and make him feel like

I cared. I didn't, of course – whiny little shit – I just didn't want him looking down. I didn't want him to notice the way my arms were moving around at the side of the car, hidden from view, as I took the crystal from my pocket and dropped it into the fuel tank.

59
Kaboom

We crossed over the river and rumbled down the road again: sedan, then the horse-drawn carriage, then the truck with Khay at the back.

These assholes were just like the cops and Thurston all over again. Folks who think that the only way to make the world better is to trim off the edges and shape it into something they understand. But this world was so far away from the one it needed to be that a bit of spit and polish wouldn't make a difference. We needed bold ideas and brave men willing to put them into action.

I wanted to believe that I was one of those men, though I had to try really hard not to look nervous so I wouldn't give the game away.

I didn't know much about how the automobiles worked, and I didn't know much about magic either, but I was well versed in destruction and I was pretty sure some kind of insanity would be coming soon.

I sat on the bench behind Linda and the Ogre. There was a heavy suitcase strapped onto the bench to my right – positioned directly behind the Ogre's head – so I untied the rope from around it. The case rattled a little more than it had before, but the others didn't notice. I gripped the back of the seat in front of me with both hands, and waited.

Linda looked back.

"You know, I asked Larry to go see you. Back in Sunder," she said.

"He never told me that."

"I instructed him not to. I wanted to find out how you were doing. Whether you'd kept your word. I expected to hear that you were still blackout drunk every night, counting every broken nose as a job well done. But you're sober, determined, proactive. Hell, you've even learned to duck a punch every once in a while."

I wondered if she could remember which of my scars had been made by her own hand.

"I don't do everything right, Linda. But I try to keep my word."

"You kept it too well, Fetch. Look at you: you're tense as a soldier about to run into battle."

She looked down at my white knuckles, gripped to the back of her chair, then back up at my clenched jaw and sweaty brow. I tried to look relaxed, but I wasn't fooling her for a moment. I was shitting myself.

"Mawrum," she said, "I think we should slow—"

BOOM!

Fire exploded from beneath the sedan, as if it had been coughed out the mouth of an angry Dragon. Blinding red light became billowing black smoke. The car landed on its nose with a crash of shattering glass, then fell back onto its burning underside, all four wheels blown out and useless.

The horses screamed. Panicked. Tripped over themselves and each other as they tried to pull away from the carnage. The Ogre hit the brakes and the carriage skidded, stopping just short of the fallen horses. The loose suitcase launched itself into Mawrum's back, knocking him down on top of them.

Linda had been slammed against the guard rail. She was stunned and hurt but still awake and extremely angry. She reached for her pistol. I stood up, took a deep breath, and kicked her in the ribs, right where she was keeping those vials of sleeping powder.

They shattered beneath my boot and I jumped away, holding my breath as Linda's yellow-green eyes rolled back in her head.

"What are you doing?" It was the Half-Elf, Jasmine, running from the truck. "What did you do?"

Her knees went weak and she fell forward. I grabbed her before she hit the ground and lowered her down slowly.

The horses pulled at the carriage, dragging on its brakes, so I used Linda's sword to slash the reigns. The horses broke loose and charged off through the trees.

My throat spasmed. I needed air.

Not yet.

The car didn't burn quickly but it burned hot, so I grabbed a handful of my jacket and used that to rip open the trunk of the car.

The crown was still there, unharmed. I put my left arm through it and grabbed a spare canister of fuel. I knew I should have checked on Larry, but there wasn't time. I passed the Ogre, who was unconscious – from fall or the powder, no way to know – and headed for the truck, which had been driven off the road to avoid hitting the carriage.

My lungs were tearing apart. Black smoke moved around me in low, toxic clouds. I got in the driver's side, slammed the door shut. Gasped. Heaved. Put it into gear.

I went around the wreckage and hammered down the highway until the plumes of smoke were out of sight, then I parked, ran around the back, and opened up the doors.

60

A Quest Complete

As soon as I lifted the handle, the doors flew open and hit me in the face. I fell onto the dirt and looked up at Khay, who stared back with gritted teeth, clenched fists and bloody wrists. Whatever restraints they'd put on her, she'd chewed through them or ripped them apart.

"Where are they?"

"Miles away," I said, getting up. "No horses. No cars. They're stranded."

It took her a moment to understand what I'd said, and another moment to believe it.

Then she jumped on me. I tried to move away – when someone launches at me like that, it usually means they're trying to knock my teeth out – but she wrapped her limbs around me and gave me a squeeze.

"Thank you," she said into my ear, before dropping to her feet. "Do you have it?"

I was surprised she didn't get whiplash, switching from grateful damsel to hungry treasure-hunter in an instant.

"I do."

I plucked the crown from the passenger seat and held it out to her. Gold sparkled in her eyes, and her face sparkled on the crown's surface. She slid her fingers through the spikes and lifted it out of my hands with fitting ceremony. She turned it around, inspected it from all sides, then pulled back her hood.

"Thank you, Fetch. Truly."

She returned it to her head, closed her eyes, and smiled.

"Does it feel different?" I asked.

She shook her head.

"Not really."

"What about . . . with Theodor?"

"I don't . . . I don't know. Do you think that counts?"

"Counts?"

"Do you think I saved his life?"

Shit.

"I'm not sure. But he'd been tortured. Experimented on. Whatever happened to Theo, you can't see that as your fault."

Khay's gloves had been lost along the way somewhere, and she looked down at her soft palms, pondering their ability to bring power or pain.

"You're right," she said. "I need to test my powers on someone healthy. A magical creature who lost their gifts in the Coda, but who will be strong enough to survive the wish."

I nodded. Before I'd thought about it, I undid the button on my jacket. I was still only wearing my underwear beneath.

Khay snorted.

"What the hell are you doing?"

"I . . . I'm letting you try out your powers. If you like."

Her smile flared up like an oil fire.

"That is a generous offer, Mr Phillips. But if you didn't know what made you magical before the Coda, how will we know if your powers have come back?"

"Oh . . . right."

"I appreciate the gesture, but I think perhaps we should look elsewhere."

"Fine. As soon as we get back to Sunder, then. Because those others – Larry and his friends in The Bridge – they'll be coming for us. We need to test your powers before they arrive. Sound good to you?"

I hoped they were okay, those bastards in The Bridge, but they hadn't given me a choice. Linda and the others, I understood –

they'd only heard the stories second hand – but Larry had met Khay. He'd traveled with us. How the hell could he betray her like that?

I didn't dwell on that question too long. I knew what mistakes a young man might make when he thinks he's doing the right thing.

"Sounds perfect," said Khay, and we got back in the truck and headed down the highway as fast as it would take us. Back to Sunder City with a treasure in our hands. A quest completed and a woman with impossible powers sitting right beside me. By the time The Bridge arrived, it would all be different. Everyone would know what she could do. They would know what was possible.

This was the first real step towards bringing the magic back, and we'd take it as soon as we got home.

61

By the Clouds

"How much longer, do you think?" asked Khay, after waking up from a nap. Her legs were on the dash, anklets clinking in the wind.

"I don't know. Two days, maybe."

"Hmm." She pondered that for a while, then said, "It all changed for me when I joined the Genie. With eternity ahead of me, I stopped marking time by the days and the weeks."

"What did you mark it by?"

"I tried a few things. You wanna know my favorite?"

"Sure."

She giggled to herself, like she knew she was about to say something silly.

"Passing clouds."

I played along with the obvious response.

"But there's no constant there. They move at different speeds. Different directions."

"Exactly. If I caught myself thinking about time, it would stress me out because it didn't mean anything to me anymore. But if I looked at the clouds and saw that it might be overcast for a while, then sunny for a bit, then some unknown weather in a few hours, it made sense again. It was real. Seconds and minutes are the least interesting way to mark the passing moments in your life."

I looked out through the windshield at the fluffy shapes above us. The lower ones were moving east quite quickly, but there were larger ones behind them that looked like they'd been painted onto the sky. I tried to put my mind in Khay's and forget about the hours ticking by, but I couldn't even pretend to disconnect from them.

"That changed with the Coda," she continued. "Now I have to worry about staying here. Staying real." She pressed her foot to the window, and I could just see the outline of the trees moving through her toes. "Now, I'm my own timepiece. The only one that matters."

We only stopped when we had to. No roadside taverns. No camps. We napped in the car until I'd rested enough to drive on, then we just kept going. We didn't have a lot to say to each other. No new stories to tell. We'd shared all our most recent memories, and they were still so overwhelming that I couldn't think about anything else.

At first, I worried about the silence. I thought she might be nervous or angry at me. Or bored – which would be worse – like I'd served my purpose. But then she'd comment on the sunset or point excitedly at some wildlife by the side of the road, or just look over and smile, and I'd relax. Relax more than I had in front of anyone in a long time. That's the mark of real friendship, I think: to be the person you are when you're alone, but in front of someone else. Just as free. Just as messy. The kind of friend where you don't have to stress over every little thing you say, because one little fuck-up in front of them won't make them think any worse of you. A single impressive act won't alter things either, because they've seen enough of your failings not to put you on a pedestal. *They know you.* The "you" beneath the bullshit. For better or worse, you can't impress or disgust them, you can't fool them or delude them, so you have no choice but to drop the act and enjoy the company. I was enjoying it so much that I felt sad when I saw a distant black shape at the end of the road.

Sunder.

It always looked different from the outside. When you couldn't smell the grease and the ash. Couldn't hear the constant clang of metal against metal and people barking out of windows and doors. Wide but not high, just the small elevation of Cecil Hill and the occasional building that went over three floors. It wasn't impressive to look at, but it had a pull. Hendricks thought that was its problem. The way it drew everyone in. The way this little mess of a place could have such sway over the fate of the once-magical, glorious continent of Archetellos.

I hit the brakes. Khay lurched forward.

"Shit, Fetch. What is it?"

"Sorry." The road ahead was clear. I looked behind us. Nothing at all. Not a car or truck anywhere on the long, straight road. I turned off the engine.

"What's wrong? Are we overheating or something?"

"No. I just . . . I just want it to last a little longer."

"Oh." She paused. Looked behind us. "I thought The Bridge were after us."

"They are. We won't wait long. Just until . . ." I looked up. A small, fluffy cloud – one of only a few in the sky – was moving overhead. It was just about to disappear behind the roof of the car on my side. ". . . just until you see the cloud. The one that looks like a Dragon."

Khay grabbed my leg. Gave it a squeeze. Sat back.

It was quiet without the engine running. The car made pinging noises as it cooled, and the wind whistled through the gaps in the metal. Beyond that, it was just wide open, silent space. Heartbeats and breath. The ruffle of cloth and leather when one of us adjusted our weight. Occasionally a little "hmm" or a "ha" – not a full laugh, really – more of an audible smile as one of us remembered something pleasant that had happened on the trip.

There was no time. No minutes. No seconds. We were free, until—

"More of a Wyvern than a Dragon, really. It only has two legs."
I wiped my cheeks before she looked over.
"Wyvern. Right."
I started the engine and we rolled back toward the city.
Our adventure had come to an end.

62

We dumped the car outside town and walked the rest of the way. It was dusk, which was good because I was still only wearing underwear and my coat. I went into a payphone and picked up the receiver.

Snap.

"Ow!"

I felt like I'd been slapped on all sides at once. I readied a punch and looked around, but there was nobody in reach.

"Did you just touch me?" I asked Khay.

"What? No."

The receiver was dangling by the cord, revealing a crack in the underside of the soft covering and a mess of frayed wires poking through. Stupid cheap Niles Company equipment. It was just the kind of accident that Portemus thought had happened to that electrified Mage, before we knew what Khay was capable of.

I avoided the loose wires and called the library.

"Hello?"

"Eileen."

"Fetch? You made it back!"

"I did."

"I've been so damn worried. What happened out there?"

"Plenty. But first, are there any other members of The Bridge in Sunder?"

"What do you mean?"

"Larry and his pack of idiots. The ones who gave you the silver badge. Did he tell you about any other members?"

"No. I thought it was just him."

She sounded sincere. Eileen was the last person I expected to lie to me, but I still needed to be careful.

"All right. How soon can you get to the café?"

"Half an hour."

"Great. I'll see you then."

There was nothing in my office but junk mail and a nasty smell. I opened the door onto the fire escape to let in some air, and was greeted by a nauseating yellow billboard fixed to the roof of the building opposite: MUSEUM OF THE FUTURE written in bold blue letters.

"What the fuck is the 'museum of the future'?" asked Khay.

"No idea."

More Niles Company horseshit. I couldn't wait to see Thurston's face when we delivered a future he never expected.

The firelight from the streetlamps bounced off the billboard and reflected yellow light on Khay's face. She seemed to be a different person to the brash young woman who'd first come into my office asking who had hired me. When I'd given her the bracelet taken from the mask-maker's basement – the one she'd asked Mora to steal from the library – and she'd first told me what she was. We'd shared so much since then, that remembering that first meeting felt strange. Like it wasn't her at all. Or me. Being back in my office, in clean clothes, looking out at the same bit of Main Street I'd stared down at for seven years, I knew something inside me had changed.

"How do we do this?" I asked both Khay and myself. "Where do we begin?"

Khay wrapped her arms around me from behind. Rested her head against my shoulder.

"We need to be careful. Start in secret. In case something goes wrong."

"Right." We didn't want another Benjamin. Another self-lobotomized Satyr. Another wild Theodor tearing up the town. "We need someone strong, someone whose body won't give out when you touch them. We need to give you the greatest chance at success."

"Of course. But when do you think the others will get here?"

"The Bridge? Days, at least. They need to find a car or rely on horses or their own feet. We have time."

"Not too much time."

She lifted her hand, held it in front of my face. The lamplight danced through her skin.

"No, not too much," I agreed. "We'll start with Eileen."

"You think she'll be up for it?"

"Oh . . . I meant that we should ask her advice but . . . I mean, we can see."

I didn't like the reality that came with being back in the city. Sharing walls with unknown neighbors and knowing there were cops, crooks and Niles Company men all around us.

I couldn't wait to show them all what Khay could do, but we couldn't risk a mistake. We had to prove to ourselves that the crown was the last piece of the puzzle, make sure Khay was back in control of her powers, and then we'd give Sunder City a performance to change the world.

Georgio dropped his mop when he saw me and wrapped me in a long, tight hug.

"WOAH! Fetch, you are a mess, even for you! You must be starving."

"Actually, I really am."

"Good! Let me cook something up."

"Make it for three, and we'd better close the blinds."

Khay was still wearing the crown under her hood. She hadn't

yet found a replacement pair of gloves, and there was a constant shimmer of transparency through her skin. Georgio sat us down and we were soon dipping crusty bread into chicken soup and slamming back cups of coffee. Eileen ducked under the blinds, saw us, and looked like she was about to cry.

"I'm so, so sorry," she said.

I had to swallow a bit of bread before responding.

"What? Why?"

She plonked herself down at the table like she was throwing herself at the mercy of a king.

"I abandoned you. I just, I don't know, I freaked out. I thought I was tougher than that, but something shook me up, you know? I wanted to get home. I thought I needed to. But as soon as I got here – hell, as soon as I got in the truck – I regretted it. I've been worried sick."

I put a hand on hers. Yes, I'd been angry at her when she'd left us, but I understood it. I'd dragged her out there. I hadn't listened to her. I'd put her in danger. If she hadn't come out with her apology first, I would have had to unload my own.

"Eileen, it's all right. You did the right thing, and it all worked out."

She put a hand on my hand on her hand.

"If you hadn't made it back, I don't know what I would have done. And look at you. Your head! Did that happen in Incava?"

"Mmm-hmm," I said, an unintentional smile finding itself on my face.

"What? The Minotaur?" I nodded. "You fought it?"

"Killed it," added Khay, and she pulled back her hood to reveal the crown.

Georgio looked over at us but didn't say anything.

"Shiiiit," said Eileen, in awe. "You got it."

"Yep," said Khay proudly. "Fetch broke into the castle, killed the beast and grabbed the treasure. He's my hero."

She batted her eyelashes like a starlet and giggled. Now that

Eileen had relaxed and our bellies were full, a giddy, celebratory energy began to bubble up.

"What about the Wizards?"

"Oh, those bastards," said Khay happily. "But we should start the story at the beginning, and we need something to drink."

I asked Georgio for a bottle of wine. He brought one out from the storeroom, but when I went to take it from him, he gave me a disappointed look.

"I know, George, but it's a special occasion. I promise."

He stared at me, and I thought he was about to say something else. Something more serious than to remind me that alcohol and I weren't the best of friends.

"Join us, Georgio!" said Khay. He waved her away with a polite but uncomfortable bow.

"Thank you, but I need to keep working. Please enjoy."

He left the bottle on the table, and we all emptied our water glasses and filled them with wine.

I started the story off, describing the walk in the woods, our time learning about the forest from Theodor, and finding the Fae bodies, before we were ambushed by the woodsmen. Eileen shed tears when I described Theodor's kidnapping, and I told her about all the things that our hired hunter had taught me: archery and hunting and how to become one with the woods.

We told her about the Constructs. The way the Wizards were mining crystals directly from the source and putting them into bodies, both flesh and clay.

"If Thurston hears about this, he'll pounce on it immediately," I warned.

"I won't say anything to anyone," she assured me. "I swear."

"We might have slowed down their operation for a while," added Khay, a glint in her eye, "but if this way of using the river gets out, it will change everything. We have to make our move first. As soon as possible."

"Of course," said Eileen, not picking up on Khay's subtle

suggestion that they should reach over the table and hold hands right now. "But what about the Minotaur?"

When I described the battle with the beast, I got caught up in the tale – perhaps it was the wine – and practically went through the whole fight blow by blow, even getting up from my chair to demonstrate some of the more exciting moments. Eileen and Khay cheered me on and raised their glasses as I brandished the wine bottle like a sword and delivered a final blow to the invisible monster.

My story fizzled out when I saw Georgio, sitting on his stool behind the register, his usually joyous face in a tired frown. Without his smile, he was almost unrecognizable. I ignored him, and assumed that he was just tired.

Khay told Eileen about Theodor – making a point to accentuate the way she'd brought him back from the brink of death, rather than focus on what he became and the way he left us – and quickly moved on to being captured by The Bridge and making our escape.

"I want you to know that I had no idea," Eileen assured us. "Larry just told me that he wanted to stay in Mira to see if he could get another car and use it to go find you. He insisted I head home as soon as possible."

"Such a little weasel," snarled Khay.

I refilled my glass and leaned back.

"Did he try to kiss you?" I asked.

I could feel the stupid grin on my face. It must have looked identical to the one that Khay was wearing. Eileen blushed.

"No," she said, with an obvious *but* hanging in the wings. "But, he did write me a poem."

Of all the explosions I've seen in my life, none of them compared to the eruption of wine that burst from Khay's nose. Closing the blinds had been useless; you could have heard our laughter halfway to the Mayor's house. We cackled like wild dogs. I was short on breath, with tears in my eyes.

"What did you do?" I asked, when I had enough air in my lungs to speak.

"I thanked him for his kind words but told him that I was partial to more feminine partners."

"Is that true?" enquired Khay.

"Not exclusively – it was mostly to get him off my back – but most of the time."

"Good to know," said Khay. "I hope this . . ." she gestured to her purple-stained lips and bloodshot eyes, ". . . is the kind of grace and femininity you're looking for."

Another trickle of wine dripped down her nose, sending us back into fits of giggles.

"Thanks for the offer," said Eileen, "but I like kissing someone who won't fry my lips off in the process."

The laughter died.

"Sorry," she said. "I'm drunk. I didn't mean that."

Khay waved the comment away. Though I could tell that it hurt her feelings, it also gave her the opening she needed to make her request.

"That's all right," she said. "It's true. At least, it *was* true. But we have the crown now. I saved Theodor's life, and he was torn to pieces before I tried it. If you're ready, we think it's time to claim the prize we all went searching for." She held out her ungloved hand across the table. "What do you say, Ms Tide? Ready to spin some spells again?"

Eileen was in shock. She looked at Khay's hand and recoiled.

"I . . . I'm sorry. I didn't know that's what I was here for."

"Oh, no, you're not," I said. "We just thought we'd offer. Thought maybe you wanted to be the first. Just an idea."

Shit got awkward. I felt like we were some free-and-easy couple on holiday inviting Eileen back to our room. Khay kept her hand out.

"Thank you," said Eileen. "But it's just a little too risky for me. I'm . . . I'm quite healthy, actually. Happy. I'm lucky enough to have too much to lose, you know? But I'll help you find someone. Someone who wants it. I'm sure you'll have them lined up around the block in no time."

Khay withdrew her hand.

"We should talk to Portemus too," I suggested, trying to reclaim some of the excitement that had so quickly dissipated. "He helped with Mora, right?"

Khay nodded. "But that was a special case. It doesn't mean I need him all the time."

"Of course. But we want to give ourselves every possible chance to make this first one count. We can't afford any more . . . well, you know . . . we want to make sure we do this right."

There was an awkward pause, and Eileen used it to excuse herself.

"I need some time to think," she said. "About who might be suitable. I'll call you in the morning."

"Of course." I was being overly warm, to make up for Khay's silence. "Thanks for coming out, Eileen."

Eileen's awkwardness was unsettling but, after she left, Georgio's silence was as potent as the stink off a sulfur mine. When I thanked him, and offered to help him pack up, he just shook his head.

"He all right?" asked Khay, as we went through the revolving door.

"Yeah, he must just be tired."

Upstairs, I lifted the receiver but there was no dial tone.

"Shit. They've cut off my phone while we were away. I won't be able to reconnect it till morning."

"Oh."

"It's all right. You stay here. I'll go and see Portemus in person."

"I'll come too."

It's hard to say what it was that made me nervous. Khay had always had a hard stare, an excitement about her, and a ready energy at all times of the day or night. She'd always been determined. I'd liked that. We wouldn't have got anywhere without it. But I knew that I needed to see Portemus on my own. Maybe it was the fact there was still blood under my fingernails and in my hair. Maybe it was because all the things we'd done on the road didn't seem to fit back into the gritty streets of this city. Maybe it was how she absently rubbed her hands together, inter-locking and stretching her fingers, sliding her palms back and forth, like she was aching to get them onto someone's skin. I had my whole mind on this case, but she had it filling up her body, and I needed some space to get my head straight.

"Best you stay here. I'll go talk to Portemus, bring him here, and we'll find someone for you to save as soon as we can."

"Promise?"

"Promise."

I showed her where the shower was, told her I'd be right back, and went downstairs. The light to the café was still on, and I was craving a coffee, so I ducked inside.

Georgio came out from the back room holding a screwdriver.

"Sorry to keep you up, Georgio, I—"

He disappeared out the side door without saying a word. Strange. Our dishes were still on the table, so I put the dirty glasses in the sink. Georgio came in, walked right up to me, and dropped something heavy onto the table.

Fetch Phillips: Man for Hire
Bringing the magic back!
Enquire at Georgio's café

The plaque from my building. I looked at it, confused, then at Georgio, who had his eyes focused on the floor.

"Georgio, what is this?"

"I don't want to work with you anymore."

You'd think with all the crazy things that had happened in the past few weeks, I'd be beyond the point of surprise, but I was more stunned than when I'd first laid eyes on the Minotaur.

"What . . . what do you . . .? Why?"

"I agreed to help you help people. That's what you said you wanted to do. *Some good*, remember? This is not good."

I felt small. Flashbacks to being a kid with scraped knees and rips in my new school uniform, or a hungover teenager returning my adopted father's broken bike; the same shame, and the same panicked desperation to make things right.

"Georgio, this is what we were working towards. Khay can help people now. *Really* help them." He kept his eyes down, shaking his head. "We went out there to make things better."

"You went to WAR!" He was shaking. I'd never seen him this angry. Hell, I'd barely seen him frustrated. "You left your home to go and murder," he continued, his voice hushed to a chillingly measured tone. "You left your home to steal. You lost a good man and you killed a creature, the likes of which we may never see again."

"I know . . . I know, but if this works then it will be worth—"

"Nothing is worth this! Nothing. It will only bring more death. This started with death, don't you remember? Your *friend*." The image of Benjamin's smiling face forced its way into my mind. "There is so much death already, and you only want to make more. I will not help you do that."

My chest burned. I felt like I was about to cry, but I smothered it. If the first sob escaped my lips, a tidal wave would follow. I choked it down. Squashed it. Spoke clear.

"I'm doing what needs to be done, Georgio. I can't just sit back and let the world die. You might enjoy making people breakfast while the world burns, but I'm actually trying to make a difference. I'm sorry you don't want to be a part of that."

It was my cue to storm out, but I missed it. I guess I wanted him to say something else. To start shouting again. To smack some sense into me. Anything but to let me leave.

But he just said: "Go."

And I did.

63

I buzzed the buzzer and waited for Mora or Portemus to answer.

"Hello?"

"Porty, it's Fetch. Sorry it's so late. Can we talk?"

A pause, then a tired, "Of course."

The gate opened and I went into the always cool and creepy lair.

"Portemus! We did it!"

He looked much the same as the last time I'd seen him: disheveled, underdressed and exhausted. He even had a beard coming in.

"Did what?"

"We found the crown! Khay's wearing it right now. Where's Mora? I can't wait to tell her."

There was that fucking look again. How many times had I been given it, or given it to someone else?

"Come with me."

We stepped through the morgue, between the slabs, and I heard music coming from the back room: a kind of sentimental tune with a sultry voice over strings and piano. It got louder as I went through the door and into what appeared to be a shrine. The room was full of scented candles. There was art on the walls. Photographs of far-off lands. Piles of books, on tables and the floor, all lying open. A crooning gramophone beside an impressive collection of records, and a bench covered in decadent treats: liquor, exotic fruits, candies, cakes and tea. There was a pipe resting on an ashtray, beside a dubious-looking bag full of some black substance. That might have shocked me, if the centerpiece of the room wasn't far more arresting.

Mora was reclining in a large leather chair, her body supported by cushions and covered by an expensive-looking quilt. Her good eye was closed. The other was still empty. What I could see of the rest of her made my eyes water.

"What . . . what happened?"

As if I didn't know the answer. I knew it the moment I walked into the morgue. Portemus was a Necromancer. He'd raised the dead. Befriended them. He still spent most waking hours with his hands in corpses, and it never stopped him smiling. Until now.

"It didn't work," he said. "Or maybe it worked too well. The undead side of Mora has overtaken the rest. It's sucking the life out of her. There are only the undead pieces of her left – still pulsing, beating, blinking – but the rest is empty."

When I'd last seen Mora, the undead parts of her body had looked like unfortunate afflictions on an otherwise healthy young woman. Now, they looked positively vibrant compared to the rest of her. Her skin was pale and yellow and stuck to her bones like wet cloth, the lines of her empty veins and arteries visible beneath. Most of her hair was gone. Her fingernails too. There was a white line of dried spit on her blue lips, and her body was so emaciated that with the quilt laid flat upon her, there appeared to be nothing of substance underneath.

I knelt beside her.

"Mora, I'm so sorry."

"Shhh," she said. "I love this part."

The music reached a crescendo, then the piano and the drums paused, leaving space for the woodwinds to take center stage. They celebrated for a few bars on their own before the singer joined in. Her voice was as rough as a shingle waterslide, but Mora's – when she joined in – was even rougher. More breath than voice, really, but she must have used every last one of her working muscles to smile that wide.

We stayed silent until the end of the song.

"Porty," she said, when the song was over, "can you open my eye for me?"

"Of course."

Portemus used a little glass circle to pry apart her eyelids. Those muscles must have lost their strength, but the eye inside was clear, and her expression was just as wry as ever.

"How are you, Mora?" I asked.

"All the better for seeing you, Mr Phillips."

"I'm sorry. Sorry it didn't work. But Khay has the crown now. She has more power. I can bring her over here and we can have another try. I—"

With effort that must have equaled anyone else hoisting a car over their head, Mora put her arm on mine.

"I'm good," she said, slow but sure. "I risked it once. I don't regret it, but I don't want to risk my last days again."

The look on my face must have divulged what I was thinking. That surely she had nothing left to lose. That if anyone should be willing to risk it, it was her.

She squeezed my arm.

"I want to enjoy whatever time I have left," she said. "My last hours. Minutes." She took a deep breath, and I could see it move through her body, from her one good lung into her shaking throat and the caverns of her face. "It's nice to be alive, Mr Phillips. I'll take it while I can."

When Portemus let me out, I knew not to ask for his help. He had a job to do. A noble cause. A duty far more important than whatever I'd been doing since the Coda happened. I tried to tell him that before he closed the door.

"You've done something really special, Portemus. She's lucky to have you."

He gave me a half-hearted nod and closed the door in my face.

I never thought I'd see the day when Portemus had had his fill of death.

64

We were running out of time to test Khay's powers, and I had no real idea where to go first. Who could we choose? What would we say to them? *Hey, can my friend put her hands on you and try to fill you with magic? It's only killed or deformed every other person we've tried it on, but maybe it'll be different for you because she has a new headpiece.*

The retirement home seemed obvious, but too risky. If they were already that close to death, then the shock of the spell might push them over the edge. One more failed attempt and this would all be over. I couldn't justify trying it again and again, hoping for the one rare result that would make it all worth it. So, we needed someone healthy enough to live through the experience, but desperate enough to give it a try. We'd have to be honest with them. No lies. No sweetening the truth.

Shit. Why was it suddenly so complicated?

"Don't move."

I ignored the order and turned around. I was in an alley between Angel Avenue and Keating Street, with a kid standing behind me. He looked about fifteen: skinny, and in a scrappy suit. He had a knife in his hand.

"What are you doing?" I asked, genuinely confused.

I'd crossed through this alley a hundred times. I practically lived on the streets. I'd seen kids like him on every corner – gangs of them – and they'd never dared stop me. Nobody did. I was more puzzled than afraid, and the kid didn't like it.

"Money. Weapons. Drop them on the ground. Now."

I laughed. This hadn't happened since my first year in Sunder, before I learned how the city worked.

Oh shit, I thought, when I realized what was going on.

My shoulders were hunched and my posture was relaxed. I'd been walking like I was still in the woods: careful footfall, meandering gait, head down and body soft. I looked like an easy mark. Poor kid. I straightened my shoulders, jumped back, and reached into my jacket.

But the pistol wasn't there. Of course it wasn't. Linda had lifted it from me and never given it back. The kid lashed out with the knife. I tried to block it with my arm – a stupid move – and it cut through the sleeve of my jacket all the way through to the skin.

I stepped back again and tripped over a trash can. He span the knife around in his fingers and stabbed.

It went in. Somewhere in my guts. Bad. Real bad.

He punched me to make sure I stayed down, but I didn't feel like fighting. He rifled through my pockets, took the brass knuckles, my wallet, keys, whatever else was in there. I didn't care. I couldn't. I was down a long tunnel, far away, watching my life like it was projected on a distant wall.

His footsteps echoed away, and as the image of the alley flickered and faded, a face slid into view: a grinning fool with five red marks across his forehead.

"Well, if it isn't the man who fixes things," said the maskmaker. "So, did you manage to save the world?"

I'd never been so happy to fall unconscious.

65

"I thought you'd learned how to dodge."

The world was out of focus but the lisp was unmistakable.

"Simms." My voice had been dragged for miles down a gravel road. I tried to move my arms, but they wouldn't respond. "What happened to me?"

"You got stabbed in an alley. A boringly predictable outcome, I know. Gone for weeks, then you're almost killed by an overeager pickpocket. You're lucky someone saw it happen and got you to hospital soon enough to save you."

I blinked. My eyes were as dry as my throat. I tried to look down at my hands, but everything hurt.

"My arms," I coughed. "What's wrong with them?"

Simms stepped closer to the bed. I braced myself for terrible news.

"They're handcuffed to the bed, you idiot. Didn't want you waking up in the middle of the night and slipping out on us."

Fear turned to relief, which turned to confusion, then anger.

"Why the fuck would you tie me up?"

"Don't hurt yourself. Here, have some water."

She pushed a straw towards my mouth. I kept my lips closed.

"Don't be a petty child, Fetch. Drink." I couldn't resist it any longer, so I put my lips around the straw and sucked it down. "Go easy. You've been out for a few days."

"I've *what*?"

Goddamn, my throat felt better.

"You almost died, Fetch. Because of your own carelessness. This isn't my fault."

"Yeah, but you tied me up."

"Because you're under arrest. Accessory to murder."

Most other days, I'd scoff at that. But not today. There were too many murders fresh in my mind. Woodsmen lying in the forest. Wizards up in Incava. A Minotaur, perhaps the last of its kind, now a corpse in a castle. Then there was the accident. I hadn't checked on Larry. What if he hadn't made it out? Or what if someone had found Linda and the others before they woke up?

Fuck.

"Which one?" I asked.

Simms raised her eyebrows. "That's not the usual response I get when I accuse someone of a crime. You want to save this conversation till you wake up a little, or would you prefer to incriminate yourself now?"

"Piss off, Simms. I thought you only cared about city crimes, anyway."

"I do." She pulled a stack of papers out of her pocket and cleared her throat. "Brother Owen Benjamin: you discovered the identity of the killer but didn't bring that information to the attention of authorities."

She held up the first bit of paper. It was a photo of Benjamin splattered on the sidewalk.

"Fuck you. That wasn't murder. It was an accident. She—"

Simms flipped to the next photo.

"Kellen Umbra. Mage. Death by electrocution. You witnessed a pattern of these murders and still refused to come forward."

"It was a mistake. She asked their permission, and—"

"Cormac Alexander. Incinerated."

"I don't know who that is."

"Pamela Lismore. Induced heart attack."

"What does that even mean?"

She threw each photo on my bed as she read out name after name.

"Judith Ash. Martin Wellington. Ishmael Amor."

"Simms, what the fuck are you going on about?"

"Tiffany Leith. Mora Abraham. Emily Christie. John Ryan. Liam Tar. Astrid—"

"Simms! What the fuck are you on about?"

"THESE ARE ALL THE PEOPLE YOU KILLED, FETCH!"

Everyone went quiet, even those in other rooms and down the halls. Silence. Simms was hissing. Her tongue was out of her lips, vibrating with every breath.

"Simms, I don't know any of those people. I promise."

"And you never will, Fetch. They're gone. Mothers. Husbands. Friends. All gone. All torn to pieces from within. Their own bodies turned against them."

"No," I said without meaning to. "She wouldn't."

The slightest hint of pity bled into Simms's anger. She turned the remaining photos around and fanned them out.

"Fetch, her fingerprints are all over them."

She was right. Every single body was deformed, twisted up, burned or broken, but they were all marked with the same slender handprint.

I couldn't catch my breath. My chest hurt. I was shaking. The cuffs cut my wrists. A pain stabbed my stomach. I tried to scream but I was beyond screaming. It hurt to move. To breathe. To think.

"Hey," I heard Simms say, her hand pressing down on me. "Hey, stop it! Stop it!"

I got some air into my lungs, but I kept shaking. Simms didn't care.

"She did this, Fetch, and you let her do it. It's all going to come down on your head." She leaned over and looked right into my eyes. "Unless you're the one who stops her."

66

A fresh shirt and set of trousers were set out for me. Simms gave me water, some plain porridge, and made me walk around the hospital ward to make sure I wasn't going to collapse as soon as I stepped outside.

"If you let him go," warned the Satyr doctor, "he could very well die."

"We can only hope," replied Simms, dragging me out of the medical center and into the blinding sun. "It'll save me the trouble of having to kill him myself if he doesn't do what needs to be done."

I covered my eyes with my hands, and even that hurt my side. It was loud. There was music somewhere. A marching band.

"What's happening?" I asked, still getting a hold of my senses.

"Year of the Phoenix. A parade to celebrate Niles bringing the fires back. But don't get distracted by the festivities, you've got work to do." Simms shoved two packs of Clayfields into my hands. "Take them all. Doctor's orders."

With a sneer, I ripped open the pack and put three between my teeth. I felt the buzz but they did little for the pain.

"Why me, Simms? A city full of cops can do more than me with a hole in my belly."

"My officers tried. You know what happened? They burned their fingers when they tried to grab her, then she grabbed them by the throat and did whatever it is she does when she touches someone's skin. A junior constable's bones stabbed her own body from the inside out. A Banshee detective screamed himself to death and burst the eardrums of a whole squad. I don't want any of my Magum officers going anywhere near her, and I don't have

enough good Humans to catch her quick enough. I could wait
for Thurston's men to track her down, but they'll shoot a dozen
civilians before they find their first clue. I need her stopped now,
before anyone else dies. It needs to be you."

The Clayfields finally had some effect on my body, though it
didn't help the mess inside my head.

"You got any change?" I asked.

She fished a few stray coins out of her pocket and handed them
over.

"What else do you need? You got weapons? Back-up?"

I walked away.

"If you don't do this," she called after me, "you're as much to
blame as she is."

Fuck off, Simms. You don't understand anything. Something's
gone wrong, that's all. Maybe they asked for it. They might have
heard what she could do, so they wanted to give it a try. There
was going to be an explanation.

Crowds were gathering along Main Street. Chairs and rugs had
been brought out onto the sidewalk and vendors roamed up and
down selling silver cans of beer, roasted nuts, frozen juice and
packs of streamers.

I went into the same payphone I'd used last time, avoided the
frayed wires, and called the library.

"Eileen, what the hell happened?"

"Fetch? You're awake."

"Where's Khay?"

She paused. "You disappeared. She came to me when she couldn't
find you. I tried to keep her calm, but she panicked. She thought
that she was fading, and she just freaked out and left. I'm sorry."

"But . . ." But *what?* I wanted some other answer. Some hint
that Simms was wrong. "Is she really doing what they say?"

"I don't think it's her. Not really. The curse wants to be used.
All magic does. It always did, but now it's . . . well, you know."
Yeah, we both knew. We'd both seen what happened to people

who tried to reclaim their powers after the Coda had taken them away. Edmund Rye, Rick Tippity, and many others. Why had we been so eager to ignore all that had come before?

Because we had to. Because we had to hope. Because what's the point of any of it if you don't believe that things can get better?

"I think it was the crown," she continued. "I mean, it was all of it, but the crown was too much. Either that or . . ."

"Or what?"

Eileen sighed heavily into the receiver, sending sadness directly down the line.

"Or she just doesn't want to die."

We were quiet for a while, sitting with the most reasonable and most troublesome explanation. The receiver made a beeping sound to let me know that I was out of money. That's the part where I should have scrambled to put more coins in, or make some kind of apology or say goodbye, but we both just listened to the sound as it beeped and beeped and went silent.

A shadow fell over me. Someone was waiting to use the phone.

"Yeah, I'm done. Just—"

I was slammed back against the wall of the booth, with five sharp points of pain around my throat.

"Linda," I choked. "You made it back."

She was filthy. Her eyes were bloodshot and her fur was matted and muddy.

"You worm." Her voice was almost drowned out by the cheers of the crowd as the lead drummer brought the parade around the corner. "You left us to die."

"Not true. I left you to sleep so I could escape, and very much hoped you *wouldn't* die." Her claws extended from her fingertips, deeper into the soft flesh around my neck. "Everyone's all right, aren't they? Larry and the others? They're alive?"

The question only made her more furious.

"They're alive. But you have no idea what we went through."

"I don't. I'd love to hear about it sometime, but you're not the only person threatening to kill me today, so you'll have to get in line."

"Fetch, you—"

I grabbed the phone cord, right where the broken wires were sticking out, and an invisible mule kicked me sideways into the wall, cracking the glass.

Linda took the hit just as hard as I did, but, as I'd been expecting the shock, I was quicker to recover. From her crumpled position, she reached out and grabbed hold of my shirt. I pulled away, ripping all the buttons, and freed myself from her grasp.

"What did you do?" she panted, still in shock.

I stepped over her without answering and slammed the door shut. There was no way to lock it, so I just ran across the road and into the parade.

The marching band was made up mostly of schoolchildren. They blasted horns and trumpets and smashed cymbals and snare drums; just what I felt like after a week in the hospital. I weaved around them, moving up Main Street towards home, but as soon as I made it through the musical kids I ran straight into a dancing girl who seemed to be wearing nothing but feathers.

"Off the road, bozo," she said as she shoved me to the side of the road and shimmied past, leading what looked like another hundred dancing girls and, behind them, the first float.

I froze at the utter audacity of what I was seeing.

A black truck pulled a trailer. The trailer was dressed up to look like a giant silver radio blasting upbeat, big band music and, on top of the radio, wearing a tuxedo and top hat and twirling a cane, was the very man who was throwing this parade in his own honor: Thurston Niles.

He was doing a terrible shuffle around a microphone stand, smiling his artificial smile at the cheering crowd.

"Happy anniversary, Sunder City!" he yelled into the mic, and the crowd roared back in adulation. What had we become?

Gargantuan beasts used to fly above our heads on a daily basis, now we applauded a middle-aged man doing the box step just because he gave us a good price on washing machines.

Thurston spotted me in the crowd and his grin became less artificial and more maniacal. He pointed his cane right at me and waved, as if I was one of the kids captivated by the whole absurd production. I turned my back on him and squeezed through the crowd, desperate to get to Khay before she used her powers again.

I couldn't feel the pain at all anymore; not the stitched-up puncture in my guts or the slit on my wrist, or the bruise that covered my entire nose. They were all blotted out by the marching band and the bellowing hellscape inside my head.

This was not how it was supposed to go. I only wanted to fix things.

I'd spent the first six years drowning in guilt. All but useless. Then I'd tried following others, and made more of a mess of things than ever before. With Khay, I'd finally, *finally*, started working. Working *hard*. And we'd fucking solved it! I'd cracked the case and gone and fought the monster and got the golden piece of shit that was supposed to make it all better, so why the hell was it still so fucking awful?

Linda thought that Khay was like Rye, but she was different. Wasn't she? She was trying to help people, not just save herself.

Or maybe that was what she wanted to believe. A reason to justify what she needed to do to stay alive.

Because she kills them, or she dies.

That's it. That's all there is. Two terrible paths and no other way to go. No turning back. Just pain.

I got back to my building, trying not to dwell on the bare square of brick, cleaner than the wall around it, where the copper plaque had once been.

Fuck you, Georgio. You're part of this too. If it's on me, it's on you.

The blinds were down again – strange at that hour – and the phone inside was ringing. Maybe Georgio had gone to the parade.

I waited outside. Listening. Nobody picked it up, so I opened the door.

The café was dead quiet, other than the telephone. It didn't smell like it usually did. Not fresh. The air was thin, like the ovens and fryers hadn't been used that day.

Ring.

I walked over.

Ring.

I picked up the phone.

I didn't say anything at first. Just listened. Far away, a male voice said something like, "Yesterday, today and tomorrow!"

Somebody breathed into the receiver.

"Hello?" I asked.

"Fetch! Oh, Fetch, I saw they let you out. I was watching. I wanted to come see you, but I can't. They're all chasing me. They don't understand."

"Khay, calm down."

"You understand, though, don't you? You're not angry?"

I didn't know *what* I was. All the emotions were there, but they were pressed down, low, under a lead ball of dread that was getting heavier by the second.

"No, I'm not. Khay, where are you?"

"I . . . I can't say, can I?"

"Yes you can. You can tell me."

"I can't. You hate me."

"I don't hate you."

She sobbed.

"You will."

The lead ball dropped lower.

"Why?"

Lower.

"I didn't mean to. I was looking for you, but he wouldn't tell me anything, and then he got angry and I . . . I'm sorry, Fetch, I—"

I left the receiver on the counter. Looked towards the kitchen. "Georgio?" I called.

Nothing.

I stepped away from the buzzing phone and Khay's desperate, panicked voice. The door to the kitchen was closed, so I pushed it open. No steam. No smell of coffee. No singing. No light.

"Georgio?"

Silence.

I stepped inside. Slowly. Light footfall, like creeping in the forest. Silence. So dark.

I reached out for the light switch. I'd never needed it before. Never been here alone.

I found the button. Rested my finger on it.

Don't do it, Fetch. Just walk away. You don't want to know.

I pressed down on the switch – only halfway – and as soon as there was a flash of light, I ripped my hand back and let the room go dark again. It was only a moment, but it was enough. Too much.

His body on the ground, leaning against the oven. His head was back, mouth open, and his face was bright red with the marks of those murderous fingers stretched across his skin.

I didn't scream. I was going to be sick. I ran out of the kitchen. Out of the café. Eyes everywhere. The parade filled the street; more floats, more music, and there were people all over the place, on the sidewalk, the doorways, the windows, the roofs. Cops. Niles Company men. All watching me. Was Linda out there somewhere? She would be soon.

Screams fill my head. Bile in my throat. I move inside. Away from them. Away from it all. Up the stairs. Not silent now. Steps loud enough to cover my moaning. The sound is too loud to stay trapped in my brain. It wants to pour out of me but I bite down on it. Smother it. I turn the knob. It's locked. No key. Must have lost it when I got mugged in the alley.

The words in front of me come into focus, painted black on frosted glass:

Fetch Phillips: Man for Hire.

I put my fist through the words and the window shatters. I reach through the empty space and turn the handle. I push my way in and fall face-first onto the bed. I stuff a pillow into my mouth and I scream.

I scream and I scream. I scream to quiet the world.

But the world just screams back.

67

When my voice was too hoarse and my lungs too empty for the screaming to help, I opened my eyes. There was blood on the sheets, less from the knife wound and more from my knuckles. That stupid goddamn window painted with that stupid goddamn name.

What a phony. What kind of asshole paints his name on the glass, puts it up on a plaque, and pretends that it means something. I didn't mean nothing to nobody. I was done.

Yesterday, today and tomorrow.

The voice I'd heard on the phone behind Khay. It played over and over in my head.

No. Not in my head at all.

I kicked open the Angel door. Stepped out onto the fire escape. The parade was going past and the float right below my building was a sickening shade of yellow.

"Yesterday, today and tomorrow!" piped the recorded message.

Right ahead of me, obscuring what was once a perfect view of the west side of the city, was that offensive yellow billboard with the same words scrawled across it. And underneath: THE MUSEUM OF THE FUTURE: OPENING SOON.

I went back down the stairs and through one of the abandoned offices into the side street so nobody would see me leave. I was sore but I walked straight. Shoulders back. Chin up. Not in the woods now. When I make eye contact, they look away.

I dare some derelict little pickpocket to try to mug me now.

The library was closed. Parade day. I broke the handle. Kicked in the door. Went all the way up the back to the storybook display that I'd designed, and all the pieces were still there, even the case with the Genie jewelry. They'd used a bit of copper to replace the golden bracelet. It did the job, I guess. Most of the other items were fakes, anyway.

Most of them, but not all.

You could never make a fake of that sword. The finest sculptor in the world couldn't craft something like that. Not anymore.

I lifted the glass from the plinth, grabbed the Fae sword from its display, and went out to find my friend.

68

Sunder City. Seven years since it all fell apart. Seven years of trying to make a difference, and what had I done? Plenty, I suppose, but how much of it was good? Any? Even a little? I'd sure as hell tried, hadn't I? Maybe not to start with. Maybe not for a while. But eventually, I really tried. Surely that counts for something.

It does, as long as you learn, I reckon. Learn when to change. Learn when to stop.

The wind moved through my hair. Moved through the Chimera fur on my collar. Moved through my patchy beard and across my bleeding knuckles.

The streets were full of life. Loud and happy. Vibrating. New colors. New smells. Nothing a string of killings could dampen. Not in a place like this.

Sunder goddamn City.

I hunched over, so as not to pull on the stitches. I was no longer the man who stands tall in the city. Not the wolf at one with the woods. Just a battered soldier with an ancient wooden sword in his bloody hands, off to tidy up one last mistake.

I chewed the Clayfield till it lost its flavor, spat it out, and put another in my teeth. The tip of the sword dragged along the cobbles. The wind danced with the lamplight and the shadows joined in. Somebody cheered about something. Someone else laughed, and it spread through the streets. There was happiness here. Hope. Optimism. A desire to move forward.

Why would we stand in their way?

The museum looked the same from the outside, except for a canvas banner that was the same shade of bile as the billboard, declaring an opening date that was still a month away. The thick front doors were closed and bolted, but I found a roller door around the side that had been cracked open.

It was dark inside, but not as dark as it should have been. There were lamplights somewhere. I lifted up the door – no way to stay silent – and ducked underneath.

"Sunder! A city of yesterday, today and tomorrow!"

The recorded voice welcomed me as I came out of the storage room into the entrance hall: a place I'd been in many times, though any semblance of the old design was gone. It was no longer a celebration of the world's most rare and vibrant creations, but more of a department-store catalog brought to life. Appliances and weapons were placed on pillars like they were something to be admired. Instead of a spectacular Wyvern skeleton hanging from the roof, there was a car engine, just like the ones we'd seen around the woodsmen's camp.

"Yesterday, today and tomorrow!"

The sound was coming from the far wall, just before the entrance to the main part of the building. I walked towards it – intending to go past, in search of Khay – but I was drawn to the three model cities set against the wall. Each of them was the size of a card table, and every building was accounted for.

It was Sunder.

Yesterday.

The first display featured Sunder as it was the night I returned from the mountain. Empty lamps up and down Main Street. Devoid of life. Back before we knew that the fires were still alive beneath us. A city drowning in loss. Amari's broken hospital. The empty Governor's mansion. The expanding retirement village and the dark curve of the sickle.

We'd believed it was over.

There was my building: 108 Main Street. The Angel door. I half expected it to be open. To see myself standing there in a tiny, fur-lined trench coat with a sour look on my face, dangling my toes off the edge of the stoop and waiting for the phone to ring.

Waiting for some kind of distraction. Waiting for someone to give me an easy way to fulfill my promise. All I wanted was a way to do some good without having to work too hard or be too smart or too sober or too brave. It was all for nothing anyway, I'd thought at the time. The good days were gone and we had nothing to do but count down the hours until the color faded from the trees and the sky. It was only a matter of days before the world stopped turning.

Today.

Electric lights pretending to be fire were balanced on the tops of the tiny little streetlights. Many of the stone buildings from the first model were gone, replaced with polished metal: warehouses, cranes and fire escapes. Brisak Reserve had been flattened and replaced by factories. Cobbles had been switched out for smooth asphalt.

They put a light beneath the streets so that it glowed through the cracks, hinting at the fire pits below. Mechanical cars span around on an endless loop, past pedestrians as big as grains of rice that filed in and out of restaurants and stores that advertised fancy new appliances.

Why did I hate this one so much? Did I just not know my place in it? Or was it pulling too far away from the world I wanted to get back to? It didn't look so bad from up here. I know that was the point – this was another specially designed piece of Niles Company propaganda – but when I thought back to what things were really like seven years ago, I had to admit that any steps that took us away from that feeling of hopelessness must be moving us in the right direction.

Of course, the curators of this exhibition had intentionally left out the even earlier version. The vision of Sunder that I'd experienced when I'd first left Weatherly. A time when the city was an overflowing explosion of color and life that stretched from the slums all the way up to the flower-filled gardens on Cecil Hill. When creatures of every kind were working, eating, dancing and fucking. Back when they set off spells and flew from rooftops.

No model of that world here. They wanted it to be forgotten. Instead, there was a plinth on the other side.

Tomorrow.

The future was fittingly unfinished. There was a kind of basic, unpainted mold that they must have used as the foundations for all the models, but the rest of the detail was yet to be created.

Perhaps they were waiting on the bureaucratic decisions from the powers above; a mandate on what kind of temptation they should dangle over the population to keep them turning up to work on time. What kind of promise would they make to inspire servitude and patriotism? What kind of lie?

We would have to wait and see.

CLANG!

Something dropped, or was thrown, in a distant room. A voice too. Was someone crying? I left the miniature Sunders behind and went down the hall. All the paintings and mosaics were gone. Now there were just posters of toasters and photographs of buildings going up: smiling construction workers instead of mighty heroes, and people holding steel beams instead of slayed Dragons.

The big painting of Hendricks had disappeared, along with all the depictions of shining knights with swords as big as their bodies, valiantly attacking enemies just outside the frame.

Good, I thought. I didn't like what Niles was doing to the city – to the world – but that didn't mean that everything that came before was perfect. Baxter had tried to tell me that nothing was worth the war, but I hadn't listened. I wanted to see myself like one of those heroes of old, wielding a sword and slaying a gargantuan beast. It wasn't the first time I'd done it, either, but the lessons we learn when we're young, when we're trying to understand what it takes to be a grown-up – to be a man – take the longest to unlearn. We deserve a better future to aspire to than just becoming soldiers – better than grubby businessmen too – but I was still waiting for someone to show me the alternative.

The next room was an armory. The museum had always had a room like this, but it had once displayed weapons from far-off lands and ancient times. Back then, there had been a sense of equality between the exhibits. No particular piece had pride of place, and no lineage or period of time was held over the others. Not anymore. Now, it was clear what we were supposed to think about the weapons on display.

Tacked onto boards and mounted along the walls were the halberds, morning stars and lances of old. Useless wands and staffs were all clumped together, as if to emphasize their lack of worth. The daggers and swords were rusty and chipped, like they were relics of a forgotten time, not weapons that were still used commonly today.

The firearms, though, were a whole different story.

The room was full of statues – new ones – of men and women in modern dress, standing in dramatic poses, brandishing various models of the Niles Company killing machines. Some I didn't even recognize, like the larger weapons with longer barrels that needed two hands to hold them. They must have been new products that hadn't hit the streets yet. Niles was clearly using the museum as a marketing tool. It was gross, but nobody would care. They'd just put in their orders and work a few more shifts to cover the cost of their toys.

"I'm sorry."

Khay was seated at the feet of one of the statues. Her robes were all torn up, and she'd wrapped them differently. The new design seemed intended to show off as much of her jewelry as possible.

For the first time, I considered how heavy the whole collection must be: the thick cuffs, the stones hanging from her neck, the countless rings, and the piercings through her ears, nose and nipples. The strings of gold that fell over her shoulders and looped beneath her arms, around her waist, and hung from her hips. Then, of course, there was the crown.

That fucking crown, weighing down her head like it was trying to sink her.

"I didn't mean to," she said. "You know that. The thing is, I can . . . I can *feel* it working. Every time, I know it can happen, I just need to work out how. That's all it will take. Just one person. Then they'll believe me. Then we can put everything back, and all the rest of the mistakes won't matter."

"Mistakes? Khay, you're killing people."

How long had this been going on? I'd spent the last few weeks trying to convince myself that a few failed attempts were worth the risk, but she was seven years deep into this endeavor, and I was sure she'd left out a few details.

"Have you forgotten what happened to this world?" she asked, finally looking into my eyes. "It's all dead anyway. Dead and dying."

As if to mock her, a celebratory burst of music caught the breeze and floated through the walls of the museum. The parade was coming uptown. Who were we to turn off the music and tell everyone that they weren't dancing the right way? That their contentment was selfish and their happiness a delusion? What had we done, with all our good intentions?

She stood up. Her tattered robes dangled from her limbs like the leaves of a willow tree.

"Why should I have to be the one who dies? I just wanted to help people."

"I know you did."

She held out her arms, presenting the cuffs. The bracelets. The rings.

"That's why I did this in the first place."

"I know."

"I would have served for centuries. I would have done so much good."

"Yeah, you would have."

She lowered her head and the reflected torchlight swirled around her crown.

"It isn't fair."

"No, it's not."

Her eyes fell on the wooden sword in my hand.

"You here to be a hero, Fetch? Have you come to kill me?"

The crowd outside cheered. I shook my head.

"I can't."

She played with the rings on her fingers, twisting them around and rubbing them together.

"I don't want to die." *Yesterday, today and tomorrow.* "Why would the world leave me this power if I can't help anyone with it? What's the point if it only hurts?" She lifted up her right hand and looked at it, considering the untapped potential of the power it wielded. "There must be some purpose."

She turned her head to the side again, and squinted at me, as if I was way off in the distance.

"Why can't I touch you?" she asked.

I swallowed. My throat dry. My arms were so heavy.

"I don't know," I said.

She stepped close. Fast. I brought up my sword arm, but I was too late. My buttonless shirt was open and the palm of her hand burned hot against my chest.

I'm a child again, approaching the walls of Weatherly.

But it's different.

It's night. I'm being carried on horseback. Wrapped in a blanket in someone's arms.

This isn't how it happened.

The person carrying me dismounts. They walk to the wall. A door opens and a man steps into the light.

Graham. The man who will become my father.

But it's different.

He's older. He has a beard. Tired eyes.

This isn't how it happened.

He takes me. Concerned. Concerned for my safety but concerned for what it might mean.

"Where did she come from?" he asks.

She?

"The mountain," says a voice. "She may be the last of them. Keep her safe."

Searing pain, like a dagger between my ribs, shocked me back to reality.

I swung the Fae sword and brought it down on Khay's arms. She screamed, and I jumped back. Khay stared at me accusingly, looked at the dent in the cuff on her wrist, then gasped as a crack appeared in the gold, all the way along her forearm. The cuff broke into several pieces and fell to the floor.

She wailed like I'd sliced off a limb, not just a piece of metal. Eileen was right: the cursed jewelry had its own drive, its own desires, and it was pushing Khay to do things she would never have done on her own.

She lashed out in anger and tried to grab me. I brought the sword back around, tapped the underside of the cuff on her other arm, then smashed it down on top, shattering it.

I didn't need to hit hard. This sword had been created by the Fae to fight back against the iron weapons of Man. All I had to do was touch the gold with it, and the residual magic did the rest. I only needed to be accurate, and keep my distance when she reached out with those slender fingers.

"Stop it!" she yelled. It didn't sound like anger. More like pain. Heartache. Fear.

"Khay, get back!" I tried to create distance between us, but she moved on me, despite herself, reaching out with her cuffless arms.

I pointed the sword out straight, but the tip wasn't sharp and I wasn't really trying to hurt her, so Khay didn't bother avoiding it. She let it press against her sternum, brushed it away with her bare forearm, and grabbed me.

She gripped the fur of my coat and pulled herself close, but I brought the sword up between us. The tip was pointed toward the ceiling, and I leaned it into her, so that the blade fell against the front of the crown.

"NO!"

She pulled her head back, but I leaned further forward. Pushed harder. The metal dented, bent and split, slowly, like a blunt knife through cold butter. She grabbed my arms, but I was stronger, and my sleeves protected me from her fingers.

CRACK.

The crown split, tumbled from her head, crashed onto the tile floor and broke into several pieces.

Khay screamed like I'd put the sword through her heart and fell to her knees. She picked up two parts of the Wizard King's crown and held them together, as if they might magically rejoin.

"No, no, no."

"Khay . . ."

One of the broken cuffs was nearby. She reached for it, but I kicked it away. Did the same with the other pieces of the crown.

"Noooo." More resigned now. Less desperate. Less angry.

"Khay, let it go."

It took her a few breaths to get herself under control, then she looked up and gave me one of her ironic eye rolls.

There you are.

"If it goes, I go," she said.

Without the crown, some part of the Khay I knew was coming back.

I tried to say "I know", but the words, too heavy, wouldn't climb my throat.

"What happens now?" she asked. "You gonna bash every piece off of me with that sword? Have that final heroic showdown I promised you?"

I didn't smile. I remembered wanting something like that. A good fight, like in the stories. The chance to run into battle with a magical sword. To slay an evil monster so the world would be a better place. Now, here it was, and it was torture.

"No," I said. "I can't."

She nodded. Bit her lip. Wiped her cheeks.

"We just wanted to save some people, didn't we?"

"Yeah, we did."

"All right then." She shrugged. Resigned. Ready. "Well, I guess this is one way to do it."

She reached up and wrapped both hands around the wooden sword. Tight. Her face clenched and she squeezed, not from the physical effort, but from the struggle of pushing against the curse. Against her own survival instinct.

"Aaaah!"

She opened her hands, and the broken rings peeled from her fingers and fell to the floor, tinkling like a drunk's last coins landing on a bar. She sat back, took a breath, and went about removing the rest. With each piece, her struggle eased. Her anklets. Toe rings. The chain that hung from her belly button and went around her body.

Piles of gold formed at her feet. A fortune in ancient jewelry, once stolen to please a queen, cursed to punish her killers, then given a new purpose by someone who dared to see the potential in items that had been marked for death.

Khay slowed. No struggle anymore. She was methodical. Ritualistic. She took the piercings from her ears, her nose, her eyebrows, navel, nipples and her lip. Then the necklaces. She slipped her fingers underneath the lot of them, lifted them up over her head, and let them drop.

Finally, there was the last bracelet. The one she'd tried to have Mora steal from the library. The one I'd given her in my office when she'd first come to ask for my help. For my trust.

It landed on the pile, and that was it. Every single piece.

She fell.

I dropped the sword and caught her before she hit the ground.

"Khay?" I looked into her eyes and saw my fingers through the back of her head. She was fading already, but . . . "I'm not burning."

She smiled. Shook her head.

"No curse anymore. There's just me." She reached up and touched my chest. Such soft fingers when they weren't full of fire. "At least you have something to remember me by."

Her handprint was burned onto my skin. Khay brushed at it with her thumb, like she was trying to wipe it away, but that piece of her was there for good. She put her hand over it instead, and I could still see the red mark through her fading fingers.

I kissed the top of her head.

"Hold me?" she asked, as if I might somehow refuse. I wrapped her up in my arms and she curled into me. Not like a child. Not like she was going to sleep. But like she was holding on for dear life. She ran her arms around my body, inside my shirt, skin against skin, and gripped tight, as if my body might somehow hold back oblivion. I gripped her right back. Tight as I could. I pressed the side of my face to hers, tears mixing with tears, and felt every heaving, fearful breath.

Do you know what you'd do to stay alive? Most of us never have to make that call. Not so clearly that we have to weigh up our life against another's. Instead, we make that choice in a hundred little decisions every day, when we put our own life, and our own comforts, over everyone else. We all live our lives off the blood of other people; they're usually just far enough away from us that we can convince ourselves that it isn't the case. We put enough businessmen, enough dollars, enough days and years between our actions and their effect to pretend that they aren't connected. That we don't have a choice. But it's always a choice. We know it deep down, and – unless anybody calls us out – we'll go on and on letting others suffer, just so we can have one more beer in the sun.

Don't you dare judge her. She did what we all do. But unlike the rest of us, she found the strength to stop.

My hands slipped past each other. My face fell forward. My body slumped to the ground. Empty.

Alone.

69

I lay on the floor until the marching band passed. Until the celebrations escalated, hit a crescendo, and faded. After a few hours, it sounded like a normal Sunder night.

I filled my pockets with the abandoned jewelry. Not that I wanted it for anything. I just didn't want it ending up in some pathetic exhibit in this conman's excuse for a museum.

I went out the way I'd come in and saw the first thoughts of the day sneaking into the eastern sky.

The streets were full of trash: streamers, cans, bottles, bones and paper plates. It was easy to turn my nose up at it, but it was a hundred times better than the morning after a battle, when it would be blood and bodies filling the gutters instead.

Main Street was the worst of all. It looked like it would take as many people to clean up this mess as it had taken to make it. A young couple, still full of booze and hormones but with nowhere to go, were on top of each other at a streetcar station, too focused on each other's tonsils to notice that the sun was coming up.

Crows, pigeons and rats were scurrying all over the place, having their own celebration now that the other creatures had gone home. A fox stopped in the middle of the street and looked at me. Knowingly breaking Theodor's rule, I looked right back. He just watched me walk and, when I got too close, took a wide berth around me and continued on his way.

I approached 108, firm in the knowledge that it was no longer home. I didn't know what I would do when I woke up, but I knew that my ridiculous Man for Hire routine was ready for retirement.

Then, I saw movement.

Somebody was walking around inside the café. Probably a looter, going through the place because it looked unattended.

I kicked open the door.

"Hey!"

Kind blue eyes stared out from the darkness. Those dual hand-prints were still there: red palms on the sides of his cheeks, thumbs under his lips, fingers reaching across his forehead. He was taller than usual – that hunch in his back had straightened out – and he stood at his full seven feet.

"Georgio? I . . . I thought you were . . ."

He smiled. Not as wide and free as he used to, but still flashing those imperfect teeth.

"I think perhaps I was. But . . . but now I'm not. At least, I don't think so."

He looked about him, as if watching a butterfly circle his head.

"Are you okay?"

"Yes. Yes, very much so. I just . . . I just *feel* something. Like I used to." He locked those warm eyes on me again, and I stared back. Stunned. "Come with me."

I followed him out the back and he collected several items: a metal pot, some contraption with a handle on top, a set of scales, a couple of different sized spoons, some mugs, cloths, soap and a bag of beans.

"I used to be able to feel the river," he said as he wiped down the stove.

"Feel it how?"

"Sense its power and, sometimes, interpret its will."

"Its *will*?"

"Yes."

My head was spinning. I couldn't yet believe that he was here, but I just kept talking, hoping the dream wouldn't end.

"You mean, like it was alive?"

"Of course it was alive. Not like we are. You don't need a brain or a heart to have life. Everything has its own momentum. Its own *will*, as I said. The river had wishes of its own. Wishes and wisdom. Some of us, those who worked very hard, could listen to those wishes and endeavor to see them manifest around us." He finished cleaning the stove and moved on to the pot and the spoons. "I am feeling it again."

"What? The river?"

He held up one long, gnarled finger.

"No, no. Not exactly. But . . . something."

Once everything was meticulously cleaned, Georgio went over to a cork board that was hanging beside the grill. Pinned onto it were countless pages ripped from the notepads he always kept stuffed in the front of his apron. He liked to make notes whenever customers complained or complimented his cooking. He unpinned one of the pages from the board.

"What is it?" I asked. "What are you feeling?"

"I don't know. But I believe I must find out."

"How?"

He shrugged. "I don't know that either. I feel it pulling me, whatever it is. It wants to be heard. So, I must go somewhere quiet and listen to what it has to say."

It was too much to take in. Not only was Georgio alive, but Khay had unlocked something in him after all. It had worked, in a way, just this once. Why? Had she not held him as long, because of her guilt and her grief? Or was it just that Georgio was such a rare being? Someone more in tune with the old ways, so more able to survive a return to its power?

I was confounded by the miracle, and the fact that it had come too late. Whether it could be replicated was impossible to know. Probably not. Not without her having to play the lottery with her deadly powers again. But goddamn, I wish Khay could have seen what I saw: Gorgoramus Ottallus, standing straight and tall, hearing sounds from a world that we all thought was gone.

"So you're . . . you're going?"

"I am." He said it like he was just taking some trivial trip to the shops, not venturing forth from the city, following an unspecified voice, for an unknown amount of time.

"What's all this stuff for, then? Some kind of spell?"

He laughed. That crazed, unfettered cackle that I loved to hear, even when it was at my expense.

"No, you silly Ponoto, I just thought I should finally show you how to make the coffee. Now, open the bag of beans and scoop some onto the scales. We want . . . What's wrong?"

"Nothing."

"Why are you crying?"

"I'm fine. Okay, how much do we need?"

Georgio took me through every step of his recipe, explaining his notes and showing me what they meant in practice. There were exact weights, temperatures, and measurements of water. There was a technique to the way he filled the pot to get the right amount of pressure on the ground beans. Though we used a timer, he made me hold the side of the pot to learn to gauge the temperature by feel, and we watched closely for the first signs of steam bubbling out of the spout.

The pot held enough for two cups, and we tasted the final product.

"See, a little bitter because we let it boil too long, but this will improve with practice. You might be tempted to fit more in the pot to save time, but don't even think about it. You stick to this recipe, train yourself, and it will be perfect."

We drank in silence. Slowly. Trying to make it last.

"Thank you," I said, when the mugs were empty.

He put a hand on my shoulder. Nodded. Then he left.

The world was quiet. The city was sleeping, the Genie was gone, and the Man for Hire had hung up his coat. The sun would rise on a new day. Less magical, perhaps, but not without its wonders.

We'd tried, hadn't we? Nobody could fault us for that. And if Georgio went out there and found something worthwhile – some way to make things even a little bit better – then maybe the fates might forgive us our failings. Or at least find a way for us to forgive ourselves.

I sat down on Georgio's chair and closed my eyes.

"Ding!"

How long had I been asleep? There was light coming in around the blinds, but it was still early.

"Hello?" Some guy had let himself into the café and was hollering towards the kitchen. Didn't he know what time it was? I poked my head around the corner.

"Hey, uh . . ." Before my half-asleep head could explain that the owner of the place had left town on a mysterious mission, the man threw a couple of bronze coins on the counter.

"Two black coffees." He turned toward another man who was standing in the doorway and continued some conversation they must have been having outside. ". . . and I told him not to have another one, but he was trying to show off to some broad and now he's puking up his late-night pigeon pie and the meeting's in half an hour."

I hovered, trying to get their attention, but without a break between sentences to let me interrupt, I just went back into the kitchen. Sure. I suppose I could make a couple of coffees before I . . . did whatever I was going to do next.

I tried making it from memory, but I must have made some mistake filling the pot because it overflowed and I had to start again. This time, I followed Georgio's instructions to the letter and the result at least looked the way it was supposed to. I took the two mugs out to the gentlemen.

"Sorry about the wait."

They didn't even stop their conversation to acknowledge me, and three more customers had already taken seats. First, there was the young couple who'd been making out at the streetcar station, still with their hands all over each other and rough skin on their chins. Then, at a table by the window, there was a dirty Werecat who was trying to stay angry instead of just being surprised.

"Hey, Linda," I said. "Just a minute." The young couple wanted their coffee with milk on the side – which seemed within my capabilities – so I jotted down their order and turned back to my old friend. "Let me get these done before you disembowel me, okay? You want one?"

She swallowed her anger and nodded.

"Black," she purred.

"Sure thing."

I took one step towards the kitchen, then turned back.

"You're not hungry, are you?"

I recognized a familiar kind of frustration, as her hard-ass plans battled her more dire needs for food and shelter.

"I'm bloody starving," she admitted.

I gave her my kindest and most welcoming smile, knowing it would need some practice.

"I'll see what I can rustle up."

Before I went back to the kitchen, I picked up the phone and dialed a number.

"Hello?" croaked a clearly hungover Richie Kites.

"When's the last time you had a meal that didn't come from a can?"

"Who is this?"

"Answer the question."

"I don't remember."

"Then come on down to Georgio's. I'll make you something proper."

I went back out to the kitchen, got the next pot of coffee off the stove, then pulled another recipe down from the cork board. *Breakfast Special*.

All the ingredients were in the cupboards, and I fired up the other burners. Linda would probably still try to kill me when her stomach was full. Then there was Simms and the law to contend with. A bunch of angry Wizards out in Incava who might be interested in revenge, and the combined forces of the Niles Company and Mortales who never could seem to leave me alone for long.

Richie was right. If I wanted to push back against Niles, I couldn't do it from the top. He had the money, the contacts, the weapons and a whole web of unscrupulous bastards working alongside him. If I wanted to win the race, I'd have to do it from the bottom: one conversation, one breakfast, one burnt coffee at a time.

And if they didn't like it, they could come and find me. Let the rest of the world go running around for a change. I had orders to fill and eggs to fry, and this city couldn't run on an empty stomach.

So I rolled up my sleeves and got to work.

Acknowledgements

The last time I wrote one of these, it was the beginning of 2020 and *The Last Smile in Sunder City* was about to meet the world. Of course, nothing has gone to plan for anyone since then, and while the release of my first books hasn't been the celebration of tours, events and signings that I imagined, the support of my friends, colleagues, fans and fellow authors has carried me through the madness and helped introduce Fetch to readers everywhere.

Jenni Hill continues to be the greatest editor I could ask for. Thank you for faith in Fetch, and in me, and for knowing that we both sometimes need a little prompting to say what we really mean.

To Nivia, Nazia, Joanna, Angela, Ellen, Melinda, Tessa, and everyone else at Hachette, Orbit and Little, Brown who rolled with the punches to deliver my debut and sequel in an unpredictable year.

To Alexander Cochran who, among other things, is responsible for my stories already being available in so many languages. These translations have been received so well that I suspect each writer must have improved on the source material, so I'm grateful to all the publishers and translators who've made this happen.

To Estefanía, whose extensive and insightful notes have once against lifted all areas of this book, and to Laura who graciously listens to me ramble out my thoughts so I can get them straight before I put them to paper, and was the much-needed cheerleader to push me through this instalment.

I can't name every person who helped get the word out about these books, but Toby Schmitz, you went above and beyond, as you always do.

Tim, Laurence, Kyle, Zach, Toby, Hannah, Jess, Hakeem, Meganne, Luke, Clara, Louise, Tom, Annie-Lou, Sarah, Jai, Soph, Jin, Jimmy, Tian, and Bronnie, thank you from the bottom of my heart for answering the call and showing up to promote my work in the madcap ways I requested. You're all beautiful, generous legends.

And thanks to everyone who has come on this journey so far. If you came to Sunder City looking for a classic detective story or a sprawling fantasy epic . . . well, I apologize for not really fulfilling those desires as yet. Instead, I hope you've enjoyed exploring the evolution of a man who feels more suited to the complicated times that we currently find ourselves in. The jaded tough guys of yesterday no longer cut it. Nor do we need overexcited warriors grabbing weapons and charging into battle. Fetch and I are still working out what is needed, so I appreciate you taking the time to walk these dark, winding streets with us. Your company makes it all worthwhile.

See you again soon.

extras

orbit

meet the author

Luke Arnold was born in Australia and has spent the last decade acting his way around the world, playing iconic roles such as Long John Silver in the Emmy-winning *Black Sails* and his award-winning turn as Michael Hutchence in the INXS mini-series *Never Tear Us Apart*. When he isn't performing, Luke is a screenwriter, director, novelist, and ambassador for Save the Children Australia.

Find out more about Luke Arnold and other Orbit authors by registering for the free monthly newsletter at orbitbooks.net.

if you enjoyed
ONE FOOT IN THE FADE

look out for

THE MASK OF MIRRORS
Rook & Rose: Book One

by

M. A. Carrick

Nightmares are creeping through the City of Dreams....

Renata Viraudax is a con artist who has come to the sparkling city of Nadežra—the City of Dreams—with one goal: to trick her way into a noble house, securing her fortune and her sister's future.

But as she's drawn into the aristocratic world of House Traementis, she realizes her masquerade is just one of many surrounding her. And as corrupted magic begins to weave its way through Nadežra, the poisonous feuds of its aristocrats and the shadowy dangers of its impoverished underbelly become tangled—with Ren at their heart.

Prologue

The lodging house had many kinds of quiet. There was the quiet of sleep, children packed shoulder to shoulder on the threadbare carpets of the various rooms, with only an occasional snore or rustle to break the silence. There was the quiet of daytime, when the house was all but deserted; then they were not children but Fingers, sent out to pluck as many birds as they could, not coming home until they had purses and fans and handkerchiefs and more to show for their efforts.

Then there was the quiet of fear.

Everyone knew what had happened. Ondrakja had made sure of that: In case they'd somehow missed the screams, she'd dragged Sedge's body past them all, bloody and broken, with Simlin forcing an empty-eyed Ren along in Ondrakja's wake. When they came back a little while later, Ondrakja's stained hands were empty, and she stood in the mildewed front hall of the lodging house, with the rest of the Fingers watching from the doorways and the splintered railings of the stairs.

"Next time," Ondrakja said to Ren in that low, pleasant voice they all knew to dread, "I'll hit you somewhere softer." And her gaze went, with unerring malice, to Tess.

Simlin let go of Ren, Ondrakja went upstairs, and after that the lodging house was silent. Even the floorboards didn't creak, because the Fingers found places to huddle and stayed there.

Sedge wasn't the first. They said Ondrakja picked someone at random every so often, just to keep the rest in line. She was the leader of their knot; it was her right to cut someone out of it.

But everyone knew this time wasn't random. Ren had fucked up, and Sedge had paid the price.

Because Ren was too valuable to waste.

Three days like that. Three days of terror-quiet, of no one being sure if Ondrakja's temper had settled, of Ren and Tess clinging to each other while the others stayed clear.

On the third day, Ren got told to bring Ondrakja her tea.

She carried it up the stairs with careful hands and a grace most of the Fingers couldn't touch. Her steps were so smooth that when she knelt and offered the cup to Ondrakja, its inner walls were still dry, the tea as calm and unrippled as a mirror.

Ondrakja didn't take the cup right away. Her hand slid over the charm of knotted cord around Ren's wrist, then along her head, lacquered nails combing through the thick, dark hair like she was petting a cat. "Little Renyi," she murmured. "You're a clever one... but not clever enough. That is why you need me."

"Yes, Ondrakja," Ren whispered.

The room was empty, except for the two of them. No Fingers crouching on the carpet to play audience to Ondrakja's performance. Just Ren, and the stained floorboards in the corner where Sedge had died.

"Haven't I tried to teach you?" Ondrakja said. "I see such promise in you, in your pretty face. You're better than the others; you could be as good as me, someday. But only if you listen and obey—and stop trying to *hide things from me.*"

Her fingernails dug in. Ren lifted her chin and met Ondrakja's gaze with dry eyes. "I understand. I will never try to hide anything from you again."

"Good girl." Ondrakja took the tea and drank.

The hours passed with excruciating slowness. Second earth. Third earth. Fourth. Most of the Fingers were asleep, except those out on night work.

Ren and Tess were not out, nor asleep. They sat tucked under the staircase, listening, Ren's hand clamped hard over the charm on her wrist. "Please," Tess begged, "we can just go—"

"No. Not yet."

Ren's voice didn't waver, but inside she shook like a pinkie on her first lift. *What if it didn't work?*

She knew they should run. If they didn't, they might miss their chance. When people found out what she'd done, there wouldn't be a street in Nadežra that would grant her refuge.

But she stayed for Sedge.

A creak in the hallway above made Tess squeak. Footsteps on the stairs became Simlin rounding the corner. He jerked to a halt when he saw them in the alcove. "There you are," he said, as if he'd been searching for an hour. "Upstairs. Ondrakja wants you."

Ren eased herself out, not taking her eyes from Simlin. At thirteen he wasn't as big as Sedge, but he was far more vicious. "Why?"

"Dunno. Didn't ask." Then, before Ren could start climbing the stairs: "She said both of you."

Next time, I'll hit you somewhere softer.

They should have run. But with Simlin standing just an arm's reach away, there wasn't any hope now. He dragged Tess out of the alcove, ignoring her whimper, and shoved them both up the stairs.

The fire in the parlour had burned low, and the shadows

pressed in close from the ceiling and walls. Ondrakja's big chair was turned with its back to the door so they had to circle around to face her, Tess gripping Ren's hand so tight the bones ached.

Ondrakja was the picture of Lacewater elegance. Despite the late hour, she'd changed into a rich gown, a Liganti-style surcoat over a fine linen underdress—a dress Ren herself had stolen off a laundry line. Her hair was upswept and pinned, and with the high back of the chair rising behind her, she looked like one of the Cinquerat on their thrones.

A few hours ago she'd petted Ren and praised her skills. But Ren saw the murderous glitter in Ondrakja's eyes and knew that would never happen again.

"Treacherous little bitch," Ondrakja hissed. "Was this your revenge for that piece of trash I threw out? Putting something in my tea? It should have been a knife in my back—but you don't have the guts for that. The only thing worse than a traitor is a *spineless* one."

Ren stood paralyzed, Tess cowering behind her. She'd put in as much extract of meadow saffron as she could afford, paying the apothecary with the coin that was supposed to help her and Tess and Sedge escape Ondrakja forever. It should have worked.

"I am going to make you pay," Ondrakja promised, her voice cold with venom. "But this time it won't be as quick. Everyone will know you betrayed your knot. They'll hold you down while I go to work on your little sister there. I'll keep her alive for days, and you'll have to watch every—"

She was rising as she spoke, looming over Ren like some Primordial demon, but mid-threat she lurched. One hand went to her stomach—and then, without any more warning, she vomited onto the carpet.

As her head came up, Ren saw what the shadows of the chair had helped conceal. The glitter in Ondrakja's eyes wasn't just fury; it was fever. Her face was sickly sallow, her skin dewed with cold sweat.

The poison *had* taken effect. And its work wasn't done.

Ren danced back as Ondrakja reached for her. The woman who'd knotted the Fingers into her fist stumbled, going down onto one knee. Quick as a snake, Ren kicked her in the face, and Ondrakja fell backward.

"That's for Sedge," Ren spat, darting in to stomp on Ondrakja's tender stomach. The woman vomited again, but kept wit enough to grab at Ren's leg. Ren twisted clear, and Ondrakja clutched her own throat, gasping.

A yank at the charm on Ren's wrist broke the cord, and she hurled it into the woman's spew. Tess followed an instant later. That swiftly, they weren't Fingers anymore.

Ondrakja reached out again, and Ren stamped on her wrist, snapping bone. She would have kept going, but Tess seized Ren's arm, dragging her toward the door. "She's already dead. Come on, or we will be, too—"

"Come back here!" Ondrakja snarled, but her voice had withered to a hoarse gasp. "I will make you fucking *pay*…"

Her words dissolved into another fit of retching. Ren broke at last, tearing the door open and barreling into Simlin on the other side, knocking him down before he could react. Then down the stairs to the alcove, where a loose floorboard concealed two bags containing everything they owned in the world. Ren took one and threw the other at Tess, and they were out the door of the lodging house, into the narrow, stinking streets of Lacewater, leaving dying Ondrakja and the Fingers and the past behind them.

if you enjoyed
ONE FOOT IN THE FADE

look out for

SIXTEEN WAYS TO DEFEND A WALLED CITY

by

K. J. Parker

A siege is approaching, and the City has little time to prepare. The people have no food and no weapons, and the enemy has sworn to slaughter them all.

Saving the City will take a miracle, but what it has is Orhan. A colonel of engineers, Orhan has far more experience with bridge building than battles, is a cheat and a liar, and has a serious problem with authority. He is, in other words, perfect for the job.

Sixteen Ways to Defend a Walled City is the story of Orhan son of Siyyah Doctus Felix Praeclarissimus and his history of the Great Siege, written down so that the deeds and sufferings of great men may never be forgotten.

1

I was in Classis on business. I needed sixty miles of second-grade four-inch hemp rope—I build pontoon bridges—and all the military rope in the empire goes through Classis. What you're supposed to do is put in a requisition to Divisional Supply, who send it on to Central Supply, who send it on to the Treasurer General, who approves it and sends it back to Divisional Supply, who send it on to Central Supply, who forward it to Classis, where the quartermaster says, sorry, we have no rope. Or you can hire a clever forger in Herennis to cut you an exact copy of the treasury seal, which you use to stamp your requisition, which you then take personally to the office of the deputy quartermaster in Classis, where there's a senior clerk who'd have done time in the slate quarries if you hadn't pulled certain documents out of the file a few years back. Of course, you burned the documents as soon as you took them, but he doesn't know that. And that's how you get sixty miles of rope in this man's army.

I took the overland route from Traiecta to Cirte, across one of my bridges (a rush job I did fifteen years ago, only meant to last a month, still there and still the only way across the Lusen unless you go twenty-six miles out of your way to Pons Jovianis) then down through the pass onto the coastal plain. Fabulous view as you come through the pass, that huge flat green patchwork with the blue of the Bay beyond, and Classis as a geometrically perfect star, three arms on land, three jabbing out into the sea. Analyse the design and it becomes clear that it's purely practical and utilitarian, straight out of the field operations manual. Furthermore, as soon as you drop down onto the plain you can't see the shape, unless you happen to be God. The three seaward arms are tapered jetties, while their landward counterparts are defensive bastions, intended to cover the three main gates with enfilading fire on two sides. Even further more, when Classis was built ninety years ago, there was a dirty great forest in the way (felled for charcoal during the Social War, all stumps, marsh and bramble-fuzz now), so you wouldn't have been able to see it from the pass, and that strikingly beautiful statement of Imperial power must therefore be mere chance and serendipity. By the time I reached the way station at Milestone 2776 I couldn't see Classis at all, though of course it was dead easy to find. Just follow the arrow-straight military road on its six-foot embankment, and, next thing you know, you're there.

Please note I didn't come in on the military mail. As Colonel-in-Chief of the Engineers, I'm entitled; but, as a milk-face (not supposed to call us that, everybody does, doesn't bother me, I like milk) it's accepted that I don't, because of the distress I might cause to Imperials finding themselves banged up in a coach with me for sixteen hours a day. Not that they'd say anything, of course. The Robur pride themselves on their good manners, and, besides, calling a milkface a milkface is Conduct Prejudicial and can get you court-martialled. For the record, nobody's ever faced charges on that score, which proves (doesn't it) that Imperials aren't biased or bigoted in any way. On the other hand, several dozen auxiliary officers have been tried and cashiered for calling an Imperial a blueskin, so you can see just how wicked and deserving of contempt my lot truly are.

No, I made the whole four-day trip on a civilian carrier's

cart. The military mail, running non-stop and changing horses at way stations every twenty miles, takes five days and a bit, but my cart was carrying fish; marvellous incentive to get a move on.

The cart rumbled up to the middle gate and I hopped off and hobbled up to the sentry, who scowled at me, then saw the scrambled egg on my collar. For a split second I thought he was going to arrest me for impersonating an officer (wouldn't be the first time). I walked past him, then jumped sideways to avoid being run down by a cart the size of a cathedral. That's Classis.

My pal the clerk's office was in Block 374, Row 42, Street 7. They've heard of sequential numbering in Supply but clearly aren't convinced that it'd work, so Block 374 is wedged in between Blocks 217 and 434. Street 7 leads from Street 4 into Street 32. But it must be all right, because I can find my way about there, and I'm just a bridge builder, nobody.

He wasn't there. Sitting at his desk was a six-foot-six Robur in a milk-white monk's habit. He was bald as an egg, and he looked at me as though I was something the dog had brought in. I mentioned my pal's name. He smiled.

"Reassigned," he said.

Oh. "He never mentioned it."

"It wasn't the sort of reassignment you'd want to talk about." He looked me up and down; I half expected him to roll back my upper lip so he could inspect my teeth. "Can I help you?"

I gave him the big smile. "I need rope."

"Sorry." He looked so happy. "No rope."

"I have a sealed requisition."

He held out his hand. I showed him my piece of paper. I'm pretty sure he spotted the seal was a fake. "Unfortunately, we have no rope at present," he said. "As soon as we get some—"

I nodded. I didn't go to staff college so I know squat about strategy and tactics, but I know when I've lost and it's time to withdraw in good order. "Thank you," I said. "Sorry to have bothered you."

"No bother." His smile said he hadn't finished with me yet. "You can leave that with me."

I was still holding the phony requisition with the highly illegal seal. "Thanks," I said, "but shouldn't I resubmit it through channels? I wouldn't want you thinking I was trying to jump the queue."

"Oh, I think we can bend the rules once in a while." He held out his hand again. Damn, I thought. And then the enemy saved me.

(Which is the story of my life, curiously enough. I've had an amazing number of lucky breaks in my life, far more than my fair share, which is why, when I got the citizenship, I chose Felix as my proper name. Good fortune has smiled on me at practically every crucial turning point in my remarkable career. But the crazy thing is, the agency of my good fortune has always—invariably—been the enemy. Thus: when I was seven years old, the Hus attacked our village, slaughtered my parents, dragged me away by the hair and sold me to a Sherden; who taught me the carpenter's trade—thereby trebling my value—and sold me on to a shipyard. Three years after that, when I was nineteen, the Imperial army mounted a punitive expedition against the Sherden pirates; guess who was among the prisoners carted back to the empire. The Imperial navy is always desperately short of skilled shipwrights. They let me join up, which meant citizenship, and I was a foreman at age twenty-two. Then the Echmen invaded, captured the city where I was stationed; I was one of the survivors and transferred to the Engineers, of whom I now have the honour to be Colonel-in-Chief.

I consider my point made. My meteoric rise, from illiterate barbarian serf to commander of an Imperial regiment, is due to the Hus, the Sherden, the Echmen and, last but not least, the Robur, who are proud of the fact that over the last hundred years they've slaughtered in excess of a million of my people. One of those here-today-gone-tomorrow freak cults you get in the City says that the way to virtue is loving your enemies. I have no problem with that. My enemies have always come through for me, and I owe them everything. My friends, on the other hand, have caused me nothing but aggravation and pain. Just as well I've had so very few of them.)

I noticed I no longer had his full attention. He was peering through his little window. After a moment, I shuffled closer and looked over his shoulder.

"Is that smoke?" I said.

He wasn't looking at me. "Yes."

Fire, in a place like Classis, is bad news. Curious how people react. He seemed frozen stiff. I felt jumpy as a cat. I elbowed myself a better view, as the long shed that had been leaking smoke from two windows suddenly went up in flames like a torch.

"What do you keep in there?" I asked.

"Rope," he said. "Three thousand miles of it."

I left him gawping and ran. Milspec rope is heavily tarred, and all the sheds at Classis are thatched. Time to be somewhere else.

I dashed out into the yard. There were people running in every direction. Some of them didn't look like soldiers, or clerks. One of them raced toward me, then stopped.

"Excuse me," I said. "Do you know—?"

He stabbed me. I hadn't seen the sword in his hand. I

thought; what the devil are you playing at? He pulled the sword out and swung it at my head. I may not be the most perceptive man you'll ever meet, but I can read between the lines; he didn't like me. I sidestepped, tripped his heels and kicked his face in. That's not in the drill manuals, but you pick up a sort of alternative education when you're brought up by slavers—

Sequence of thoughts; I guess the tripping and kicking thing reminded me of the Sherden who taught it to me (by example), and that made me think of pirates, and then I understood. I trod on his ear for luck till something cracked—not that I hold grudges—and looked round for somewhere to hide.

Really bad things happening all around you take time to sink in. Sherden pirates running amok in Classis? Couldn't be happening. So I found a shady doorway, held perfectly still and used my eyes. Yes, in fact, it was happening, and to judge from the small slice of the action I could see, they were having things very much their own way. The Imperial army didn't seem to be troubling them at all; they were preoccupied with fighting the fire in the rope shed, and the Sherden cut them down and shot them as they dashed about with buckets and ladders and long hooks, and nobody seemed to realise what was going on except me, and I don't count. Pretty soon there were no Imperials left in the yard, and the Sherden were backing up carts to the big sheds and pitching stuff in. Never any shortage of carts at Classis. They were hard workers, I'll give them that. Try and get a gang of dockers or warehousemen to load two hundred size-four carts in forty minutes. I guess that's the difference between hired men and self-employed.

I imagine the fire was an accident, because it rather spoiled things for the Sherden. It spread from one shed to a load of others before they had a chance to loot them, then burned up the main stable block and coach-houses, where most of the carts would have been, before the wind changed direction and sent it roaring through the barracks and the secondary admin blocks. That meant it was coming straight at me. By now, there were no soldiers or clerks to be seen, only the bad guys, and I'd stick out like a sore thumb in my regulation cloak and tunic. So I took off the cloak, noticed a big red stain down my front— oh yes, I'd been stabbed, worry about that later—pulled off the dead pirate's smock and dragged it over my head. Then I pranced away across the yard, looking like I had a job to do.

I got about thirty yards and fell over. I was mildly surprised, then realised: not just a flesh wound. I felt ridiculously weak and terribly sleepy. Then someone was standing over me, a Sherden, with a spear in his hand. Hell, I thought, and then: not that it matters.

"Are you all right?" he said.

Me and good fortune. How lucky I was to have been born a milkface. "I'm fine," I said. "Really."

He grinned. "Bullshit," he said, and hauled me to my feet. I saw him notice my boots—issue beetlecrushers, you can't buy them in stores. Then I saw he was wearing them, too. Pirates. Dead men's shoes. "Come on," he said. "Lean on me, you'll be fine."

He put my arm round his neck, then grabbed me round the waist and walked me across to the nearest cart. The driver helped him haul me up, and they laid me down gently on a huge stack of rolled-up lamellar breastplates. My rescuer took off his smock, rolled it up and put it under my head. "Get him back to the ship, they'll see to him there," he said, and that was the last I saw of him.

Simple as that. The way the looters were going about their business, quickly and efficiently, it was pretty obvious that there were no Imperial personnel left for them to worry about—apart from me, lovingly whisked away from danger by my enemies. The cart rumbled through the camp to the middle jetty. There were a dozen ships tied up on either side. The driver wasn't looking, so I was able to scramble off the cart and bury myself in a big coil of rope, where I stayed until the last ship set sail.

Some time later, a navy cutter showed up. Just in time, I remembered to struggle out of the Sherden smock that had saved my life. It'd have been the death of me if I'd been caught wearing it by our lot.

Which is the reason—one of the reasons—why I've decided to write this history. Under normal circumstances I wouldn't have bothered, wouldn't have presumed—who am I, to take upon myself the recording of the deeds and sufferings of great men, and so on. But I was there; not just all through the siege, but right at the very beginning. As I may already have mentioned, I've had far more good luck in my life than I could possibly have deserved, and when—time after time after time—some unseen hand scoops you up from under the wheels, so to speak, and puts you safely down on the roadside, you have to start wondering, why? And the only capacity in which I figure I'm fit to serve is that of witness. After all, anyone can testify in an Imperial court of law; even children, women, slaves, milkfaces, though of course it's up to the judge to decide what weight to give to the evidence of the likes of me. So; if luck figures I'm good enough to command the Engineers, maybe she reckons I can be a historian, too. Think of that. Immortality. A turf-cutter's son from north of the Bull's Neck living for ever on the spine of a book. Wouldn't that be something.

Follow us:

f **/orbitbooksUS**

🐦 **/orbitbooks**

▶ **/orbitbooks**

Join our mailing list
to receive alerts on our
latest releases and deals.

orbitbooks.net

Enter our monthly
giveaway for the chance
to win some epic prizes.

orbitloot.com